Hunt for The
ROSES

Hunt for The
ROSES

DREA SCOTT

DISCLAIMER

Ideally, I'd prefer for you to dive into this book blind so as not to spoil the twists and turns, but I know many people like a warning. Some triggers of this story include the following:

The loss of a loved one, the coping stages of dealing with this loss, and explicit sexual content only suitable for adults who are 18 and older.

Reader discretion is advised.

This story is for all those who have lost.
Know that the transformative power of love exists.
xo Drea

Contents

"When life throws thorns, hunt for the roses."

—anonymous

PROLOGUE

ARIA

The ivy-covered roof of the gazebo stares down at me as I lie in the middle of the rose garden. I think about how one moment, one single moment, can change everything. It changes how we feel, how we live, and the direction of our journey.

Some people are lucky enough to experience a moment that brings greater meaning to their life. A moment that brings joy, hope, and purpose. But what about those of us who aren't so lucky? Those of us who experience a devastating moment that shatters our entire world. A moment that wreaks havoc on all of our hopes and dreams that once were.

It's like that single moment morphs into invisible shackles around your wrists and you're chained to the corner of a dark room. The door closes, and as your eyes adjust to the dimly lit space, you see the key to your shackles on the other side. It's like that scrappy piece of metal represents the wonderful moments that were once within your reach.

At first, your instinct is to tug at the restraints with every ounce of strength you possess, even though you know your efforts are pointless. And as time goes on, you start to tire physically, and eventually your mental exhaustion catches up. At some point, you're not tugging frantically at the restraints, but you're embracing them. Accepting them as your fate and wardrobe accessory for life. Finally, you lay limp on the floor with your cheek flat against the cold concrete, and you stare at the door to the room. As time starts to slow down, you're willing someone to walk through that door and pick up the key to release you. But when minutes turn to hours, and hours turn to days, despair starts to consume you and you forget what it ever felt like to live unchained.

These are the ripple effects of just one moment.

One moment that's caged me for so long, it feels surreal to be lying flat on this wooden bench, surrounded by endless beauty. I can see hints of the starlit sky above, and I feel my lips tip up ever so slightly at the corners. I inhale as I turn to look toward the green rose pathway, keeping my eyes trained on the bold, green petals. Flashes of scenes from the past couple of months shine in my mind. Moments I thought I could never experience again.

And then I think of *him*.

I think of how his arms were wrapped around me as we danced under this very gazebo that night, savoring every second together. The images are so vivid, like the memories have been inked into my veins and forever etched into my soul. It was the first time we listened to our hearts instead of the sand pouring in our hourglass. Some would say you can't hear the sand anyway, but when you're on borrowed time, it's the loudest sound of all. And if I had to relive that night again, I would make the same decision every single time.

Because that night, the door to my dark room finally opened.

He represents my liberation.

My salvation.

My key to freedom.

CHAPTER
One

ARIA

One Year Earlier - Friday, June 11, 2021

"Wooooo!" Kyle is cupping his mouth with his hands, making sure everyone in the karaoke bar can hear him cheer Kate and me on before we hit the microphones. Holding his gaze, I blow him a kiss with my hand, and he winks back at me.

Trent is sitting next to Kyle in the booth as he yells some inevitable nonsense. "Give us a good show, ladies!" Then Trent makes a gesture with his hands like he's lifting his shirt up, implying that Kate and I should flash everyone.

Kate gives Trent a hard stare and flips him off from the stage we're on. In reaction, Trent makes it like he's catching Kate's middle finger in his hand, and shoves his fist in his jeans pocket. Looking at their exchange, I can't help but laugh as my hand goes to my forehead.

"We got the dollar bills ready!" Dane yells as he waves a few dollar bills at us.

I roll my eyes and turn to Kate. "I seriously can't with them," I say as I grab a microphone from one of the stands in front of us.

Kate grabs her microphone and talks into it as she points to where the boys are sitting. "This song is going to be dedicated to the gentlemen in the booth over there. The blond one is Aria's boyfriend," she says as she hikes a thumb over to me, and then she points between Trent and Dane. "And the other two gentlemen have just started a relationship together. Sorry ladies, if you were thinking of taking one of them home, they're off limits."

I put a hand over my mouth as I chuckle, and Kate just winks at the boys in the booth. Dane and Trent are good sports, and play along by toasting with their beer glasses as if they are actually celebrating being a couple.

As Kate and I are laughing, the man running the karaoke asks if we are ready to start the song, and we both turn around to give a thumbs up. We start to hear the instrumental introduction to "Come to My Window" by Melissa Etheridge, and Kate and I start side stepping as we sway to the music. One thing about the two of us is we never miss our chance to dance and live through music when we go out. It's honestly our greatest pastime, and not for nothing, we're pretty good at it if I do say so myself.

When the first verse of the song kicks in, the microphones immediately go up to our mouths, and we stare intently at our audience like we're putting on a real concert. Along with our dancing ability, Kate and I are decent singers given the right song, so naturally we chose a song we can sing pretty well in tune.

As we start singing, people in the crowd become more vocal and receptive to us, which encourages us to really sell this karaoke. When the pre-chorus kicks in, Kate and I face each other to sing through it, and then once the chorus finally kicks in, we're standing back-to-back as we wave our arms in the air and sway our hips in sync with each other.

"Owwwwww!" We hear Kyle, Trent and Dane screaming for us from their booth, and Kate and I turn to face each other again as we laugh before the next verse comes on. Given the fact that both of us had two cocktails before singing, Kate and I feel like absolute superstars up here, so to put it simply, we're having the time of our lives.

We repeat the same routine for the next verse and pre-chorus, but as we're singing "Just to reach you," I start to point to Kyle from the stage. Kyle throws me a wide smile, and I return the favor his way. Kate and I belt out the chorus a little harder, knowing our favorite parts of the song are just around the corner. We dramatize our motions as we bend our knees and tilt our heads up, both of us raising an arm in the air as we hold out the note to sing the line "Anyway."

Finally, we shake our heads eagerly side to side as we sing through the last pre-chorus, and we're smiling, giggling, and giving it all we have for the home stretch. The crowd erupts in applause, and as expected, we hear Kyle, Trent, and Dane over everyone.

"Work it, babe!" Kyle yells.

"When's the World Tour?!" Trent shouts.

"Sign my ass!" Dane hollers.

Kate and I are laughing as we put the microphones back on the stands and step down off the wooden stage to head to the booth where the guys are. Trent gets up so I can slide in next to Kyle, and Kate slides next to Dane, who's sitting across from the three of us. Kyle brings me in for a tight side-hug as he kisses my forehead, and before the five of us even start conversation, a waiter comes over to our booth with two sex on the beaches. "On the house, ladies."

Kate and I do a little victory dance in our seats as the bartender places the drinks in front of us, and we clink glasses before we each take a sip.

"Perks of being a woman," Dane says before he takes a sip from his beer.

"Yep," Trent agrees as he takes a sip of his.

I look at Dane. "Did it ever occur to you that we're just that good of singers?"

"And dancers," Kate chimes in as she vaguely points a finger.

Dane turns to Kate. "And good at having tits?"

"Oh please," Kate says as she waves Dane's comment off to take another sip of her cocktail.

Dane gestures a hand between Trent and Kyle. "Guys? Help here?"

Trent is the next to speak. "Okay, what Dane is so eloquently trying to say is that if he and I went up there to perform karaoke, we're pretty sure we'd still be paying for our drinks right now."

"Thank you," Dane says as he taps his beer bottle with Trent's and takes a sip.

I turn to look up at Kyle with a smirk. "You're quiet over there."

He exhales as if he's been found guilty. "Sorry, babe, I may have to agree with the boys on this."

I wave him off playfully. "Ugh, what good are you?"

He chuckles as he nips my ear. "I'm good for a lot."

I giggle as his breath tickles my ear, and then Kate looks between Dane and Trent. "Well, if what you're saying is true, I love reaping the benefits," she gloats as she stretches a victorious smile across her face.

Dane downs the rest of his beer before he gets up from the booth. "Alright, I'm going to head to the bar to buy another drink. Anyone want one?"

The rest of us shake our heads in response, and as Dane walks away, Trent says, "That may be the last we see of him tonight."

Trent is implying that Dane is most likely going to find a girl to bring home and hook up with. To catch you up, Dane Hudson is the epitome of a womanizer. He has no problem charming women between his quick wit and good looks, so it's only inevitable that he leaves without a trace sometimes. Dane's stark hazel eyes, one-to-one ratio lips, and aristocratic nose directly contrast his square, stubbled jaw line and dark wavy brown hair that's thicker on the top. Not to mention his six-foot-two athletic and lean build that keeps the girls flocking to him. He's a Casanova alright, so I guess I can't really blame him for taking advantage of his blessed looks.

I turn to Kyle. "Do you ever miss it? The single life?"

Kyle narrows his eyes. "Is this a trick question?"

"No." I laugh.

"Ari, how can Kyle possibly miss the single life when he has you?" Kate asks.

I place my hands over my heart. "Aww, thanks, babe." Kyle grabs my chin to kiss my cheek, and I smile as I roll my eyes playfully. "Yeah, yeah."

"I'm surprised you're not on the prowl like Dane is," Kate says, as she turns to Trent.

Trent finishes his sip of beer and shrugs. "Not really feeling up to it tonight."

Kate feigns shock. "Wow, I'm impressed."

"Hey, I have standards sometimes," Trent claims as he holds his hands out in defense.

"Are we not going to mention the girl you picked up at Shippers a couple of weekends ago? The one who was practically giving you a lap dance at the table in front of all of us?"

Trent looks between all of us with a tight-lipped smile. "Not my proudest moment. Definitely misjudged that."

Kyle and I laugh as we both take sips of our drinks, and for the next hour or so, the remaining four of us engage in more conversation and laughs before heading home. To say the least, tonight is just one of the many nights that make life worth living.

CHAPTER

Two

DANE

I groan as I lean back on my forearms against the mattress. I'm sitting at the foot of my bed with my boxer briefs pulled down, while Chelsea's naked on her knees. Chelsea is the smokeshow I met at the karaoke bar, and I'd say this blow job is probably worth dipping out early on my friends.

They'll get over it, trust me.

I grab the condom sitting next to me on the mattress and rip it open. "Stand up," I rasp as I tug on her upper arm, and then roll the condom down my shaft. When Chelsea stands, I wrap my arm around the small of her back to flip us so she's lying down, and I settle myself between her legs.

Chelsea whimpers as I pump into her, tilting her head back into the mattress, and her response only encourages me more. I hook my forearms around the back of Chelsea's thighs so she's spread wide for me, and I'm on my knees now.

I grunt as I take in the vision of Chelsea's body, and the feeling of her around me is just as fucking good as I imagined it would be. It's only a matter of time before I feel Chelsea shudder below me, and when she cries out in sheer pleasure, I brace one forearm next to her head on the mattress and finally chase my own release.

My forehead is now dipped into the mattress at the side of Chelsea's head, and the only sound filling my bedroom is the sound of our ragged breathing as we descend from our highs. When I'm finally able to get my breathing under control, I gently slip out of her and get up from the bed, leaving Chelsea naked on the mattress. I dispose of the condom in my wastebasket in the corner, and find my jeans on the floor to put back on. Once my jeans are buckled around me, I find Chelsea's yellow mini dress in the corner of the bedroom, and retrieve it to hand it to her.

"I believe this is yours," I say as I hold Chelsea's dress out to her.

"Thanks," Chelsea says with a satisfied smile as she takes the garment from my hand.

I pick up my t-shirt that was also tossed randomly on the floor, and walk to my dresser to look through my phone for any messages I may have missed. I hear Chelsea shuffle off the bed to walk up behind me, and then I feel her palms sliding up my back to land on my shoulders. "You were *incredible*," she moans in my ear.

I turn my head over my shoulder to look at her with a smirk. "Glad I could be of service."

Chelsea continues with a seductive grin. "I wouldn't be opposed to another round sometime." With her fingertips, she's tracing the length of my black and gray phoenix tattoo that covers the entire right side of my torso and wraps around the back of my shoulder so the flames dip onto my pec. But as much as her tender touch is trying to persuade me to see her again, her convincing falls short.

Survey says…

Not going to happen.

I place my phone back on the dresser to put my shirt back on, and turn around to cup Chelsea's hips in my hands. I bite my lip as I smack her ass cheek one time, causing Chelsea to yelp in a wide grin. "Oh!"

I smile back as I grab her chin between my thumb and forefinger to bring her in for a kiss, and when I pull back to look at her, I say what I really want to say. "Do you need me to take you home?"

I'm single, don't judge me.

Chelsea responds with a timid smile. "I can set up an Uber."

"Alright, I'll let you get your things together." I release my hold on her and walk toward my bedroom door, but once I reach the handle, I turn around to look at her. "Take your time. I'm going to be in the living room." Then I exit my bedroom and walk to plop down on my living room couch, praying Chelsea sets up the fastest Uber known to man.

Saturday, June 12, 2021

The next night, I'm entering the local dive bar, Shippers, to meet up with Kate, Trent, Kyle, and Aria. I met Kyle Reid seven years ago during our sophomore year of college at Dupont University. We were both in the architecture program, and as fate would have it, we were set up by our professor to complete a presentation for his class. We actually came to find out we have a lot of similar interests; craft beer, cars, working out, traveling. The list can go on, but you get the idea.

Kyle and I didn't meet Trent Palmer until a year later at Dupont. Trent is the odd man out, having studied business and marketing, but we still like him, I suppose. The three of us met at a mixer on campus, which was the same night we discovered Trent had a girlfriend in one of the sororities. So naturally, Kyle and I took advantage of that real quick. Trent had introduced us to his then-girlfriend Casey, sorority sister of the Kappa Delta house, who introduced us to her friends. As you could guess, Kyle and I were able to reap a lot of benefits for the rest of our college days where girls were concerned.

However, one of the best things about being introduced to the sorority was getting to meet Kate Crowley, who also happened to be a sorority sister at Kappa Delta. Kate had the biggest crush on Trent back then, and I definitely think she still has one now, but she'll never admit it. Trent gives off more of a surfer vibe with his shaggy light brown hair, clean-shaved face, and broad and bronzed physique. Maybe it's the baby blues of his that gets Kate every time. Who knows?

Anyway, Kate's a hoot. Of course, Kyle and I would never think of her as more than a great friend. Not to say she isn't attractive, because she's certainly a looker. Kate's a five-foot-six brown-eyed blonde, always bubbly, trying new things, and encouraging people to tag along for the ride. She is the definition of an extrovert, which sometimes is a little overbearing, but we love her in spite of that.

The four of us were happy to discover that we actually live within a half hour of each other, and have continued to hang out past our college years. Shippers was our place of choice, and we would try to come here at least once every weekend. Friday or Saturday night, whichever worked best for the whole group.

Our group of four became a group of five when Kyle was introduced to Aria Tate about four years ago. One of Kyle's coworkers set him up on a blind date with Aria, and they've been inseparable ever since. We all gave a stamp of approval when we first met the brown-haired, brown-eyed teacher. Aria can be just as funny as the rest of us when she wants to be, so she can keep up with us pretty well. Not to mention, she's probably one of the sweetest people I've ever met. It's no surprise Kyle was infatuated with her from the very beginning.

So that's the background of how my four best friends and I met, and why I have a big smile on my face as I open the door to Shippers. The thing with us is we don't need anything glamorous. We just need these wood walls, dim lighting, and neon bar signs. A simple night like tonight is our staple of being twenty-six years old, and we wouldn't trade it for the world.

Once I walk through the entrance to Shippers, I go straight to the bar to grab a beer and spot the crew in the corner of the bar at a high-top table. To make their presence known, they all raise their hands and shout, "Eyyyyy!"

I love these people.

When I reach the table, Kyle and Trent are sitting on the outside, so we exchange the typical "bro" handshakes to greet each other, and I take the head seat at the table.

HUNT FOR THE ROSES

Kate is the first one to speak as she slides her beer to me. "Dane, you must try this new IPA they have on tap."

I gratefully take a sip of her IPA and raise my eyebrows as if I'm thoroughly impressed. "Shit, that's good."

"Right?!" Kate exclaims.

"Okay, you literally just started liking IPAs. Now you think you're an expert or something," Trent cuts in.

Kate plasters a smug grin on her face as she looks at Trent. "I'm an expert in a lot of things. Too bad you'll never find out what some of those things are."

Narrowing my eyes with a smile, I chime in. "So, do you guys need a minute? Or are you going to go at it like rabbits in front of us?"

"Dane!" Aria cuts in as if she's offended.

Kate narrows her eyes back to me. "Ugh, seriously Dane, you're such an idiot."

"Well, if Trent isn't gonna bite, I will," I say and throw her a wink.

Kate scrunches her face. "With the amount of girls you hook up with? No thanks."

"You'd love it," I say, and then quickly throw her a kiss with my lips.

Kate rolls her eyes.

"Okay anyway! I have great news," Aria interrupts. "My dad is opening his own restaurant here in Crestside. It's going to be located in Dawson's Marina. Bistro Eighty-Six."

"Eyyyy!" Kate, Trent, and I all praise in unison as all of us at the table raise our glasses.

Kyle throws his arm around Aria as she nuzzles into his side, and then he's the next one to speak. "And Aria just finished her last professional development class to get her salary advancement."

"Eyyyy!" Kate, Trent, and I all exclaim.

"Well, I won't be getting my salary advancement until the fall, but my goal was to finish by the beginning of June, and here we are," Aria says with a wide smile.

"That's amazing, Ari. You've worked so hard, you deserve this," Kate says.

I take another sip of my beer before interjecting my usual joke. "Well, now you have no lame excuse to not come out with us Friday or Saturday nights."

"I resent that. My excuses were always valid," Aria challenges.

I shake my head and give her an accusatory look. "Not when you could have chosen to save the school work for a weeknight."

Kyle chimes in next. "Hey, if the woman I love is neurotic about schoolwork and I accept it, you all have to accept it. It's just who she is."

Playing along, Aria raises both palms outward. "It's just who I am. Take it or leave it, guys."

I chuckle as I bring the glass of beer to my lips when Trent turns to me. "So, Dane, care to share some juicy details from last night? You dipped out on us pretty early."

"Ooooo," Aria and Kate say at the same time, their eyes lighting up with curiosity. As much as they'll deny it, the girls thrive on gossip and drama. Aria and Kate never want to be a part of it, but if it has nothing to do with them, they think it's fair game.

Girls.

I lift my backwards snapback and run my fingers through my dark locks as I respond. "I may or may not have brought home the knockout blonde."

"Eyyyy!" Kyle and Trent say in unison as they clink glasses with me.

Rolling her eyes, Kate looks at Aria. "Men."

Aria shrugs with a defeated expression. "But we love 'em."

These are the moments I cherish most. Sitting in a dive bar with my very best friends in a quaint coastal town in South Carolina. Life just doesn't get any better than this.

CHAPTER
Three

ARIA

Sunday, June 13, 2021

Kyle's arms are wrapped around my waist from behind, and he's nuzzling his nose in the crook of my neck as we walk barefoot on the beach. We just finished dinner at a Peruvian restaurant, and we always like to enjoy the beach when we can. It's a Sunday night in June. I'm not terribly busy with lesson planning anymore now that school is almost done, so this works out perfectly. When the wind picks up, I have to adjust the hem of my floral mini dress, which is a little difficult since I'm holding my nude wedge sandals in my hand at the same time.

Kyle playfully pinches my butt. "Trying to give me a sample of what's coming later, huh?"

I laugh as I try to wiggle out of his touch. "Stop! I was just trying to adjust my dress, you animal."

Repositioning his arms around my stomach and holding me tighter as we walk, Kyle's lips hover over my ear. "You love it though."

That's when I stop walking to turn around and put my arms around his neck. "I love *you*."

"I love you too," Kyle says before leaning down for a kiss.

Our lips and tongues connect like second nature, molding into one another like it's the only thing our mouths were meant to do. Our foreheads press together when we pull away, and we just let the breeze whisk between us as we treasure the beauty of a night like tonight. When we resume our original walking position, I tilt my head back to lean on Kyle's shoulder and look toward the starlit sky as I ask, "How do you picture our life in ten years?"

"Well, let's see," Kyle starts off as he lifts his head up from my neck. "I see us living in a colonial-style house, with two dogs, and three children."

"Three children?" I peer back over my shoulder and look at Kyle with questioning eyes. "Who do you think is carrying all these babies?"

Kyle's face scans mine for a few silent moments before he whispers, "I want as many of your babies as you can give me."

His words encase my heart in the warmest embrace, making it forget to beat for a second. I love this man without a shadow of a doubt. He is my other half, my best friend, and my hero. I stop to turn around again, and slide my fingers through his wavy, dirty blond hair while staring into his blue eyes. "I'll give you as many babies as you want, Kyle," I whisper back.

"Mmm, guess we better start practicing," Kyle murmurs against my lips.

I smirk against Kyle's mouth. "So there's an ulterior motive. I see."

Kyle smiles as he spins me around one last time, wrapping his arms around my stomach again, and I place my hands over his. "Yep. I couldn't possibly want anything more from you than just incredible sex," he jokes.

I laugh as I nod my head and play along. "I thought so." Kyle laughs with me as he places a kiss on my cheek, and I smile widely at the loving gesture. "So colonial-style house, huh? I've always wanted to live in a vintage Victorian," I say.

"They look much better than they are practical. Trust me," Kyle replies.

I roll my eyes playfully. "Your knowledge of architecture is both a blessing and a curse."

"Just wait until we start house hunting."

"Oof, I didn't even think of that. Maybe you should go solo, so I won't have my hopes crushed every time I want pretty houses that happen to be dysfunctional," I say as I look over my shoulder with a smile.

Kyle places his lips on my forehead as he speaks, "I would never dream of making a life decision without you involved, so stop talking crazy."

His soft lips against my skin provide a solace no other man could ever give me, and I close my eyes as I take in the comfort of his words. I reach behind me to grab Kyle's upper arms, gently clinging to the cotton fabric of his long-sleeved shirt, and we hold each other the rest of our walk in the sand.

Luckily, our townhouse is only a ten-minute walk from the beach, so we don't have to wait too much longer to get home. Our one-bedroom townhouse is on a quiet street lined with sidewalks, and although it's called a townhouse, it's not connected to the neighboring townhouses. They all look more like tiny cottages than anything. Each townhouse is a different pastel color, paying homage to our beach town. As you look down the line of cottages, you see light blue, sea green, salmon, light yellow, then the colors repeat in that same order.

Our two-story townhouse is light blue with vinyl siding. On the first level, there is an offset white entrance door, and a concrete roofed-over porch lined with a white wrap-around PVC fence. Once you step onto the porch, you enter through white-capped column covers, and next to the front door are two double-hung windows. The porch has a gable-end roof, and on the upper level, there is a centered double-hung window with black shutters, a circular attic vent above it, and a gable-end roof with eave returns. It's truly picturesque, and every townhouse on the block looks exactly the same in style.

Once we reach the top of the porch of our townhouse, I grab Kyle by the shirt and pull him into me as I lean back against the porch column. "Hey! None of that while I'm out here."

We're caught off guard when Dane interrupts us as he walks down the steps of his neighboring townhouse. A year ago, Kyle and I had decided we wanted to move in together, and when Dane found out that the house next door to him was up for sale, he told us right away. As if the stars aligned, this house is within a reasonable distance of our jobs, and still keeps us close to our family and friends. Needless to say, it was the perfect fit.

As Kyle and I both look to see Dane, he's wearing a black pullover hoodie and gray gym shorts, with a black backwards snapback.

"Where are you going?" Kyle asks with furrowed brows.

Dane walks up to us on the porch. "I wasn't able to get a workout in today, so I figured I would now. Kind of like you guys are going to in a minute," Dane says with a smirk.

I playfully shove Dane.

Dane grins. "Okay, fine, truce."

"It's nine o'clock at night," Kyle counters.

"Gym closes at ten, and I'm already behind, so I'm gonna get going," Dane responds as he goes to give Kyle a handshake-hug.

"Night, Dane," I say.

"Night, Ari," Dane responds as he turns around to walk down the porch and to his car. His back is still to us as he shouts out some final words. "Enjoy the orgasms!"

Kyle and I both chuckle as we turn to face each other, and then Kyle cups the side of my face. "Dane's got a point."

"Mmm, yes he does," I moan as I lean forward to kiss Kyle.

CHAPTER
Four

DANE

Saturday, June 19, 2021

I wake up to my phone buzzing, groaning as I roll over and lazily open my eyes to look over at my nightstand. I see "Mom" on the homescreen of my iPhone, and I clumsily pick up my phone as I sit up to lean my back against the headboard of my bed.

I run my fingers through my disheveled hair as I answer the call with a groggy voice. "Hey, Mom."

"Oh, I'm sorry, did I wake you?"

I yawn as I start to respond. "I was sleeping, but I should probably get up anyway."

"I haven't heard from you. I wanted to make sure everything was okay. You know, see what's new with my one and only son."

I run my fingers through my hair, feeling like a real asshole for not texting or calling my mom in a while. My dad left us when I was just seven years old, and has been completely out of our lives ever since. Dad was caught cheating, Mom found out and kicked him out of the house, and then he went on to live a whole different life with his lover. Couldn't tell you what he's doing or where he is. Nor do I give a shit. So knowing the life my mom built for me on her own, I always feel I'm in debt to her, and I always want to make her as happy as I can.

"Shit, I'm sorry, Mom. I've been caught up at work with a few aggressive clients this past week."

"Oh, no, I'm sorry to hear that. Did everything turn out okay?"

"I was able to smooth over two clients, but the other is not budging. Flipped out over the pricing of building materials. The usual. Just one of the many perks of being a Project Manager," I say sarcastically.

"You're amazing at what you do, and your bosses appreciate you. That's all you need to keep you going. Except maybe a *girl*…" My mom emphasizes the word "girl" at the end of her sentence.

Here we go.

My mom is just waiting for the day I tell her I've settled down. I'm twenty-six years old and the last time I had a relationship was when I was twenty-three. It was for about a year, and I cared for the girl, but she just wasn't the one. So I broke it off, and here I am living my mighty single life. It's not like I'm with a different girl every night, but I definitely have been racking up my head count the past few years.

"No girls in my field of vision yet. Sorry to disappoint," I say.

"She'll come sooner than you think. Don't count out every girl you meet."

"Don't worry. You'll be the first to know when she comes into my life," I assure her.

"I better be! But alright, I won't push anymore. I'll push for a mother-son date instead. What do you think?"

I smile. "Sounds great."

I can hear her large smile as she responds. "Yaaayyy."

I chuckle. "I'll text or call you this week to set something up. Promise."

"I'm holding you to that," my mom states.

"Cross my heart," I say as I make an "X" gesture across my bare chest.

"Okay, hun, I'll let you be. I'm sure you have plans other than talking to your mom on a Saturday morning. I need to run some errands anyway. Love you."

"Love you too," I say and hang up.

I place my phone back on my nightstand, then exhale as I run both hands down my face. Even though I was planning on sleeping in later, I guess I'm up now.

After hanging up with my mom, I knock on Kyle's door to see if he's still up for going to the gym this morning. We both take a lot of pride in staying physically fit, which is great because we keep each other company while working out, and it makes the time go by faster.

When we make it to the gym, Kyle and I head straight for the kick-boxing floor, throw on some gloves, and start punching and kicking away.

"So Aria wants to take a trip to Montauk this summer. Are you inter-ested?" Kyle breathes out between punches.

"Depends when," I pant.

"Any weekend that works for everyone," Kyle responds.

I punch and kick a few more times before standing to look at him, and then I shrug. "Shouldn't be a problem. Just let me know specific details so I can take off if I need to."

Kyle finishes a punch and kick before standing to face me. "Cool. I'll ask Trent and Kate too."

I nod, then go back to my assault on the body bag. Between punches and kicks, I ask, "Do you and Ari have any big summer vacation plans?"

"Not this year. We're trying to save money right now, so I think we're stalling on big trips for the time being."

"Better not be because you're buying a new house. I'll kick your ass," I respond.

Kyle stops with his hands on his hips as he breathes out his response. "First off, we're not moving. Secondly, you couldn't kick my ass."

I stop what I'm doing to look at him. "So, what are you saving up for?"

Kyle pauses, then responds with a smile. "I want to ask Aria to marry me."

"Seriously?"

"Seriously."

I run a glove through my hair. "Holy shit, man, that's awesome."

"I don't have the ring yet, but I'm going to start looking within the next week or so." Kyle just shakes his head with his hands on his hips as if he's mesmerized by something I can't see. "She's the one. I can just feel it."

My hands are also at my hips as I stand facing Kyle. "I'm really happy for you. Aria's great."

"Yeah, it's incredible. I mean, I know you're enjoying your single life, but when you find that person, it just makes everything make so much more sense."

I vaguely hold out a hand. "Okay, let's pump the sensitive brakes. I said Aria's great. We can leave it at that."

Kyle chuckles. "Well, it's helpful you approve, because I actually wanted to ask you something else."

"I already had strippers planned before you told me this," I joke.

Kyle just throws me a wide smile. "I can't think of anyone else I'd rather have as my best man."

I pause for a split second, and my facial expression becomes more serious once I fully register what he's asking me. I take a glove off and go in for a handshake-hug as Kyle does the same. "You know you don't have to ask me twice." When we step back, I continue on. "Of course, my only request is that you introduce me to the hot single bridesmaids. Aria better come through on that."

Kyle laughs at my joke. "Will do."

I start slipping my other glove off as I narrow my eyes at him. "Now, what was that you were saying about kicking my ass?"

Kyle slips his other glove off as well. "Let's go."

Both of us throw our gloves in the corner and start to circle around each other. Kyle goes to wrap his arms around my legs, but I fall forward on his back and hug my arms under his stomach, and we hit the ground. I have Kyle in a hold and we're laughing through breaths, but then he surprises me by flipping us over so he's now on top. We're wrestling back and forth like this for another five minutes before we realize we should probably pack it up before other people start coming in.

When Kyle and I are in the locker room, both of us are dripping with sweat from our workout and wrestling antics. I take a sip of my water before turning to Kyle, and offer a fist out to him. Kyle returns the pound with a smile, and after we change into dry t-shirts, we make our way out of the gym to head home.

On the ride back, I think about Kyle getting married and how insanely elated I am for him. I know how much he loves Aria and how happy she makes him. They're perfect together in every way, and when the time comes, I look forward to standing beside my best friend at the altar. Many people don't get to experience friendships like ours, and to have a friend like Kyle is a gift. There's no denying how incredibly fortunate I feel to have him in my life.

Maybe I should have counted my blessings sooner.

CHAPTER

Five

ARIA

Saturday, June 19, 2021

As per usual, the gang's all together to kick back on a Saturday night, and since summer is officially right around the corner, we decide to have a bonfire out on the beach. By gang, I mean the typical five of us, with two additions–my brother Ronnie and his wife Cheryl.

Ronnie is the staple of an overprotective big brother. He's five years older than me and lives almost an hour away to be closer to the city area where he works as an electrician. While we both still lived at home, Ronnie would interrogate any guy who came to the house to pick me up for a first date. Asking questions like "Where are you going tonight and what time will you be back?" and "Do you think I care what happens to you if you break my little sister's heart?" You know, the typical "big brother" complex. So I guess it bodes well for me that Ronnie doesn't live as close, but even so, the fact that he wholeheartedly approves of my relationship with Kyle is just the icing on the cake.

As we're all sitting in our camping chairs around the fire, I see my brother and his wife approach us. "Hey, you made it!" I scream as I get up from my chair to hug the both of them. Kyle follows suit, shaking Ronnie's hand and hugging Cheryl after me.

Ronnie and Cheryl already know Kate, Trent, and Dane, so there are no need for introductions. They all just say their hellos as my brother and his wife set up their own chairs around the fire.

"How was the drive out?" I ask as I sit back down and take a sip of my hard seltzer.

Cheryl responds first. "Not bad, actually. We purposely left later in the day, so that definitely helped."

Ronnie is cracking a beer open from the cooler, and chimes in after he takes a sip. "I also have impeccable driving skills."

Cheryl makes a deadpan expression. "Knew that was coming."

Ronnie smirks and then directs his attention to Kyle. "So how's the house? Everything up and running there, or do you need my help with anything?"

"Knock on wood, everything is running smoothly," Kyle says.

"Glad to hear," Ronnie responds, and then he taps Dane on the arm since he's sitting next to him. "So I haven't seen you in a minute. What's new?"

Dane shrugs. "Not much. Grinding at the architecture office during the week and letting loose on weekends."

"I hear you were promoted to Project Manager, so congrats," Ronnie says as he clinks his beer bottle with Dane's.

"Thank you, sir. Going to start taking my exams to get licensed, so we'll see what happens from there. There are a lot of opportunities to consider afterwards," Dane answers.

"Good for you, that's awesome."

"How many exams are there again?" Trent cuts in and asks.

"Six," Dane replies.

"Geeze, I thought three exams was a lot for teaching," I chime in as I hike my bare feet up on the seat of my chair.

"Yeah, it's pretty brutal," Dane responds with a tight-lipped smile.

"So how long are you both in town for?" Kate asks Ronnie and Cheryl.

"We're staying with my parents and leaving tomorrow night. I figured I'd go over what work needs to be done for my dad's restaurant so I can give him reputable contacts and help him plan accordingly," Ronnie responds.

"Aww, Mom's going to be so happy to see you. Her only son–the golden child," I tease with a smile.

For the next hour, more conversation and laughs occur over the Bluetooth speaker that's bumping eighties classics from the playlist I chose. The wind is starting to pick up as the night goes on, and I cover my head with my sweatshirt hood to rest it on Kyle's shoulder next to me. As I angle my head in this position, I see two girls walking along the beach that I hadn't noticed before. One is a brunette with a cute navy romper, and the other is a blonde with a flowy pink sundress.

Dane places his beer in the cup holder of his chair and then gets up to walk in their direction. "You two interested in a drink?"

Both girls look confused at first, but as they walk closer and see Dane, they don't seem as confused anymore.

Typical.

"That depends, whatcha got?" the brunette answers with a smirk.

"Pick your poison," Dane says as he walks to the cooler on the sand and lifts the cover up.

"White Claw, now we're talking," the blonde says as she grabs two out for her and her friend.

When the brunette throws Dane a wide smile, he grins as he gestures to his chair. "All yours." I'm throwing Kate the eyes that say "I can't wait to watch all this unfold," as she does the exact same to me. Then, Trent gets up from his chair to offer the blonde his seat, and it seems like our friend Trent is going to get lucky tonight too.

"Wait, you guys brought cornhole? Let's play!" Dane's girl of interest says enthusiastically. She grabs Dane's hand and leads him toward the cornhole boards we have set up outside our circle of chairs.

"Yes!" the blonde shouts as she follows suit and leads Trent to join in on the game with Dane and his girl.

While Cheryl, Ronnie, and Kate are engaged in conversation, I turn to look at Kyle. "Don't you just love nights like this? They're so simple, yet they make for amazing memories."

Kyle puts an arm around me. "Agreed, nothing better. Except maybe if you were doing a strip tease for me," Kyle jokes as he wiggles his eyebrows at me.

I laugh and grab the side of his face. "Well, maybe if you play your cards right, I can offer one when we're home."

"Mmm, I love when you talk dirty to me."

I laugh again and give him a quick peck on the lips. "Ugh, promise when we're old, saggy, and wrinkly, that we still have this same sexual energy," I say.

Kyle shakes his head with a smile. "With you, I don't think that's a problem."

I cuddle into his arm again and rest my head against his shoulder. "Dane's girl looks like an actress, but I can't put my finger on it," I say as I'm watching the cornhole events unfold.

Kyle takes a swig of his beer before responding. "Mila Kunis."

I jump up and look at Kyle. "Oh my god, yes! That's it!"

Kyle chuckles. "Seems like you like her as much as Dane does."

I shrug, considering her beauty as I look her over. "She's pretty hot. And so is the blonde, apparently. I may be a little jealous of Trent too."

"But they've got nothing on you, babe," Kyle says.

I turn around to look at him and cup the side of his face. "Aww, thanks, babe. But you still aren't winning the car battle. We're going with an SUV for our next vehicle, not another sports car."

"Damn," Kyle mutters, feigning defeat.

I laugh and wave my hands in the air to emphasize my point. "A sports car is not a family car!"

"We could totally make it work. You're not even giving it a fair shot," he accuses.

I roll my eyes. "Uh-huh."

"Hey! Who wants the next round?" Trent calls out from the cornhole game.

"We do!" I shout back as I tug my hoodie down and grab Kyle's hand to lead him toward the cornhole extravaganza.

I stand next to Dane's girl, and Kyle stands next to Dane across the way. "Is she carrying you or what?" Kyle says to Dane. She giggles and then Kyle introduces himself. "I'm Kyle, by the way."

"Lauren," she says with a small wave.

I turn to her with a smile and extend my hand. "Aria. Nice to meet you."

"I love that, that's such a pretty name," Lauren says.

I put a hand over my heart showing I'm flattered by the compliment, and then I look over to Dane. "Thank you for bringing Lauren into our lives tonight."

Lauren laughs, and Dane looks at her while shaking his head. "Don't mind her, she doesn't get out much."

"It's true," Kyle adds.

I make a face at Kyle before we start a game of cornhole, and we start out with a lead on Dane and Lauren, but then Dane sinks three bags into the hole consecutively. I point at Dane, but speak to Kyle as I shout, "You better be watching where he steps! Make sure he's not going out of bounds!"

Dane holds a hand up as if to say "time out." "Hey, don't try to downplay my amazing cornhole abilities."

"Don't tempt me to take out the measuring tape," I say with narrowed eyes.

Kyle turns to Dane. "If you think she's kidding, she's not."

Lauren looks at Dane and acts fearful. "Maybe you should let me take control. She means business."

"If control is what you want, I'm happy to give you the reins, girl," Dane says with a suggestive smirk.

Kyle and I give each other deadpan looks over the cornhole boards, but start to chuckle at how much fun we're all having. When the game is over, Dane and Lauren win by two points, and we all start to walk off. With one arm draped over Lauren, Dane tells us they're leaving, and Trent says the same with him and Julie while Kate tags along.

"Alright, we're going to get out of here too," Ronnie says as he walks up to me to give me a hug.

"So glad you could make it," I say as I revel in his hug. When I pull back, I ask, "So we're coming over to Mom and Dad's for dinner tomorrow right?"

"That's the plan. Just come on time, otherwise Mom is going to ask me ten times in a row if I know where you are," Ronnie says.

"Yep. I got you." I sigh, knowing how neurotic our mom can get at the smallest things.

When he releases me, Ronnie and Kyle exchange goodbyes, and then Kyle and I say goodbye to Cheryl. Kyle throws one camping chair over his shoulder and picks up the cooler, while I throw the other camping chair over my shoulder, and then we walk back home.

As Kyle and I walk into our bedroom, we immediately start changing into our pajamas and wash up for bed. I am the last one out of the bathroom since I have a strict skincare regime, which takes some time, especially in the summer when I'm sweating a lot. When I exit the bathroom, Kyle is sitting on the bed with one knee bent up, and one leg stretched out in front of him, looking like sex-on-a-stick in only his black boxer-briefs. His tan, rippled stomach is out on display, as well as the bulge behind the black fabric. I give him a smile in appreciation as I lean against the doorframe of the bathroom, and Kyle just gestures a "come hither" motion with his finger.

When I reach the bed, Kyle grabs me by the waist to straddle his hips, and cups the sides of my face so that our foreheads touch. "I love you so much, Aria," he breathes against my lips.

"I love you too. You're my one and only," I whisper back as I entangle my fingers through his hair at the back of his head. Our lips lock eagerly as Kyle slides the straps of my camisole tank top down my shoulders, and his lips start placing a trail of gentle kisses from my chin, down my neck, and to the top of my breasts. I feel the flick of his tongue every so often, causing my skin to break out in goosebumps from the velvety touch, and setting off sparks of electricity in random areas underneath my skin.

After a few moments, I pick his head up so that his eyes are peering up at me. "I can't wait. Make love to me," I whisper. My wish is his command as Kyle flips us over so I'm lying on my back and he's parked between my legs, and eventually, we make slow and passionate love to one another.

Little did I know, this was the last time we ever would.

CHAPTER

Six

ARIA

Monday, June 21, 2021

It's now Monday, and back to the grind it is. I'm always up before Kyle, and I'm throwing on a black fitted tank top dress before my fingers tousle with my long dark waves in the mirror. Kyle is still sleeping soundly, but as I always do, I make sure to kiss him goodbye before I head out. I rub his arm that's resting above his head to wake him, and I whisper over him, "Hey, babe, I'm leaving. I love you."

I kiss Kyle's lips, and he lets out a groggy, "Love you too, babe."

With that, I walk out of our bedroom, and close the door behind me.

I'm sitting at the desk of my classroom shoveling the last bit of my turkey and Swiss sandwich in my mouth, when I see a text pop up from Kyle.

Kyle: After work, I'm going to run to the store so I can replace some of our high hats in the house. I should be home around 6:30 the latest.

Me: Okay, babe, dinner will be done by then. Chicken cutlets and asparagus sound good?

Kyle: Sounds perfect :)

Me: Kay, see you later. Love you.

Kyle: Love you too.

Not too long after I put my phone down, the bell rings to indicate that it is the next class period. I start to see some of my seventh graders flooding into my classroom, and I get up to turn the projector on to display their "Do Now" and "Agenda" for the day.

"Ms. Tate! You wanna see the new TikTok Kara and I just made?" Morgan says as she rushes into my personal space, waving her cell phone in front of me.

I chuckle as I respond. "Sure, why not."

One of the many reasons I love my job. The randomness of my middle schoolers never ceases to amaze me or keep me on my toes. After I watch their fifteen second TikTok, I give my two cents. "Impressive. Hopefully you can keep that same energy during class today? Yeah?" I tease.

"Ms. Tate, we always bring our A-game to class. We're your favorite students. In fact, you need to do a TikTok with us on the last day of school. Please?" Morgan asks.

I look upward with my hands on my hips, as if really contemplating, and then extend my hand out to shake Morgan's hand. "Deal," I say with a wide grin.

"Wait, really?!" Morgan exclaims with excitement.

I shrug like it's no big deal. "Sure. But the only stipulation is that it's appropriate."

"I swear it'll be appropriate! Oh my god, you're the best teacher ever!" Morgan says before taking her seat.

Oh the simple things that make my students the happiest people ever.

HUNT FOR THE ROSES

It's six o'clock, and I am placing the breaded chicken cutlets in the oven, along with the seasoned asparagus. Kyle should be home within the next half hour, so I pour two glasses of Cabernet, and start setting the table. While dinner is cooking in the oven, I pass time by taking out the load of laundry I put in the wash earlier, and hang specific clothes up on the drying rack. When I come back upstairs, I check on dinner periodically until it's done, and I take the trays out of the oven to place them on trivets.

Figuring I still have some time left to kill, I take my glass of wine and sit on the couch in the living room to start flipping through Netflix. Once I spot that there is a new thriller movie in the "Top Ten" that looks semi-decent, I leave the movie highlighted on the screen, and scroll through social media on my phone until Kyle makes his appearance.

But before I know it, it's seven o'clock. I look out the window behind the couch to see if Kyle's car has pulled up or if he's going to pull up any minute, but there is no sign of him at all. I decide to call Kyle, and after his phone rings for what feels like forever, I leave a voicemail message. "Hey, babe, just wanted to check in and see where you were. Me and dinner are waiting for you. Call me when you get this," I say into the phone, then hang up.

I get up to serve the chicken cutlets and asparagus on plates, and place the plates on our dining room table. I start to rinse off the bakeware and pots I used to cook dinner, and load them into the dishwasher to save time after we eat. Afterwards, I resume my position on the living room couch to scroll through Instagram and TikTok again.

Before I know it, it's now seven thirty, one hour after Kyle said he would be home and I still have not heard from him. Taking a sip of my wine, I look out the window behind the couch I'm sitting on to check to see if his car is outside.

Still nothing.

Maybe my voicemail from earlier didn't go through or he overlooked my missed call. I put my wine glass down on the coffee table and try to call Kyle again. But once again, the phone just rings for what feels like an eternity until it goes to voicemail. I decide to leave another voicemail, then open my text message log with Kyle to type him a text as well.

Me: Everything okay? Call me when you get this.

It seems like I'm going to be waiting for some time, so I turn on *Friends* on HBO Max and watch a couple episodes in the meantime.

Another forty minutes pass by.

I look back out the window again.

Nothing.

Two hours after Kyle said he would be home, and I haven't heard a single thing from him since this afternoon. I decide to pick up my phone again and call the person who may have heard from him.

After a few rings, Dane picks up on the other line. "Hey, what's up?"

"Have you heard from Kyle?" I ask immediately.

Dane hesitates for a second, seemingly a little thrown off by the fact that I didn't even greet him with a "Hello." "No? Why?"

"He's not home. I tried calling and texting him, but he hasn't responded to me," I explain. It's evident from my voice that I'm hoping Dane has answers for me.

"Maybe he got caught up at work?" Dane suggests.

I sigh into the phone. "He didn't sound super busy today. He said he was stopping by the store after work and was supposed to be home by six thirty," I respond.

"Alright, I'm sure there's a reason. Let me see if I can get in touch with him," Dane suggests.

"Okay. Thanks," I say.

"You got it," Dane says before hanging up.

I place my phone down on the couch, before sitting up straight and looking out the window behind me.

Still nothing.

I see a text pop up from Dane a couple minutes later.

> Dane: Just tried calling him and I sent a text. Will let you know if I hear something.

An eerie silence starts to fill the room, and I feel like the walls of my living room are starting to close in on me. I decide to shake the feeling and call Kyle's mom, and luckily she answers after a couple rings.

"Hi, sweetie," Pamela answers.

"Hi, Pam, I'm sorry to bother you so late. Have you heard from Kyle? He was supposed to be home a couple hours ago, but he hasn't come home yet," I explain.

Pam pauses before speaking into the phone. "What? No, I haven't. What's going on, you sound nervous…" she trails off.

"I don't know, maybe I'm overreacting. It's just, I tried calling and texting Kyle, but he hasn't gotten back to me, and he said he would be home by six thirty," I say.

"Okay." Pam sighs. It seems like I'm making her on edge now, and as much as I don't want to make Kyle's mom worry, my nerves are getting the best of me right now. "Let me try calling him and I'll let you know if I hear from him."

"Okay," I say in a hushed voice. I can't even muster any other words because it feels like I suffocate a little more as everyone I talk to makes me lose more hope.

Hope that everything is okay.

I swallow a nervous lump in my throat, and just flip my phone face down on the couch to try and relax a little. I continue to look out the window every couple minutes as time passes by excruciatingly slowly. I start to become more aware of each passing minute and second without Kyle walking through the front door of our home. And with each minute and second that ticks by, I start to feel a shadow casting over my heart, dimming the sunlight that's been shining over it.

Minute by minute.

Second by second.

Tick tock.

Tick tock.

When the clock reads nine thirty, I start to pace around my living room and kitchen. I hear my phone vibrate, and I race to my phone on the living room couch. My heart sinks when I see Dane's name on the screen, but in the same breath I think he may have answers now.

"Have you heard from him?" I ask.

"No. You sure he wasn't going anywhere else after work?" Dane asks.

I let out a nervous breath. "I'm sure. At least he didn't mention anything." I put my hand to my forehead. "I'm starting to get worried, Dane," I say in a shaky voice.

"Alright, calm down. Have you tried calling his mom?" Dane asks.

"Yes, but she hasn't heard from him either," I say.

"Okay, calm down. Let me try calling Trent and I'll call you back," Dane says before hanging up. But just as I hang up with Dane, I hear a knock at my front door.

The dark cloud that was hovering over my heart before is here to stay. I pause my movements, like I'm frozen in time. My heart sinks into the pit of my stomach, and I feel like I'm going to vomit as my breathing starts to become erratic, and tears threaten to trickle out of my eyes.

Tragedy is knocking, and I know once I answer the door, there is no turning back.

CHAPTER
Seven

ARIA

Monday, June 21, 2021

"There's been an accident."

Four words that shattered my entire world in two seconds.

A four-car pile-up on the main highway and t-boned on the driver's side, Kyle's injuries are severe and critical. I'm in a trance while I'm sitting in the hospital waiting area, praying with every cell of my being that Kyle makes it through this. The policeman who came knocking at my door drove me to the hospital that Kyle was taken to after the car crash. I have my forearms crossed across my stomach as I'm doubled over, clutching to the sleeves of my sweatshirt hoodie, like I'm clinging on for dear life.

Kyle's life.

Dane is in the chair next to me. He came outside his house when the cop showed up in front of mine and followed us to the hospital. His elbow is on one knee with his head in his hand, while his other hand is on my shoulder to just let me know he's there for me. I called my parents, and Dane called Kyle's parents, as well as Trent and Kate.

When my parents come through the hospital waiting room doors, they spot me right away. I jump up and throw my arms around my mom who's already holding her arms out to me. I fall apart as I wrap a vice grip around her, tears freely running down my cheeks as she hugs me back as tightly as she can.

"He's going to be okay, shh," my mom whispers as she strokes her fingers through my hair.

"He can't leave me, Mom. He can't," I sob profusely into her chest.

My mom continues to comfort me with her touch, as my dad embraces me from behind. Kate and Trent rush around my parents and I, seemingly just entering the waiting room, and I notice Dane starts to crowd around us as well.

"Any news?" Trent cuts in while looking frantically back and forth between my parents and Dane.

"Not yet," Dane answers, and I don't miss the hint of fear etched in his voice.

"How long has he been in there?" Kate asks.

Just as Kate asks her question, Dr. Kline comes out of a set of double doors and heads our way, and we all stand up straight to face him.

Dr. Kline purses his lips as he says the next words that crumble my entire existence.

"I'm very sorry. He didn't make it."

I grab my mom's arm and fall down to the ground as she tries to soften my fall with her body. Everyone closes in around me as everything goes black.

Tonight, my wrists were shackled to the corner of a dark room.

A room that is my new home.

My new reality.

CHAPTER
Eight

DANE

Sunday, June 27, 2021

My plans for this weekend were that of any average twenty-six-year-old–kick back with good friends and make everlasting memories. Instead, I'm sitting here in a black suit and tie, watching Kyle's casket be lowered into the ground.

I'm hollow. Empty. Like a piece of my heart has been gouged out, and the blood pumping through my veins is no longer rhythmic. Even though I'm witnessing Kyle's burial right in front of my eyes, it doesn't seem real. I'm thinking any minute, someone is going to pinch me from this nightmare. Any minute, I'm going to wake up in a cold sweat in my bed.

But this isn't a nightmare.

It's real.

And it's the toughest reality I've ever had to accept.

I'm looking around me in a trance-like state as the priest speaks above the somberness. I look to my side to Kate and Trent. Kate's cheeks have tears streaming down them, and Trent is fighting back tears of his own. My eyes go to Aria sitting between her mom and Kyle's mom. She's tightly holding both their hands on either side of her, and she mirrors my trance-like state. She looks like the shell of the person she once was. Just a shadow. Ronnie and her father sit behind her, and Ronnie has his hand propped on Aria's shoulder to silently express his support.

I take a deep breath as I draw my attention back to the priest who is speaking. I'm trying to find some solace in the words he's saying, but the meaning of his words fail me. I can't process the senselessness of all of this.

When the ceremony ends, people start making their way to their cars at the curb of the cemetery to chat with each other. I stand from my seat and turn to my mom who was sitting next to me. She brings me in for a tight hug, and I rest my chin on her shoulder. Somehow, she's more emotional than I am right now, and we're at *my* best friend's funeral.

I just stare blankly in front of me.

When my mom pulls away, she grabs the sides of my face. "Are you going to be okay? Do you want me to keep you company back at your house?"

I shake my head with a tight-lipped smile. "I'll be fine, I promise."

"You let me know if you need anything, you understand?" She hugs me again. "Oh honey, I'm so sorry," she whispers.

"I'll let you know. Thank you for being here, Mom," I say, and I kiss her on the cheek to say goodbye to her.

I watch my mom walk off as I let out a long breath, and then I make my way over to a tree away from where the crowds of people are. I lean back against the tree with closed eyes, shoving my hands in my suit pockets as I cross one foot in front of the other. This is all too much, and I just need these few minutes alone. I don't want to mingle with anyone again just yet. So many thoughts are coursing through me, I don't even have a clear vision of what's going on in my head. Everything in my mind is so blurry that I just feel numb. Like my emotions are iced over. I feel like I should be crying or getting angry, and the fact that I'm not makes me concerned. How could I not be feeling much of anything right now?

"Hey, man." Ronnie's voice interrupts my thoughts, causing me to open my eyes. I tilt my head forward to see Ronnie walking toward me with two hands in his pockets.

"Hey," I respond in a faint voice.

"How are you holding up?" Ronnie asks once he's standing in front of me.

I look off to the side and let out a sigh. "This fucking sucks," I breathe out.

Ronnie throws me a tight-lipped smile as he places a hand on my shoulder, and I mirror his tight-lipped smile as if to say "thank you" for the comfort.

Ronnie brings his hand down and shoves his hand back into his pocket. "I'm really sorry, Dane. I can't imagine what it's like to lose a best friend."

I drop my head and nod. "Yeah, I wouldn't wish this on anyone. Not even my worst enemy."

"I know 'sorry' doesn't seem like enough, but that's really all it comes down to," Ronnie says.

I look up at him. "I appreciate it. Just you being here is enough." I pause before continuing. "Especially for Ari."

Ronnie gives a slow nod in understanding. "My parents and I think it's best for Aria to stay with them for a while. We don't think it's good for her to be in that house right away."

I gulp nervously just thinking about what Aria is going through. "How's she doing?"

Ronnie shakes his head. "Not good."

I just stare at him and inhale a long breath.

He rubs the back of his neck. "This isn't going to be easy for her. No other way to put it than how you did before. This fucking sucks."

I vaguely gesture a hand out. "Hey, listen, whatever I can do, let me know."

Ronnie nods. "For now, just worry about yourself. You have healing to do too."

I nod and we say goodbye with a hug. I'm glued to the tree as I close my eyes again and listen to the crowd of mingling people for the next few minutes. I can't convince myself to move from this tree because if I move, everything starts to become real. If I start conversing with people and exchanging apologies, everything just becomes more real. Saying sorry to Aria was just the cherry on top of the miserable day this is. I told her whatever she needs from me, I'll be there for her. You know, the typical things you say to someone who is grieving. I really did mean it, but I just can't face her again. At least not right now, it's just too much to bear. So I wait for the voices of the mingling people to die down, and once people start clearing the green field, I find my way to my black Mustang to drive home.

Once I am back in my house, I place my keys on top of the foyer table to the right. I stand in place as the silence in my house consumes me. I'm now completely alone with my thoughts, being forced to confront them head on. It's like the foggy haze that I was seeing in my mind slowly parts, and my new reality comes into focus.

Kyle is dead, and he's never coming back.

With this revelation, I pick my keys back up off the foyer table, and ricochet them across the living room area as hard as I possibly can. The keys crash into a picture frame on the wall, and shards of glass explode onto the carpet.

CHAPTER
Nine

ARIA

~Two Weeks After~

It's been two weeks since Kyle's burial, and my childhood bedroom has become my physical prison. I'm lying in a fetal position on my twin bed, just staring numbly out the window at the tree branches blowing in the gentle wind. My emotions have been coming in waves, but the one thing that remains constant is my broken heart.

Each passing day without Kyle has torn a piece of my heart off. My heart is no longer a complete organ that beats inside my chest, but a box of broken pieces that serves no meaningful purpose. When I move around, it's almost like I can hear the rattling of the box, and the sound is so loud that I'm reminded every second Kyle is gone. The only way to not hear the clanking of the box is if I don't move, so I choose to lie down most of my days. Silence is the soundtrack to my life right now, and I kind of like it here.

A knock on the bedroom door kicks me out of my own thoughts. "Ari, I have lunch for you," my mom says as she comes through the bedroom door.

I don't speak or move at all as my eyes focus on a single tree branch dancing in the breeze. My eyes move in sync with the twig, and I become taunted by the energy and happiness that emits from its movement and bright green leaves.

I hear my mom set the plate of food on the nightstand and feel her sit behind me on the bed. "Ari, you have to eat. You've hardly eaten anything these past two weeks."

I say nothing and just continue to stare out the window. I don't want to deal with the real world. If I deal with the real world, I am accepting Kyle's death.

I feel the bed shift as my mom lies down and cuddles me from behind, wrapping an arm around my stomach. I finally break my silence in a strained whisper. "I don't know how I can go on without him. My heart hurts so much, Mom." A single tear falls out of the corner of my eye, but my face doesn't contort with the emotion or scrunch an inch. Even my grief has become as deadening as my joy, and my soul is vacant.

When my mom kisses the back of my head and hugs me even tighter, another wave of crying wracks my entire body, and the sound of the rattling pieces inside my chest haunts me once again.

~Two Months After~

Ronnie and Cheryl are forcing me to go out tonight, and it's the first time I'm leaving my parents' house since Kyle's death. Well, I've left my parents' house for short walks outside and quick trips to the grocery store, but I haven't left the house for any substantial reason.

I'm on autopilot in the mirror, not really consciously thinking about getting ready, but just going through the motions. I don't feel like going out, so I feel no need to look the part as I throw on a black hoodie, leggings, and sneakers. I don't even bother to style my hair, so I just leave it straight down, and not a stitch of makeup touches my skin.

When we enter Shippers, Ronnie and Cheryl lead me to a booth where Kate, Trent, and Dane are sitting. The three of them stand up and hug me hello, and I throw a forced smile their way.

When we all sit down, Ronnie looks at me. "What do you want to drink?"

"Water is fine for now."

"Do you want to try this sour I just ordered?" Kate offers as she slides her beer across the table.

I throw her a tight-lipped smile. "Sure." I take a small sip just to appease Kate, and look up to her after. "What is it?"

"Very Berry Lady," Kate says. "Do you want me to get you one?"

I shake my head. "No, that's okay. I'm not really in the mood for drinking tonight."

Everyone throws awkward eyes at each other, and I want nothing more than to scream. Scream at Ronnie and Cheryl for making me come out. Scream at Kate, Trent, and Dane for agreeing to thinking this night out would be successful. Scream at all of them for trying to help me at all.

I take a sip of my water that was ordered for me before I got there, and Dane's the next to speak. "Can we get you something to eat?"

"I'll look at the menu," I respond. Silence commences once again, and I tuck a loose strand of hair behind my ear as I look at the menu I could recite in my sleep. Right now, looking anywhere but everyone's faces is good enough for me. I despise feeling like a charity case, and I hate knowing that anything my family or friends offer won't bring Kyle back to life. Their efforts are to no avail ever since I became the shell of the person I was two months ago. I'm physically here on Earth, but my emotions have been hollowed out of my body. There's a black hole where my soul used to reside, and my spirit is nonexistent.

I forgot what it feels like to *live*.

Conversation starts to pick up between the others, and they exchange a couple jokes. I stretch a half-ass smile their way every now and then, trying to save face, but the loudest sound among the chatter is still the clanking pieces of my broken heart. Roaring in my ears as it deafens my other senses.

When I get back to my parent's house and close the bedroom door behind me, I lean against it and let out a long breath. Tears well up behind my eyes, and I feel a rage start to brew inside me. I lock eyes with a picture frame on my bedroom wall, and look at it like a predator hunting down its prey.

I roll up one sleeve of my hoodie as I walk up to the picture frame, and punch the glass repeatedly, using every ounce of anger I possess to shatter it to pieces. My fist bleeds from the explosive contact, and blood begins to trickle down my hand and forearm. As I watch the bright red lines slide down my arm, it's like I'm watching some of my fury leave my body, and for a split second I feel relief.

This feels good.

I fall to the ground on my butt, relishing in this newfound satisfaction. My fist is still clenched, so I slowly open it, then gradually close it back up again. I'm savoring every bit of physical pain I feel with each contraction, unexpectedly thankful for this moment.

Thankful that I am able to feel something that can challenge the agony of my broken heart.

CHAPTER

Ten

DANE

~Three Months After~

It's nine o'clock at night on a Friday, and I'm sitting on my porch as I look over at Aria and Kyle's house. I start to envision the times I would see them holding hands leaving for a dinner date, or making out on their front porch. Then if I caught them, I'd always chime in with some joke, and we'd all have a good laugh. Man, I miss those days. It's amazing how before you lose something, you don't really understand its value until it's gone. No matter how small.

I miss the small moments.

I miss our nights at Shippers.

I miss our nights at the beach.

I miss us.

All of us.

I lean back against the wooden bench, propping one foot up on the small table in front of me, and run my fingers through my hair as I sigh. I start to feel guilty for wallowing in my own sadness when I know my sorrow pales in comparison to Aria's.

Aria.

I haven't seen or spoken to her in a month since we tried to take her out to Shippers, and I find myself thinking about her when I have a free moment. I think about how Aria is, what she's doing, and how she's learning to cope. It still feels like some horrible nightmare we're all going to wake up from, and just brush off in the morning. But that morning never comes. The sun never rises in this situation. There's been a dark cloud hovering over my life for the past three months, and I can't seem to run fast enough to escape the rain.

I wonder if I ever will.

I inhale a breath as I take out my phone from my jogger sweatpants pocket, and go to Aria's contact information to compose a message.

> Me: Hey, I'm still here if you need anything.

I usually send her a few texts a month just to check in. My texts pretty much always say the same thing, they're just paraphrased. To be honest, I dread sending these texts to Aria because I know there's nothing I can say in a situation like this to alleviate her pain. It feels pointless and uncomfortable, but deep in my heart, I know it's the right thing to do.

Kyle was my best friend. I know how much he loved this girl, and I know how much she loved him, and I feel this is my way of honoring Kyle in his wake. Making sure the person he loved and adored the most is going to be okay is reason enough for me to send these texts to Aria. No matter how dreadful they might be.

> Ari: Hey, how have you been? I appreciate you reaching out.

I narrow my eyes as I momentarily focus on the fact that Aria asks me how I've been. I didn't even ask her how she's been. Here she is grieving over losing the love of her life, and she's asking me how I am. See what I mean? These texting conversations are always awful.

> Me: I'm okay. But "okay" is a relative term these days. How are you doing?

Ari: I'm getting by. I try to keep myself occupied.

Me: Well, I meant what I said earlier. Anything you need, just let me know. I'm here.

Ari: Means a lot. Thanks, Dane.

Me: Anytime.

And that's the end of our conversation. I blow out a breath as I sink back into my patio bench, staring at the dark, lonely street that reflects exactly how I feel.

CHAPTER
Eleven

ARIA

~Four Months After~

It's Saturday afternoon when Ronnie and I pull up to mine and Kyle's townhouse. I decided today would be the day that I fully face reality, and I start to tackle my struggles head on. But I couldn't do it alone, so I asked Ronnie to come with me. I let out a long, nervous breath as we step out of his car, and I look over at my front porch.

It appears the same, but somehow *different*.

Ronnie turns to look at me. "You okay?" I nod when I look back at him, but I'm honestly not sure if I am.

Ronnie is in front of me as we walk up the porch steps, and when he opens the door to my townhouse, I walk inside the foyer first. Although it's a bright and sunny day, there is not one ray of sunlight that seeps through the windows. At least I can't notice because the gloominess that's resided in this house for so long remains prominent, and as I look around, the walls and shelves are stripped of any photos of Kyle and I.

This house looks exactly like my heart.

Empty and broken.

I knew that Ronnie and my father had cleared the house of pictures of Kyle and I, and they packed up whatever possessions Kyle's parents didn't take. I told my brother and dad I couldn't stand to put Kyle's stuff away because it was just too big a burden to bear, so they took that burden off of me. As grateful as I am for that, looking at my former home makes me feel lonelier than ever before.

Ronnie comes next to me and brings me in for a side-hug with one arm, and tears threaten to leave my eyes. "You're going to be okay. I'm here," Ronnie assures me.

I just nod, and then continue to walk cautiously around the living room and kitchen. Memories start pouring into my mind like a waterfall. Kyle and I cuddling on the couch, making dinner together, wrestling each other for the remote in the living room, playing board games on the coffee table while sipping on delicious red wine.

When I find it difficult to keep my composure, I put my head in my hands to try and gain some control back, and I feel Ronnie's hand rubbing the outside of my arm in an up and down motion. Once I lift my head back up, I look at Ronnie. "Let's go upstairs."

Ronnie nods and starts walking toward the stairway as I follow his lead. He knows exactly where I want to go, and when he gets to the top of the stairs, he slowly opens the door to the bedroom. I take a moment before entering the room myself, and when I finally walk through the bedroom door, the first thing I notice is the bedding.

This is where Kyle and I made love.

I walk over to the bed and start to graze my fingertips against the duvet. I just want to feel something that Kyle once touched because somehow, it makes me feel closer to him. Like he's still with me.

I turn back to Ronnie who's leaning against the doorframe. "Where did you put his things?"

Ronnie clears his throat and points to the closet. "They're in there if you want to take a look."

I walk over to open the closet door, and find a brown box in the corner on the floor. I go to my knees and pick up the box flaps to find framed pictures, and some of Kyle's clothes. The top picture is a photo of Kyle and I on our third date together. We went out to dinner at this Mexican restaurant where we discovered our love for peach-mango margaritas on the rocks. We're clinking glasses in the picture, and we both have smiles on our faces that stretch from ear to ear. A tear slips out of my eye, no longer being able to fight the constraint.

I hold the picture to my heart and with my free hand, I pick up one of Kyle's golf polos to hold it to my nose. When his scent invades my senses, another tear falls freely from my eye, and then another. I feel Ronnie come up behind me, and he bends down to grab my arm to help me get to my feet. Once Ronnie spins me around and tightly embraces me, I completely lose it as I sob uncontrollably in my brother's arms, until I've exhausted all of my tears for the day.

~Five Months After~

It's Sunday, and Kate has convinced me to go to brunch with her. I'm starting to care a little more about what I look like when I go out, so I decide to throw on a beige, ribbed long-sleeved crop top with mom jeans, and feel *okay* about today. But like Dane said, "okay" is a relative term these days.

When I hear my phone buzz, I see a text from Kate letting me know she's here, and I go downstairs to answer the door. When I open it, Kate greets me with a bag held out to me. "I brought you a doughnut. Can't say that won't put a smile on your face."

I chuckle as I take the bag. "Thanks, you really didn't have to."

Kate shrugs. "I know. But I wanted to." I just smile back at her, and then I'm grabbing my purse off the dining room table and heading out the door with Kate.

Luckily, we're seated within ten minutes of putting our name in, and we scan the QR code on the table to look through the menu on our phones. After the waitress comes and takes our orders, Kate looks over to me. "So how's work been?"

"It's okay. Holiday vacations are approaching, which normally I would be stoked for." I shrug before continuing. "But all it means is I have more free time for my mind to wander."

Kate gives me a sympathetic look. "Those days off could be good for you, Ari. You know we're all here for you, and we want to see you."

I nod. "I know, I don't doubt that. You guys have been great." I look out the window next to our booth. "It's just hard to be around you guys sometimes. And I'm not saying that to be mean, it's just the truth, and I'm sorry."

Kate nods in understanding, and when our waitress comes over with our lattes, we're able to fill the awkward silence with sips of our drinks. I lick my lips after the first sip, and decide to be the first to resume our dialogue. After all, Kate's really trying here. "I'm going to start therapy tomorrow."

Kate's eyes light up. "Ari, that's great."

"Yeah, well, I'm not really looking forward to it. My family is pushing it."

"I think they're pushing you in the right direction," Kate says.

"I know." I swallow a lump in my throat before continuing. "I know logically this could be a way for me to get my life back, but it all seems like it will be futile," I respond.

"You don't know that. I mean, you have to try, right?"

I give Kate a small smile. "Yeah. I'm going to try."

Dr. Connelly sits across from me in her arm chair as she starts our first therapy session. "Talk to me about what you're feeling."

I'm sitting up straight on the couch as I play with my hands nervously. "Anger. Pain."

"It's a normal part of the grieving process. But the intensity of what you're feeling will not always be this strong," Dr. Connelly responds.

"Knowing these emotions are normal provides me no solace," I say, frustration evident in my tone.

Dr. Connelly takes a moment before speaking. "I think what you should start doing is consciously try to refocus your attention. Go for a walk outside, read, bake, hang out with friends. Maybe even meet new people."

"If I'm being honest, I don't want to be around people that much. Their happiness just reminds me of what I don't have," I respond.

Dr. Connelly nods. "That's understandable. And you may not be ready for that right now, but you can start smaller. What are your hobbies?"

I shrug as I look out the window to the right of me in my therapist's office. "Reading, dancing. Not dancing in a professional way, or that I take classes or anything. But I like it. It's freeing for me."

"That's wonderful. Maybe try to channel some of your energy into music." Dr. Connelly gestures her hand out to me. "For example, make a playlist that you could listen to from time to time, and put songs on there that will comfort you."

I laugh-sigh as I look back at Dr. Connelly. "It sounds ridiculous. I don't mean to criticize your suggestion; it just seems so small to try and help cope with something so big."

"There are a lot of people that find comfort in the smallest things. This journey for you is about new self-discoveries."

I look back out the window again, trying to digest the conversation my therapist and I are having.

Maybe therapy will help.

Maybe it won't.

But like I said to Kate, I'm going to try.

CHAPTER
Twelve

ARIA

~Six Months After~

It's one o'clock in the morning on a Saturday night, and I'm walking out the door of my former townhouse. I've visited a few times since my first visit with Ronnie, trying to slowly adapt to my new life. I still don't feel ready to live back here yet, but I'm becoming more hopeful that I can. The truth is, I loved my life in this house and I loved my life in this town, so I'm not ready to completely close that chapter. With my salary advancement, I've been able to continue making the monthly payments on my own, and my parents and Ronnie have offered to help me out when they can. I feel very fortunate that when Kyle and I bought this house, it was during a hot time in the real estate market, so our mortgage was much cheaper than it would have been normally. I'm not ready to completely let go of this house, and it almost feels like I would be completely letting go of Kyle if I did. But Kyle's still a part of me, and I still feel his soul braided around my own.

I came here tonight after having dinner with my family, and I just laid in our bed for a few hours, clearly losing track of time. When I walk down the porch steps and take a few steps down the pathway to my car, I hear a door open and people talking. I turn my head in the direction of the sound, and notice Dane hanging outside his front door as he kisses a girl goodbye. I'm stuck staring at the scene in front of me since I haven't seen Dane in so long. It's almost lost on me how to even act around him, or what to say. He's reached out to me over the last few months, and he's probably going to be completely confused when he sees me. I can't even try to hide from him now, so I guess the best thing to do is just face this situation head on.

When the brunette walks into the Uber parked in front of Dane's house, Dane catches sight of me and does a double take. I start to feel extremely nervous and uncomfortable, wishing I had darted for my car instead of standing where I am, especially after he seemingly just had a rendezvous with a girl.

"Aria?" Dane asks with narrowed eyes.

I anxiously give a small wave in his direction. "Hey."

He holds a finger up. "Wait, give me one second." Dane goes back into his house momentarily and comes back out as he's throwing on a black crewneck t-shirt. He was shirtless before in gray joggers, so I guess the awkwardness goes down a notch. Dane walks down toward me, and his hands are on his hips as he stands in front of me. "I had no idea you were here."

I gesture with my hand as I look toward my townhouse. "Yeah, I've been starting to visit," I begin to explain, and then I look back at Dane. "Just to get used to being in the house before I fully move back this summer."

Dane nods in understanding and just stares at me for a few moments, almost like he's trying to figure out what to say next. At least I'm not the only one who feels super uncomfortable right now. "Is there anything I can do? Do you need anything?"

I shake my head and wave off his offer. "No, I'm fine." I smile as I change the subject. "So, how are you?"

Dane rocks back on his heels as he shoves his hands into the pockets of his sweatpants. "I'm alright. Work's been busy as spring and summer approach with new projects. I've been making time for my mom more, which

is nice. I don't see her often." He swallows before continuing. "It helps…
having her to talk to."

I give Dane a tight-lipped smile in understanding. "Yeah, I know. Family helps a lot."

We just stare at each other for a few more seconds before Dane speaks next. "So, how are you doing?"

I look down as I play with my hands in front of my stomach. "I'm in therapy now." I look back up to him and shrug. "It's actually somewhat helpful. Who would have thought?" I say as I let out a shaky laugh.

"Yeah, Ronnie told me that."

I cock my head in surprise. "You've spoken with Ronnie?"

He shrugs. "Yeah. If I don't hear from you, sometimes I'll reach out to him just to make sure you're alright."

I smile, and suddenly the awkwardness fades for a brief moment. "That's really sweet. Thank you." Dane gives a small smile as if to accept my gratitude. "But I think I'm going to be okay. I'm slowly starting to piece my life back together."

"You'll be fine," Dane confirms.

I throw him an appreciative smile, and Dane sheds a nervous smile as he looks off to the side. Taking that as my cue, I hike a thumb over my shoulder. "I should get going."

Dane waves a vague hand gesture. "Listen, it was great to see you."

"You too," I say as I start to walk backwards a few steps to signal that I'm going to leave.

Dane quickly waves a hand at me. "See you later."

I throw a quick wave back at him, and then turn to my car. As I drive off, I notice that Dane is still standing in the same position I left him.

~Seven Months After~

Dr. Connelly starts our therapy session off from her infamous brown leather arm chair. "So how have things changed since the last time we spoke? And there's no pressure here. It's okay if nothing has changed because we can talk about that too."

"I think I've been better at refocusing my energy. I'm eating more. I go on small outings with my family. I read."

"This is good."

I nod with a shrug, not as convinced with my progress as Dr. Connelly is.

"You mentioned family, but what about friends?" Dr. Connelly asks.

I shake my head. "It's too difficult to be around them a lot."

"Why is that?"

"All of us were friends, and we have so many memories with Kyle. It's too much to be around them as often as I used to be. Especially as a group. I can handle hanging out with them individually, but as a group…" I sigh when I trail off. "As a group, I feel the empty chair that much more."

"Do they reach out to you? Your friends?"

"Yes. Kate reaches out to me weekly, and I've seen her briefly a few times. Dane reaches out a few times a month to see how I'm doing or if I need anything, and Trent does the same."

"It's nice that you have friends who care about you so much. That's a beautiful thing."

"I guess."

My tone is not confident at all, and Dr. Connelly looks at me curiously. "You don't seem like you agree. Talk to me about that."

I look out the window. "It's just so hard. It's so hard to see good in this world after everything that's happened." I look back to my therapist. "I feel betrayed. I feel betrayed by *life*."

Dr. Connelly considers me for a moment before responding. "I think anyone in your position would have the right to feel that way. But what you're doing is you're putting blinders on over good things in your life. You don't want to accept that life can be good to you because you feel wronged. You feel owed."

I look at her with a hard stare. "Yeah, I do feel wronged." I know she's going to try and tell me that I shouldn't feel that way, but she doesn't get to tell me that. I've been let down by life in one of the worst possible ways, and I have every right to be bitter.

"Aria, the problem with that is that it's counterintuitive. You're setting yourself up for more sadness. You've accepted that life is against you, and you refuse to see life's beauty." I slightly roll my eyes as I look out the window again. Sometimes, I can't take these inspirational speeches she gives because most of it is crap if you ask me. But in true therapist fashion, Dr. Connelly continues on anyway. "I want you to think about this quote, and we'll end today's session with a discussion on it."

I look back at my therapist. "Like what? 'Everything happens for a reason'? No offense, but I'm not sure I'm going to find much meaning behind a quote with all that's happened to me," I admit.

"You're stuck with me anyway," Dr. Connelly retorts, and I guess she does have a point.

"Can't argue with that. Do your best," I say.

"'When life throws thorns, hunt for the roses.'"

I blankly stare at Dr. Connelly for a couple seconds, not expecting such a unique quote.

"Who's it from?"

"It's from Anonymous, actually."

I feel my brows slightly furrow at my therapist, waiting for her to give the inevitable inspirational speech. "Aria, you've been thrown a lot of thorns in your life. But if you put the effort in to embrace the battle through the thorns, you'll see that there's still beauty to be found."

I swallow as I listen to Dr. Connelly's words. I stare at her for a few moments before looking out the window again, and it makes me beg the most important question of all.

Are there even any roses left for me to find in my world of thorns?

CHAPTER
Thirteen

DANE

~One Year After~

Saturday, June 4, 2022

About a year has passed since Kyle's death, and I've gradually been putting the pieces of my life back together. Over the past six months, Kate, Trent, and I have been starting to resume our weekly routine of going to Shippers. The first six months, all of us struggled to continue our traditions without Kyle, so we hung out less often, but it's nice to know we're starting to build some normalcy back into our friend group. That being said, I haven't seen Ari since the night I found her outside her townhouse when she told me she was starting to visit. I've continued to text her, but the conversations always remain the same. Brief and uncomfortable.

My mom has been a huge help, turning our lunches together into therapy sessions, so she's been a solid rock throughout my journey. Not to mention the increase in my random hookups. Not to say I've racked up a different woman every night, but my headcount rate has definitely increased this past year. But every hookup was for one purpose and one purpose only–to feel something other than pain.

As I'm punching and kicking the boxing bag at the gym, I hear my phone buzz. When I step away to pick up my phone from the floor, I see there's a text from Ronnie.

> Ronnie: Hey, I was wondering if you were going to be home in the next hour. I wanted to swing by.

> Me: I'll be at the gym for another twenty minutes, then I'll be on my way home. Everything okay?

> Ronnie: Sounds good. Yeah, I just wanted to talk to you about a few things.

I furrow my brows as I reply.

> Me: No problem. See you in a bit.

I put my phone down on the floor mat, and take a sip from my water jug before going back to the body bag. I break a sweat for another twenty minutes, rinse off, and then head home.

The ten-minute drive home turns into a twenty minute drive due to an accident on the main road, so by the time I'm pulling up to my townhouse, I see Ronnie's car parked along the curb.

I get out of my Mustang at the same time Ronnie steps out of his car. "Hey, it's good to see you," I say as I extend my hand so we can have a handshake-hug.

"Hey, man, you too," Ronnie replies.

I hike a thumb over my shoulder toward my house. "Want a drink?"

"Sure," Ronnie replies as he gestures for me to lead the way.

When we get into my house, I drop my car keys on the foyer table and go to the kitchen to retrieve a beer from the fridge. I place it on the kitchen island and open the top with a bottle opener, before handing it over to Ronnie who is standing on the opposite end of the kitchen island.

oning donening do onene

I walk over to a cabinet to get a drinking glass for myself, and then go to the fridge door. "So what's up? What's new?" I ask as I fill up the glass with water.

A few silent moments pass before Ronnie speaks behind me. "Aria's coming back to live at the townhouse." I pause momentarily registering his words. I knew her living arrangement at her parents' was temporary, but I guess being that a year has passed, I've sort of forgotten.

I turn around when my glass is full with enough water. "When?" is all I can think to say.

"Tomorrow," Ronnie says.

I walk over to stand across from Ronnie at the kitchen island. "Do you need me to help with anything?"

"Actually, yes. That's why I came to talk to you."

I take a sip of my water, then wave a vague hand gesture. "Anything you need."

"Dane, she needs someone to be there for her. She's made some big leaps these last six months being in therapy, and my family and I need to make sure she continues on that path." I nod as I furrow my brows, not fully understanding where he's going with this, so I just take another sip of my water and wait for him to continue explaining. "Can you just make sure she's okay? Check in on her and keep her company? Help around the house with maintenance if she needs it?"

I'm silent for a few seconds, wrapping my brain around this responsibility I would be taking on. "Oh, man," I breathe as I run a hand through my hair. "I've been reaching out to her, but I never know exactly what to say." I laugh thinking back at our awkward conversations. "To be honest, I don't know how much help I'm going to be. I mean, I will be there for her, I just don't know how well it's going to go."

Ronnie shakes his head and holds out a hand. "Trust me, just her knowing you're a shoulder she can lean on, that's all she needs." Ronnie places his beer on the island, and he's leaning with two palms. "Look, the only reason I'm asking you is because you live right next door, and it's easier for you to check in on her. I'm not saying this has to be every day, but maybe a few times a week, knock on her door to see what she's up to and make sure she's alright. That's all I'm asking. She's been living with my parents for the past year, and having people around her and knowing someone is there for her, it's really helped. I don't want to see her regress, because she's made so much progress up until this point. And now that Aria's coming back to live in her former house, she's going to need new support."

I nod more certainly this time because I can understand his concerns as an older brother, and I can understand why he's asking me to do this. "Hey, I once told you that anything you need, I'm here. That hasn't changed."

"I really appreciate this, Dane," Ronnie says thankfully.

"You got it," I say. I take another sip of my water as I ponder what I just agreed to. I mostly feel anxious because I haven't seen Aria in six months, and it's been a whole year since Kyle passed away. Yeah, I've texted Aria to check in, but I always knew she had her family as a backbone and support system. It almost feels like I would be taking on their duties, and I wasn't entirely sure if I wanted this baton to be passed to me.

Can I even handle this responsibility properly?

Time will tell I suppose.

CHAPTER
Fourteen

ARIA

Sunday, June 5, 2022

I step into my old home, and the gloomy fog has lifted a little from the first time I came back here. Occasionally, my mom and I have come here to redecorate to bring life back into this house, and it seems like our work paid off in a tiny way.

Small victories count a lot these days.

I drop my keys on the table in the foyer, and look to my left at the living area where the gray sectional sits on the beige carpet, facing the SMART TV that's mounted to the wall. I walk further down the hallway to enter the kitchen, and lean my palms on the island. I try to control my emotions by firmly gripping the edges of the countertop and inhale deep breaths when I start to feel overwhelmed. My boxes of clothes and toiletries are in the car, but I just needed this moment to step inside this house by myself.

My parents and Ronnie begged to come with me, but I refused the offer. Therapy has encouraged me to continue facing realities head on and confronting them on my own sometimes, so I am choosing to do just that.

I eventually walk upstairs to the bedroom and am extremely grateful we've replaced the sheets and comforter on the bed. I turn to go into the bathroom and look at myself in the mirror, recognizing how far I've come. My long, dark hair is styled down in loose beach waves, I have a touch of makeup on, and I am wearing a white fitted tank top tucked into a pair of high-rise denim shorts. Keeping my eyes on my reflection, I delicately rest my fingertips over my chest as if to comfort the fragmented pieces of my heart. Although I've made strides these past six months, my heart is still healing, and sometimes the smallest trigger sets off the blaring sound of the rattling pieces again.

Fortunately my time in therapy has helped lower the volume of the noise, and some days I feel like the broken pieces of my heart aren't necessarily hundreds of tiny flakes anymore, but rather fewer larger sections. I may have given up hope that my heart will completely mend, but I have faith that it can improve. That it can feel better than it did before.

As I run my fingers slightly through my hair, I hear a knock at my door that snaps me out of my thoughts. I furrow my brows as I make my way downstairs, and when I peek through the beveled glass to see who it is, I notice Dane on my front porch. I haven't seen him in six months, but he still looks the same. Tousled dark hair smoothed back under a backwards black snapback, and he's wearing a gray crewneck t-shirt with a pair of black gym shorts.

I inhale before reaching for the door handle, and open it with a smile. "Hi."

He has his hands in the pockets of his shorts as he greets me. "Hey, so you're back," Dane says with a smile.

I nod as I look around my house. "Yep."

Dane hikes a thumb over his shoulder to point to my car. "Can I help you move some of your things inside?"

I immediately respond. "No, don't be silly. It's just a few boxes."

"And I insist. Keys?" Dane responds as he holds out his hand.

I throw him a tight-lipped smile, knowing Dane won't take no for an answer, and turn to get my keys off the foyer table. Dane and I head to my car to take out the several boxes in my backseat, and we walk them back to the house. Once we drop off the boxes on the living room carpet, Dane stands up straight and rubs the back of his neck as he speaks. "I know a thing or two about appliances and household maintenance, so if there is ever something you need fixed, I'd be happy to take a look anytime."

I decide to make a joke. "Don't tempt me, you might regret that offer," I say with a smirk.

"Luckily I'm right next door, so it's not a huge inconvenience." Then he narrows his eyes as he plays along. "Unless you're planning on micro-managing me?"

I shake my head with a smile. "I won't, I promise."

He smiles back. "Alright, then."

I chuckle as I start bending to take clothes out of the boxes we just placed on the floor, but there are a few beats of awkward silence between Dane and I, so I fall back on basic conversation. "How are Kate and Trent? I haven't seen them in a couple of months."

Dane bends to help me pick out clothes from the box I just opened. "They're good. I'm actually planning on seeing them this Friday if you'd like to join?"

I stand up straight to look at Dane and nod in agreement. "Yeah, that sounds fun."

Dane gives me a surprised look like he didn't expect my answer, but then smiles wide once he realizes I'm being serious. "Great. I'll let them know."

I nod once to confirm plans. "Great."

Dane bends to lift the rest of the clothes out of the open box, and when he stands up, he has his hands resting on his hips as he looks at me. "I'm glad you're back. It's been pretty lonely around here."

I slowly nod as I say, "Me too." Awkward silence falls between us once again as we hold each other's eyes, and I decide to end both our misery as I vaguely gesture a hand out in front of me. "So thanks for the help. I really appreciate it."

"Of course." Dane takes my cue and starts walking toward the front door, but is half turned to me as he says, "Anything you need, just let me know alright?"

I smile. "Deal."

Then Dane waves goodbye before walking out my front door.

Band-Aid ripped off.

CHAPTER
Fifteen

DANE

Friday, June 10, 2022

Friday night, Kate, Trent, and I decided that we would take Aria out to the Annual Summer Kick-Off Festival in town. Seeing as it's her first time out with all of us in some time, we figured we would do something out of our element. Something fresh.

There is no need for Aria and I to take separate cars since we live next door to one another, so I offered to drive us over to the festival to meet up with Kate and Trent. When Aria opened her front door, I was happy to see her dressed in a pair of high rise denim shorts and a flowy, yellow off-the-shoulder crop top. Her long, dark brown hair is down in soft waves, and although it seems silly to notice her appearance and make a big deal of it, there's a lot to be said about it. She's dressed like she used to dress, and she looks more like the person she was *before*. I guess I'd be lying if I said that didn't make me smile inwardly.

The festival was more inland than where we live, so it was about a fifteen-minute drive to get here. At first, the car ride was a little too silent for my liking, but eventually, Aria and I were able to fall into a natural conversation about work, and have a little venting session about crabby clients and misbehaved students.

When we reach the parking field of the festival and meet up with Kate and Trent, we can see tents set up for shopping, food trucks, and a few standard carnival rides and games. Luckily, Kate and Trent do not have as much of an awkward introduction with Aria as I did last Sunday, so I'm hoping that's an indication that tonight will go smoothly.

As the four of us make our way through the entrance of the festival, Kate turns to us with an "Oh my god" face. "Guys, there is a Locos Tacos Food Truck." The rest of us look at each other with confused expressions, and turn back to Kate to silently ask her to explain. "You guys have never had Locos Tacos?" We all shake our heads to answer her. "Okay, we're fixing that right now," Kate says as she grabs Aria's arm, and Trent and I follow suit.

I shove my hands into my jean pockets as I look up at the menu board, and wait in line with Trent behind the girls. Kate turns around with her arm still weaved around Aria's. "The Locos Nachos are a must."

"You two can have fun with that. I chose to have my cheat day yesterday," I say.

"Same. Except mine was Wednesday," Trent chimes in.

Aria rolls her eyes, thinking it's the most ridiculous excuse. "*Whatever* you self-disciplined moguls."

"Again, perks of being a woman," I say.

Kate and Aria look at each other in confusion, and then turn to Trent and I. Trent looks over to me, and I gesture my palm outward to give him the floor. "No woman wants to go home with a guy who has a flabby gut," Trent says.

Kate bobs her head in agreement, waiting for Trent to explain further. "So what does that have to do with women getting the upper hand?"

"Well, a guy is less picky when choosing to sleep with someone," I chime in.

Kate furrows her brows. "So? That sounds like your problem."

"Seriously," Aria adds, and then she points between Trent and I. "And we've seen the women you both take home. You guys aren't exactly un-shallow."

"I guess that's why we're *self-disciplined moguls*," I say while emphasizing the phrase Aria used earlier.

Aria just smirks and shakes her head as she faces forward again. Once Kate and Aria order, they wait a few minutes for their loaded nachos to come out while Trent orders, and then I place my order after him. I grab my black bean and rice burrito from the food truck counter, and then I make my way over to Kate and Aria who are now standing off to the side eating.

"You guys gonna breathe at some point?" I say as I eye them devouring the nachos in generous handfuls.

Aria's holding a couple loaded nachos between her thumb and forefinger as she speaks mid-chew. "I know I have a line of chili sauce dripping down my chin and hand. Just ignore it, I'll clean it up later."

She definitely does, but I smile at her admission and careless attitude. It's endearing, actually, and refreshing to see a girl not be so timid while food is in front of her. "I see nothing," I say, and then take a bite out of my burrito. "Where's the beer around here?" I ask.

"I think I saw a sign for beer that way by the Ferris wheel," Trent answers as he points to the right of us. I finish my burrito in three more bites, then throw out the foil in a nearby trash can before walking back over to the group to see if anyone wants anything.

"Wait, I'll go with you," Aria answers while wiping her chin and fingers with a napkin.

Kate and Trent let me know what they want, and Aria and I trail off to go get some beers. "Ugh, I think I'm going to regret that later," Aria says with a scrunched face while putting her hands over her stomach.

"Woah," I say as I place a hand on Aria's shoulder to stop us both in our tracks.

Aria seems genuinely concerned as she looks at me. "What?"

"I should have you know that feelings of nausea or other stomach issues won't be well received in my Mustang."

Aria looks up at me through squinted eyes. "This is my 'homecoming' welcome? Letting me know you're not putting your car at risk if I happen to get sick?"

"Okay, first off, I welcomed you home on Sunday. Second, she's a GT Three Fifty," I counter.

"Is she?" Aria says with a bored expression. "Well, thankfully, I wasn't referring to throwing up or *stomach issues*."

"Then what are we talking about?"

Aria throws her head back with a chuckle as she starts walking again, and I step in line with her at her side. "I was referring to eating like crap and cheating on my own diet." Then she turns her head to look up at me and pats my shoulder. "Your car is safe around me, Dane. Don't worry."

I turn my head forward. "Ah, got it." A few seconds pass by before we reach the end of the line at the beer tent, and I turn to look at Aria as I shrug and say, "For the record, it's not like I'd kick you out of my Mustang and make you walk home."

Aria raises her eyebrows in surprise at me. "No?"

I shrug playfully. "I mean, I may call you an Uber or-"

"Hey!" Aria says.

I laugh as I put my arm around Aria's shoulders and pull her close to my side. "Come on, you know I'm kidding."

Aria looks up at me knowingly. "The thought of me throwing up in your precious car?

You're *at least* half serious."

I slightly scrunch my face in discomfort as I look off to the side. "God, just thinking about it makes me uneasy."

"Yeah, exactly," Aria says with a chuckle.

I laugh with her as I remove my arm from around her shoulders and place my hands in my jeans pockets. Eventually, I turn to look back at Aria's side profile, and just think for a few seconds. I know she knows I'm kidding with her and we're having a fun time joking, but after everything she's been through, I want to say something meaningful. For whatever it's worth.

"But I think I could get over it quickly," I say, and then slowly stretch a genuine smile across my face to let Aria know that with all kidding aside, she can rely on me to be there for her. I know we're talking about a specific scenario, but when Aria returns a smile, I know she knows what I'm trying to say.

When we turn our heads to read the beer list, Aria asks, "So what are you getting?"

"I'm between the IPA and the sour they have on tap."

"I didn't even see the sour. Okay, decision made," Aria says.

"Is that what I'm ordering for you?" I ask.

"Sure, just let me know how much I owe you."

I start reaching for my wallet in my back pocket just as the person in front of us finishes their order. "You would owe me nothing."

"Dane, no," Aria chimes in.

Just as Aria tries to fight me on paying for her beer, the counter is vacant for me to walk up to, and I order all of our beers. Aria stands beside me and waits until I'm done talking to the person at the counter to try and slip me money. I hold my palm out to resist her attempt, and luckily enough, the beers are poured fast enough that we can scatter away before she becomes relentless. I grab mine and Trent's beer, while Aria grabs hers and Kate's, and then we walk off to the side to make room for the people behind us.

When we stop, Aria places one beer on the ground and holds her money out to me. "Dane, please just take it."

"Okay, Ari, there are two things very wrong with this scenario. One, your efforts are pointless. Two, there may be people watching this display who think I can't pay for some girl's cheap beer."

Aria sighs as she tucks her money away in her back pocket, and then bends to pick up the beer cup she placed on the ground. "Well, thank you," Aria says as she stands back up.

I smile as I raise my cup to tap hers. "Welcome home."

Before taking a sip of her beer, Aria's lips tip up in the corner as she holds my gaze for a couple moments. After I swallow my first sip, I decide to change the subject to keep the easy conversation going. "I'm actually impressed with the Nachogate display. Can't fault a girl with an appetite."

She laughs, realizing I'm referencing her devouring nachos with Kate earlier. "I have no bedside manner when it comes to junk food. I'm actually surprised I'm still as tiny as I am."

"Good genes," I reply.

She furrows her brows. "Hey, give me credit. I work out too." She holds the plastic cup of beer to her lips as she mumbles, "Once a month."

I laugh. "Well if you ever want a workout partner, let me know."

"Okay, but it's more of a chore to me than anything, so consider yourself warned."

"Considered," I say with a smile, and then I lead us back to where Kate and Trent are. But as we start walking back over to them, it turns out Kate and Trent are coming our way. "Geeze, you alcoholics couldn't wait five seconds," I joke as I hand Trent his beer and Kate takes hers from Aria's hand.

"Let's go on the Ferris wheel!" Kate exclaims.

"Oh, no." Aria shakes her head in fear.

I take a sip from my cup and look at Aria questioningly. "You're scared of the Ferris wheel?"

"I don't like heights," Aria explains.

"Oh, come on, it'll be fun," Kate says while wiggling her eyebrows.

"*Or,* I can be like the mom who holds everyone's things and watches from the ground."

I'm sipping on my beer as Kate and Aria go back and forth, and then I get an idea. "Okay, tell you what, Ari. If you can chug your beer faster than me, we won't go on the Ferris wheel. But if I chug mine faster than yours, we do."

Aria narrows her eyes at me. "That's so ridiculous, you'd obviously win."

"Then chug half the amount Dane has to," Trent suggests.

Aria's eyes go back and forth between Trent and I, seemingly thinking we've concocted some sort of secret plan with this chugging contest, but we definitely didn't. Suddenly, I have this urge to push Aria out of her comfort zone tonight. Maybe it's because of my promise I made to her brother, or maybe it's the fact that this is the first night in a year Aria can truly let loose and have fun. Whatever the reason, I know I want to push her on this and I'm absolutely going to.

Aria finally gives in as she throws a hand up in defeat. "Alright." She sighs.

I look down at how much beer I have left in my cup, and then point to a specific area on the outside of Aria's cup. "Drink to about there, and then we'll chug."

Aria gives a mocking thumbs up, and starts to drink until the amount of beer in her cup is half the amount I have in mine.

"Okay, raise 'em up!" Trent exclaims.

"Come on, Ari, kick his ass!" Kate yells.

Aria squints her eyes as she raises her cup out in front of her, and I smirk as I hold my cup up to hers. "Cheers," I say.

"Cheers," Aria says as she taps my cup. We both start chugging our beers, and we both eye each other out of the corner of our eyes. Within a few seconds, I down my beer before Aria, but by practically one gulp considering she had half the amount of liquid to drink.

"Okay, let's go!" Kate shouts as she takes Trent's hand and walks with purpose to the Ferris wheel.

Aria finishes the rest of her drink and throws her cup in the garbage can next to her. "Wow, I lose a chugging contest and get to go on a Ferris wheel all in one night? Tonight must be my lucky night," she says sarcastically as she makes her way to the ride.

The Ferris wheel is lit up with purple, teal, and pink LED light bulbs that decorate the length of the steel spokes. There are sixteen buckets for passengers to ride on, each with an awning held up by a pole in the middle of the cart. I follow Aria, and once we pay admission for the ride, Aria and I take a seat inside a bucket right after Kate and Trent have been lifted in their own cart. The wheel rotates into action when our bucket starts to rise in a swift motion, and Aria is gripping the bar in front of her with white knuckles as she purses her lips.

I'm casually leaning back next to her with my arm around the length of the top of the seat. "Jesus, you're going to give me anxiety," I say.

"Good, I hope you're suffering too," she quips back.

I give a smirk as I look out at the view of the nighttime sky that's dusted with stars and the colorful lights of the festival that come into view as we dip back down through the circular movement. But when I look back at Aria, her eyes are closed. "You know, that's not the best way to get over your fear." Then I gesture to the air as if she can see me. "You're missing this entire aerial view."

"You'll give me the Cliffs Notes," Aria says with her eyes still shut.

"Okay, how about I hold your hand while you keep your eyes opened? You can even hold it with a vice grip," I suggest.

"I'll probably crush your bones," she responds.

I chuckle. "Not likely, so come on."

I hold my palm out next to her on the handlebar, and Aria opens one eye to scope out the scene. "Fine," Aria says as she cups my palm with hers. The grip isn't bone crushing, but it's definitely firm. Turns out, Aria's clever when she wants to be because even though Aria's eyes are open, she's looking up at the sky.

"Okay, now you're just cheating," I say.

She shrugs as if she doesn't know what I'm talking about. "You said nothing about where I should be looking when I open my eyes. I'm keeping my end of the bargain."

"Touché, Ms. Tate," I praise with an impressed tone, and then I lean back to get more comfortable in the seat as the ride catapults us up over the peak of the wheel and dunks us back down.

"Just so you know, I'm throwing up in your car on the way home," Aria says.

I smile at her sass. "Somehow, I highly doubt it's because you have motion sickness right now."

"Your intuition is astounding," Aria retorts, and I can't help but laugh.

"You think so? Maybe I should read tarot cards in the psychic tent when we get down," I joke as our bucket swings over the highest point of the ride and dips back down.

Aria's head is still tilted upward as she slightly shakes her head, and I can tell she's trying not to smile. "You're ridiculous."

I look at her side profile. "Would you rather be stuck on a Ferris wheel with someone who was boring? Come on, you know I'm the lesser of two evils."

"I'm sorry, but do you ever miss a chance to stroke your ego?" Aria asks.

"No, it just comes naturally when it's true," I quip back.

When Aria finally tilts her head down and turns to face me, my lips slowly stretch into a shit-eating grin, and Aria just eyes me with a deadpan stare. "I can't believe I'm stuck on a Ferris wheel listening to you gloat about yourself," she admits in a monotone voice.

"Right, because wallowing in your panic would have been less dreadful," I tease.

Aria's eyes narrow at me as her jaw slightly tenses, and I raise my eyebrows at her to suggest that she knows I'm right. I feel the rotation of the wheel start to slow down, indicating that the end of the ride is near.

"I wasn't panicking, I was coping," Aria says, and as soon as she finishes her response, the wheel stops its motion and as our luck would have it, we get stuck at the very, very top. Aria bobs her head once to the side in realization as she holds my eyes. "Now I'm panicking," she admits as she gives my hand a squeeze.

I smile at her confession as I turn and lean back in the seat. "Okay, twenty questions it is. Dream vacation?" I ask as I look up at the sky.

I feel Aria shift at my side as she presumably tilts her head up to the sky to enjoy the view with me. "Italy," Aria answers.

"Most embarrassing moment?"

"Uh, probably getting caught peeing under the pier at the beach with Kate."

I laugh. "That's gold. Favorite color?"

"Pink."

"Favorite TV show?"

"*Friends*. Was that a serious question?"

I smile. "Hey, I'm asking the questions here. Froot Loops or Trix?"

"Froot Loops."

I'm now the one scrunching my face. "Really? No way, Trix are superior. Doughnuts or cake?"

"No contest. Doughnuts."

"I fully support that." Then I decide to throw caution to the wind and have some fun. "Wait, is that Charlie Hunnam?" I whisper-shout as I lean forward and point aimlessly toward the ground.

"What?! Where?!" Aria shouts as she finally looks down. We're not as high up as we were, but still high enough for her not to find my joke as funny as I do. Aria tucks her lips in as she turns to me and darts daggers at me with her eyes.

I shrug with a smirk. "I had to take the opening, sorry."

She eyes me carefully, but seems to be getting more comfortable exploring her surroundings. "I would take my hand away, but you're my lifeline right now," she jokes.

I squeeze her hand once as I look into her eyes. "I can learn to live with that," I say as I draw a small smile on my lips.

Holding my gaze, Aria's lips tip up at the corner in an appreciative expression. I'm assuring her she's going to be taken care of around here, and I can tell she finds my gesture and comment sweet.

I'm still smiling as I look off to the side, and it's another couple minutes until we are safely on the ground. Afterwards, the four of us all grab another beer, and walk around the festival for another hour. For the first time in a really long time, I witnessed Aria smile. Not because she had to save face, and not because she felt forced to. She smiled because she felt *happy*, even if it was just for a moment.

CHAPTER
Sixteen

ARIA

Thursday, June 16, 2022

"I'm so glad you had a lot of fun with your friends," my mom says over the phone.

"Yeah, it was definitely a long time coming."

"How is everyone doing?" she asks.

"They're all doing well. Dane is still at the architecture firm, and Kate and Trent are still flirting as usual. The normal stuff, you know," I say with a laugh.

"Aw, I'd love to see those two together. Are you guys hanging out again soon?"

"I'm sure we'll make concrete plans in the near future, don't worry. How's Dad and Ronnie?" I ask.

"Dad's restaurant is almost ready for the Grand Opening. We're only a couple months out now," my mom says.

"Wow, I can't believe how fast time flew. How's Dad feeling?"

"Excited and stressed. The business of working with contractors is not always the smoothest sail, but the project is at the finish line, so he's at least grateful for that."

"Well, when you guys are ready to decorate and get the place ready for opening night, let me know because I want to help," I offer.

"Of course. Listen, your father is calling me on the other line so I need to go, but we'll talk soon?"

"Yes, definitely. Love you," I say.

"Love you so much. I'll talk to you later," my mom replies before we both hang up.

It's Thursday evening, and I'm making dinner in my loungewear. My hair is tousled down, and I'm wearing a light pink crewneck sweatshirt with black spandex biker shorts. I'm pan-frying cubed chicken breast and vegetables in teriyaki sauce when I hear my phone ping from the kitchen counter. When I look over at the screen of my iPhone, I see a text message from Dane.

Dane: Hey, what're you up to?

I turn my attention back to sauté the chicken and vegetables for another few seconds and then place the wooden spoon on the spoon rest to reply to Dane.

Me: Making chicken and veggies for dinner.

Dane: Sounds wild.

Me: Always living my best life. :)

Dane: I'm scrolling through Netflix. In case you cared.

I laugh as I shake my head and type out another text.

Me: Sounds wilder.

I place my phone back on the counter and resume sauteing my dinner in the wok. As I lower the heat from the medium to low setting, I hear my phone ping again.

Dane: It's been unsuccessful so far.

Me: If you haven't eaten yet, I could make you a plate.

Dane: That's tempting…

Me: Ha ha. Well if you decide to come on over, just knock.

I put my phone down to take a sip of the Cabernet I poured earlier and continue sauteing the chicken and vegetables. I place the lid of the wok back on, and turn to lean my lower back against the counter as I continue to drink from my wine glass. A few minutes later, I hear a knock at the door, so I guess Dane didn't find anything on Netflix after all.

I answer the door and joke with him. "Fell into the Netflix trap of just scrolling?"

It seems like we're in the same mood right now because Dane's in comfy clothes like I am. He's wearing a black crewneck and gray jogger sweatpants, and it looks like he must have been lying down too because his hair is a little wild on top. Not that I'm judging.

He leans with one shoulder on the door frame as he responds. "To answer your question, no I didn't eat."

I smile as I gesture for Dane to come in, then close the door behind us and walk past him to continue cooking on the stovetop. "What do you want to drink?" I ask.

He's walking further into the kitchen as he responds. "Water's fine, but I'll get it since I'm already making you cook for me."

Dane starts to retrieve a drinking glass from the cabinet, and I'm focusing on cooking as I respond. "Well to be fair, I was cooking for *just me*. You're taking what would be my leftovers."

I hear Dane filling his glass with water from the fridge. "Wow, it's like a warm hug around here," he says sarcastically.

I turn away from the oven and lean my back against the kitchen counter as I smile. "I digress. Your company is worth more than my leftovers."

"Well, obviously. What would you do without my jokes?" he says as he takes a sip from his glass.

I shake my head at him with a smile. "Hell would freeze over, I guess." Then I turn back to continue cooking.

Dane's voice cuts through from behind me again. "What plates do you want to use? I'll get them."

I point at the cabinet to my left where he can find the dinner plates. "In there, thanks."

Dane sets two dinner plates on the countertop next to me, and then he pulls out two forks from the silverware drawer. I turn the gas burner off and pour a serving of stir fry onto each plate, and Dane brings the plates to the eat-in kitchen table.

As I'm rinsing off the wok in the sink, I call out to Dane. "If you like it, great. If you don't, tough luck. Enjoy!"

"Thanks?" Dane says, like he's unsure if he should be thanking me.

I turn the water off and wipe my hands on the dish towel over my shoulder. When I make my way over to the table where Dane is sitting, I place one hand on the table as I place my other hand on my hip, looking down at him with raised brows. "Well?" I say.

"Okay, no offense, Ari, but you're being a little weird."

"I didn't just slave over a hot stove to not hear your feedback."

Dane holds his hands out in surrender. "Okay." He takes a forkful in his mouth and chews it as he looks at me.

When he scrunches his face, my eyes widen. "That horrible?"

He swallows the bite and nods his head in agreement. "No," he admits, and then smirks.

"Ugh, I should have known." I brush Dane off with a hand gesture as I take my seat across from him, laying the dish towel on the table. I take a sip of my wine, and start to dig into my plate as Dane takes another forkful from his. "Any plans for this weekend?" I ask.

"So far, just going for a run Saturday morning. The rest is still to be determined," he responds.

"You run?" I ask as I furrow my eyebrows.

"Tell me I look out of shape, without telling me I look out of shape?"

I laugh as I put my palm to my forehead. "I'm sorry, not what I meant," I laugh out. "I know you kickbox, I wasn't aware you took up running too."

He takes a sip of his water before responding. "I've gotten into it more the past year, especially during the warmer months," he explains. "You could join me if you want."

I look off to the side, considering his offer. "Hmm, maybe I will. I'll let you know."

"How about you? Any plans?" Dane asks.

I shrug as I hold a forkful of stir fry in front of me. "I may just stay in, watch a few movies. Sometimes it's nice to just kick back and relax."

Dane nods. "Well if you feel like getting out of the house, let me know."

Finishing my bite, I say, "Only if you promise not to drag me on a Ferris wheel again."

"Such torture I put you through, I know," Dane jokes.

I pick one leg up so my foot is resting on the seat of the chair, and I'm collecting another forkful of stir fry as I respond. "Make fun all you want, but I'm sticking to the fact that it's the scariest ride at the carnival." Then I whip my forkful of stir fry to the side. "It's basically a death trap." When I feel the contents on my fork fall to the floor, I purse my lips as I look down at the food next to my foot.

"Uh oh, she's flinging food now," Dane comments.

I bend over to pick up the bite of chicken and two pepper strips that fell, then shrug as I look at Dane. "I cleaned my floors yesterday. Whatever," I say as I pop the food in my mouth with my fingers.

As I'm chewing and wiping my fingers on my napkin, I notice Dane resting his elbow on the table as his chin rests in his palm, and he's eyeing me with a smirk.

Mid-chew, I decide to pry. "What? Why are you staring at me like that?"

He shakes his head in his palm with that same smirk. "Nothing. You're just…entertaining."

I smile as I chew the rest of my mouthful and flip my hair to one side. "Look at that. You didn't need Netflix after all."

"No, I definitely didn't," Dane says with a chuckle as he resumes digging into his plate. We continue eating our dinner together, and once both of us clear our plates, I stand up to take his, but Dane gets up from his seat instead. "I got it. It's the least I can do for you after you *slaved* over a stove for me," Dane says with a wink as he grabs my plate from me.

While Dane is at the sink rinsing our plates and loading the dishwasher, I'm clearing off the kitchen counters. But just as Dane shuts off the water and turns to face me, I grab the Disco Doughnuts box out of my fridge and hold it up. "Have you ever been to heaven?" I ask with raised eyebrows.

"That good, huh?" he eyes curiously.

"Oh, yeah," I gasp. I take the chocolate frosted with sprinkles out and take a bite, not even bothering to sit down at the table or grab a plate.

"Well, when you put it that way," Dane trails off as he walks over to look into the box I'm holding. He winds up taking a vanilla frosted with sprinkles, and I smirk up at him as I chew.

"What?" Dane asks.

I swallow my bite and start to close the box to put it back in the fridge. "If you were going to take the other chocolate frosted one, I would have pummeled you to the ground. So you're lucky." When I close the refrigerator door, I take another bite of my doughnut and start talking mid-chew. "Yeah, I'm definitely on for that run on Saturday."

Dane chuckles. "One doughnut won't kill you, but it sounds like a plan."

We exchange a few more laughs in the kitchen before saying our goodbyes, and I think about how nice it was to have company in this house again. For the first time since I've been back in this house, I didn't go to bed feeling so *alone*.

CHAPTER
Seventeen

DANE

Saturday June 18, 2022

On Saturday, Aria and I are jogging along the boardwalk of the beach, sweating bullets on this June morning. We run side by side most of the way until the last quarter mile when I am jogging alone. When I reach the end of our run, I look back and see Aria has stopped jogging, and is now walking. I'm standing there with my palms resting on my hips, dripping sweat through my white tank top and black basketball shorts.

As Aria makes her way within shouting distance, I tease her. "Really? You're going to jog the first two and three-quarter miles, then just walk the last quarter?"

Aria shouts back with no shame. "Yep!"

I'm still controlling my breathing as I throw a smile her way, and just stare at her as she walks closer into focus. I've actually never realized how petite and naturally fit Aria is. She's five-foot-five with a lean physique, but has just enough muscle in her stomach, legs, and arms, probably from all the dancing she always engages in.

Aria's voice cuts into my thoughts as she stands in front of me. "Do you think I did enough cardio today to let me off the hook for the month?" she asks through ragged breaths.

"Not quite," I say with a chuckle as I peer down at her, and then I gesture a hand up and down her stature. "Look at the bright side though, you're already small, so you don't need to put in a lot of effort."

She looks out onto the beach, still trying to regulate her breath as she responds with a shrug. "I guess that's true."

We start walking along the boardwalk side by side so we can head back home, and I speak first. "Excited for the school year to end this week?"

"Oh, yeah, so ready to be done. These kids have officially lost their minds," Aria responds.

"I could only imagine what little bastards they are right now," I say.

"You're telling me. One kid started dancing in the back of my room the other day, trying to make a TikTok when he was supposed to be doing work."

I'm laughing out loud. "Okay that's kind of amazing. I could just picture the sheer horror on your face."

She shakes her head as if to say she can't believe that happened, and we walk a few more strides before Aria speaks. "Well, I definitely want to spend more time on the beach this summer. I miss it."

A silence falls between us, because we both know why she's missed it. However, I'm not going to open that can of worms unless she wants to take the conversation further, so I side-step her comment as best I can.

"We'll go," I say nonchalantly.

"Okay," she responds, and then she looks over to me. "But I have some terms."

"What's that?"

"We get Kate and Trent to skinny dip, then take away their clothes and run," Aria says with a devious smirk.

I extend my hand to her. "Deal."

We both laugh as we shake hands, and then head home.

Later that night, I'm sitting at the bar at Shippers with Trent, drinking a beer, and listening to live music as we catch up.

"So how is she doing?" Trent asks after sipping his beer.

I stall in answering his question by sipping my own beer. The truth is, I don't know how Aria is doing. She seems like she's doing fine, but I know there's a great possibility she's masking her emotions just to appease her family and friends. "I think she's just taking everything as it comes," I finally let out.

Trent nods knowingly. "Kate wants to spend July Fourth together. Are you doing anything?"

"Oh you guys are finally gonna get it on?" I say as I raise an eyebrow at him.

Trent smirks at me, then he looks away. "I don't know, we'll see."

"Whatever, man. You two go back and forth like dogs in heat," I say.

"Listen, there's no denying she's hot. I just don't want her to catch feelings the second we cross that line. I'm also trying to figure out what my feelings are for her. Not to mention, I also like keeping my options open." He lifts his chin to gesture at something in the distance. "For example, your nine o'clock."

When I turn to my left, I see exactly what Trent's referring to. Long blonde hair, perky tits, flat stomach, legs for days. She's standing in a light blue form-fitting mini dress with beige strappy sandals that lace up her calves, and the sight of her is making my mind dive into the gutter. I turn back to rest my forearms over the bar. "Wasn't really planning on having sex tonight, but I think I've been convinced otherwise."

Trent laughs at my side. "Don't let me stop you. I've had my eye on the red head in the back corner."

I'm resting my chin in my hand and peeking over at the blonde every now and then to contemplate the right time to make my move. It's been a couple weeks since I've gotten laid, so I feel like I deserve this.

I take my beer off the bar counter, and head over in the mystery blonde's direction as she's standing against the wall on her phone, seemingly messaging someone. I don't see a drink in her hand yet, so I go for a generic introduction.

"Hey, can I buy you a drink?" I ask as I walk up closer to her.

When she looks up at me, I can tell she's pleased with what she sees. I know I'm a decent looking guy, and I dress pretty well if I do say so myself. My hair is gelled a little on top just enough to clean it up, but it's still a little messy. I shine my pearly whites at her in case she needs more convincing, and luckily she shines a wide, pretty smile back at me.

"Sure. I'll have whatever you're having."

I extend my hand out to her to bring her to the bar with me, and I order her a drink. We're both leaning over the bar as I take a sip of my beer, and then turn to her. "So what's your name?"

"Tara. You?"

"Dane. You meeting friends here?"

"I was supposed to, but it seems like plans have fallen through."

The bartender hands me Tara's beer, and I hand it to her as I say, "Sorry to hear that."

As she puts the cup up to her lips, she throws me a seductive grin. "I'm not."

Score.

Tara and I get out of my Mustang at the same time, and my arm is draped over her shoulders as we make our way up the pathway to my front door. Just as we reach the top of my porch steps, I notice a sleeping figure on Aria's porch in my peripherals, and I do a double take. When I squint my eyes to focus in, I realize the sleeping form is Aria.

What?

She's cocooned herself in a navy plaid blanket, and is fast asleep on the wooden bench on her porch. I decide to unlock my front door, and push the door open just enough to let Tara in. "Hey listen, I'm going to check on my friend next door. I'll be back in a few minutes, but make yourself comfortable." I gesture to the living room couch.

Tara smiles as she kisses my lips. "Mmm, don't take too long."

When Tara walks inside my foyer, she starts untying her sandals so she can relax on my couch, and I lick my lips as I resist the urge to pounce on her right then and there. But I know the right thing to do is check on Aria first. Maybe karma will be good to me, and tonight will be the best sex of my life.

Who knows?

When I close my front door, I walk down my porch steps to cross my lawn over to Aria's, and then step carefully up Aria's porch.

"Aria," I whisper, but she just stirs in her position on the bench. "Aria," I whisper louder.

Aria's eyes pop open this time, and she seems disoriented for a second until she looks up at me, and then jolts up to a sitting position. "Shit, Dane!" she gasps as she puts a hand over her chest to get her mental bearings.

I put a hand out in front of me. "Sorry, I didn't mean to scare you." When I notice her breathing starts to regulate, I shove my outstretched hand back into my jeans pocket, and furrow my brows. "What are you doing out here?"

Aria rubs her temples and eyes for a few seconds to wake herself up, and then she shrugs. "I don't know. Sometimes, I like to be out under the stars at night."

Not really knowing how to respond to that, I just say what comes to mind. "Oh."

I know, I'm really deep sometimes.

Feeling like she has to give an explanation, Aria continues on as she hugs the blanket tighter around her body. "I feel closer to him when I do."

Fuck.

I crouch down in front of Aria as I touch her shoulder, and I stroke my thumb across the fabric of the blanket that's over her body. "If you ever want company, I'm here," I offer with a small smile.

She's looking down in her lap as she smiles and shakes her head. "No, that's alright," she says before looking back at me. "I've come a long way since last year, and I'm able to handle most of these moments on my own." I give her an understanding nod, and then Aria looks at me questioningly. "Besides, if you have nothing better to do than sit under the stars with me, we need to go over your event calendar immediately."

She's making a joke. She's making light of the unfortunate situation she's in, and it inspires me. Aria's kindness and strength radiate off of her so effortlessly that it's almost crazy to me that I never noticed these qualities about her before.

After a few seconds, we turn our heads to the sound of the door opening from my porch, and a female voice. "Dane? Are you coming inside?" Tara is standing halfway out my front door, looking directly at me and Aria on Aria's porch. I stand up and nod my head, which thankfully makes Tara go back inside with no further explanation needed.

Aria stands up with a palm on her forehead and gasps. "Oh my god, I'm so sorry. I didn't know you had company." Aria's blushing, seemingly thinking she's interrupted my hookup for the night, when she's forgetting I was the one that came to see her. Aria starts to fold the plaid blanket and lay it on the bench, but her movements are rushed and quivery.

"Aria, it's okay. I came to check on you," I assure her.

Her cheeks are still a bright shade of pink, and she turns to look at me as she shakes her head with a smile. "You didn't have to, but thank you. I'll see you soon?" Aria's hand is already gripping the handle of her front door, waiting for me to end her embarrassment, so I decide to have mercy on her and not push farther.

"Sure," I say.

"Great, good night," she says as she throws one last smile at me, and takes refuge in her home.

I stand alone on Aria's porch, staring for a few seconds in silence, just processing the last few minutes. When I reluctantly come to terms with the fact that some days are going to be tougher than others, I turn to go down the steps of Aria's porch to walk over to my own house.

As soon as I walk through my front door and shut it, Tara is walking up to me in the foyer. My mind is a little distracted from sexual thoughts at the moment, but as soon as Tara starts kissing my neck, I cup the side of her face to bring her lips to mine and readily fall into the moment with her.

CHAPTER

Eighteen

DANE

Thursday, June 23, 2022

It's Thursday after work, and I haven't seen or heard from Aria since Saturday night on her porch. So I shoot her a text message to check in and make sure she's alright.

> Me: Hey, what are you up to?

> Ari: About to head out to the pier for a stroll.

That's interesting.

> Me: By yourself?

> Ari: I'm a big girl, I think I can handle it. ;)

> Me: Cute, Ari. What I meant was, why are you going by yourself?

Ari: I like to look out over the pier sometimes. Watch the sunset.

Me: But maybe it would be less boring with someone? Just a thought.

Ari: [eye roll emoji] Dane, would you like to come?

Me: Omg, I can't believe you read my mind. It's crazy.

Ari: I don't know how we're friends. See ya in a bit.

Me: [thumbs up emoji]

I throw on shorts and a shirt, and since I don't really have time to address the mop on my head, I put on a black backwards snapback. I walk out my front door and over to Aria's to knock. When she opens the door, she's wearing high-rise mom jeans, and a red square neck crop tank top. Her long dark hair is down in beach waves, but slicked back with a thick pastel yellow floral headband. Since her hair is completely out of her face and she hardly has any makeup on, I'm able to see her almond, light brown eyes, button nose, and her plump lips.

Has she always been this naturally pretty?

Before I can answer my own question, I'm snapped out of my thoughts at the sound of Aria's voice. "Hey," she says as she stuffs her phone in her back pocket and steps out onto the porch with me.

Once she locks the door, we both head down the stairs at the same time and walk toward the boardwalk. My hands are in the pockets of my shorts as we walk side by side. "So not to be needy, but there better be more incentive than just a stroll along the pier. We do live here, and it's nothing new for me."

"Of course there is. Disco Doughnuts," Aria assures as she looks up at me with a smile.

I look away from her. "Ah-ha. So you've used the pier excuse to indulge. I see."

She holds her arms out to drive her point home. "It's called balance. After I eat a doughnut or two, I walk off the calories. Makes perfect sense."

I narrow my eyes down at her as I shake my head. "I don't think that's exactly how that works."

"To each their own," she says with a shrug, but then she looks up at me and points. "And you're crashing *my* night plans, so hush."

I chuckle. "Okay, that's fair. So why are you coming out here so late anyway? On a Thursday night, nonetheless."

"There's less people on a weeknight, and I like to watch the sunset when it's quieter," she replies.

"I won't argue with that."

Aria doesn't look at me as she responds, and just looks straight ahead. "My therapist actually gave me advice about consciously finding beauty in the world. I thought it was a ridiculous notion at first, but I'm starting to come around to the idea. It's like seeing the world from a different perspective. Or maybe for the first time," Ari confesses.

I lick my lips, almost nervous to venture into this conversation because I don't want Aria to get upset, and I'm not exactly sure what's going to trigger her. "I think that's great. It seems like your therapist has really helped you a lot," I say honestly.

She smiles, still looking forward as she walks. "Yeah, she has." Then Aria narrows her eyes as if she's in thought. "But I want to start standing on my own. I'm not knocking anyone who relies on therapy, but it's time for me to just take her advice and make my own good fortune."

"I don't think that will be a problem. You're probably one of the strongest people I know."

Aria looks over to me with a smile. "That means a lot." Then she turns her head forward and changes the subject. "But the idea of standing on my own sort of brings me to my next topic." Aria stops walking and faces me completely with her hands shoved in her back pockets. "I don't want you to feel obligated to me."

"What?" I ask, completely confused.

She sighs as she turns to continue walking, and I follow alongside her. "I'm talking about the night you had a girl at your house. I don't want you to feel like you need to cut time short with someone to cater to me. I'm fine, you don't have to worry about me."

I stop Aria by placing a hand on her upper arm. "I chose to check on you that night. I *wanted* to check on you."

Aria slightly scrunches her face as she looks off to the side. "I don't know. I just don't want to feel like someone's charity case." Then she looks over to me with a grateful smile. "But I appreciate you telling me what you just did. So, thank you."

"If it makes you feel any better, she wasn't even a good lay," I joke.

Aria playfully shoves me. "Dane! Ugh!" I'm smiling at her as we both resume walking side by side. "*Anyway*, this breeze feels nice," Aria says while holding out her arms and closing her eyes.

"Yes, the perks of living in a coastal town. Not many humid summer nights," I say.

Aria is still in the same position so she can fully feel the breeze. "Mmhmm, you don't have to convince me twice." When she opens her eyes, she walks with her hands stuffed in her back pockets as she asks, "I love living here, don't you?"

I tilt my head to the side. "It's definitely got its advantages, but I don't think I'd mind trying to live in a big city."

"No, look at this," Aria responds as she walks over to the wooden railing of the boardwalk. She rests her forearms over it to look out at the view, and I come up to her side. We're just looking at the lowered sun illuminating the evening sky, and the waves crashing against the shore. "It's so peaceful here. Quaint. You get to enjoy the simpler things in life, not just expensive restaurants and lounges," she says.

I take a moment to look at Aria and appreciate the fact that she isn't a high maintenance girl. I'm looking at her with the evening glow casting on her face, and the breeze catching strands of her long hair, but I can see just how beautiful of a person she is on the *inside*.

I turn to look over the railing with her. "I think you might be onto something. There's a crowd of teenagers underage drinking around that small fire over there," I say as I point to what I'm talking about.

She chuckles. "Yeah, well, sometimes getting drunk is a beautiful thing."

I laugh, and then tap her upper arm with the back of my hand as I start walking away from where we are standing. "Alright, show me where these doughnuts are."

It's another ten minutes until we reach the doughnut shop and head in. "Which doughnut are you getting?" I ask her as we wait in line.

She puts a hand up and turns to face me. "I'm getting half a dozen. I need some for the rest of the week."

"*Okay*, well which *six* are you getting?"

"Five of the chocolate frosted with sprinkles, and one strawberry frosted with sprinkles." When I give Aria a confused look, she elaborates. "Everyone knows the chocolate frosted with sprinkles is the best."

"I don't know. Double chocolate with sprinkles is a good time," I argue.

Ari throws me wide eyes. "Oooo, I forgot about those," she says, and I nod my head with a tight-lipped smile. "Okay, four chocolate frosted with sprinkles and two double chocolate with sprinkles," she says matter-of-factly, as if this is very serious business.

"So, can I just pay you for the one double choc-"

"No." Aria is then called up to place her order, and I guess I'll be placing a separate order. The girl loves her doughnuts, and I can't deny how adorable she is about it.

Once we have our doughnuts, Aria and I start digging in as we walk toward the pier. "So good," Aria moans through her mouthful, and then she does a little shake with her walk like she's the happiest person ever.

I can't with this girl.

"Did you know there's a 'Dance Party' night at Duke's scheduled for later this month?" Aria asks as she swallows her bite.

Once I swallow my first bite, I respond to her. "Well, no, I normally don't keep tabs on the themed events at Duke's. I'm usually there for drinks and women."

"Well, free your schedule for July seventh because we're going. You, me, Kate, and Trent. If they're available."

"What time is this ridiculousness between?" I ask.

"It's between seven and ten o'clock. I promise, whatever or *whoever* you want to do afterwards, I'll leave you alone."

"Sounds amazing," I mutter sarcastically as I chew.

"Woo!" Aria throws her hands in the air as she does a small dance with her feet, and I can't hold back the light chuckle that escapes my lips.

When we reach the pier, we start to walk down it as I take the last bite of my doughnut, but as I'm chewing, I notice that there're darker clouds drifting toward us. "Looks like there is a summer storm coming in."

"Crap," Aria says as she looks up at the sky, and then pops the last piece of her doughnut into her mouth. "Guess we gotta beat it," Aria says as she walks backwards in front of me, creating more distance between us. Then suddenly, she turns around and takes off in a run down the pier.

"Ari, hey!" I call to her.

When I realize she's on a mission, I just jog after her as my feet move on their own accord, too intrigued to stand still. It's only another twenty seconds until I reach Aria at the end of the pier, and she's placed her box of doughnuts on the ground while she catches her breath over the railing. "Oh my god, that felt good," Aria breathes out.

"That's shocking. You were so annoyed with me at the end of our running workout the other day," I say as I lean over the railing beside her.

"Well, that's because I didn't actually *want* to do that. Sometimes, I just look for an adrenaline rush," she explains before looking out in the distance. "I wish this was the view from my backyard and I didn't have to walk a half hour to get here," she adds.

I feel a rain pellet land on my head, and then my forearm. "Yeah, well, your appreciation may be short-lived because it's starting to rain."

"So? When has a little rain hurt anyone?" she says with a smirk.

All I can do is smile back at her, and then turn my head to enjoy the scene with her. But unfortunately, I start to feel the raindrops come down more consistently, and then it turns into a downpour.

"Shit!" I yell as I grab Aria's hand and move us under the side of a small building structure along the pier. The roof of the small building hangs over the side just enough to allow us shelter, and of course Aria prioritizes grabbing the doughnut box from the ground, so that comes with us too.

When we seek shelter, Aria starts bursting out laughing while leaning her shoulder against the brick of the building. Everyone else has also sought shelter along the sides of the pier, so the pier is clear of people at the moment. Aria turns to lean her back fully against the wall, and her laughing fit diminishes as she considers something in her mind. I notice her swallow thickly, and her eyes are trained on the rain like it's a corridor to another universe.

Before I even have time to guess what she might be thinking, Aria turns to me. "Will you hold this?" she asks as she holds her box of doughnuts out to me.

I furrow my eyes, but extend my hand in acceptance anyway. I have no idea what she's up to, but once Aria hands the box to me, she peels herself off the building, and walks out into the rain on the pier. When she's met with the downpour of rain, she crosses her forearms lazily over the top of her head, and tilts her head back while she spins around in a circle. Once she completes a full rotation, she takes her headband out, and runs her hands through her hair as she just stands there with her head tilted up to the sky.

What the hell is she doing?

I decide to go with my instinct and jog toward her to drag her off the planks of the pier. When we come back to our original location under the roof overhang, she leans her back against the brick wall of the building with one hand on her head.

"Okay, that felt *great*," she pants out as she is drenched from head to toe, looking like she just jumped into a swimming pool with her clothes still on.

"Yeah, well it won't feel great when you catch pneumonia," I counter as I use the hem of my shirt to wipe down her arms.

Aria leans her back against the brick wall as I lean my shoulder against it right beside her, but she doesn't look at me. She just continues to look out at the rain as she says, "Sometimes I just want to feel alive again. Just feel *something* other than the emptiness that's consumed me for so long."

I blink as I stare at Aria because I don't know what to say. I never know what to say, and I feel like I fail her in these moments. But I understand what she's saying about wanting to feel something. I've definitely felt the void spaces in my heart this past year and have looked for ways to fill those voids. That's all Aria is trying to do right now.

She wants to *live* her life again.

Silence hangs between us as Aria continues to look out onto the pier, and I swallow a nervous lump in my throat as I look at her soaked body. Her ragged breathing pulls my eyes to her crop top that is slick against her flat, toned stomach. The outline of her full breasts are stretching the fabric, and her denim is hugging the sensual curves of her thighs even tighter now. There are loose strands of her hair that are slick, and sticking to her silky, sun-kissed skin, which is now glistening from her short-lived adventure.

Her beauty never waivers from head to toe, and it entices me, drawing me closer with every new detail I notice about her. But as I feel myself being reeled in, the moral threads in my mind pull me back to my original position, and I'm reminded of my place. A place that has *no* business being attracted to this woman.

Like clockwork, Aria's voice cuts through my thoughts. "You think I'm crazy, right?"

I look at her for a few seconds before responding. "Not at all." And that was the truth. I've seen Aria at some of her lowest points when dealing with Kyle's death, and I've seen her become just a cloak of the person she once was. But now? Now she's trying to take back control. It's admirable. "Aria, if you set your mind to do something it'll happen. So if you're looking to *live* again, just do it. You deserve that much," I say. "I'm here for you. Always," I whisper.

Aria turns to look at me, and I see her eyes slightly narrow as she ponders what I just said and the weight of my words. She's quiet, but the silence isn't awkward as I usually fear it will be. It's peaceful. We keep our eyes locked on one another as the pitter patter of the rain against the wooden planks of the pier provide white noise and solace to our tangling thoughts.

Finally, Aria steps toward me and wraps her arms around my neck, placing her head on my chest. "Thank you, Dane," she says.

I hesitate to return Aria's embrace, before placing my palms gently on the small of her back. When her words infiltrate my ears, it feels like they reach my heart, and I feel content knowing I did something right. Knowing Aria trusts me enough to confide in me, it makes me want to continue to be there for her. It makes me want to continue to breathe life back into her, and get to know this side of her. A side I guess I never really knew. They say that curiosity kills the cat, and I think my curiosity is starting to get the best of me.

I want Aria to keep surprising me.

Let's hope I don't self-destruct in the process.

CHAPTER
Nineteen

ARIA

Saturday, July 2, 2022

School's officially out, and it's Fourth of July weekend. Me, Kate, and the guys plan to have a bonfire out on the beach tonight, while we drink and watch the fireworks over the pier. Dane's been texting me more frequently to check in and crack his usual jokes, and as great as that is, I can't help the thoughts that take over my mind when I think of my friendship with Dane.

The last thing I want is Dane to feel obligated to me, let alone halt his own date with someone else to make sure I'm okay. I know he reassured me that this wasn't the case the other night, but the discomfort still claws at the back of my mind every now and then. I'd like to think my growing friendship with Dane is genuine and not just a contrived relationship born out of guilt and sympathy. How depressing would that be? I shudder to think.

To add to this miserable thought, seeing Dane and the blonde on his porch made me realize that I haven't had sex since Kyle. Or for that matter, any physical contact with the opposite sex whatsoever. Truthfully, I miss sex, and I think I'm starting to come around to the idea of being intimate with someone again. Not entirely, but I'm starting to.

I'm immersed in my thoughts as I'm helping move tables and chairs around in my dad's new restaurant. Speaking of, my dad transformed this building into one of the best looking modern farmhouse restaurants I've ever seen. The open floor plan allows dining to be located in the middle of the restaurant with oak surface tables and gray padded armchairs, while booths outline the perimeter of the space. The bar is located in the back left-hand corner, and the white shiplap paneling on the outside of the bar matches the white shiplap paneling of the walls. Large picture windows with sliders decorate the rear of the restaurant to give a panoramic view of the dock at Dawson's Marina, and above the sliding doors are transom windows with green wall planters underneath the length of their frames. Two exposed timber posts and frames are located in the center of the restaurant, attached to the ceiling where there is exposed ductwork and round trunks. To say the restaurant is eye-catching is an understatement.

As I'm fixating four chairs around one table, Ronnie comes over to me. "Need any help?"

"No, I'm good," I say as I push the last chair in, and then I check in with my mom and dad behind the bar. "Okay, I'm here, so what else do you need me to do?"

My dad speaks first. "Ronnie and I need to arrange the rest of these tables, so I need you to unload some boxes from the truck outside. Some are heavy, so just stick to the lighter ones until Ronnie and I grab the rest."

"I'll come with you," my mom says as she walks out from behind the bar.

We start an assembly line of me picking up the boxes in the truck, and my mom taking them from my hands outside the truck. "Are most of these boxes light fixtures?" I ask.

"Yes," my mom says as she takes a large box from my hand. "Ronnie's going to start installing these over the next couple weeks."

"I'm curious to see what Dad picked," I say as I crouch and lift the flaps of one of the brown boxes. "Oh, these look great. You sure Dad picked these himself?" I joke.

"Francesca definitely swayed your father from his original plans on quite a few things," my mom says.

I laugh as I look over the image of the intimate pendant light on the manufacturer box. "So I'm assuming these lights will go over the dining tables? Are there any for the ceiling?"

"No, just the dining tables. Have you seen the amount of natural light flowing in the restaurant?"

I nod. "True, that makes sense. Plus there're lights out on the marina to shine through the windows at night, so point taken." I close the flaps of the brown box back up and stand to hand the box to my mom.

"What kind of decor is going on the walls?" I ask.

"Recessed wall art to the side of the bar. Less is more, don't you think?" my mom asks as I hand her another box from the truck.

"Honestly, you probably don't even need decor with how detailed and styled the space is. The green wall planters can even be considered decoration."

"Your father and I thought the same, but we'll see." My mom takes another box from my hand when she continues. "Are you doing anything tonight or tomorrow to celebrate July Fourth?"

"Going with Kate and the guys to Crestside Beach tonight. Bonfire, fireworks, the whole nine," I say. I'm breaking a sweat in my flowy crop tank top and black spandex biker shorts, and it's a good thing I'm wearing a sports bra because I have boob sweat. Awesome.

"Well if those plans fall through, Ronnie and Cheryl are having a barbeque at their house. But I know it's been a long time since you've spent time like this with your friends," my mom responds.

"Yeah, it definitely has been," I say as I pass the last box to my mom, and then I look down at her from the truck. "I spent all of last summer away from the beach, and I honestly just miss it so much."

She nods with a tight-lipped smile. "You know I'm proud of you, right?"

I step off the truck. "I know, I love you," I say as I pull her in for a hug and kiss on the cheek.

I'm tying my American flag bandana into a headband after I just used my curling wand to make beach waves in my hair. I have on a white, V-neck short-sleeve romper with frill trim around the shorts and sleeves, and a keyhole back with an adjustable waist tie.

Once I get downstairs into the kitchen, I grab a twelve pack of hard seltzer from my fridge, and put it on the floor next to my camping chair. When I hear the knock at my door, I open it to see Dane dressed in a navy zip-up hoodie and shorts.

"Went all out, I see," Dane says as he eyes me up and down.

"I'm in a good mood, don't ruin it," I playfully warn as I turn back around.

"Okay, I'll stop. What do you need me to do?" he digresses as he walks through the door after me.

"I guess we can put the seltzers in the cooler now."

"You got it," Dane says as he grabs the White Claw pack from the floor and starts loading up the cooler he brought.

I'm leaning one palm on the counter as I look down at him. "Not for nothing, but do you ever wear flip flops to the beach?" I ask.

"No, I don't wear them ever. I figure I'll just take my shoes off if I'm going in the water," Dane says as he continues his task.

"It kind of seems like a cardinal sin while living in a beach town, no?"

Dane chuckles as he looks up at me. "I guess I live on the edge."

"Yeah, I get it," I breathe out as I bend to hike my camping chair over my shoulder. When Dane closes the cooler and stands up, I continue on my rant because I just can't help myself sometimes. "Men's feet—no one really wants to look at that," I add.

Dane laughs as he shakes my head. "Okay for the record, my feet are well groomed." Then Dane pulls his own chair over his shoulder and bends to grab the handles of the cooler to lift it. "I just choose not to display them if I don't have to."

"Honestly, in a woman's world, that's like top tier consideration," I say. Then I walk past him only to half-turn to place my hand over my heart dramatically. "I guess that's why you're such a ladies' man."

Dane smiles as he follows me, and I smile in reaction as I turn back to walk to the front door. "Oh yeah, sneakers are the new aphrodisiac," he says.

When my hand cups the door knob, I look down at Dane's feet, then back up at him critically. "I mean, I'm more of a Nike gal, but I guess you'll get by with Puma," I tease.

"We're talking about feet," Dane states.

I shrug nonchalantly as I turn to open the front door. "I am who I am."

"That you are, Ari," Dane says, and I can hear the smile in his voice as he follows me out of my house.

Once we make it to the beach, we start the bonfire, grab a drink, and let eighties classics flow through the bluetooth speaker. It's seven o'clock, so the sun is still out, but it's an evening glow as lines of lavender and orange layer between the clouds. We purposely wanted to be here at sunset, and as any Fourth of July would be, there are swarms of people on the beach at this hour.

As I'm grabbing a drink from the cooler, I'm interrupted by a casual voice. When I stand up to see who's speaking, it seems this voice belongs to a handsome man who has "surfer dude" written all over him, between his shaggy dirty blonde hair, and hazel eyes that stand out against his bronzed skin. Not to mention, he has a lean muscular build that shows through his white t-shirt and mint colored board shorts.

Naturally, my eyes light up as I stretch a wide smile across my face. "Hey."

"Is this your campfire?" mystery man asks.

"Yes, but guests are always welcome," I say.

"Nice. I'm hanging out with some of my boys a little further down, but thought I'd swing by and say hello."

I can feel myself grinning like a teenage girl. "I'm glad you did. But I have two questions for you. Do you have a name? And can I get you something to drink?" I ask.

"Blake, and I'll take whatever you're offering me," he says with a grin.

Feeling my cheeks blush from his insinuation, I distract myself by grabbing a Corona from the cooler and handing it to him. We "cheers" to take a sip of our respective drinks, and then I gesture with my head in the direction of my friends standing around the fire.

"Come on, I'll introduce you." When we reach Trent, Kate, and Dane, I take it upon myself to introduce Blake. "Hey, guys, this is Blake. Blake, this is Kate, Trent, and Dane," I say as I point to each of my friends.

"Nice to meet you," they all say in unison as they throw a wave.

I turn to Blake. "I'm assuming you plan on being out late tonight like the rest of us?"

"It's the only proper way to celebrate."

"Awesome, us too," I say. "We brought cornhole to set up later, and I can use a partner if you're interested?"

"I can't promise a wipe out of the other team, but I'm pretty decent," Blake jokes.

"I'll take my chances," I laugh out. Then I take a sip of my seltzer as I contemplate my next question to keep the conversation moving. "So how old are you?"

"Twenty seven, you?" he says.

"So am I. Did you grow up in Crestside?"

"I actually grew up in Plainstone, but moved out here after I finished college. I have a few friends that live out here and once they gave the recommendation, I had to see what the hype was all about."

I look at Blake as he praises Crestside, thinking of all the ways this town has changed my life for better and for worse. Even though I've spent such a small part of my entire life here, it's the only place that truly understands who I am and knows all of my secrets.

"Yeah, this place is special to me," I finally draw out.

Blake smiles back before taking a sip of his beer. "So what do you do," he asks after he swallows.

"I'm a teacher."

"That's awesome, what grade level?" Blake asks.

"Middle school. Seventh and eighth grade," I answer.

Blake makes a face. "Yikes. You deserve an award."

I laugh. "Everyone says that, but middle school is my niche. I couldn't picture myself teaching high school students."

Blake shrugs. "Hey, you get the summer off so that's reason enough to deal with everything you deal with, right?"

I raise my can of hard seltzer to him. "Eyy, someone who appreciates teachers! Can't find many of those these days."

Blake laughs as he clanks my can with his beer bottle, and we both take generous sips of alcohol to christen the night we're about to endure together. I think back to my first few therapy sessions with Dr. Connelly, and maybe this is what she was talking about. Meeting new people, inviting new adventures into my life spontaneously, and finding reasons to smile again.

No matter how small.

An hour passes amongst everyone's conversations and the music, and Blake and I fall into easy conversation. He's actually really funny, and that goes a very long way in my book. But at some point, Kate and I are three White Claws deep when we hear "Girls Just Wanna Have Fun" by Cyndi Lauper, and we give each other the *look*.

"Oh boy, here we go," Trent says as he looks at Dane.

I'm feeling *good*. Yes, it may be alcohol-induced, but I embrace the feeling as I grab Kate's hand and drag us away from everyone. Off to the side, we start singing along to the Cyndi Lauper classic and twirling each other around as our feet sink into the sand. I can't remember the last time I had this much fun or laughed this many times, and I'm not about to let the night slip away from me.

I'm holding on tight.

CHAPTER

Twenty

DANE

I take a sip of my beer as I watch Kate and Aria dance to the music. It's clear they're starting to feel buzzed, and Aria's laughter rings in my ears well after the sound has left her mouth.

"Hey, I have to ask…are either of you involved with Aria?" Blake stands in front of Trent and I as he asks his question.

"No, definitely not," Trent responds.

I remain silent and choose not to answer right away. I'm strangely overcome with an urge to protect Aria, and the idea of him being with Aria rubs me the wrong way. Blake has no idea what she's been through this past year, and I'm not about to let him blindly crumble all the progress she's made if he's just looking for some quick action.

I narrow my eyes slightly. "No we're not. But she's been through a lot, so I wouldn't overstay your welcome."

Blake throws his hands up in defense. "I was just thinking about a date. That's all."

I ignore his reply as I finish my beer, and walk away to grab another, but mostly just to get away from Blake.

"Hey!" Aria exclaims as she comes up behind me. Her hands are on my shoulders, and she's peeking over them to see what's inside the cooler. "You better be gettin' me another drink."

I smile as I grab a mango flavored hard seltzer from the cooler, and turn to offer it to her. "Make it last, will ya?"

She gives me a devious smirk as she takes the can from my hand. "Woah," I say as I grab the bottom of Aria's can, noticing she's guzzling her drink. "Slow down there."

Aria turns her head to the side as she lets out a belch, avoiding burping in my face, and I sigh out a laugh. She just shrugs it off like it's no big deal, and then grabs my hand and spins herself under me. "I've always wanted to take ballroom dancing classes," she coos, and yeah, she's definitely getting more drunk by the minute.

"Oh, yeah?" I play along and spin her a couple times, but I'm sure Aria would be amazing at ballroom dancing if she took a few lessons. Hell, I may even go with her if she asked me. I've actually taken a class before with my mom for her birthday, and it wasn't as painful as I imagined. Go figure.

When Aria releases her hand from mine, she stands in front of me as she says, "Yeah, it would be fun." Then she bobs her head side to side as she considers something. "Embarrassing, but fun, nonetheless."

"I think you'll manage just fine," I smirk as I take a sip of my beer and hold her gaze.

Aria stares at me for a few silent moments in concentration as she studies my face. "You have hazel eyes," she blurts out.

I'm thrown off by her random observation, let alone the fact that she's known me for years and this shouldn't be brand-new, riveting information. But then again, Aria's tipsy, so a change in subject within conversation is not totally abnormal. "Yes," I say with a question mark on the end, not too sure how to respond.

Aria's lips tip up at the corner as her eyes scan back and forth between my own, like she's mesmerized. "They're green."

The popping and crackling sound of fireworks turns our attention to the pier in the distance as long cascading bursts of stars embellish the dark sky. One after another, weaving clusters of light appear in shining golds, blues, and reds, and Aria and I just stand there watching. I peek over at her, and when I see Aria's contemplative expression, I assume her mind is going haywire with memories.

Out of nowhere, Kate comes up from behind Aria and tackles her into a hug, knocking her a little off balance and both of them into a fit of giggles. "They're so pretty!" Kate yells as she refers to the fireworks.

Aria turns around to tap her can of White Claw with Kate's as she raises her free hand up in the air. "Happy Fourth of July!" Aria shouts.

When they finish their cheers, Kate starts to walk past me with Aria following behind, but Aria pauses for a brief moment to look up at me. Her lips are still curled up in the corner, and her elegant fingers come up to brush a few strands of hair off my forehead. The contact startles me when I feel a shiver run down my back, and I'm stunned speechless as my sneakers remain grounded in the sand.

"Your eyes give me hope," Aria softly says as she pulls her hand away from my face. I think I let out the slightest exhale, but I can't be sure. Her light brown hues entice me, persuading me to look longer and deeper beyond the surface and peel back her outer layers.

Before I have time to fully comprehend what's happening, Aria stretches a playful smile across her lips and walks off to follow Kate. I swallow thickly when Aria steps out of view, but the floral and amber scent of her perfume is caught in the gentle breeze around me, provoking and teasing my senses. And as soon as the fumes invade me, I quickly wipe a palm down my face as if to wash them away, and I go to catch up with Trent by the fire.

Another hour passes, and Aria and Kate are drunk as they're sitting side by side in the sand and looking up at the sky with their canned drinks in hand.

"I'd pay money to hear the gibberish coming out of their mouth right now," Trent says.

I laugh as I sink back into my chair. "They're constructing a new language as we speak."

"I'm getting another beer, do you want one?" Trent asks.

"No, two is my limit tonight," I say as I tilt my head back and close my eyes. "Not to mention I'm probably going to need my energy to take care of Aria later."

"Take care?" Trent asks. As soon as I hear the confusion in Trent's voice, I realize just how misleading my choice of words were.

I open my eyes and turn my head to him with my palm turned upward. "Oh, come on, I didn't mean I was going to kneel at her bedside. I mean that I'm going to make sure she gets home and into bed safely."

"Got it," Trent says as he gets up from his chair and grabs another beer for himself from the cooler.

I inwardly roll my eyes as I turn my head forward, only to be greeted with Kate walking up to our chairs. "Helllooooo," Kate greets.

"Hey, Kate, why don't you lay off the Claws," Trent suggests as he walks back up to his chair.

"No, it's mine." She frowns as she hugs the can in her hand.

My lips tip up at the corner, only to tip down when I look over to where Aria and Kate had been sitting. "Where did Aria go?" I ask Kate.

She shrugs. "I don't know, somewhere down there, I think," Kate responds as she slurs her words and points to her left.

"Shit. I'll be right back," I say as I get up from my seat. I walk in the direction Kate pointed to, and that's when I see Aria stepping into the water. It's pitch dark out, and she's completely drunk, so I start jogging in her direction and yell out to her.

"Ari!" I quickly rip my sneakers and socks off to jog into the water, splashes of water crashing against my legs as I do, and when I reach Aria, I pull her arm back. "Come on, this isn't safe." But my words don't have the effect I want them to have, and she aggressively jerks her arm away to step further into the water. I waste no time getting in front of her and tugging both her arms down at her sides. "Ari, this isn't fucking funny. You're drunk."

Aria's looking off to the side, unmoving, and there are a few moments of silence before she speaks. "We always spent Fourth of July here."

I bring my hands up to cup her face so she can look up at me. "Ari, listen to me. We can talk about this, but you need to get out of the water." We've been pulled in a little more by the current, and the waves are crashing against us in higher places. The lower half of my hoodie is starting to stick to me, and because Ari is shorter, 90 percent of her romper is soaking wet.

As if a switch turns on inside her, Aria's back to being aggressive. "Leave me alone!" she yells as she pushes past me, but I don't let her get far when I scoop her up with one arm around her stomach, and hold her backside against my side. I carry her back to the dry sand, and when I put her down, Aria shifts around trying to balance herself on her feet. I place my hands on her shoulders to help her stay steady, and once Aria finds proper footing, she's standing in front of me as she hugs her arms across her stomach. "I'm sorry. I'm sorry," she breathily chants.

I immediately bring Aria in for a hug as my arms cross behind her shoulders and kiss the top of her head. I hold her for a few silent seconds, resting my chin on the top of her head as I stare out at the beach behind us, and figure my actions speak louder than words at this point. When I release her, my palm rests on the back of her neck and my thumb subconsciously draws lazy circles on her skin there in an attempt to continue comforting her.

"What are you doing?" Aria whispers.

As if her words physically burn me, I release Aria to interlock my hands behind my head and take one step back from her. I don't say anything as Aria looks off in the distance somewhere.

"I haven't been touched or been with anyone *since*," she whispers.

What. The. Fuck.

Aria's confession pulls my eyes gradually downward, and I notice the way her delicate curves are painted against the wet fabric of her romper. Against my better judgment, I'm unable to tear my eyes away, and I swallow a nervous gulp as I drink her in. Her nipples are now standing taunt behind the soaked white material, and her breathing is becoming shallower with every heave of her chest. Seeing how affected Aria is by a simple touch, my body instantly springs to attention, and I'm turned on just the same. As fucking shameful as I feel to admit it, it wouldn't take much for me to cut the moral thread that's holding me back from touching her in every way I shouldn't.

But that's not even the worst part.

What's even more alarming is that I'm *satisfied* to know Aria hasn't been intimate with anyone since Kyle. I feel relieved, but the relief isn't because Aria's remained "loyal" to Kyle. The more I focus on Aria's innocence, the more I realize how much I don't want her to fool around with just any random guy. The idea frustrates me, and I don't have a single rational reason as to why it does.

As if Aria is mine to claim.

As if she has some unspoken duty to remain loyal to *me*.

Me of all people.

The truths Aria's revealing to me tonight are making my mind twist with unfamiliar emotions, spinning them into a cyclone of thrill and defeat. I swallow as I stare at Aria for several more seconds, and then tip my head to the side as I change the course of this discussion for good.

"Come on, let's get you dry and home." I wrap one arm around Aria's shoulders as her arm snakes around my back, and I walk us safely back to our homes.

CHAPTER
Twenty-One

ARIA

Sunday, July 3, 2022

My eyes are difficult to pry open as the sunlight from my bedroom window starts flooding in and hitting my face. I don't have a terrible hangover with a pounding headache or anything, but the struggle is real. I remember chugging hard seltzers on the beach with Kate, dancing to Cyndi Lauper, and after Dane gave me my fourth drink, last night's events started to become hazy.

I hear my phone vibrate from my nightstand, and I grunt as I shift my body to see who's calling me. Dane's calling at 11:45 am.

Wow, I overslept.

"Hello?" I answer groggily.

"Been at your front door for the past five minutes. Should I send a SWAT team?" Dane says.

"Coming down now," I grumble and then hang up the phone.

I put my phone down on the nightstand and throw my head back on the pillow as I rub my eyes and groan. When I decide to get up, I'm throwing my covers off of me and notice I'm in my pink plaid pajama pants and an oversized black t-shirt. I furrow my brows momentarily because I don't remember changing into these clothes at all.

Did Dane walk me home?

Oh my god, did he have to change me?

I feel so confused and embarrassed as I reluctantly make my way downstairs to my front door. When I open it, I am greeted with Dane who is dressed in a pair of navy gym shorts and a gray t-shirt. His skin looks damp, indicating he just finished working out, but he's also holding a small cup of coffee out to me.

"This should help wake you up."

"Thanks," I mumble as I take the cup, and then I look at him questioningly. "Did you bring me home last night?"

"Yeah, I was on 'damage control' duty by the end of the night," he jokes.

I scrunch my face apologetically. "Sorry. I hope I wasn't too annoying."

He shrugs. "No more than usual."

I laugh and nod my head as I lift the flap to the top of my coffee, and then I take a sip. Once I swallow my first gulp, I ask him another question. "This is kind of embarrassing, but how did I get in these clothes?" I ask as I point at my wardrobe. "I literally don't remember much after the Cyndi Lauper dancing."

"You can relax, you dressed yourself. Apparently, you're on autopilot when you're drunk," he says with a smile.

I take another sip of my coffee before responding. "Wow, I'm impressed with myself."

"I was too."

I squint my eyes accusingly at him, but Dane holds his hands out in defense. "You were in the bedroom with the door closed. I was in the hallway."

"Good. I thought I'd die of embarrassment if you had to dress me like a toddler, or watch me try to dress myself."

"No need. You're in the clear."

I smile as I look Dane over for a few moments and then say what I really want to say. "Thank you."

He knows I'm thanking him for taking care of me last night, and Dane nods back in acceptance. Then he places a hand on the top of my head as he says, "Just stay out of trouble today, yeah?" Dane smiles as he turns away to head back to his house, and then I decide to retreat into my own home to plop myself on the couch with my surprise coffee.

Today is definitely a Netflix day.

DANE

I ring my mom's doorbell, expecting her energetic self to greet me at the door because I'm following through on plans to have dinner with her and her boyfriend.

When the door swings open, my mom doesn't disappoint. "You made it!" she exclaims as she brings me in for a bear hug.

"Even remembered to pick up the hamburger buns," I say as I return my mom's hug.

My mom pulls back with a smile and then turns to walk in the house. "You saved me a trip. Thank you."

"No worries. Just not sure I'll go back to the grocery store on a Sunday," I say as I set the rolls on the kitchen counter.

My mom takes a sip of her coffee, then leans one hip on the kitchen counter as she faces me. "Yeah, it's always a madhouse on the weekends. Doesn't help that it's a holiday weekend either."

"Yep. Chaos automatically ensues," I say as I walk to the kitchen island and grab an apple from the fruit bowl. When I take a bite, I start to talk mid-chew. "Where's Chris?"

"Upstairs getting changed. I think he just showered."

"So, how are things with him?"

My mom just started dating Chris a couple months ago, and I never feel weird about her dating men, just protective. If there is one thing I can promise, it's that if the guy my mom's dating decides to hurt her, he'll have to answer to me.

My mom stretches a wide grin on her face. "Great, actually. He's... refreshing."

I take another bite of my apple as I saunter back over to my original position at the kitchen counter, next to my mom. I lean my hip against it as I face her and say, "Good. Wasn't exactly in the mood to play the over-protective son tonight."

My mom rolls her eyes. "Oh, you're being ridiculous, Dane. I can take care of myself."

"Doesn't mean I can't care," I say before taking another bite of my apple.

"Well, you're off duty for the night," my mom jokes.

"Great, because last night kicked my ass," I say.

"Oh, that's right! You and your friends celebrated on the beach. How was it?"

I shrug as I chew what's left in my mouth and swallow. "Unsurprisingly, a good time. Drank, kicked back, watched fireworks going off over the pier."

"Doesn't sound too chaotic for you to be exhausted."

I shrug again as I take the last bite of my apple, and go to throw the remnants of the fruit in the garbage under the sink. "Aria got a little carried away with her drinking, so I looked after her."

"I'm sure the holidays are hard for her. But she's lucky to have you as a friend," my mom says from behind me.

When I hear the word "friend" come from my mom's mouth, a tinge of irritation flares within me. After last night, I've been thinking about how the friendship between Aria and I has evolved. How I'm getting to know little details about Aria I never would've known if it weren't for Ronnie asking me to look out for her. As happy as I am to be there for Aria and spend time with her, there's a part of me that is resentful of being given this task. It almost feels like I've been pulled too deep into something I may not be able to dig myself out of. Because the more Aria opens up to me, the more my interest is piqued.

I can hold an honest conversation with her, and she's so damn funny and carefree at the same time. I laugh effortlessly when I'm around her, and she keeps up with my own humor better than most women I know. It's unexpected, and I don't think I've ever found someone so…sexy. And I'm not just referring to her looks, even though Aria's undoubtedly beautiful.

It's her *soul* that draws me in.

But a "friend" can't act on these types of feelings. There's nothing for me to do with these new emotions brewing within me, and I feel like my hands are tied behind my back with the position Ronnie put me in. And for that matter, the position I've been in ever since she dated Kyle. All that's left for me to do is admire Aria from afar while other men admire her up close.

Great.

Tired of thinking about this any longer, I close the cabinet under the sink and make my way to the fridge to start getting out the hamburger meat to grill.

"Yeah," I say, keeping my response short and simple.

"Hey, Dane, how are you?"

I close the fridge door once I retrieve the packages of meat, and turn to see Chris standing at my side. I extend my free hand to shake his. "Hey, not bad. You?"

"Can't complain too much," Chris responds.

I start walking toward the spice rack on the kitchen counter. "Hopefully my mom's not causing you too many headaches," I joke.

"Oh, please," my mom interjects.

I smile as I look through the spice rack for what I need. "I kid, I kid."

"Well the latest would be that your mom wants a puppy," Chris says from behind me.

I pick out a couple spices and turn around to face both of them with furrowed brows. "A puppy?" Chris leans himself against the fridge with his palm as he smirks at my mother, and I look to my mom as I say, "You do know that you need to actually train it, right?"

My mom throws her hands up as if she's offended. "Why is it such a ridiculous idea to think I can properly train a dog?"

I chuckle. "Because you don't have the time. I know you."

"Well, maybe I just need a change in routine," my mom counters, but it sounds like she's trying to convince herself.

I give an unsure smile as I look over at Chris. "Well, good luck with that." Then I peel myself off the counter and make my way to the sliding door in the kitchen that leads to the patio. "I'm going to start grilling."

"I'll bring out the cheese and other toppings!" my mom calls out as I walk onto the patio and start gassing up the grill.

With one hand on the handle of the grill lid, I feel a vibration in my jeans pocket and fish out my cell phone with my free hand.

Aria: This was me the whole day.

There's a GIF of a disheveled looking cat under Aria's text, and I laugh out loud.

Me: Next time, I'm just going to refill an empty hard seltzer can with water. You'll never notice.

Aria: [neutral face emoji].

Me: [thumbs up emoji] Did the coffee at least help a little?

Aria: For a hot minute. Thanks again.

Me: I guess I should've gone with my first instinct and got a doughnut too.

Aria: There's only one instinct to follow on that [unamused emoji]. I'm disappointed.

I'm grinning from ear to ear when my mom walks through the patio door. "What are you smiling about?"

I place my phone back in my pocket and open the lid to the grill. "Nothing, just texting."

"Who were you texting? I don't think I've ever seen you smile so big," my mom questions.

I give her a deadpan expression as she comes beside me. "Calm down, it's not a girl. Aria and I were just having a good laugh."

"Really?" my mom says with a surprised expression.

I start putting the hamburger patties on the grill as I respond. "I take offense with your surprised tone. As boring as you may find me to be, I can actually be very entertaining from time to time."

"You know that's not what I meant," my mom says as she lets out an exhausted breath.

I smirk as I put the last of the burger patties on the grill and close the lid. When I turn to face my mom, I say, "I know. But I also know you're about to overanalyze the situation, so maybe just save us the time and skip that part."

My mom shrugs as if she has no idea what I'm talking about. "I wasn't overanalyzing anything. I just commented on how big your smile was."

I let out a laugh as I turn my head forward, but as I feel my mom's eyes still on me, I run a hand through my hair as I let out an exhausted sigh. "She makes me laugh. It's no big deal."

My mom holds her palms up in defense. "Again, I didn't say anything."

I look at my mom with a bored expression, knowing exactly where her mind is going, but I decide to change the subject for not only her sake, but for mine as well. Apparently, my sanity these days is slipping little by little, and this conversation is helping none.

"You want cheese on your burger?" I ask.

My mom chuckles. "Yes."

I smile as I turn to open the lid and continue grilling, but the whole time my hands are moving, my mind is somewhere else.

And there's probably a thousand other places my mind should be.

CHAPTER
Twenty-Two

DANE

Thursday, July 7, 2022

It turns out Kate and Trent are both busy tonight, and it's just Aria and I going to Duke's for the "Dance Party" themed night. I put together a white three-quarter sleeve henley, gray jeans, high-top black Converse, and my hair is gelled just enough to tame my waves.

When Aria opens her door, she's all decked out. Her long beach waves are tucked loosely back in a half up half down hairdo, with loose strands framing her face. She's wearing a black crop tank top, and a black floral maxi skirt with a thigh high slit. To complete the outfit, she has silver hoops dangling from her ears, and she's wearing black wedge sandals.

I respond before thinking. "You look great," I say.

"Thanks! It's a dance party, so naturally I had to pull out all the stops," Ari responds.

I involuntarily check her out as I say, "I approve."

She narrows her eyes at me curiously. "You're being too nice."

Snapping my eyes back to hers, I chuckle as I shove my hands in my pockets. "Are you implying I'm not nice normally?"

She's still narrowing her eyes at me. "You are. You just normally open with jokes, so I was thrown off for a second."

"Well that's because I'm unpredictable. One of my many charms," I say as I place a hand over my heart.

She points to me. "Ah, there we go. That's what I like to hear." I just laugh, and Aria smiles as she grabs her clutch off the foyer so we can head down her porch steps to my Mustang.

We arrive at eight o'clock, and just as we enter Dukes, we hear the DJ playing "Hot in Herre" by Nelly. "Okay, song choice is strong from ·the start, so that's a good sign," I joke from behind Aria as I follow her to the bar.

She turns back to me, but keeps walking forward. "Oh my god, I'm so happy right now," she says with an excited smile.

I smirk as I continue to follow her, and luckily there are two free stools at the bar for us to sit at. "So, what're we having tonight?" I ask her as we take our seats.

"I think this night calls for at least two shots," Aria says with suggestive eyebrows.

"Oh wow, we're going hard tonight. What'll it be then?" I respond.

She squints her eyes and purses her lips as she thinks about what she wants. "Fireball?"

"Really?"

She sighs in frustration. "Well what would you suggest?"

"Tequila. For sure," I say.

She slaps and rubs her palms together. "Let's do it!"

I laugh and call the bartender over to order two shots of tequila and two waters. The bartender pours the shots in front of us and places a lime slice on top of each little glass. I hand one over to Aria as I take the other, and I raise my shot glass up to hers. She taps her shot glass with mine, and we both down our tequila shots in one smooth gulp.

When we are both done sucking the juice out of our limes, we place them in the empty shot glasses, and Aria does a small shake with her body. "Ugh, I haven't done a shot of tequila in years," she says as she winces.

I furrow my brows. "Yeah come to think of it, I probably haven't done one of those since college. Shit, we're getting old."

Just as I finish my sentence, I feel someone bump into my shoulder at the bar. I turn around to apologize, but when I do, there's an attractive blue-eyed brunette standing next to me.

A distraction.

This is what I need.

"Sorry," she apologizes as she places a hand on my shoulder.

"If you wanted my attention so bad, you could've just asked for my name," I say with a side grin.

She smiles shyly as she asks, "So what is your name?"

"Dane. You?"

"Sarah," the brunette responds, and then notices Aria sitting next to me. "Are you here alone?"

I turn to Aria who is sipping her water, and she's trying to look like she's not listening to this exchange, but I know Aria too well to know she's definitely listening in. I turn back to Sarah to respond. "I'm actually with a friend tonight. Maybe I can catch you later if you're around?" I say as I throw her a smirk.

"Great. Come find me later," Sarah says before she bites her bottom lip and walks away.

I'm grinning as I turn to Aria, but Aria isn't smiling. Instead, she's throwing me a hard stare. I play dumb. "What?"

She grabs my arm with both her hands as if she's begging. "Dane, could you please just give me this hour or two, and I promise, whatever sexual escapades you want to do afterwards, won't offend me in the least."

I hike a thumb over my shoulder. "Did you not just witness me tell her I'm with a friend?"

She purses her lips as she removes her hands from my arm. "That's true. You did."

"Thank you." I turn to face the bar and take a sip of my water. "So let's get actual drinks now. What do you want?"

"Sex on the beach, please," she says. I order a sex on the beach and then a gin and tonic for me. Once the bartender passes the drinks to us, "I Wanna Dance with Somebody" by Whitney Houston plays, and Aria's eyes go wide. She takes her drink off the bar as she gets up from the stool.

"Where are you going?" I ask.

"To dance," Aria states like it's no big deal.

"By yourself?"

She leans closer to my face as she says, "Sometimes you just have to seize the moment. Right now, I feel like dancing." And with that, Aria raises her arms in the air, with her drink in hand, and she starts dancing with a couple other people in front of the DJ.

Aria's quick to make friends with another woman up there, who seems older than her, but just as fun apparently. Aria takes the woman's hand and spins her around, and then the woman spins Aria around. Before you know it, they just sway their hips to the beat of the music.

I take a sip of my drink as I watch Aria move on the dance floor. I'm finding that I'm learning a lot about Aria I never knew before. Like how spontaneous and *fun* she is. To top it all off, she's a natural beauty, and she has *great* rhythm. Talk about a total package, I can't take my eyes off of her.

Once the chorus comes on, Aria's arms fly high in the air, and she's singing right along at the top of her lungs with everyone else on the dance floor. I can't help but stupidly grin from my seat at the bar, and I almost wish I was dancing with her.

Not almost.

I *definitely* wish I was dancing with her right now.

When the song ends, Aria walks toward me as she's fanning herself. "I forgot how much I break a sweat," Aria says. "I hope I don't smell," Aria adds as she tips her nose down to her shoulder.

My elbow rests on the bar as my chin is in my palm. "Did you just sniff your armpit?"

Aria takes a seat in her bar stool, and grabs her crossbody bag to sift through it. "Yes," she responds as she takes a travel size deodorant out, and uncaps it before slouching down and sneaking a few swipes under her armpits.

"Okay, this is happening," I comment.

"What? Nobody likes body odor," Aria retorts as she sits up straighter and puts the deodorant back in her bag.

I chuckle. "You could have just asked me how you smelt and saved yourself the trouble. You smell nice."

"My sweat glands are out of control when I dance," she says in her defense.

I briefly look over to the dance floor. "Yeah, you weren't exactly holding back over there."

"Okay, go ahead. Make fun of me."

My elbow is resting on the bar counter as my temple leans on the knuckles of my fingers. "For once, I wasn't going to make a joke."

Aria eyes me suspiciously. "Uh-huh."

I sit up as I laugh and tip my palms outward. "What, I'm incapable of complimenting you?"

"Yes," Aria says with a playful smile as she defends her point.

I return her smile, and just as I'm about to respond to her, I'm interrupted by some random guy who slides in at the bar next to Aria.

"Hey, can I buy you a drink? Least I can do after the great show you gave on the dance floor," he says.

Seriously?

Aria smiles shyly, and I can tell she's a little uncomfortable. Aria doesn't have a mean bone in her, so I know she's about to entertain this clown. On the other hand, maybe my instinct is wrong, and maybe she is interested. Thinking rationally, I'm going to need to feel the situation out before I step in. But if she gives me the eyes that tell me to save her, it's game over for Homeboy over here.

Aria puts a palm over her forehead like she's embarrassed. "Oh good lord, a show?" Then Aria turns to face this guy. "Well hopefully my dancing wasn't too obnoxious," Aria jokes.

"Not at all. You're a sight for sore eyes. Even off the dance floor."

Wow.

Aria bites her lip on a smile as she briefly turns her head away, but then she turns back to him. "What's your name?"

"Chris. You?"

Aria holds out her hand. "I'm Aria. Nice to meet you, Chris."

"Likewise."

Is she actually interested in this guy?

I take a sip of my drink as I watch this unfold, but act unknowing at the same time. My discomfort level is increasing, but I'm not sure if it's because I feel awkward being a third wheel, or if it's because I feel...*jealous.*

I can't help but think back to what Aria and I were talking about right before Chris walked up, and the irony of this entire scenario. Aria was telling me how it would be weird for me to compliment her, even though all I really wanted to tell her was how amazing and sexy she looked on the dance floor. I want to tell her how I find her quirkiness to be absolutely adorable, and how she's unlike any woman I've ever met. But as luck would have it, someone else beat me to the punch, and now I'm sitting here practically being friend zoned. And even though it's the only zone I should be occupying when it comes to Aria, I feel frustration creeping up on me anyway.

"So how about that drink?" Chris asks Aria.

Aria shakes her head with a grateful smile. "I really appreciate the gesture, but I already have a drink."

"How about if the next one's on me?"

Aria playfully brushes him off. "No, you don't have to. Thank you though."

I notice Chris bend his head lower and turn his head so his lips are hovering over her ear, speaking directly into it. I can't hear exactly what he's saying, but I'm pretty sure it's a sexual proposition. When I see Aria's smile completely drop and her body stiffen, I notice his hand at her lower back, caressing her through the fabric of her crop top.

Then it hits me.

It isn't just the fact that some random guy is touching her. It's the fact that she hasn't been touched like this in a whole goddamn year, let alone by some random guy she doesn't know at all. I don't even think before I stand up from my seat at the bar.

"Hey," I say to get Chris' attention.

Chris furrows his brows at me. "Was I talking to you?"

"I'm talking to you." I don't waste any time with a rebuttal.

When he peels his palm off Aria's back and stands up straight, he says, "My bad. Wasn't aware she had a boyfriend."

I shove my hands in my pocket and eye him with a tight jaw. "She doesn't. But the next time you touch her in front of me, we're gonna have a big problem."

I feel Aria place a hand on my elbow. "Dane, it's fine," she says.

I ignore her efforts as I hold Chris' eyes, and he lets out a laugh, making it a point to laugh at me. Then Chris turns his attention to Aria. "Hey, babe, how abo-"

"I'm not playin', bro. Leave her alone." I don't even give him the chance to finish his sentence when I place a hand to his chest and get only inches away from his face.

Aria is now the one to get up, and she snakes her arm between us, placing her hand on my chest. "Dane, stop it."

When I look down at Aria, she's pleading with her eyes for me not to make a scene, and when I catch a glimpse of her bright, brown eyes, I become more aware of her small palm touching my broad chest. And the longer I stare into those gorgeous eyes, my alpha streak starts to recede.

"You sure? I could've wound her up for you. Seems like you want to tap that more than me," Chris says with a smug grin.

Blind rage takes over.

My fist connects with this prick's jaw in one blow, knocking him off balance.

"Dane!" Aria shouts.

"HEY! OUT!" one of the bouncers shouts as he comes up to me and nudges me to start walking.

"We're going," I say as I quickly take Aria's clutch off the bar and grab her hand. We make our way to the exit of the bar all the while being shadowed by the bouncer.

Once we're out on the sidewalk, I hand over Aria's clutch to her.

"Gosh, Dane, that was so stupid," Aria gasps.

I shake the sting from my knuckles as I say, "That's an odd way of saying thank you."

"Thank you? Dane, you went full blown 'Gorilla'! What the hell?" Aria counters.

I stop as I turn to her, throwing my arms out in front of me. "Well excuse me for giving a shit about the way he touched you and spoke to you. Clearly, I was the only one that did."

Aria swallows a nervous lump as she stares at me, and I see her angry walls start to lower as her face softens. When she looks down at my knuckles, Aria squints her eyes as she reaches for my hand with both of hers. "Let me see," she whispers.

I turn my head with a tight jaw. "I'm fine." When I feel her soft fingers stroke the small cut and swelling on my knuckles, I feel my stomach flip at her touch, and I'm so freaked out that I automatically pull my hand from hers. "I'm fine," I say in a sterner tone.

Aria hugs her arms across her chest nervously and looks down at the ground, then back up to me. "Thank you," she says in a faint voice.

I give her a small smile, and decide to alleviate the tension between us. "Do you still think I'm incapable of complimenting you now that I've defended your honor?"

"No. As long as your compliments are better than those lines that douchebag was using on me," Aria jokes back.

"I was in physical pain. More than my knuckles right now."

Aria laughs. "Same. Besides the knuckles part." Then Aria's face gets more serious, and she scrunches her face. "I'm sorry."

"You're actually not permitted to say sorry in this situation," I say.

Aria rolls her eyes at my corniness, and then she turns to start walking.

I follow suit by shoving my hands in my jean pockets, and smile as I look over at her. "Shippers?"

"So you can get in more tussles?" she jokes.

I chuckle. "No," I say, and then I shrug as I look forward. "I just know how much you were looking forward to tonight."

Aria turns to face me with a smile. "Lead the way."

ARIA

When we walk through the door at Shippers, it's a quarter to ten, and luckily the bar is dead with only a few people scattered about. Random music plays in the background through the speakers, and Dane and I make our way to the bar.

As we both take a seat, I ask, "So another shot of tequila? Clearly, we're going HAM tonight."

"Clearly," Dane echoes as he hails the bartender over.

Once the bartender pours our shots, we knock them back, and then order a couple beers. My arms are crossed over the bar counter as I turn to Dane. "Despite the small mishap, I hope you're having *somewhat* of a good time. I definitely owe you one though."

Dane turns his body on an angle to face me while his forearm drapes over the back of the barstool. "So you're gonna punch a girl in the face if they start hitting on me?"

"*No*," I say like it's the most ridiculous thing, but then I think about the idea and shrug as I look off to the side. "I mean…maybe."

Dane raises his eyebrows. "Aria, I never knew you were such a fighter."

I give Dane a deadpan stare. "I'm not. But if she was a high mainte-nance brat who gave me an attitude, I might have to throw some hands."

"Could I throw some Jell-O on the two of you and watch from afar?" Dane asks as he wiggles his eyebrows.

I playfully shove Dane. Dane chuckles as he turns so his elbows are over the bar again. "Alright, all joking aside, I wouldn't take home a girl who gave you an attitude or was nasty to you."

I look at Dane with bored eyes. "Yeah, okay."

Dane holds his hand to his chest. "You think I'd choose sex over friendship?"

I continue with my bored expression. "Dane, I know you."

"I think you're underestimating our friendship."

I stretch a smile as I say, "No. I just think you're a typical guy who enjoys sex."

"Doesn't everyone enjoy sex?" Dane asks.

"Yes, but you're kind of a womanizer."

Dane stares at me for a few silent moments, letting my last comment sink in. "Does that bother you?"

I furrow my brows and shake my head. "Of course not. I wasn't judg-ing you, Dane."

Dane turns to lean over the bar as he runs a hand through his hair. "No, I didn't think you were judging me."

"Sometimes it intimidates me a little. How effortless it is for you."

Dane lets out a small laugh, but doesn't look my way.

"Can I ask a question? But you have to answer honestly," I ask.

"Shoot," Dane says.

I hesitate for a few seconds as I look at his side profile. "Is it fulfilling?"

Dane's lips tip up ever so slightly. "Temporarily."

"Well I know *that*. I'm asking if it satisfies your heart."

Dane finally turns his head to look at me with a tight-lipped smile. "No. It doesn't."

I smile at his honesty, finding Dane's vulnerability charming. I've always known Dane to be this confident Casanova, and the fact that he's able to be so transparent with me allows me to see a new part of him. It makes me feel closer to Dane, like I know something no one else knows.

In a way, I feel *special*.

I hold Dane's eyes as I say, "I think if you allow yourself to open your heart up, you'll find what you're looking for."

"What makes you so sure?"

"Because I see who you are. You're confident, funny, intelligent, and you're a great friend. Your heart can't be wasted," I say with a friendly smile.

Dane eyes me curiously as his elbow rests on the bar counter and he rubs his thumb lazily back and forth across his chin. I guess I've struck some kind of chord that he's left with nothing to say, so I just shrug at him and avert my gaze as I lean over the bar counter.

I inhale, becoming more uncomfortable with the silence that feels like it's lasting eternally. "Sorry if I talk too much, or I talk nonsense. It's a habit."

"It's not a bad habit for you. It's kind of cute," Dane says.

I roll my eyes with a smile. "Thanks."

"What's that for?"

I turn to look at Dane. "Cute can just be a nice way of saying I'm annoying."

"Out of all the things I find you to be, annoying is not one of them," Dane assures me.

"Oh," I say, and then I narrow my eyes. "What else do you find me to be?"

"Well, there's neurotic."

"Oh, great," I say sarcastically.

Dane smirks as he continues. "Kind. Determined. Fun."

I slowly nod my head as I eye him carefully. "Okay, you're redeeming yourself."

"Talented," Dane adds.

I put a hand to my heart and look up toward the ceiling. "Stop it, you're making me blush," I joke. When I look back down at Dane, we both smile at each other, and then he squints his eyes as he turns his head toward the small dance floor by the stage where the live music is typically played.

After a few seconds, he turns to face me. "Speaking of talent, why don't we end the night with some dancing?"

I look at him inquisitively as I hear Shakira's "Me Gusta" softly play through the speakers. "You want to dance to this?"

"I think I can manage," Dane says as he gets up from the barstool and holds his palm out to me. I'm still questioning Dane's intentions with my eyes, but stretch a small smile across my face as I accept his invitation to the tiny dance floor. Once he guides us to the middle of the space, he holds our palms up in frame, and places his free palm around my waist while mine goes to his shoulder.

Dane tilts his chin up. "Step forward on your right foot." I hold the smile on my face as I look down and follow his instructions, and as soon as I do, he steps back on his left foot. "When you step back, stop with both feet together." Once I complete his next direction, I look up at him with a wider smile, waiting for him to continue coaching me. "Step back on your left, then come back to the middle again," he says while looking between us. When I step back on my left foot, he steps forward with his right, and then we come back to the middle, both of us planting our feet together. "Now we just repeat," he says.

I look back up at him and chuckle lightly, then look down again to watch my feet carefully as I try and remember the steps. I slowly step forward on my right foot, and he confidently steps back on his left.

"Now together," he mutters to remind me of the next move.

Once my feet are planted together, I take a second to remember to step back on my left foot, while he steps forward on his right. After a few stumbled salsa moves, I start to pick up the steps quickly, and we get in a groove that is in sync with each other.

As we continue to follow the steps to the music, my excitement never falters when I look back up at Dane. Dane returns my expression, and we hold each other's gaze for a few seconds before he releases my waist to spin me around in his hand. Dane's smoothness on the floor takes me by surprise, and when I'm facing Dane again, I land closer to him, leaving only inches between us.

I'm still grinning like a kid on Christmas morning as I avert my eyes downward between us, and my free palm goes to his bicep. When I feel the hard muscle beneath his shirt, I feel a wave of heat scroll over my body for a fleeting moment, but our proximity doesn't make me uncomfortable.

In a strange way, it almost feels *too* comfortable.

When the rough pad of his finger touches the exposed skin of my lower back, his gentle touch differs so much from the demeanor he showed earlier. Another flare of heat bursts under my skin, thinking about how passionate Dane was to stand up for me. And as I'm embraced in Dane's arms now, he feels like my safe haven. Like shelter from the rain in a raging storm, he gives me hope that I'm going to be *okay*.

My eyes lock with Dane's again, and our facial expressions mirror one another's. We eventually fall into the salsa steps naturally, and it's really a shame we haven't danced together before.

"How did you learn to salsa?" I ask through our movements.

"My mom was always talking about taking dancing lessons, so I bought her a lesson for her birthday," Dane says.

I stare at Dane in awe for several seconds as we continue alternating stepping forward and back to the rhythm of the music. Not knowing what to really say as our eyes are locked on each other's, I smile shyly as I tip my gaze downward.

Dane lightly chuckles at my timidness. "Does that surprise you?"

I shrug as I pick my eyes back up to meet his. "A little. But in a good way."

While the last lines of the song are playing, Dane spins me around in his one palm and I can't help but tilt my head back in laughter. When we're back in hold, we're chest to chest as we laugh together and execute the final salsa moves.

"Consider this a start to your ballroom dancing lessons," Dane says when the song ends, and we're standing in each other's arms.

I furrow my brows in confusion. "What are you talking about?"

"Fourth of July. You told me you wanted to take ballroom dancing classes as you were spinning under my palm. Tipsy might I add."

My face softens as I study his green hues for several moments. "You remember that?"

Dane averts his eyes between us as he nods. "Yeah, I do. I guess I want to make sure you get to do all the things you want to do." Then he picks his head up to look at me. "I think it's time you start living for *you* again. Do what makes you happy."

I swallow a lump in my throat as I take in what Dane's saying. I haven't lived for myself in over a year. I've lived for my tears, my pain, and my sadness. But I've yet to live for my happiness again. I guess I never thought about it until now.

Until Dane.

How can he see me so clearly and understand what's going on in my mind without me voicing it? Has he always been this intuitive?

Dane clears his throat as he slowly releases me and gestures his chin to the exit. "Ready?"

I'm caught off guard for a second, seemingly too deep in thought to recover from the conversation whiplash, so I just nod my head.

Once I grab my purse, we walk through the double doors of the bar, and we're walking side by side when I turn to him. "Dane, I can call an Uber if you wanted to stay out."

Dane turns his head toward me with furrowed brows. "What?"

I vaguely twist my palm out. "If you want to pick up a girl tonight, don't let me stop you."

Dane smiles as he turns his head forward. "I'm already with a girl tonight."

I roll my eyes as I look at his side profile. "You know what I mean."

"I do." When we reach his car that was parked at the meter, he stands in front of the passenger door with his hands in his jean pockets, and turns to look at me. "But can I be completely honest with you?" he asks.

"Sure," I say with a questionable tone, not knowing what truth he's going to lay on me.

"You're a lot more fun than I expected you to be," Dane says as he looks carefully over my facial features, like he's trying to understand what he's talking about.

"Well, thanks," I say as I place a hand on my hip, feigning offense.

Dane smirks as he looks down to open the passenger side door of his car, and as he's opening it, he looks back up at me. "Well, I'm sure you didn't expect to have as good of a time with me either," he starts off, and then when the car door is opened all the way, Dane rests his forearm on the top of the open car door, and shoves a hand in his jeans pocket.

I narrow my eyes at Dane. "It's so typical of you to assume I enjoyed my time with you."

"Are you saying you didn't?"

I scrunch my lips to the side as I make it like I'm debating my answer, and then I finally shrug as I say, "Well, you did teach me salsa."

"That I did."

"How did it go?" I say before I step forward on my right foot, then back together, then back on my left foot. "And then I think it went something like this," I say before breaking out a few ridiculous dance moves with my hands in the air and rolling my body.

Dane lets out the loudest laugh I've ever heard from him, and I stop and laugh with him as loose strands of my hair are whipped around my face chaotically. I continue to chuckle as I brush my hair from my face and walk closer to him at the passenger side door.

Then Dane shakes his head at me, breathless from laughing. "You're so sexy."

At first, I think Dane's playing along and being sarcastic, but as I look into his eyes, Dane's playfulness seems to have faded and been replaced with something else. Something I'm not used to seeing from Dane.

I feel my own laughter start to die down as I hold his eyes, and my smile dips as words get caught in my throat. Dane runs a nervous hand through his hair and looks off to the side as he clears his throat, almost like he got caught saying something he knew he shouldn't have said, or slipped up by saying the one thing he was trying to refrain from saying all night.

"I'm sorry. That was out of line," Dane says with his eyes still diverted from mine.

I shake my head as I let out a nervous laugh. "No, don't worry about it."

I decide not to make a bigger deal of the situation, so we can just move past this moment as quickly as possible. When Dane turns his head back to me, I tilt my head toward the car as I change the subject. "We should head home," I suggest.

Dane inhales tensely. "Yeah. Let's go."

Dane closes the car door after I hop in his Mustang, and then he gets in on the driver's side. The first few minutes of the drive home are a little awkward and slow, but once Dane turns on some music, the discomfort dissolves, and we fall back into easy conversation like we always do.

I'm not entirely sure what happened outside on the sidewalk, but whatever it was, I'm hoping we can just forget it ever happened. Because the more I think about Dane's comment, the more aware I become of a mysterious shell inside of me.

A shell that harbors new emotions that are threatening to spill out.

A shell that should remain unbroken.

CHAPTER
Twenty-Three

ARIA

Friday, July 8, 2022

My phone is buzzing as I'm getting ready to go to Shippers with Kate, Trent, and Dane tonight. It's my mom of course. She's probably just checking in on me like she normally does.

"Hey, Mom," I answer. "Everything okay?"

"Yeah, everything's great, just wanted to check in," my mom replies.

"I'm actually going out with Kate and the boys to Shippers tonight," I say.

"Oh, that sounds like a lot of fun. I was a little late to the party, but I saw pictures from Fourth of July posted on Facebook. Seems like everyone had a great time."

I pause thinking of how obliterated I was by the end of that night, but choose to omit that information. "Yeah, it was much needed fun. I met a guy."

"You did? Tell me about him," my mom says.

I shrug. "I don't know. It's not much of anything, so there's no need to make a big deal of it. But he's great to talk to, makes me laugh, and he's also very cute."

It feels strange to talk about another guy besides Kyle, and what's making me more anxiety-ridden is the inevitable judgment that will be passed by me.

"I'm assuming you're going to keep seeing him?" my mom asks.

I nod with the phone to my ear. "Tomorrow night, actually. He texted me a few days ago and asked me out."

"So how are you feeling? Do you feel ready?"

I fall silent for a few moments before responding. "I don't think I'm ever going to be completely ready to take the first dive back into romance, but my therapist also reminded me that going on dates can be about companionship more so than it is about romance."

"I think it could be great. Finding friendship with someone new, someone who doesn't relate to your past, and can give you a third-party perspective."

I nod again. "Yeah, exactly. It's worth a try, right?"

"You deserve to be happy. If you feel like this is something that will make you happier, then I'm your biggest supporter. You know that," my mom says.

"That means a lot, Mom."

"Well, alright, I'll let you get back to getting ready. Maybe we can set up a brunch date soon?"

"Sounds great. I'll ask Kate for suggestions since she always knows the best places."

"Yes, I'd love to try something new! Okay, I won't keep you. Love you."

"Love you too," I say and hang up.

Once I place the phone down, I look in the full-length mirror to tousle my long beach waves, and I'm adjusting my yellow crop tank top and high-rise denim shorts. Once I feel pleased with my look, I grab my crossbody, then head out the front door to meet up with Dane.

DANE

"Single Bull, let's go!" I yell as my last dart hits the outer ring of the bulls-eye on the dart board.

Trent is removing the darts from the board as he says, "What did you have, Wheaties for breakfast this morning?"

I lift my backwards snapback and run a hand through my hair as I respond. "Don't hate the player, hate the game."

When Trent comes back to where I'm standing, he throws me a smile. "We're gonna get cocky over darts now?"

"Since it's the highlight of my week, yes."

After Trent throws his first dart at the board, he glances my way. "That shitty, huh?"

I lean my lower back against the table where our two beers are sitting, my palms gripping the edge of the tabletop. "Yep. My boss has been riding my ass to get two projects completed this week, both of which were set to be completed in the next month. So I worked through my lunch most days, while getting yelled at by these entitled assholes I have to call 'clients.'"

"Sorry to hear that. At least you know next week will be a lighter load."

I look behind me to grab my beer to take a sip. "Let's not jinx it just yet," I say. "So how's everything with you?"

Trent shrugs. "Not much, honestly. Work hasn't been as eventful or fun as your job, and my personal life still consists of just me." Then Trent throws his third dart, which lands on one of the far outer layers of the board. "Did you wind up going out with Aria the other night?"

"Yeah, I wound up connecting my fist with some guy's face. Good times."

Trent gasps in a laugh. "What?"

I shrug nonchalantly. "Some guy was being a complete douchebag to Ari, so I stepped in."

"Wow, are you having a midlife crisis living out your early twenties again?" Trent jokes.

"Okay, I definitely wasn't in that many brawls in my early twenties. And if I was, the receiving end always had it coming."

Trent chuckles as he faces the circular board again to throw his last dart. "Just try to keep it civil tonight, Rocky."

I step toward the dart board and gather the four darts Trent just threw. "I'll behave. Besides, my knuckles stung for a good day. What is that?"

"Old age," Trent jokes.

I adjust my backwards snapback on my head as I walk back to where Trent is standing. "Guess so. Damn."

"Did Aria have a good time at least?" Trent asks.

"I think so. Looked like she did," I respond as I throw the first dart at the board.

"Looks like she's having a good time right now too," Trent says as he gestures his chin in the direction of Kate and Aria.

When I turn to take a look, I see Kate and Aria both laughing with some preppy blond-haired kid by the bar, who might as well star in a remake of *Gossip Girl* with how clean cut he is. I notice Aria's big smile and how her eyes are lit up from the conversation they're having. I swallow as I continue observing, a little disappointed that I'm not the only one who can make her smile like that. The other night, I felt separated from the rest. Like I was the only person who could bring laughter back into her world, and genuine happiness. But now? Now I feel like any other person who's entered her world. I feel ordinary, and it sucks.

I inwardly roll my eyes and focus back on the board as I whip the next dart harder than usual.

"Easy there killer," Trent chimes in.

"Maybe someone should call his fraternity. I'm sure they've sent out a 'missing persons' report," I quip.

"Oh, come on, you remember being young and loving the attention of older girls."

I look back at Kate and Aria, and then squint my eyes as I look back at Trent. "I'd like to think I was smoother and way better looking."

Trent pats my shoulder playfully. "You were. You were."

I hold my palm out. "Thank you. Now that that's settled, I'm about to hit a Double Bull for good measure." Before I throw my last dart, I hear Kate and Aria's laughter from the bar, and turn my head to see both girls with their hands to their chest and their eyes closed. I tighten my jaw as I turn my head to face the dartboard, and narrow my eyes on my target. I whip the dart as hard and fast as I can, and the tip of it lands exactly where I want it.

I smile in victory as I turn to Trent. "Some people just have it."

ARIA

Kate and I see Dane and Trent walking over to us after their game of darts, so we say our goodbyes to Josh, and the four of us grab a table. Kate and I sit next to one another while Dane and Trent sit across from us.

"So are you guys going to give everyone a dancing show like you did on the Fourth of July?" Trent jokes.

Kate responds immediately. "I think Ari and I would be doing everyone a favor if we gave them a dancing show. If you find it so horrible, maybe just don't look."

Trent puts a fist to his chest as if he's heartbroken. "Hitting me where it hurts."

Kate playfully shoves Trent's forearm across the table, and we all continue sipping our beers.

"Not to brag, but you both missed out on a *great* time the other night," I say as I point between Kate and Trent.

"Really? Even with Dane's T.K.O?" Trent jokes.

"Wait, what?" Kate chimes in.

My elbow is resting on the table as I place a palm to my forehead and grumble. "Let's not talk about it."

"Oh we're talking about it. Dane, spill," Kate insists.

"Aria was being hit on by some asshole, so I gave him what he had coming," Dane explains.

Kate's eyebrows raise in surprise. "You punched someone?"

Dane sits back as he places a forearm over the back of his chair. "Yes. Can we move on now?"

"No we cannot. I need details," Kate says as she looks between Dane and I, and I decide to be the one to explain the story.

"I don't know. The guy was nice at first, but then he started getting handsy and making sexual innuendos. The creepy kind, not the smooth kind. So Dane said something, and when Chris tried to be smart with him,

Dane threw a solid punch." I clap my hands together. "And then we got kicked out of Duke's."

Kate's mouth hangs open as she looks at Dane.

"Alright, it wasn't my finest moment," Dane digresses.

"*Anyway,*" I interrupt. "Dane was able to salvage the night by teaching me salsa."

Kate and Trent both furrow their brows as their eyes focus on Dane.

Dane looks over to me with a deadpan expression. "Really?"

I smile and shake my head to egg him on. "I'm not sorry."

He playfully rolls his eyes as he looks back toward Kate and Trent, and lets out a sigh before giving them an explanation. "I took a salsa class with my mom for her birthday."

"So now you just salsa wherever you go?" Trent jokes.

Dane turns to me. "I'm gonna kill you for this."

I make a face at him and then turn to take a sip of my beer. Once I swallow my sip, I turn to smirk at Dane. "Let's not ignore the fact that Dane enjoyed the dancing."

Dane just wears a tight-lipped smile as he stares back at me, then looks to Trent with the same expression. "Fuck it. She got me."

"Noooo," Trent says, feigning disgust, and Kate and I are laughing at Dane's admission.

"Trent, you better watch out because I'm coming for you too," I joke.

Trent places a hand on Dane's shoulder. "Well, unlike my friend over here, I have *zero* rhythm on the dance floor. It won't be a pretty sight." I smile as I take a sip of my beer, and Dane and I just hold each other's stares across the table. It's clear we're both reminiscing about how fun that night was with just the two of us.

When I bring my glass to rest on the table, Kate places her palm on top of mine. "In all seriousness, it's great to see you smile like this again."

I turn to grab the side of her face, and rest my head on top of her shoulder. "Well it wouldn't be possible without any of you."

"I'll toast to that," Trent says as he raises his beer, and we all clink glasses to take respective sips.

When I swallow my sip, I lick my lips and say, "Okay, enough sappiness. I don't want to spoil the mood tonight."

Kate touches my shoulder. "Sorry, Ari, I didn't mean to bring-"

"No, I'm okay. I promise," I interrupt with a genuine smile. I look between Kate, Trent, and Dane as I explain myself further. "I just don't want to make this about my emotional baggage, that's all."

"That's not how we see it," Trent chimes in.

"I know. Thinking about Kyle doesn't automatically make me cry or upset. I can look back on memories of us and smile now. It's just, sometimes I feel like if I think about him too much, I'll take too many steps back."

Kate gives me a sympathetic shrug. "I don't think anyone can blame you for thinking that way, but you have so much to look forward to. I promise."

I decide to rip the Band-Aid off, judgements be damned. "Speaking of looking forward to things, I have a date tomorrow," I say.

"You have a date?" Dane asks.

I nod at Dane before speaking. "With Blake." Dane looks at me with furrowed brows, and I gather he doesn't remember who Blake is. "The guy I met on the Fourth of July."

"Oh," Dane says, but his facial expression only gets slightly softer. Once he takes a sip of his beer, he casually sinks back into his seat and asks, "So where are you guys going?"

I make a face as if I'm thinking to myself. "I'm actually not sure of the exact place, but he promised me drinks, greasy food, and live music."

"Fancy," Dane says sarcastically.

"Hey, why are you judging?" I respond.

"No judgments. But if I actually liked a girl, I'd bring her to a more romantic place," Dane quips back.

I roll my eyes while bobbing my head as if to say "yeah, yeah, yeah," but Dane's eyes linger on me tentatively for a few seconds, and I'm a little thrown off by Dane's reaction. I assumed he would be the last one to judge me out of my three friends.

Luckily, Kate chimes in next with a wide grin. "You're going to have a great time. In fact, I think we need some girl talk in the bathroom. Shall we?"

I just shake my head and laugh at Kate as we get up from the table and make our way to the restroom.

"You think you're gonna kiss him?" Kate asks as she closes the bathroom door behind her.

"Are we in sixth grade now?" I joke.

Kate rolls her eyes. "You know what I mean."

I sigh as I turn my head to look off to the side. "If you're asking me if I'm ready to be with another man, the answer is that I don't know if I am."

"He's so cute though," Kate emphasizes.

Now I'm the one rolling my eyes. I turn to one of the two empty stalls in the bathroom, and close the stall door behind me as I get ready to pee. "Cute is only going to get him so far on a first date."

I hear Kate enter the stall next to me. "Uh-huh. That's what they all say."

"You're crazy." I chuckle.

"Not as crazy as you if you don't take advantage of this guy. *But*, I can respect the fact that you aren't ready. The main thing I want is to see you happy again," Kate responds.

"I'm making a heart with my hands. I promise to give you all the gossip tomorrow night," I call from my stall.

Kate laughs. "I fucking love you."

Then we're both laughing at our ridiculousness, and once we're done peeing, we wash up and head back to Trent and Dane.

After another hour hanging out at Shippers, Dane and I are driving back to our townhouses, and I look over from my passenger seat at Dane. He has one hand on the steering wheel, and his other hand to his mouth like he's thinking about something, and he's been strangely quiet.

"Are you alright?" I ask.

"Never better," he responds, but he doesn't take his eyes off the road.

I roll my eyes and let out an annoyed sigh. "Okay."

"What? You asked me a question, and I answered."

"It wasn't an honest answer," I say in a low voice while looking out the passenger side window.

There is a silence that consumes the car the next ten or fifteen seconds until I hear Dane's voice again. "Do you actually like this guy?"

I'm still looking out the window as I shrug. "I like him as a friend for now. He's good company."

"Are you thinking of pursuing a relationship with him?" Dane asks.

I turn to look at Dane with narrowed eyes. "Why am I getting interrogated right now? I think I'm old enough to pick and choose who I go out with, thanks."

His eyes still don't leave the road for a moment. "I'm not interrogating. I'm asking questions you should probably be asking yourself."

"What the hell does that mean?"

He hesitates before answering. "Maybe you should be guarding your heart more."

I just look at him, stunned by the audacity of his comment, and then I turn to lean back in the passenger seat. "Drive faster, Dane. I want to go home."

I stay silent as mixed emotions course through me. Am I jumping the gun here? Is it wrong for me to go on a date with a guy? Even if I know it's just to have some good company, and I have little intentions of pursuing a romance?

Dane lets out a frustrated sigh, then faces his palm upward on the steering wheel as he speaks. "Come on, you're overreacting."

I let out a sarcastic chuckle. "I love how I'm the one who's overreacting when you're the one butting into my personal business."

Dane lets out a soft laugh of his own, eyes still trained on the road. "I hardly think I'm asking you personal questions. In fact, if memory serves me correctly, you were the one that decided to share personal information with me when you were drunk on July Fourth."

I turn my head to look at Dane through squinted eyes. "What are you talking about?"

Dane swallows a nervous gulp before speaking. "You told me you hadn't been touched by anyone, let alone *been with* anyone…since." With Dane's emphasis on the words "been with," I know he means having sex with a guy, and I can't help the overwhelming amount of anger that rushes over me.

I can only gasp at Dane's audacity. "I can't believe you," I say as I stare at him for several moments in disbelief, and finally turn my head to stare out the windshield in front of me, unable to look at him. "The nerve you have to bring this up…" I trail off trying to find the words I want to say, but I'm so mad I can't think of how I want to finish my statement.

Dane exhales a laugh, but I know it's a mocking laugh and not a genuine one. He casually leans back in his seat, leaving one hand on the steering wheel and his other hand on his upper thigh. "It's amazing how I'm getting scolded for mentioning something that you told me in the first place."

As much as I want to lash out at Dane and scream at him, I decide to meet him tit for tat. If he wants to play this game and try to shame me for going on a date with a guy, I may as well go all in on this. He's treating me like a child. Like I can't make my own decisions and need his permission to take steps forward in my life.

Screw that.

I kick my snarky tone into high gear as I turn to look at Dane's side profile. "Maybe you should make a Do's and Don'ts list for me."

Dane furrows his brows. "What?"

"Well I'm not sure I remember how to fuck a guy, so I'm going to need some tips," I retort.

Dane concentrates on pulling the car up to the curb in front of our townhouses, and he smirks knowingly. Like he's confident he's about to come back with a wiser remark than mine, and I'm a fool to have ever challenged him. When he shuts the car off, Dane shifts back into his seat, one palm still on the steering wheel and one on his thigh. He looks forward as he says, "Then it's a good thing all men love tight pussy." Then Dane looks over at me with a smug grin. "You won't disappoint in that area."

My palm connects with Dane's cheek so hard the contact causes my skin to vibrate uncomfortably, but I don't feel the throb just yet. The sound of the slap lingers in the air as I stare at Dane's side profile, just shocked. He tries to alleviate the sting by adjusting his jaw, and I just ponder in disbelief at the turn of events within the last five minutes. I'm fueled with anger as I quickly turn and reach for the door handle to exit Dane's car, and I make sure to slam the car door obnoxiously.

Once I am inside my house, I let out a heavy breath as I lean back against my front door in my foyer, trying to settle my raging emotions. How could Dane speak to me like that? I peel myself away from the door and run my hands through my hair, closing my eyes to try and sort through tonight's chaotic events. Up until tonight, Dane has been nothing but kind, supportive, respectful, and a genuine friend to me. Never in a million years would I have envisioned him talking to me like he did.

I open my eyes and stare aimlessly down the hallway as I inhale. I let out a long and slow exhale as I try to make sense of everything that transpired tonight, but the hazy fog in my mind doesn't part enough for me to see clear answers. It's like the path Dane and I were on this summer has been clouded over, and we're going to have to find our way through the mist to get back on track. But the fog in my mind feels like it's growing thicker as I continue to think about our friendship, and it's getting more difficult to see when and where we may have made a wrong turn from our original course.

The most dangerous part is, I'm not sure we're ever going to find our way back on the original route.

CHAPTER
Twenty-Four

DANE

Saturday, July 9, 2022

I'm going out tonight. There's no way I'm staying home to watch Aria potentially bring this guy back to her house. Things between us got extremely heated last night, and neither of us has said a word to each other since. I have no clue what to do with these feelings that I'm having, to the point where I'm starting to unravel around Aria unexpectedly. Every time I see her, her beauty is no longer lost on me. I notice every detail of her perfect face and body. Every time I hear her laugh, I want to hear it a thousand more times, and every time she smiles, I think about how much I want to make her smile every moment we are together.

But Aria has a date tonight, and I'm doing what I do best and going to look for a distraction.

Thankfully, Shippers is more crowded than yesterday, giving me a better chance of bringing home some much needed company. I go straight to the bartender, order a beer, and take a seat. I scope the scene as I take a sip of my beer, and I'm looking around for about five to ten minutes before I feel someone squeeze in next to me.

Lucky for me it's a good-looking redhead, so I shoot my shot. "Well, my night just got better," I say and then throw her a smirk. She smiles wide, and I've landed myself a distraction for the night.

I'm leaning shirtless against the headboard of my bed as Lisa straddles my hips and cups my face in her hands. Our tongues find one another through desperate kisses, and I lift the hem of Lisa's dress up and over her, leaving her in a blue lace bra and thong. My hands grab handfuls of her ass cheeks, and I let out a groan as she slowly grinds on the erection through my jogger sweatpants. When Lisa trails her lips down my neck and over my shoulders, I find myself staring at my bedroom ceiling and walls.

I start to get lost in my own thoughts and think about what Aria might be doing on her date. I think of Blake laying Aria down on the bed, and Aria giving him what she hasn't given a single man in over a year. What the fuck makes Blake so special? I internally wince when I imagine Blake's hands inching up Aria's thighs, eventually touching her most sacred part. He'd get to hear and taste her moans of pleasure while being inside her, not fully knowing what she's been through, or how incredibly innocent she is.

My blood starts to simmer at the images that scroll through my head, and I feel a blunt sense of possessiveness take over my mind. Blake wouldn't know how to take care of Aria like I would, that much I am certain. I'd make sure to kiss every inch of her body, and pay attention to her every need. Every desire. Her wish would be my command, and I'd fall to my knees before her to give Aria anything she wanted from me. I'd take her with tenderness and passion, making sure every part of her mind and body came alive under my touch. If she was with me, Aria would be reminded just how powerful intimacy between two people could be, and I'd make it my life's mission to restore her faith in that.

"Is something wrong?" Lisa's agitated voice cuts into my thoughts as she stares down at me.

I inhale as I rub my palms up and down Lisa's back. "No, I'm fine," I breathe.

"You seem distracted," Lisa counters.

Lisa's words draw my attention to my softer state below, and I'm a little confused on where to go from here. As much as I really need a distraction tonight, I foresee this night continuing to dip further south. I exhale as I run a hand through my hair and say, "I'm sorry. I have a lot on my mind."

The corner of Lisa's mouth tips up as she lightly grazes her fingertips up and down my abs. "Let me help take your mind off of whatever's distracting you."

Lisa's fingers curl into the waistband of my sweatpants, and I welcome her attempt to successfully divert my attention. I close my eyes with a groan as I feel her silky palm cup my length, and start to stroke me from base to tip. I feel myself start to get harder, and I bite my lip at the sensation as I open my eyes to look at Lisa. Her smile of victory is sexy, but just as I revel in the pleasure she's giving me, I'm also very aware that the woman stroking me right now is not the woman I want it to be. As I stare into Lisa's green eyes, I feel let down that I'm not staring into a pair of light brown ones, and that notion terrifies me more than anything. The reality is that although the physical feeling of this moment is amazing, my head is just not in this.

"This isn't going to work for me," I say as I wrap my hand around Lisa's wrist.

"Are you serious?" Lisa asks as she narrows her eyes.

"Look I'm sor-"

Lisa doesn't even wait for me to finish my apology as she hops off the bed, and retrieves her mini dress and wedge sandals from the floor. "Asshole," she mutters as she walks into my master bathroom.

Saw that coming.

When I re-adjust myself and get up from the bed, I lean a shoulder on the doorframe of the closed bathroom door and talk through it. "I'm not enough of an asshole to let you walk home alone, so do you need me to take you home?"

I hear her laugh out loud. "No thanks. I'm setting up an Uber right now."

I run a hand through my hair and then turn to grab my jeans and shirt from the floor to dress myself. I sit down at the foot of the bed to tie my shoelaces, and then just wait for Lisa to come out of my bathroom. I lick my lips as my elbows rest on my knees and I look down at the floor.

How did I get here?

I stare at the carpet of my bedroom, just trying to pinpoint when my life became a soap opera. Trying to target how my mind suddenly became occupied with one person. Let alone, the last person who should ever consume it.

When I hear the door to my bathroom open and see a fully clothed Lisa, I sigh and stand up. She doesn't even acknowledge my presence as she beelines it to my bedroom door, storming out to make her exit. Luckily, I can keep up with her and follow Lisa down the stairs and through the foyer. When I reach the front door just as Lisa's walked through it, I'm standing halfway out when I see Aria stepping out of a car. Lisa's Uber is parked in front of my house, and as my luck would have it, Aria and Blake are exiting his car in front of her house. Aria looks over to Lisa entering her Uber and then looks back to my porch to see me standing halfway out my door. It takes a second for her to put two and two together, and she rolls her eyes as she turns around and regards her date instead.

I watch intently as Blake and Aria seem to be exchanging a few smiles and laughs before hugging each other goodnight. Before my mind can catch up with my legs, I walk through the door, making sure it slams hard enough to get their attention. I smile inwardly as they break their hug to turn their heads in my direction, and I walk down my pathway to my mailbox.

"Didn't mean to disturb," I say as I open the small door to my mailbox, making a show of looking for the mail I know I already picked up today.

"No worries. Dane, right?" My jaw tightens when I hear Blake speak.

Why the fuck does he have to be a good guy?

I close the door to the mailbox and lean myself with a forearm propped over the top of it. "Yeah," I say, and then I tilt my head to the side. "Thought I missed the mail today. Guess I forgot I picked it up before."

I'm looking at Aria who's not in the least bit humored, and then she turns to Blake. "Thank you for a great night. We'll talk later?"

He nods with a grin that I wish I was wearing, now that I know the reason behind his smile. "Of course," Blake says, and then gestures his chin upward over Aria's shoulder. "I'll wait 'til you get inside."

"I'll be out here," I interject, and then I point to Aria. "I needed to talk to you anyway. Remember?"

I can visibly see Aria's jaw clench as she turns her attention to Blake again. "I'll text you in a little bit. Get home safe."

Blake smiles at her with a nod, and then turns his attention to me as he rounds his car to the driver's side. "Have a good night," Blake says with a small wave.

I throw him a tight-lipped smile and a small wave back. "Good night."

When Blake starts the engine, Aria waves him off, and as soon as his car is all the way down the block, I notice Aria immediately turn around to power walk up the pathway to her porch.

"Hey!" I call after her as my legs take me across my lawn to hers. Aria pays me no mind and doesn't even spare a glance my way as she picks up the pace to her front porch. "Aria," I say as I lightly jog up her porch steps to catch up to her. When Aria goes to open the storm door, I reach from behind her and lay my palm against it. Aria stills as she feels my presence hover over her, and I make sure to keep my voice low and calm. "When I'm speaking to you, I expect you to answer me," I say.

"Get off the door." I can hear Aria speak the words through gritted teeth.

I continue to keep my voice controlled. "Before we make a scene for our neighbors, I suggest you open the door so we can talk."

"I have nothing to say to you."

I dip my head lower so my lips linger over the back of her ear. "Well this isn't a one-way street, and I'd like to speak to you *inside*," I say in a low voice.

I hear Aria sigh frustratingly, and she purposely pulls back the storm door harshly to knock into me. Fortunately my reflexes are fast enough that I catch the door frame in my palm, and once Aria turns the key in the lock and opens her door, I follow right behind her.

When Aria enters her house, she slams her keys and crossbody on the foyer table, and just continues to walk straight ahead. I close the front door, then follow behind Aria as she makes her way into the kitchen, and I lean my shoulder on the wall of the entryway of the room. I shove my hands in the pockets of my jeans as she purposely keeps herself busy by putting a few plates and glasses away from the drainboard.

"I can wait all night, so if you think ignoring me is going to force me to leave, it won't," I say from behind her.

Aria closes her cabinet a little harder than necessary and turns to face me as she scrunches her face. "My god you have the biggest ego on the planet." Then Aria sighs as she runs one hand through her hair before throwing her arm in front of her. "Why do you think you even have the right to barge in *my* home, after fucking some girl, nonetheless?"

Now that she's faced toward me, I notice her slim body in her low-cut, short-sleeved black romper. Between the short hem of her romper and her beige wedge sandals, her tan legs look longer than usual, and I can see the slight contours of her thigh muscles that show her dedication to staying fit. Her long brown hair is down in beach waves, framing her beautiful face, and I'm suddenly unashamedly overcome with jealousy. Jealousy over the fact that Aria dressed like this for another guy, and he got to lay his eyes on her like this all night long. Maybe he even got to touch her.

"*For the record*, I didn't fuck her," I say.

"Good for you," Aria responds as she walks to the kitchen island to grab a clementine in her fruit bowl.

I watch her start peeling the layers of the orange fruit, refusing to look at or acknowledge me. With each ticking second, I lose my will to filter the words that come out of my mouth, and decide to voice them before thinking it through. "Did you sleep with Blake tonight?"

Not the best plan of attack, but I have nothing to lose here.

Aria slams her hands down on the counter of the island and picks her head up to look at me with an intensity that recharges my madness. This is all so fucked up, but I'm past the point of caring. The fact that I think I have the right to invade Aria's privacy like this, and the fact that Aria thinks it's none of my business to know what she does with other men has me spiraling out of control. I seem to think Aria is mine.

Mine.

Aria starts to shake her head before speaking. "Why are you doing this?"

"Because he doesn't deserve you."

She dips her brows as she says, "You don't even know him."

"I know you," I challenge. Aria turns her attention back to her fruit in a weak attempt to get rid of me. I see her inhale as she keeps her eyes trained downward, and I can tell she's intentionally avoiding eye contact. I gradually lift myself off the doorframe and walk the few steps to Aria, who doesn't budge an inch. I lay a palm on the counter as I come up beside her, barely grazing my body with hers as I'm hovering over her. "I don't want him around here," I confess.

I feel Aria shiver at my demand, and as I'm watching her peel her fruit, her fingers are slowing down to clumsy movements and seem to have lost focus of what they were trying to do in the first place. "It's not your concern."

I lick my lips as I swing my arm around Aria's back, letting my other palm rest on the other side of Aria on the counter. I'm caging her in from behind, making sure to leave a few inches between us as I curl my fingers into my palms against the granite. "Seemed to be my concern when all I thought about tonight was some guy's hands all over you," I say from behind her, my voice just above a whisper.

Aria lowers her fruit to the counter, resting her hands on top of it as she slightly turns her head to the side, sneaking a glimpse of my body behind hers. It's apparent I've caught Aria off guard with my comment, and the wheels in her mind are turning to make sure she heard me correctly and decide how to proceed. When she turns her head forward to resume stripping her fruit, it's apparent she's dismissing my comment. Aria's mentally running from the admission I just made, and it frustrates me to my core.

I gently place my palm over the top of her hand that's cupping the fruit, and lower it to rest on the counter. "Stop with the fruit," I demand.

I hear the faintest breath escape her lips as I pull the fruit out of her hand, purposely grazing my fingertips along her skin, until I place it to the side on the counter. On instinct, Aria raises her palms to her chest, holding one palm in the other hand, as if to physically hide them from me.

"I'm not really used to a woman shying away from me," I taunt.

I notice Aria's breathing gets slightly shallower. "There are boundaries here, Dane," she whispers.

"As far as I can tell, I'm not touching you, and I'm certainly not *fucking* you, so you're going to need to be a little more specific," I retort as my palms grip tightly around the edge of the counter.

Aria swallows a lump in her throat as she turns around to lean her back against the kitchen island. She slouches against it, creating as much distance as possible between us, while looking up at me with lost eyes. "You can't talk to me like this," she breathes. Aria's chest rises and falls in deeper breaths, making my eyes drift downward, where her skin is flushed red. I notice her hardened nipples pressing against the fabric of her romper, and it takes every ounce of restraint to hold me back from taking one of them between my lips.

I lift my eyes up to meet hers. "Because I'm the last person who should talk to you like this?" I ask. "Or because I'm the last person who should get you this worked up?"

Aria swallows thickly. "I need you to leave," she whispers. I hold her gaze for a few moments, and the longer we stare at each other, the more flustered Aria becomes. Aria hugs her arms across her chest as she nervously licks her lips. "Dane, please just go," she pleads in a hushed voice.

I can tell I'm making her uncomfortable, and my need to exude my alpha persona takes a backseat. Eventually I inhale as I peel myself off the counter, and then turn to walk away and walk out her front door.

ARIA

My palms are glued to the edge of the kitchen island behind me as I stare blankly in front of me. My mouth is slightly parted, and my body feels like it's overheating from the whirlwind of emotions that's been spun into overdrive. Part of me is so livid with Dane for thinking he has any right to micromanage my life when he does whatever the hell he wants, whenever he wants, with no questions asked. But the other part of me defies rational thought. Anyone in my position would feel pure frustration, and they should only feel rage and resentment towards Dane.

But not this other part of me.

This part of me is cracked from a forbidden shell. A shell I wasn't aware was lying dormant inside my body. I can almost feel the new emotions ooze out of the shell in a slow-moving current, and time seems to stand still around me as I try to focus in to get a closer look. This part of me isn't irate with Dane. Instead, this part of me is curious to know how far he'll keep this up. How far he's willing to go to push the boundaries of our friendship and test the limits. It excites me. It captivates me and holds my attention longer than it should. Because when Dane's body was caging mine in and he started becoming vulnerable, there's no denying the revival I felt in the blood pumping through my veins. Like my body had been jolted awake, and made aware of something that's been there for a while. Dane's confession affected me in a way a friend should never affect another friend.

We're *friends*.

He's Kyle's best friend.

But the more I feel the liquid of emotions pouring out of the cracked shell, the more I feel frightened. Because the invisible line that's been drawn between Dane and I is fading, and it seems like it's only a matter of time before we step out of bounds and suffer the penalties.

CHAPTER
Twenty-Five

ARIA

Saturday, July 16, 2022

I'm sweaty from working out and need a shower, but I promised Ronnie I'd help him with the light fixtures today at Dad's restaurant while our parents are at the bank sorting out the loan plans. Turns out, I did not manage time accordingly beforehand. I came straight to the restaurant after my run, and I'm wearing black spandex shorts and a black sports bra covered with an off the shoulder white tee. My hair is high in a ponytail, and I feel like I smell, but whatever.

"Ronnie! I need help with this box!" I call out from the main seating area of my father's restaurant. It's Saturday afternoon, exactly one week since Dane and I saw each other, and I haven't heard from him or seen him. I think we've both been staying off each other's radar.

"Here, I got it," Ronnie says as he takes the heavy box from my hands and sets it on the floor. The tables and chairs have been placed, and the light fixtures are being mounted today. But since I know nothing about the electrical trade, I'm only here to hand out tools. Easy enough.

Ronnie uses a box cutter and starts ripping the cardboard open to retrieve the light fixture inside, and I'm at his side as he's stepping on the ladder working whatever magic he needs to work in the ceiling.

"Your stocky ass better stay up there because I'm not about to die from your body falling on mine," I say as I look up to my brother.

"Yeah, well, sometimes shit happens," Ronnie jokes.

I chuckle. "Okay, seriously, what do you need me to do?"

He puts his hand out to me. "Pliers. They're on the bar countertop."

I feel like a medical assistant as I hand him the appropriate tool, and then I start to mindlessly shuffle around from foot to foot, spinning slowly on my heels since I'm bored. "I promised Mom I'd make the centerpieces for the grand opening. Now she won't stop asking me about them, and I guess I should have seen that coming from a mile away," I joke.

Ronnie laughs. "Yep. You only have yourself to blame."

I throw my hands in defeat. "Well, I feel useless doing nothing while you help with important jobs. What was I supposed to do?"

"Not give Mom any opening to start harping on stupid shit," Ronnie says.

"Yeah, I guess that would have been the way to go," I admit. "But I did find some great ideas online, so I'm actually looking forward to keeping my mind occupied."

"Haven't you been going out with your friends more lately?" Ronnie asks.

I start to feel nervous Dane's name is going to be brought up, so I respond indirectly. "Well, when I'm home, I like to keep my mind busy, I guess."

"So maybe Mom's nagging will be worth it," Ronnie says brightly.

I laugh. "We'll see."

"Can you hand me the pendant? I think I'm ready to connect it," Ronnie requests.

I bend down to grab the light fixture and place it in my brother's outstretched hand. "One down, only eleven more to go," I cheer optimistically.

"Uh huh," Ronnie echoes as he connects the wires of the pendant to the ones in the ceiling. It's a few minutes until Ronnie finds the proper wiring, and when he wraps them successfully, I smile wide. But just as soon as I draw a smile on my face, it starts to frown when I see Dane entering the restaurant in my peripheral.

"Need some help?" Dane's strolling into the restaurant looking between Ronnie and I, but I'm pretty sure he's directing his question to Ronnie since I'm not doing much of anything at the moment.

"Hey, what's going on?" Ronnie says as he looks down for a quick second.

Since Dane and I haven't spoken civilly recently, this is kind of awkward. I choose not to say anything, frankly because I don't know what to say, and I just look at the ceiling pretending I'm micromanaging Ronnie's work.

"Are there any other boxes I can grab?" Dane asks.

"By the bar," Ronnie responds as he points.

Dane just accepts the job, and he brings a couple more boxes near us, setting them down on the floor. "Need me to cut these open, or do you want to hold off?"

"No, I'm getting these done today, so open 'em up," Ronnie says. His eyes are focused on covering the wiring with the fixture plate as Dane grabs the box cutter off the bar counter and gets into action. "So what do you think so far?" Ronnie asks.

"Looks great. I'm sure your dad is psyched," Dane says.

"He's in his *glory*," Ronnie says as he steps down the ladder and pulls his phone from the back pocket of his jeans. "I'm going outside for a second, I need to call Cheryl back."

I wave Ronnie off with a tight-lipped smile and once the coast is clear, I look at Dane as I shake my head. "Dane, what are you doing here?"

"I imagined you'd slam your door in my face if I came knocking on it. I also assumed you wouldn't have answered a text or call from me either."

"You're correct. You're actually the last person I want to see right now," I confirm.

"Look, I know I've said some really shitty things to you, and I wish I could take them back, but I can't. So all that's left for me to do is apologize to you, and if you give me the chance to explain, we can move past this."

I narrow my eyes, ignoring his apology. "How could you treat me like that?"

Dane peeks out the windows of the restaurant to make sure Ronnie is still occupied talking on the phone, and then he turns to look at me. "Ari, I've been thinking a lot about us and how close we've become," he says before running a hand through his hair. "I think I had a moment of weakness that made me *jealous. Curious.*" When I open my mouth to respond, Dane puts a hand out. "A moment that is now fleeting. I'm not going to act on it or say anything else that might make you uncomfortable. I promise you that because I know what's at stake here. So just tell me what I need to do."

I swallow as I just stare into Dane's eyes for a few moments. I can feel the sincerity of his words from his tone and facial expression, and I don't doubt that he is sorry. As relieved as I am when he says his moment of weakness is fleeting, I also feel a tinge of disappointment. And I'm not entirely sure where that disappointment stems from. Does it stem from the fact that Dane's moment of weakness was just about wanting to have sex with me? Or does it stem from the fact that he's not going to try and pursue me anymore? Not that he was "pursuing" me, but he definitely challenged me in ways I haven't been tested before. If there is one thing I know for sure, it's that Dane is *different.* He thrills me and he pushes me. I'm not quite sure if I want to put out the fire that's burned between us recently. Instead, I think I may want to fuel it. But now that Dane's pulling back, am I still going to feel that delicious burn?

Once these questions flood into my mind, I realize that the answers to them don't matter because our circumstances don't permit us to be together. And if Dane and I were to be anything other than friends, my life would rumble into instant chaos. Naturally, everything will go back to how it once was, and all of this will be a mere afterthought.

Great.

But why does that sadden me?

I swallow a lump in my throat before speaking. "I just want things to go back to the way they were."

"Done," Dane says.

I'm a little surprised at Dane's submission and am reluctant before responding back.

Aria, what exactly is the problem here?

"Great," I finally say.

Both of our heads turn toward Ronnie's walking form, and then we both make eye contact with each other again. Dane throws me a small smile before bending down to grab a light fixture out of one of the boxes he opened, and he and Ronnie get to work.

For my date with Blake, I chose to wear a ruched off-the-shoulder floral dress where the hem hits mid-thigh, and I've paired it with nude strappy sandals. My hair is down in beach waves, and I've applied a soft shade of pink to my lips, along with the usual natural eyeshadow and black mascara.

"Two for two so far? What do you think?" Blake says as he shines a smile my way. Blake and I are strolling along the pier after having dinner at an Italian restaurant.

I smile as I look at him. "I'd say so. The live music last week was great, and that shrimp scampi tonight was probably some of the best I've had."

Blake touches his chin as if he's considering something. "Okay, live music and shrimp scampi. Noted."

"Don't forget doughnuts are the key to happiness."

"Is that what they say?" Blake teases.

I shrug. "That's what I say."

"Then we should probably get doughnuts once we're off this pier," Blake replies.

I smile at him, then take in the beautiful night view from the pier. I start to walk toward the wood railing to overlook the beach, and just watch the waves as Blake comes next to me. Everything feels *serene*. It's nice.

"Uh oh, am I that boring?" Blake says.

I softly laugh as I shake my head. "No, I just love watching the waves. People. *Life*." I'm staring out in wonderment, and although I'm on this date with Blake and I like him, I still don't feel *it* with him. I start to wonder if I will ever have that feeling again.

Hunger.

Desire.

Passion.

"What're you thinking about?" Blake asks.

"I never told you about my past relationship," I simply state. I think Blake senses I am going to tell him something important, so he remains quiet. "I was with Kyle for four years. He was the love of my life."

When I don't continue on right away, Blake speaks. "What happened?"

I turn my head to look at Blake with a sympathetic expression. "He was in a car accident a little over a year ago."

Blake holds my eyes as he places the pieces of the puzzle together in his mind, and then I see him visibly inhale. "Wow, I'm really sorry to hear that, Aria," he breathes out.

I give Blake an appreciative smile. "It's okay. I'm not bringing this up for you to feel sorry for me. I just wanted you to fully understand where I'm coming from and what my past is."

"It means a lot that you're letting me in," Blake says.

I turn my head back to look into the distance. "You're the first guy I've gone out with since. But I'd be lying if I said I feel one hundred percent emotionally available." Then I turn to look at Blake again. "I just want to be honest with you."

Blake shakes his head. "I wouldn't rush you on anything. We can take this as slow as you need to take it."

I smile at Blake's consideration. "That means a lot."

"Of course," Blake says. I look out over the pier again and I can sense Blake shifting on his feet, probably carefully contemplating his next question. "Are you still in love with him?"

The million-dollar question.

As easy as it would be to say I am, this question is a lot more complicated than it appears to be. When you lose someone you love, a part of your heart dies, and being in love with someone is a present tense action. You experience it in real time *with* your heart.

"I still love Kyle just as much as I did when he was alive," I admit. "But being *in love* with someone is a feeling you live through. It's life-altering and riveting, and no amount of memories can replace that feeling. Sadly, they'll never compare to the real thing."

Silence hangs in the breeze between us. "I'm really sorry," Blake says.

I decide to go on one of my rants to alleviate the awkward direction this conversation can go. "Time is an extraordinary concept. As much as you despise it in the beginning of your mourning and view it as the enemy, you wind up being so grateful for it later on and it becomes your best friend. Time heals you. Maybe not entirely, but it stitches some of the bigger wounds back up, making it tolerable to live your life again. I *hated* the concept of time when Kyle died."

"You're a warrior," Blake says.

I tip my lips up at the corner, still looking out at the beach. "I'm human. But I'd like to think I can fight more battles than I could a year ago."

I feel Blake's palm rest on my shoulder. "That's a sure thing." I turn to look at Blake with a small smile before he speaks again. "Thank you for sharing this with me."

I choose to make a joke to lighten the mood and take the attention off me. "I promise to keep our next date cheery and bubbly. I owe you."

Blake smiles. "No worries at all."

I let out a small laugh before responding. "You'll find I'm not great with dealing with sympathy or attention. I can either go on long rants or make silly jokes."

"That's admirable. I don't see myself getting offended by that."

I smile wider. "Good. Because I was about to demand we go get some doughnuts from all the sappy talk."

Blake squints his eyes as he purses his lips and looks off to the side. "I think you're just using our conversation as a persuasive device," he teases.

"Is it working?" I ask with a smirk.

Blake looks back at me. "That depends. How good are these doughnuts?"

I hold out a hand and my face gets serious. "They're *the best*. And I'm like a doughnut guru. Trust me on this."

He laughs, then gestures his head to say, "Let's go."

We walk away from the wooden railing and make our way toward Disco Doughnuts. As we're walking, I start to think that maybe I'm not giving Blake a fair shot, and that maybe I need to take a leap and start to *make* things happen.

"Blake?" I ask as we walk side-by-side.

"Yeah?"

"Will you hold my hand?" I ask as I look at him.

"Of course." Then he takes my hand in his and we interlock fingers. I don't like to admit it, but I'm slightly let down when I don't feel electricity as we touch. It's just comfort that I feel. Friendly comfort.

I keep my eyes forward as I think about how I felt when I first started dating Kyle, and how I was like a moth drawn to a flame with him. When Kyle first held my hand, I felt butterflies. When he first kissed me, I felt a surge of warmth in my lower belly. Kyle ignited so many desires and feelings within me, and a smile slowly stretches across my face as I'm reminded of him.

"If I knew holding your hand would make you this happy, I would have held it sooner." Blake's voice slices through my thoughts. I feel guilty that Blake thinks he's the reason a smile is on my face, when in reality, it's the memories of my past love that have me smiling ear to ear.

I decide to play along as much as I can without being dishonest. "Well, there's more you'll get to know about me," I say.

"I look forward to it," he says.

I smile back at Blake as we make our way to the doughnut shop, and when we get there, I buy a half dozen assortment as usual before we head back to my house.

When Blake pulls his car up to the curb, I turn to him in my passenger seat. "Thank you for a great night."

"My pleasure. I'll text or call you?"

I'm thankful Blake's not specifically asking for another date because I'm honestly not sure what I want to do yet or how I would respond to him. "Sounds good. I'll talk to you later," I say as I hug him goodbye, and then exit his car.

I smile and wave Blake off, then turn around to walk to my porch. When I look up, I see that the lights are on in Dane's house, and I get an idea. I decide to walk up the pathway to his front porch and knock on the door with my box of doughnuts in hand. I'm waiting a few moments before the door opens, and I'm hoping my peace offering buries the hatchet between us once and for all. Dane was mature enough to come to seek me out to smooth things over, so why couldn't I do the same?

But when Dane finally greets me on the other side of the door, words are lost on me. His dark wavy hair is a bit messy on the top, and he's shirtless while wearing black jogger sweatpants that hang just below the waistband of his boxer briefs. Now, I've always known Dane was a good-looking guy and that he was fit, but I don't think I've ever really *looked* at him. I find myself momentarily admiring his bronzed skin that's stretched taut with hard, lean muscle. He has sculpted pecs, and a rippled six-pack that dips into an appetizing "V" at his pelvic area. My eyes trace up his black and gray phoenix tattoo that runs the entire length of the side of his torso and wraps around the back of his shoulder to drip down his pec. I start to feel hot sparks flicker across my skin as I look over Dane's body, and I swallow a nervous lump in my throat to keep down an involuntary gasp.

"Ari?" Dane's voice breaks me from my thoughts.

"Oh, sorry. I brought doughnuts." My response is a statement but comes out more like a question.

Dane just narrows his eyes at me, a little bit confused at my awkwardness, and then my eyes go wide at the idea that I may have just interrupted something. I feel red immediately paint onto my cheeks and I plant my free hand on my forehead. "Oh, my god, I'm so stupid. I didn't know you had company."

I go to turn around, but I feel Dane grab my upper arm. "Ari, stop. I'm alone."

I blush as I respond. "I'm sorry, I just assumed," I explain as I gesture my hand up and down his body to reference his half nakedness.

Dane just smiles as he pushes the door all the way open, and steps aside for me to go in his house first. I enter the house as Dane follows me in, and I turn around to face him in the foyer. When Dane looks up from closing the front door, I hold up the box in my hand. "Doughnut?"

Dane just stands with his hands on his hips and furrows his brows. "Why are you dressed up?"

I sigh as I turn and walk toward his kitchen to place the box of doughnuts on the island. "I had another date with Blake. If you couldn't already guess, it went amazing." I turn to face him as he's walking into the kitchen. "That's obviously why I'm here," I add, sarcasm evident in my voice.

Dane stands at the opposite end of the kitchen island, and plants his palms down to lean over a little. "So what happened?" he asks, and it actually sounds like he's genuinely interested to hear about my date.

"Chemistry just isn't there."

"Sorry to hear that."

I wave a hand as if to brush off the pity. "It's not a big deal," I say as I open the box of doughnuts and retrieve a chocolate frosted with sprinkles. "Nothing a doughnut can't make up for. Cheers." I raise my doughnut toward Dane, then take a bite of it.

Dane smiles and leans further over the island to peek into the box. "Am I going to get my hand cut off if I try to take one of the chocolate frosted with sprinkles?"

"I'll let it slide for tonight," I say mid-chew.

Dane chuckles as he retrieves a doughnut and walks around the island so he's standing next to me. He leans his lower back against the counter and takes a generous bite of his doughnut. "So was Blake that awful of a kisser?" Dane asks while chewing.

I swallow my bite and respond. "Actually, he was a complete gentleman. He didn't try to make a move." Dane takes another bite of his doughnut and just stares at me like he's pondering his next words. "What?" I ask.

Dane swallows his bite. "I just thought he would have at least tried to kiss you." He shrugs before he continues. "If you ask me, he's a fool." Then he pops the last bite of his doughnut in his mouth and makes his way to the cabinets to get a drinking glass, as if what he said is the most casual statement ever.

I take another bite and am looking at him as he goes to the fridge water dispenser. "Well, maybe you should give him dating pointers from your handbook, Mr. Rico Suave."

Dane's eyes are focused on pouring his water as he speaks. "You don't need a handbook to know to take the opportunity to kiss a gorgeous woman." Once the glass is filled with water, he takes the glass away to take a sip.

As I'm looking over at Dane, my eyes start to take notice of the contours of his bicep and tricep muscles, and I start to think about how it would feel to be in his arms. For a fleeting moment, I'm envious of the girls I've seen Dane take home, knowing they've been held in those arms before. Arms that are strong, protective, and all masculine. I notice the way his large, rough hand dwarfs the glass he's holding, and I start to feel myself flush thinking of him touching me, caressing intimate parts of my body. Then, my eyes slowly trail down to his carved stomach, and I begin to wonder how it would feel to touch him there. How it would feel to graze my fingers over the ridges of his abdomen I know he works hard for. Dane's been such an amazing friend to me these last two months, and we've grown so close, that I start to think about how he is as a lover. Is he gentle like he is with me and our friendship? Or is he rough and untamed like he showed glimpses of last week? The thought surprisingly stimulates me, and I start to think about how he's really been there for me this summer. How kind and thoughtful he's been. I've seen a whole different side to Dane, and it's like I'm meeting him for the first time, and I'm more curious to know other parts about him. But what's really overwhelming my mind right now is how I feel being in his presence. I feel *turned on.*

Attracted.

Wait, what?

"You're staring." Dane is smirking as he leans one shoulder against the fridge and crosses one foot in front of the other.

I shift on my feet as if to physically shake the thoughts away. "I zoned out. Sorry."

Dane looks at me for several seconds like he's contemplating something. "It's only ten o'clock. You want to go somewhere?"

I lift the corner of my mouth, and I give the only answer I want to give. "Yes."

Dane quickly threw on a pair of dark denim jeans and a black zip-up hoodie over his bare chest to drive us to Crestside Landing. Once Dane parks on the gravel, I exit the car to take in the surroundings of the small dock on the bay. We're the only car in sight considering it's ten thirty, and the sky is lit with stars, illuminating the still water in a sparkling, peaceful glow.

"This is beautiful," I say as I walk closer to the wood planks bordering the gravel lot. When I look back over to Dane, the only part I can see of him are his denim covered legs and white sneakers. It seems he's connecting his phone to the car stereo, so I just smile as I turn to look out over the water again. "There better be some songs I'm fond of on that playlist," I say.

I hear Dane's car door shut behind me. "I think you'll like some of the country hits I have on there."

I turn and walk toward him. "Country works. I would even choose it over eighties music for this setting. Crazy, huh?"

Dane shoves his hands in his pockets as he closes the space between us. "Absolute madness."

I chuckle. "So, what now?" Dane tilts his head toward the hood of his car, indicating we should walk toward it, and once we both do, he holds a hand out to me. I grin as I take his hand and step on the hood of his car, then sit up by leaning my back against the windshield. Dane is tall enough that he just sits on the side of the hood and swivels his legs around to sit next to me. A few inches separate us as I sit with my legs curled to my side, and Dane with one leg straight out and one bent upward at the knee.

"So what made you want to come here?" I ask.

"I know you like to look at the stars at night," Dane answers as he's looking up at the sky.

I turn my head toward him and slowly tip the corner of my lips up, then settle my gaze back on the dark sky above. I close my eyes, listening to the music flowing through the speakers of the car, and enjoying the tranquility that kisses the air. "Mmm, I could fall asleep right here."

I feel Dane's gaze on me. "Well don't spoil the fun, we just got here."

My eyes are still closed when I respond. "Then think of something to do."

"Alright, twenty questions." I can hear the smile in his voice.

"You're activating my PTSD from the Ferris wheel extravaganza. Why would you do this?"

Dane laughs. "Well what would you suggest?"

"Dancing, obviously," I answer.

"So weird for you to suggest. Would have never thought."

"Just kidding, you're spared my dancing for tonight."

"I'd say there are definitely worse things in the world than watching you dance, Ari," Dane says. His voice isn't as laced with humor as it was a minute ago, so I open my eyes and turn my head to face him.

"Oh, really?" I ask.

Dane looks over to me, and I can sense his playful demeanor has lifted slightly. "You look genuinely *happy* when you dance," he confesses.

"I'm always happy to provide entertainment when I can," I say with a smirk. I turn my head and look back up, my eyes tracing designs created by the arrangement of the stars, and then I let my mind wander to familiar thoughts.

In my side view, Dane turns his head to look up at the sky with me. "I think about him too," he says.

"What do you think about?" My eyes are still looking up at the sky as I ask my question.

"How much I miss my best friend. The good times we shared. I try to focus on the *good* because I'm at least grateful we got to experience those moments together."

My eyes are still scanning the atmosphere above when I answer. "Yeah," I breathe out as I linger on images and memories of Kyle. But when I catch myself falling deeper into a rabbit hole, I decide to pull myself out. "When I was in therapy, my therapist read me a quote that really resonated with me." I don't say the quote right away, but when I sense Dane turn his head to face me, I answer his silent question. "'When life throws thorns, hunt for the roses.'"

Silence falls between us before Dane speaks, and I can feel Dane's eyes bore into the side of my face. "There's plenty out there for you. I don't have a single doubt in my mind about that."

I smile as I rotate on my side to face him, propping my head up in my hand. "I think you're still trying to make up for the last couple days."

"I guess I deserve that," Dane jokes as he turns his head to look back up at the sky, and vaguely throws an arm over his head. Realizing he's getting more comfortable, I close my eyes and allow the music to replace conversation.

When I hear the next song start to play, my eyes flash open with excitement as I say, "Oh I like this song. What is it?"

"'Long Way Home' by Canaan Cox," Dane answers, and then turns his head to face me with a knowing smirk. "Why? You gonna start dancing on the hood of my car?"

"I just might," I say, and then I resume closing my eyes while tapping my hand at the side of my hip.

"I'm disappointed. You're going to have to really commit here," Dane interrupts.

I open my eyes to look at Dane with raised eyebrows, and he raises his eyebrows back at me as if he's waiting on me to make my move. I purse my lips as I consider Dane's challenge and raise myself up on my knees. "But this can't be a one-woman show," I say as I grab Dane's hands in mine. I start swaying my hips to the rhythm of the song, and with that adorable smirk, Dane starts to mouth the lyrics to me as he taps his foot on the hood. A giddy laugh escapes through my lips, and I close my eyes as I tilt my head back to sink into the music and embrace this feeling of being unchained.

Unbound.

Free.

My hands act on their own accord, and I release Dane's to vaguely raise them above my head and continue moving my body to the beat of the country hit. I don't have to look at Dane to know his eyes are following my every move, and truthfully, it doesn't bother me at all.

In fact, it's exhilarating.

As the song reaches its last verse, I feel Dane rest one palm at the side of my hip, and I instinctively cover the top of his hand with my own palm. I'm completely immersed in what I'm doing when Dane sits up straighter to grasp my other hip to pull me closer to him. I let out a playful laugh as I tilt my head forward to look at Dane, who's staring back at me with something unfamiliar woven into his bright green hues.

Somehow, they look *darker* to me.

Starved.

I swallow hard when I realize I'm straddling one of Dane's thick thighs, and I have to rest my palms on Dane's shoulders to brace myself. My sex is all too aware of his denim-clad leg that's inches away from creating electrifying friction, and I feel my heartbeat quicken and my tongue start to feel too big for my mouth.

"Do you feel alive yet?" Dane's voice is low and husky. The pressure of his palms on my hips scorches me through the fabric of my dress, and a crackling heat begins to pop repeatedly underneath my skin. But regardless of our compromising position on top of his Mustang, it's Dane's words that set my soul aflame.

All I can do is stare at Dane with parted lips, admiring and appreciating him. My hands subconsciously fall to his chest, and heat singes my back as my small palms gently press into his steel muscle. His hoodie is unzipped just enough to make out the well-defined indent in the center of his chest, and I have to lick my lips to satiate the need to drag my tongue across it.

Dane reaches up to tuck a loose strand of hair behind my ear, and my body vibrates with adrenaline. His fingertips lick the shell of my ear, and my breaths become shallow as he cups the side of my face with his large, rough palm. "I refuse to believe that you've already been given all life has to offer," he whispers as his thumb caresses my jawline.

I exhale the smallest breath as the pulse between my legs throbs uncontrollably, but what surprises me the most is how his words spring me to life. It's like I'm taken under a powerful spell, and it's all-consuming and inescapable. And there's nowhere else I'd rather be than right here on the hood of Dane's car with an umbrella of stars above us.

My eyes flutter closed when his fingertips drop to my neck, tracing down the length of it, creating goosebumps in their wake. My body hums with need at his skilled touch, and I tilt my head back just enough to invite him in. I'm scared that if I voice what I want, I'll come to my senses and lose this intoxicating moment, so I silently beg him to take the leap for both of us.

"Is this what you were thinking about earlier?" he whispers. Dane slides his hands under the collar of my oversized cardigan to drag it down my shoulders and to my elbows. "How I'd touch you if I ever got the chance to?" A breathy whimper escapes my throat when Dane's soft lips connect with the sensitive skin of my neck. He marks a path downward and gently nips in random spots, each teasing kiss and bite lighting a new flame under my skin.

Right when Dane's mouth reaches my collar bone, his lips abandon their assault, and I lift my head forward to hold his gaze. His fingers wrap tightly around each side of my waist, giving it a squeeze that holds warning. "You'll find that being a gentleman isn't really my style."

My blood cools in the streams of my veins at his suggestion. "You just want to fuck me? Is that it?" I ask with accusation.

The corner of Dane's mouth tips up as he takes my hand off his chest and brings my fingers to his plush lips. "Any guy can fuck you, Ari," he rasps. His eyes never leave mine as he kisses the tip of my pointer and middle finger, and when I feel the tip of his tongue flick against my skin, my stomach somersaults and a surge of warmth pools in the apex of my thighs. "I want you to surrender," he breathes against my skin, placing another kiss on my fingers. Then he gently brings my fingers against my own lips. "Surrender every part of yourself to me so that when I'm inside you, I consume every pocket of your body and soul."

Mint and cinnamon invade my senses, and all I can do is flutter my eyes closed and place a kiss exactly where Dane's lips were two seconds ago. The warmth between my legs transforms to liquid heat as the tip of my tongue grazes my skin, and tasting the evidence of Dane's kiss only makes me want to devour him whole.

Like a lion hunting a gazelle.

"How do I taste?" he whispers.

I exhale against my fingers as I open my eyes and respond with the most honest answer I can think of. "Like you can ruin me," I whisper.

Dane's eyes are glued to mine as he releases my fingers to gently drag my bottom lip down with his thumb, and I instinctively wrap my hand around his wrist. The tension is palpable, and I can practically see the frayed moral thread between us that's preventing us from closing the distance. The sound of my heartbeat drums in my ear as my breaths become desperate against Dane's thumb, and I know that if he says one more word, the thread that keeps us apart will finally snap.

"Tell me to," he says.

The thread splits in two.

"Shatter me."

Dane's large hand engulfs the side of my face, pulling my mouth to his, and when our lips collide, I feel color seep into my veins. We part our lips at the same time to deepen the kiss, and Dane's velvety tongue dips into my mouth, teasing my own with every expert stroke he makes. His lips are pillowy, soft, and *made* to do this, but his kiss is intoxicating and poisonous. Like I know I shouldn't be drinking from the glass he's handed to me, but I'm too stubborn to think that the liquid will destroy me. Both my hands firmly lace around Dane's neck and into his hair, refusing to let go as our tongues fall into a slow, sensual dance. Our stifled moans fuse together as our bodies mold into one another, and our lips interlock in quicker, more fervent movements. Dane's palm at the side of my face wraps to the back of my head so he can weave his fingers in my hair and angle my head right where he wants me. His touch is mixed with tenderness and dominance all in one, and it's like I'm his possession to *worship*.

His kiss is *out-of-this-world*.

But just as I'm taking in the rapture of this moment, the sound of ambulance and firetruck sirens blare in the distance and catapults me from the lust-filled haze I've been lost in. The color drains from my veins, and the currents are now streams of icy water that freeze my heart. I slouch my body away from Dane's as I look off to the side with one palm covering my mouth.

What am I doing?

This is Dane.

I wipe my palm down my lips, as if to physically erase our kiss and any evidence of the last minute.

"Ari." Dane's hard tone interrupts my thoughts from my peripheral vision.

I don't risk a look at him as I swing my leg from around Dane's thigh and sit next to Dane on the hood of his car. I re-adjust my cardigan by pulling it back over my shoulders, as I say, "Please don't make this more difficult."

I hear Dane sigh a frustrated laugh. "I can't believe this." At my side, I see his face turn to look at me. "So was this your plan tonight?"

I turn to look at him through squinted eyes. "What?"

Dane has his elbows propped up on his bent knees as he gestures vaguely with his hands in between his legs. "Come to me for some instant gratification, only to have a moral dilemma once we're all over each other and caught up in an incredible moment. Because if so, that's a really shitty plan."

"I didn't come to you with the intention of any of this happening," I say as I shake my head.

Dane raises his eyebrows to challenge me. "No? It seemed pretty convenient for you to run to me after your lackluster date tonight."

"I came to you as a *friend*. But it's clear that was the wrong decision."

"It was the wrong decision," Dane retorts. My mouth parts slightly at his harsh admission and tone, but when words don't leave my mouth, Dane continues on. "I don't think I'm really cut out for the 'friend' role when it comes to you."

I swallow thickly as I hold his gaze, trying to make sense of what he's saying. "I'm not going to sleep with you just because you want to fulfill some sexual conquest," I retort.

Dane exhales a laugh as he turns his head away from me and looks out at the water. "That's the worst part about it. I don't want you for just one night."

I stare at Dane as the weight of his words register in my brain. I feel like I'm suffocating from the overwhelming emotions that crash over me, like a tidal wave wiping out any happiness or clarity I once had about mine and Dane's relationship. Those feelings are now replaced with confusion, fear, and guilt. Feelings that I want no part of, especially after the strides I've made this past year. No matter how Dane or I feel about one another, it doesn't change the fact that we could never become anything more than friends.

"We made a mistake tonight," I say, my voice just above a whisper.

Dane shakes his head at me. "I don't believe you," he says confidently, like he can see right through me. I narrow my eyes when Dane challenges me and calls my bluff, but he elaborates anyway. "If you can look me in the eyes, and honestly say you felt nothing for me while I was touching and kissing you, then I'll take you home right now. No questions asked."

I open my mouth to say something, but quickly change my mind because I know I'll give myself away if I try to avoid answering his question. Dane's trying to get me to admit that I enjoyed kissing him, and that there are mutual feelings between us. But the harsh reality is that none of that matters. The only thing that matters is what is right and what is wrong, and I'm the one that has to live with my conscience the rest of my life.

I decide I'd rather live with a conscience that is free of guilt than one that is plagued with regret. "I felt nothing."

I see Dane's jaw clench, and he holds my eyes for a few moments before he turns his head away from mine. He hangs his head down as he stares at his hands hanging between his bent knees and licks his lips. I hug my arms tightly around my chest, trying to mask my discomfort and act as casual as possible. Like what I said didn't phase me at all or didn't prick my heart just the same as it pierced his.

"Okay," Dane says, and then swings his legs around so he can hop off the hood of his car.

"Dane-"

Dane's eyes meet mine, and he automatically interrupts me. "I'm a man of my word, so I'm taking you home." Dane gestures to the passenger side of his Mustang. "But it would help if you sat *in* the car."

I'm stunned as I hold Dane's stare for a few moments. It's hard to ignore the sudden change in Dane's face and body language, and the distance he's creating between us makes me want to scream.

Maybe even cry.

I feel helpless. Like my hands are bound behind my back. The words that I spoke tonight didn't come from my heart, but instead, the moral part of my brain. I almost feel robotic, like I have no control over my feelings anymore, and my true emotions have become prisoners in my own body.

Acknowledging I've probably spent way too much time dissecting our tiff, I slide off the hood of his car. I don't dare look Dane's way as I hop right in the passenger side of his Mustang, fearful that looking at him will cause me to say something I probably shouldn't. And once Dane gets in the car and starts driving, we never look or speak to each other once the whole ride back.

CHAPTER
Twenty-Six

DANE

I lay restless in bed that night as I drape one arm over my head, and stare at the ceiling, allowing my thoughts to wash over me. I've never experienced something like kissing Aria on the hood of my car tonight. I didn't have to be naked with Aria to feel it, and I didn't need to touch her in a sexual way either. The simple act of holding her in my arms, caressing her face, and kissing her lips, made my heart stumble a beat or two. Like it was unsure how to respond to this newfound feeling inside of me.

I felt *connected* to Aria. Knowing the person she is, all I wanted to do was *show* her how much I admired her soul. I wipe both hands down my face as my thoughts start to make my emotions unravel. My relationship with Aria was always so natural and effortless. She never felt like a responsibility to me. She never felt like a burden. I'm fascinated by the person she is, and who she wants to become. I *want* to bring her happiness. I *want* to be the person to put that infectious smile on her face and make her laugh every single day of her life. I *want* to be the one who restores her faith in life and reminds her of her purpose in it.

Because that's what she deserves.

I want to be hers. I want her to be mine. But even if Aria felt the same, there is one detail that crushes any hope of mine.

I can never have her.

And that's just it.

That's where our story ends.

ARIA

I lay on my side in bed as I stare out the window at the nighttime sky. How is it possible for a moment to feel so morally wrong and so incredibly perfect at the same time? It's like my heart and head are at war.

My heart wants Dane.

Dane energizes my mind and body just the same. Dane is as loyal as they come, always putting me first and making sure I'm taken care of. I feel safe with him. Protected. And if he disappointed me with his kiss, I could convince myself that my feelings for Dane stem from the comfort I feel with him as a friend.

But his kiss was *intoxicating*.

Like a syringe that injected a drug into my veins, slowly awakening me from a coma where feelings of passion and pleasure were frozen in time. I didn't even have to strip my clothes off, but he handled my body with such a seasoned expertise that it thrilled me to my very core. Made me yearn for more.

And I want more.

So much more.

I start to think about how soft his lips felt, and wonder how they would feel against my breasts, and how his tongue would feel working my sex. I bite my lip at the thought of his fingers sliding inside of me, the same fingers that caressed the side of my face.

But these thoughts are the extent of what this can be, because my head is the victor of this war.

How did I manage to develop feelings for the one person I shouldn't fall for?

What would our friends think?

What would my family think?

What would Kyle think of me?

Kyle.

I feel tears well up behind my eyes, and I turn to lay on my back to stare at the ceiling. I think of how I've betrayed Kyle, and how careless I've been to dishonor our relationship. I suddenly feel the familiar tightening of my invisible shackles around my wrists, and I start to wonder if I'm meant to escape them at all.

CHAPTER
Twenty-Seven

ARIA

Thursday, July 21, 2022

I haven't seen or spoken to Dane since Saturday, and it is now Thursday night. To be honest, I've purposely been avoiding him, and I intend to keep it that way until I feel ready to face him with a clearer and stronger mind. To my dismay, I can sense he's doing the same.

Thankfully, I won't have to consciously avoid Dane tonight because I am going by my parents' house for a family dinner. When I pull up to the driveway, I head up to the front door on the wrap-around porch and ring the doorbell holding the tray of brownies I made for dessert.

My mom opens the door. "Hi, honey!" she exclaims as she hugs me.

"I've missed you," I say while in her embrace.

I enter the house to greet my dad, Ronnie, and Cheryl, and dinner is ready by the time I am there with the table already set up. I place my brownie tray on the kitchen counter for later, and we all take our seats as soon as we're done with greetings.

When we all start digging in, I am the first to speak. "How are the light fixtures working in the restaurant? Did Ronnie drop the ball at all?" I joke.

"Really?" I hear Ronnie say, and I throw him a smirk.

"So far, so good," my dad responds.

"I bought the materials for you to put together those centerpieces you showed me on Pinterest," my mom tells me.

"I would have ordered them, you didn't have to do that," I say.

"We're about a month out. You need time to get them done," my mom answers.

I finish my bite of pot roast and swallow it before speaking. "Mom, they'll take two or three nights maximum to get done."

My mom waves me off. "Oh, whatever. You know I like crossing things off my 'To-Do' list."

"To be fair, that was my 'To-Do' list item," I counter.

"That wasn't being done," my mom adds.

I purse my lips. "Okay. Not exactly, but I swear I was going to order them this week."

"Uh-huh," my mom says.

"Mom, I love you, but you get stressed *way* too easily," I say as I take another forkful of pot roast.

My mom holds her palms out. "Why does everyone keep saying I'm like this?"

"Because you are," Ronnie chimes in.

"What is this? 'Gang up on Mom Day'?" my mom asks.

I smile as I finish my bite, and it seems we're all having a good laugh about the conversation.

"How's your summer vacation been Ari?" Cheryl asks.

I take a sip of water. "Pretty eventful, actually. Luckily, the weather has been perfect for me to enjoy being outside."

"Yeah, this is definitely one of the mildest summers we've had in a while," Cheryl says.

"Yeah, Kate and I have been able to enjoy sitting outside at some waterfront restaurants. We actually just went to The Block a couple weeks ago. It's a fairly new steakhouse, and it was really good," I respond.

Cheryl turns to Ronnie. "Guess we'll have to go."

Ronnie rolls his eyes playfully. "Someone says one good thing about a new restaurant, and you have to go."

Cheryl turns to me. "Is it so awful I want to try new places?"

"I'm totally with you," I say, and then I look at Ronnie. "Stop being annoying and diverge from the same five restaurants you eat at."

Ronnie faces Cheryl. "I promise we'll go, okay?"

Cheryl smiles and raises her glass to me as if to thank me, and I just lightly chuckle as I raise my glass back before taking a sip.

"How's Dane?" Ronnie cuts in.

I pause as I stare back at him. The mention of Dane's name makes me feel like this casual question implies my brother may know something. I make a slight frown and shake my head. "The usual. He's Dane," I answer, and then I take another bite of my pot roast as if that will prevent me from having to go on with this conversation.

"Have you seen him recently?" my mom asks.

I swallow nervously. "Not the past week, no." Ronnie takes his sip of water, then looks at me as if he's contemplating saying something. "What?" I ask.

Ronnie shakes his head. "Nothing."

I feel my heart rate start to pick up from fear that he's about to tell me he knows about Dane and me, even though that's impossible. I avert my gaze as I take a sip of water but am interrupted by Ronnie's voice. "Alright, the reason I ask about Dane is that I asked him to do me a favor."

I furrow my brows waiting for him to continue. "I asked him to look out for you when you moved back to the townhouse, just to check in every once a while."

"You begged him to be a friend to me?" I ask, annoyance evident in my voice.

"Ari, he was always your friend, don't twist my words around," Ronnie says as he shakes his head.

I let out a frustrated sigh before speaking. "Well, this is kind of shitty. I thought the time I spent with Dane this summer was genuine." Then I look away from everyone's faces at the table, almost like I'm embarrassed.

My mom cuts in immediately. "Your brother is right. Dane has always been a good friend to you. This doesn't change that."

I know the words they are saying make sense, and if they told me this information before Dane and I kissed, I probably would have thought nothing of it. But for some reason, this information bothers me. It saddens me not knowing if all the great times we've spent together were because Dane actually wanted to spend them together, or if those times were just a burden to him. Did it feel like a job to him to keep me company? I even remember our conversation on the pier when I told Dane I didn't want him to feel obligated to me, and I didn't like feeling like a charity case. He assured me that wasn't the case, but was that a lie? Was he just telling me what I wanted to hear? It feels like Dane's been keeping this small secret from me, and that I've been kept in the dark this whole time our relationship has been blossoming. The thought makes me lose my appetite, but I know I can't overreact in front of my family right now. It would throw too many red flags in the air.

I look back at Ronnie. "I know you were looking out for me. I guess I'm just sick of sympathy," I say matter-of-factly.

"It's not sympathy. We all care about you," Ronnie says.

I half smile back at him, and we go through the rest of our dinner talking about work, Ronnie and Cheryl's house renovations, and other summer events. Although I'm physically engaged in all these conversations, my mind is still marred by disappointment.

It's then that I realize my feelings for Dane may run deeper than I thought.

Friday, July 22, 2022

The next night, I'm throwing on a white, square neck crop tank top with a high-waisted floral ruched mini skirt. My hair is down in beach waves, and I finish the outfit with nude strappy sandals. I told Kate I wanted some girl time, so we're going to Shippers alone, and I'm looking forward to some much-needed drinks and laughs.

Once Kate picks me up and we enter Shippers, we order drinks at the bar and find ourselves a table quickly.

"So how are things with Blake?" Kate asks.

I just shrug with a scrunched face in response.

HUNT FOR THE ROSES

"Nothing, huh?" Kate asks.

I let out a sigh before explaining. "He's a really nice guy, and we had a fun time on both of our dates, but I just didn't feel *it*."

"I'm sorry, hun," Kate says as she places a hand over mine. "You're still healing, and maybe you just aren't ready. You'll know when you're ready."

When Kate says this, I can't help but think of how ready I felt when I was touching and kissing Dane, but I can't exactly tell her that, so I keep my response short and simple. "Yeah," I say.

Kate raises her glass, and I smile as I clink mine with hers. After I take a sip, I'm the next to speak. "So what's new with you? How's the accounting firm?"

"Ugh, we're always so busy toward the end of the month, so it's starting to get swamped. But my boss has pretty much guaranteed me a promotion by September," Kate answers with a wide smile.

"Oh, that's great!" I exclaim.

Kate nods her head in agreement. "Yeah, I'm really excited. It's definitely a long time coming. Now I can do what I do best and order people around."

We both laugh and I'm about to say something before we're interrupted.

"Hey, can I interest either of you in another drink when you're finished with those?" There is a handsome stranger that has approached our table. He's got brown hair, blue eyes, and his hair is tied back in a low man bun. He's wearing a navy crewneck and light denim, which both fit his muscles perfectly, and Kate and I give each other a knowing smirk.

Kate is the first one to take the bait. "I think our interest is very much piqued," Kate says with a flirtatious smile, and then she pulls her V-neck crop top down a little more.

Mystery man smiles back and puts out a hand to Kate. "Brad," he introduces himself, and then extends a hand out to me. "Nice to meet you girls."

Kate and I give him our names and ask him to take a seat with us, and Brad sits next to me. "So is there just one of you, or do you have any friends who would like to come join?" Kate asks.

Brad chuckles. "Sorry to disappoint, it's just me tonight."

I'm now the next one who speaks. "Well, you're brave to come here outnumbered. We'll do our best not to bore you with too much girl talk."

We're all taking a sip from our drinks and moving through conversation pretty easily as Brad throws some decent jokes around, and tells us stories of fishing trips gone wrong. Once Kate and I finish our drinks, Brad keeps his promise and gets up to go to the bar to buy us another round.

Kate grabs my hand. "Oh my god, he's so hot."

"I know, it should be sinful to look that good. I don't even like man buns," I say.

When Kate doesn't respond right away, I notice she's looking past my shoulders at something in the distance. "Well, I guess our girls' night is going to be tainted in five seconds." I furrow my brows as I look behind me in the direction she is staring. That's when I see Trent and Dane walking in.

Shit.

I immediately start feeling anxious. I haven't seen or spoken to Dane since we kissed, and more than that, I found out he's only been hanging out with me because my brother asked him too.

Fuck my life.

I don't contain the frustration in my voice too well when I turn to Kate. "Kate, I thought you said it was just girls tonight."

Kate defends herself. "I didn't tell them we were here. They must have had the same idea as us."

"Well, now they're going to come over here," I say in an annoyed tone.

"So? We always hang out with them anyway," Kate asks while looking confused. I realize how ridiculous I sound from Kate's perspective. She's right, we always hang out. But she has no idea about anything that has happened the past week, so she still thinks everything is normal. I try my best to compose myself to save face. I lick my lips and lean back in my chair, trying to physically control my nerves as my hands play nervously in my lap.

Trent and Dane eventually make their way to our table when Trent says, "Fancy seeing you guys here. Thanks for the invite, by the way."

Even though Trent is the one speaking, it's Dane who I look at, and I'd be lying if I said he didn't look *good*. *So good*. His dark wavy hair is tousled on the top, he's wearing a navy button down that hugs his muscles in all the right places, with the top two buttons undone and the sleeves rolled up his forearms. He's paired his shirt with tan shorts and white sneakers, and he's donning the perfect amount of scruff on his face. Both of us seem to be rewinding last week's events in our heads because neither of us says a word as we hold each other's gaze.

I finally throw Trent and Dane a tight-lipped smile and look away, hoping Kate does all the talking. But to my surprise, it's Brad who cuts into the silence first. "Hey, can I help you two?" Brad asks as he comes up next to Trent and Dane with mine and Kate's beers.

Trent and Dane immediately furrow their brows and look back and forth between us and Brad. Dane is the first to speak. "I think you have it backwards. Can we help you with something?"

"I was just buying these girls another round."

"Trent and Dane, this is Brad," Kate cuts in trying to diffuse the rising testosterone levels.

"Well they're taken care of already," Dane says as he steps closer, leaning one hand on the table.

"Whatever, man," Brad says with a shake of his head as he walks off.

"What the hell Dane?!" Kate yells.

Dane rubs the back of his neck. "Here we go."

"Yeah 'here we go' is right! He was hot and bought us drinks. You're such an asshole sometimes," Kate says with a sigh as she leans back in her seat.

I don't speak. I'm just watching this banter unfold between Kate and Dane because I honestly don't even know what to say with how overwhelmed I feel.

Dane leans both hands on the table and levels his eyes with Kate. "Kate, get over yourself." Then Dane stands back up and turns to Trent. "Let's get drinks."

They both walk away, and Kate is left with her mouth open in shock. "What the fuck?!"

I look away from her eyes as I respond. "No idea. So weird."

But Kate's right. What was that about? I mean, it's not like Brad was doing anything offensive or inappropriate. He was just buying us drinks. There was nothing to defend our honor about, and Dane and I haven't even spoken recently. I was actually taken aback by how worked up Dane was just now.

I'm thinking about all these things as I stare at Dane's back at the bar. As if he senses my eyes on him, Dane turns around for a second, and when he catches me staring back at him, we lock eyes for a moment as he swallows hard, and I do the same.

"If Dane sits next to me, I'm punching him in the face." Kate's voice averts my gaze from Dane's.

I put a hand over my head and lean on the table. "I don't think we need any more drama for tonight. Let's keep it PG please."

Kate narrows her eyes. "Aren't you pissed too?"

"I don't know," I breathe.

Just as I respond, Trent and Dane take a seat at our table with their drinks, and drinks for us. Trent sits next to Kate and Dane sits next to me, so maybe he heard Kate's threat about punching him in the face. Who knows?

"If you think this is making up for your ridiculous stunt, you're sorely mistaken," she says as she refuses to take the drink Trent tries to hand to her.

"Right, because you'd refuse a free drink on any given night," Dane deadpans before taking a sip of his drink.

Kate rolls her eyes in defeat and pulls the drink closer to her as Trent throws an arm around her. "Besides, now you get to hang out with me instead. We both know I'm a much better time than that guy is," Trent says as he wiggles his brows at Kate.

Kate playfully punches him, and Dane and I don't say anything. We just stare at their flirtatious banter because we don't actually have anything to say to each other. It's so painfully awkward, so I take a large gulp of my drink, trying to erase any thoughts with alcohol.

"Ari, I guess that leaves you with Dane for the night," Trent jokes.

I give Trent a mortified look. "What?"

Trent looks at me curiously at first. "It's a joke. Chill."

Kate and Trent exchange confused looks, and that's my cue to physically escape the situation. "Yeah, sorry. I'm actually going to go to the bathroom." I get up from the table without waiting to hear any of their responses, but once I'm out of view of the gang, I make my way to the front door of Shippers, and step outside to get fresh air.

I walk through the crowd of people on the wooden deck, and down the steps to the side of the building. I lean back against the building wall, and let out the unknowing breath I've been holding in. I have no clue what's going on with Dane and I at this point. We said absolutely nothing to each other back there, but I feel like so much was said in the silence at the same time.

I look up at the nighttime sky above, and just think. I think about the start of summer when Dane and I were on the Ferris wheel. When we had dinner together at my house. When we were on the pier. Those moments between us were special to me, but was it as special to him? Or did he just keep me close company those days because my brother told him to? Then I think about Dane's fingers on my skin, his lips on mine, and how handsome he looks tonight. I think of how much our relationship has grown, and how wonderful it was to be with him in such an intimate way.

"Thought you said you were using the bathroom."

I look to my side as Dane walks closer to me with his hands in his pockets. When he's only inches away from me, he leans a shoulder on the wall, and crosses one foot in front of the other as he stands next to me.

I turn my head to look straight ahead and let out a sigh. "Great."

Dane drops his head. "Ouch. I'm just getting it from all angles today."

I just stare straight ahead, refusing to look at him, and Dane runs a nervous hand through his hair. "Look, I've kind of been going out of my mind thinking about the other night."

"Yeah, well, you don't have to worry about it anymore," I snap.

"What?" Dane questions.

I peel myself off the wall and hold out my arms as I look at him. "You can be done with your charity case," I say as I start walking past him. "You're off the hook, Dane, don't worry about me anymore."

I feel Dane's hand grip my wrist, and I spin around. "What the hell are you talking about?" he says with furrowed brows.

"Get off me," I say as I yank my wrist out of his grasp and start walking away again.

I gasp when Dane grabs my upper arm and leans me against the wall of the building. "No. You're going to tell me what the hell you meant by that." His aggressive and dominant tone startles me.

My breathing starts to pick up, and I'm peering up at him for several seconds before I respond. "My brother asked you to look out for me. That's why you've been spending time with me."

Dane takes a few seconds to comprehend what I'm talking about, and then he starts to slowly shake his head. "That's not the reason I've been spending time with you, Ari."

"But you wouldn't have started unless Ronnie asked you to, right?" I counter.

Dane furrows his brows at me. "Why would that matter to you?"

I'm offended he would even ask me that question because it seems to tell me just how little he cares for me. "It wouldn't. So get off me," I say sternly as I shake my arm out of his hold. But as soon as I do, he's caging me in with both of his palms on the wall behind me.

"I don't believe you," Dane challenges.

"I don't give a shit what you believe," I say as I knock his arm out of the way to storm off.

I head back inside Shippers, knowing Dane won't be too far behind me, but I don't care enough to look back. I find Kate and Trent sitting at the table, but I'm so angry with Dane that I don't want to hang out with the three of them anymore tonight. I'm ready to play fire with fire, so I look around for Brad, and when I spot him at the bar, it's game on.

I walk up to tap Brad's shoulder. "Hey!"

When he turns around, he throws me a wide grin. "Hey! I was hoping to see your cute face again."

I blush at his compliment and egg him on. "So can I buy us another round, considering your gesture was compromised earlier?"

He smiles at my offer. "Sure thing."

Just as I'm about to get the bartender's attention, Dane comes in between Brad and I, and he shifts me away from the bar a little bit. "We're going. Say goodbye to your friend."

I narrow my eyes at him. "You're not my father. Get out of my way."

Dane leans down so he can talk into my ear. "You have three seconds to move out of this bar, or I'm going to physically remove you from it. And I mean it, Ari."

His tone is cold, and it sends a shiver through my body. Without looking back at him, I start walking out of the bar with Dane right behind me. There are too many people outside that I don't want to make a scene, especially since Kate and Trent are here. So as much as I'm furious with Dane and don't want to get in his car with him, I swallow my pride and do it anyway.

When we reach his Mustang, I get in the passenger side and position my body so that my knees are leaning on the door, and my elbow is leaning on the windowsill. Once Dane pulls out onto the road, we drive for a few minutes in silence until he's the first to speak. "I'm not apologizing for ruining your hookup plans. So if you're expecting an apology, don't hold your breath."

Is he kidding me?

Okay, two can play this game.

I continue to look out the window as I say, "What else is new? You're always trying to cock block me. Come up with something original next time."

Dane laughs as if I'm being ridiculous. "Yeah, I'm keeping you from *real* winners," Dane says sarcastically.

I turn to face him, even angrier now. "Yeah, because the girls you fuck are just *gems* right? That's why you always kick them out the second you get what you want, huh?"

"At least those girls know I can get the job done. Must be the reason you came running to me last Saturday after Blake couldn't satisfy you," Dane says.

I slam a palm on his glove compartment. "You bastard!" I yell as rain starts to drizzle on the windshield.

"But despite all your mixed signals and mind games, I'm more than willing to be of service to you," Dane says as he flashes a cocky grin at me. I can tell his voice carries a bitter edge with it, and I suddenly feel what Kate felt before.

I want to punch Dane straight in his face.

Just one good hit.

I look at him with narrowed eyes. "Get off your high horse, Dane. The last person I want right now is you."

"I find that hard to believe with how eager you were for me the other night," Dane retorts as he keeps his eyes on the road, his jaw visibly tense.

I huff back into the seat and choose to stop talking for now. I'm getting too worked up, and nothing I say is phasing Dane in the slightest. You can cut the tension in this car with a knife, and even then, I'm not sure a knife is sufficient to cut through it entirely.

The rain starts to pick up a little as we drive, so Dane has to activate the windshield wipers. The sound of the wipers is all we hear for the next several minutes as both of us sit in silence, but when Dane turns on our street, I decide I want to have the last word. I want to stick it to him where it hurts.

When Dane puts the car in park, I have my hand on the door handle as I turn to him and say, "I'll be sure to call Blake tonight for a night cap considering my first option was shot to shit." Then I throw him a smug grin, and storm out of the car and into the drizzle of rain.

I jog around the car to the pathway leading to my front door, but as I'm about to walk up the pathway, I hear Dane's car door slam shut. "Hey!" Dane shouts from behind me, and then I feel his hand grip around my upper arm, and he whips me around to face him.

"What?! What Dane?!" I shout back as the rain picks up, and our hair and clothes start to become damper. Our breaths start to become shallower as we just stand there and look into each other's eyes. Dane's proximity is dominant, making me feel at his mercy. I'm so willing to give Dane every ounce of control just so I don't have to make the decision to walk away again, and ironically enough, that feeling makes me feel a sense of empowerment. Finally, Dane's gaze lowers to my lips, then trails back up to my eyes again, and our eyes speak a language of their own.

A language only the two of us understand.

We combust.

Dane grabs the side of my face with his hand and pulls me into a raw and passionate kiss. I instantly wrap my hands around Dane's neck, and we attack each other's mouths like they're going to escape from us any minute. I eagerly open my mouth to Dane, and he inserts his tongue to massage my own. I let out a moan as I feel his warm, wet tongue caress my own, and it sends an electric current through my entire body. I feel like I am on fire despite the fact that there is water pouring down on us, and I start to feel my nipples strain against the wet fabric of my shirt as an aching need brews at my core.

Dane bends to wrap his palms around the back of my thighs and hoists me up quickly. I let out a gasp as I instinctively wrap my legs around his waist, and we continue to deepen our kiss. Between the rain and my lips entangled with Dane's, I'm not really aware of my surroundings, but I do feel Dane start to walk. I'm not sure where he is taking us, but I don't care. I just want to keep living in this moment forever.

I need this passion that's been absent from me for so long.

Nothing else matters right now.

I need his touch.

I need him.

CHAPTER
Twenty-Eight

DANE

I walk up the stairs of my porch with Aria wrapped around my waist. Reluctantly, I break our kissing escapade and place my forehead against hers. "Give me a second," I say breathlessly as I put her down.

I'm holding Aria's hand behind me, and I fidget trying to get my key out of my pocket to turn it in the lock of my front door. Once successful, I lead Aria inside while we still have our fingers intertwined, and when I close the door, I'm on her in under a second. I cup both sides of her face, our mouths opening hungrily and desperately as I walk Aria backwards until she's braced against the wall of the hallway. I push my body flush against hers, bringing both my palms down from her face to harshly knead her breasts, making sure to tweak her puckered nipples that are straining against the damp, thin white material. The moan that I wring out of her is mixed with pain and pleasure, stirring something primal within me.

"How should I make this pussy come?" I breathe against her lips as our breaths coil together and her chest heaves in anticipation.

"However you want," she pants, both fear and excitement etched into her light brown hues.

I hold Aria's gaze as my palms ease their grip on her breasts, and I slowly slip both hands under the hem of Aria's crop tank top. My movement is not as ravenous, but rather calculated and stealthy, and she instantly raises her arms so I can pull the shirt over her head.

When I toss her shirt on the floor, Aria resumes leaning back against the wall, and I stare at her for a moment, just looking at her olive skin glistening from the rain pellets, slick pieces of hair sticking to the side of her face, and her perky, full tits on display in that white lace bra.

She's so fucking lovely.

I nest her chin between my thumb and forefinger and take her bottom lip in between my teeth, gently biting into the soft cushion with just enough pressure. Aria lets out the faintest exhale, some of her breath catching in her throat as she's trying to release it, and I can practically feel and hear her heart thumping out of her chest.

"Take off your skirt," I whisper against her lips.

When Aria moves shaky fingers to the back of her garment, I rest both my palms on either side of her against the wall, towering over her small frame. My eyes follow the movements of her hands as she drags down the zipper behind her and slides her fingers into the waistband of her skirt to trail it down her thighs. Once the skirt reaches her knees, it no longer needs her guidance, and it drops to a puddle at her feet. As Aria steps out, I bite my lip as I catch the back of her knee under my palm, and curl her leg around my waist, keeping my palm under her thigh.

Aria gasps in surprise, peering up at me like prey that's just been caught by its predator. Her back is still glued to the wall when I yank her bra cup down with my free hand, and my greedy mouth latches onto her hardened nipple, mercilessly sucking on it and lavishing it with my tongue. Aria writhes beneath me as she moans, her fingers immediately lacing through my hair, and her hips timidly grinding against the angry bulge underneath my shorts. I can feel her wet heat seeping through the material of her underwear, radiating onto my crotch, causing the pressure in my groin to tighten painfully.

I stand straight as I tug her other bra cup down, making sure both Aria's breasts are bare to me. "Come on, get nice and wet for me," I rasp. Aria whimpers, and the erotic nature of seeing her almost completely naked in my arms is electrifying. I hook my fingers in the waistband of her white lace panties, then harshly tug the flimsy fabric all the way out to the side until it tears in a visible crescendo.

"Oh god," Aria breathes as she throws her head back against the wall, and her creamy arousal drenches my shorts. As soon as she grinds her sex against me, I push on her lower stomach to back her away, and graze two fingers against her slick folds.

"You're dripping for my cock like a naughty fucking girl, huh?" I growl. Aria bites her bottom lip as she nods her head in agreement.

I tauntingly shake my head as my lips hover above her own. "You better settle down, because it's not happening like this," I say gruffly, and a flash of disappointment shines over Aria's face when she realizes I'm not taking her the way she wants me to take her.

As much as I'd love to bury myself deep inside her and show Aria every shred of what I feel for her, I need to take this slow for her sake. Aria's mind is clouded by lust right now since she hasn't been touched in over a year, and as crazy as it sounds to me, I don't want her to want me just for pleasure or a release.

I want her to want *me*.

I graze the tip of my nose with hers, slightly snapping her out of her own head that's probably going a mile a minute right now. "But I'm gonna wreck this pussy just as good," I rasp, and then I plunge my fingers through her tight, velvety walls.

Aria cries out at the unexpected invasion, bracing her small palms on my broad shoulders as I pump in and out of her in a slow and even rhythm. Once she settles into me, I curl my fingers in a "come hither" motion, stroking that sensitive barrier inside her.

"How's that?" I whisper as I hover over her lips.

"So good," she breathes out. I slightly increase the stroking of my fingers against her tight walls, her arousal lathering my digits like I'm washing my hands with liquid soap. But her snug walls suffocate my fingers, defeating my efforts to create more fluid movements.

My left palm bruisingly presses into her right thigh I've been holding up as I jerk my chin toward her left side. "Let's go. Spread this tight pussy out for me," I demand.

Aria gasps as she takes her left hand off my shoulder and spreads her fold out to the side. Completely opened for me, my fingers move with more ease, stroking that delicious spot for her, and her pussy glistens so fucking beautifully I feel like I'm going to come in my pants like a goddamn teenager. Aria curls her right hand into my shoulder as I pump my fingers inside her in hot and fast thrusts, pulling a short breath out of her lips with each plunge.

When I start to feel Aria's leg tremble in my palm, I lower myself so that I'm on a bent knee, resting her already raised leg over my shoulder. My face is now aligned with her sex, and I peer up at Aria with an evil smirk. I gently tug her swollen button between my teeth, making sure to avoid flicking it with my tongue.

"Dane, please," Aria pleads breathlessly.

I continue to hold her eyes as I lightly wrap my lips around her clit to kiss it, and then flick my tongue for one brief swipe over it. "Oh god," Aria whimpers as she throws her head back in pleasure and frustration. Then I flatten my tongue against her clit for a few drawn out licks and eventually start sucking on her clit unapologetically as my fingers fuck her pussy. "Oh god, yes," Aria pants out as she starts to slowly grind against my hand and mouth.

I slap her bare ass cheek to encourage her to keep riding me. "*Goddammit,* yes, ride my tongue baby," I grunt against her pussy.

I don't just want to see Aria come undone.

I *need* to see her come undone.

I'm feasting on her swollen button like it's my last meal and curling my fingers until they're knuckles deep in her. "Come on, give it to me," I rasp.

When I resume eating at her clit, I feel Aria's legs start to tremble around me, and then finally, I feel Aria's walls clamp down on my fingers as she arches her back off the wall. She cries in oblivion as her stomach contracts with shockwaves of pleasure, and I have to place a hand over her lower stomach to steady her body as her orgasm wracks through her.

It's without a doubt the most thrilling sight I've ever seen as I witness Aria come alive under my touch, and I'm absolutely positive I want to witness it infinite more times in my lifetime.

I take my time lapping Aria's juices up, savoring the flavor of her like it's a goddamn souvenir. I continue to slowly pump my fingers inside her, letting Aria fully ride out her high, and her palm is over her forehead as she tries to control her disorganized breathing. Her body jerks a few more times as she swipes her fingers sloppily through my hair, before I pull my mouth away from between her legs.

I gradually let down her leg that's draped over my shoulder and come up to a standing position to cup the side of her face firmly. Aria starts to reach both her hands down to the belt of my shorts, but I halt her movements by grabbing one of her wrists. "You don't have to," I whisper.

Immediately Aria shakes her head as she pants out her next words. "I want to. Let me touch you." I place both palms on the wall behind her in defeat, my arms caging around her. The temptation is too great for me to take control of, and there is no way I can resist her right now.

We're already past the point of no return.

She looks at me as she tugs my shorts down over my erection, and then she repeats the same movement by pulling my boxer briefs down. As soon as my cock springs free, she doesn't hesitate to grab it in her small, silky palm. "*Holy shit,*" I breathe out. I place my forehead against hers as I groan, while she strokes me from base to the tip.

"Never knew how jealous I'd be of all the girls I've seen you with," Aria whispers against my lips. Her sultry words make my dick jerk in her palm, but she doesn't let up on pumping me, making sure to swirl the pre-cum with her thumb when she reaches the head.

I lift my lips up to one corner in a smirk. "Is that your way of telling me I have a nice cock?" I whisper against her lips.

She smirks and nods her head in agreement as she continues to stroke me from base to tip. Then she leans in for a kiss, our mouths opening instantly to invite each other's tongues inside, and between Aria's hand on my dick and her mouth on mine, I'm not going to last long. I need release so fucking bad right now, it's like the air I need to survive.

I break our kiss and drop my head into the crook of her neck, and Aria allows me better access as she tilts her head slightly backward. I cup the side of her face again as I start trailing light kisses down her neck, letting my tongue slip out to lick her damp, soft skin. "I'm not going to last much longer," I pant against her skin.

She touches the side of my face with her free hand. "Come for me," she whispers. The way she says it is so innocent and genuine, it makes my control break. I feel a slow pressure build in my balls, and after a few more firm strokes, I release my hot liquid into her hand.

"*Fuck*," I grunt. My head drops back down to the crook of her neck as I ride out the waves of my orgasm through spastic jerks of my body. Aria starts to slow her pumps as I come down from my high, and I stay in the crook of her neck for the next several moments before picking my head up. When I look at Aria, she licks her lips nervously at me, and I know exactly what she's thinking because I'm thinking the same thing.

We've crossed a line we can't uncross, and neither of us know how to untangle it effectively.

We just keep staring at one another.

Looking for an answer.

A sign.

A direction to go.

Aria is the first to break our silence. "I should go wash up," she whispers as she readjusts her bra over her breasts with her clean hand.

"No, give me a second," I say. I slowly stand up straight and start to situate my boxer briefs and shorts back over my hips. When I look at Ari, she's still biting her bottom lip as she nods.

I walk into the kitchen behind the wall we're on and wet a hand towel with warm water. I walk back in front of Aria, who is in the same exact position I left her in, and I gently grab her wrist to start to wipe myself off of her palm. When I've made sure I've thoroughly cleaned her hand, she slowly releases it from mine as she looks up at me. "Thanks," Aria says in a faint voice.

I fold the hand towel and throw it on the floor for now, then grip either side of her waist with my hands. Aria leans back against the wall, her ample breasts and tight stomach on display in her white lace bra and high-waisted ruched skirt. Aria cups either side of my face, and before we know it, our mouths find each other again.

No words have to be spoken about what just transpired against the wall of this hallway, and for this single moment, we choose each other.

What a beautiful moment it is.

CHAPTER
Twenty-Nine

ARIA

Sunday, July 24, 2022

It's ten o'clock in the morning, and I'm peeking out the window to make sure Dane is nowhere in sight before I leave for my run on the boardwalk. As incredible as last night was for us, my heart is no longer in control of my emotions. Instead, my mind has seized control, and familiar feelings of guilt force my temporary happiness to crash and burn.

Once I realize the coast is clear, I quickly step out my front door, down my porch steps, and start jogging toward the boardwalk. My body is on autopilot as it moves my legs to exercise, because the only thought consuming every inch of my mind is Dane and me.

Dane and I against the wall of his hallway.

Dane and I clawing at each other for sexual relief.

It was raw, primal, and untamed.

I haven't felt that kind of passion in over a year, and my need for Dane scares me more than anything. I fell into his touch like it was second nature, and air I needed to breathe. His touch was tantalizing and dug up something that's been buried deep inside of me for so long. When I was with Dane last night, it was the first time I felt like I was freed from the prison I've been caged in for over a year, and I'd be lying if I said I didn't want more than just last night.

I do want more.

So much more.

How could something so wrong, feel so damn right at the same time? How did it happen that the first person I have intimate feelings for, turns out to be the very person I shouldn't have those feelings for at all? I know the right thing to do here is to stop this before it gets out of control. My feelings should be put to the side because the reality is, my loyalty to Kyle still matters to me. He's gone, but he's still a part of me. I refuse to betray him, and if I continue to act on my feelings with Dane, what does that show? It would show that Kyle didn't mean that much to me. Almost like he was just an obstacle in my way while he was alive, and now that he's gone, I can have who I want to have.

I feel my eyes start to swell, and I feel mentally exhausted and drained, but I keep moving my legs across the wood of the boardwalk. I start to jog faster, trying to physically escape the emotional torture I'm subjected to by life's turn of events. I stomp my feet harder on the wooden planks of the boardwalk and breathe heavier with every push forward. I start to feel the physical effects of my run, and my breaths are coming out shorter as I exert more energy. Between thoughts of Dane and I, and trying to catch my breath, I make an abrupt stop at the wooden railing of the boardwalk, hanging my forearms over it to steady myself.

I inhale and exhale with deep, intentional breaths. I keep my head and eyes trained at my feet on the boardwalk, unable to look at the scenery or people around me. It's a warm and cloudless sunny day, and I hear conversations and laughs all about. This day could not be any more beautiful when looking from the outside-in. But the truth is, my invisible shackles have reclaimed my wrists today, and it feels like I'm being taunted by the happiness around me.

When I make it back home, I'm profusely sweating from the hot summer day and my cardio. I strip my clothes off as soon as I make it to my bedroom, and I hop in the shower. As the warm water rains over me, I place two palms against the tile and just stand under the falling water, almost in a trance-like state. It feels good to be boxed in this shower and not have to face reality.

Like a small cocoon hiding me from the rest of the world.

The cloud nine I was floating on last night has officially drifted away, and I'm left haunted by feelings of shame and disappointment. But the worst part of it all is that my feelings of shame don't come from regretting last night. Instead, I feel shameful for wanting and needing Dane as much as I did.

As much as I still do.

I turn around and close my eyes as I run my hands through my drenched hair. Are these feelings I have for Dane momentary? Or do these feelings run deeper than I had planned?

Like clockwork, I hear my phone vibrate on top of my bathroom sink counter, and I push the shower curtain aside to peek at the name and number on the screen.

Ronnie.

I stretch my arm out for the phone and pick it up.

"Hey," I greet my brother.

"Hey, you busy?"

"Just showering, everything okay?" I ask.

"Yeah, I'm at the restaurant right now helping Dad with a few things. I was going to drop by in about a half hour to say hi. And also, Mom won't stop hounding me about giving you the supplies for the centerpieces," Ronnie replies.

I exhale a laugh. "Sounds about right. I'll be around, so drop by whenever," I say.

"Cool, I'll see you soon."

"See ya."

I place my phone back on the counter to get back under the running water, grateful I have something to keep my mind occupied for the rest of the day.

When I open the door to my house, Ronnie greets me with a huge cardboard box.

"Relentless doesn't even begin to cover Mom's antics back at the restaurant," Ronnie greets.

I open the door more so he can step in. "Uh oh. How many times did she remind you to bring me the materials?"

"Probably a good ten times," Ronnie replies as he walks through the foyer to the kitchen.

When he places the box on the kitchen island, I open it up to view its contents, and start to take out the wooden lanterns. "Don't you know by now that if you just do her chore the first time, she won't have to repeat herself?" I ask.

Ronnie is leaning against the counter with one palm. "This is *Mom* we're talking about."

"This is true," I say as I keep digging through the box of contents.

"So what are the centerpieces anyway?"

"Lanterns with tea light candles. Didn't really want the centerpieces to be over the top since it's not really our style, and it also goes well with the farmhouse theme of the restaurant," I say.

"They didn't have any that were pre-made?" Ronnie asks.

I shrug as I keep my eyes averted. "I thought it would be a good idea to keep myself occupied. Something I've learned the past year."

"Makes sense. I mean if you ever need to be occupied anymore, you can repaint the walls of my house. Would save me a ton of time and trouble," Ronnie jokes.

I look up to Ronnie with a smirk. "Hard pass on that."

"Worth a shot," Ronnie says as he peels himself away from the counter, and opens my fridge door, grabbing a bottle of water.

I turn around to face Ronnie. "So, anything else happen?"

After Ronnie swallows his first sip of water, he shakes his head. "Nothing worth mentioning." Ronnie takes another sip and then asks, "What's new with you?"

I shrug as I look off to the side. "Exercised today. Going to do laundry after you leave. I'll probably binge watch some trash TV."

Ronnie laughs. "My god, you and your reality television."

I point at him. "Don't knock it 'til you try it. Plus, they say highly intelligent people watch crappy shows."

"That's definitely not what they say."

"Well they should."

"Anything you need fixing around the house?" Ronnie asks.

"Not yet, thankfully. I guess that's good karma for having such a shitty year. It's about time I have it easy," I joke as I shift the lanterns in the box to make sure all the contents are there.

When Ronnie doesn't respond right away, I realize he probably thinks I'm going to spiral emotionally, but I reassure him as I turn around. "I'm trying to make a joke. Clearly it was a bad one."

Ronnie walks up to me and wraps one arm around me to pull me into him. He gives me a kiss on the top of my head as he says, "Well, if ever you need anything, you know I'm here."

"I know," I say with a grateful smile.

When Ronnie releases me, he starts to make his way out of the kitchen. "Well, I don't want to keep you from your wild night, so I'll get going."

"Thanks for stopping by," I say as I follow him to the foyer.

"You got it. I'm sure we'll talk soon," Ronnie says as he makes his way to the front door.

Once Ronnie exits my house, I start to make my way back to the kitchen, but the sound of a couple car doors, and two familiar voices makes me freeze my movements.

DANE

As I'm pulling up to the curb of my townhouse, I notice Ronnie about to get into his car that's parked outside Aria's house. That is until he notices my car slowing down the block. Part of me really wishes he didn't see me, because the last person I want to see right now is the brother of the girl whose legs I was between last night.

Last night.

If someone ever asked me the purpose of my existence, I would describe last night to them. But ironically enough, as amazing as our night was, Aria didn't spend the night, and we haven't spoken to each other all morning. I guess I could have sent a text her way, but I'm not sure what she's feeling, or what would make her most comfortable in this situation. Aria seemed so sure of us last night, but I can't help this dreadful feeling in my gut that says today's a different story.

Before I can get too wrapped up in my own thoughts, I see Ronnie approach my car, and I turn the engine off to hop out.

"Hey, what's up?" I say.

Ronnie stretches his hand out to me so we can bring each other in for a hug-handshake. "Not much, just had to drop something off for the restaurant."

I close my car door and lean my palm against the roof of my car. "Anything I can help with?"

"No, actually. Aria's determined to keep herself occupied with those centerpieces. I think we're good."

I'm a little thrown off by Ronnie's comment, not entirely sure what he means by that, and unfortunately, I can't help the slight dip in my facial expression. "Oh…" I trail off.

Ronnie shrugs with a smile. "She was just speaking in general. I wouldn't worry too much."

I try my best to brush off my concern nonchalantly, and just throw a small smile with a nod. I feel like for this scenario, the less I speak the better off I'll be.

"Listen, I don't think I've ever properly thanked you for looking out for Aria this summer. But man to man, I really appreciate it. It seems like you've really been a great friend to her, and have helped her continue to heal," Ronnie says.

Fuck me.

I'm no genius, but I'm almost positive Ronnie won't be appreciating me much longer once he finds out about Aria and me. I should own up to the truth right now. I know that. I should explain what's going on between us, but I realize it would be a whole lot easier if I knew exactly what was going on myself. Instead, I feel estranged from Aria. Like we're two strangers who didn't just make a passionate display of our feelings against a wall. It's truly a mind fuck that I want no part of, and for a split second, I feel angry. Angry that I wouldn't even know what to explain to Ronnie if I chose to do so. Shouldn't I know? The typical answer would be yes, but there are so many blurred lines and taboos written in our story, it's hard for me to see through all the gray and black of our relationship.

When I realize I haven't responded to Ronnie, I inhale before speaking up. "You never have to thank me," I say. It's the most honest answer I can think of without having to say too much, and I feel it's sufficient.

For now.

Ronnie nods in understanding and puts his hand out to me again. "Alright, well I better go. It was great catching up with you. I'm sure we'll see each other soon."

"Definitely," I say.

I can only stare at Ronnie retreating into his car and driving off as I try to sort through the pile of emotions that crash into me. When Ronnie's car is completely out of sight, I find myself walking up to Aria's front porch and knocking.

ARIA

Shit.

I really didn't want to do this now. I wait several seconds, part of me stupidly thinking that Dane will leave if I don't respond right away. But he knocks a second time, and I'm forced to take a deep breath before walking toward my front door and opening it.

When I open the door, Dane's wearing a black tank top and black basketball shorts, with a backwards snapback, seemingly home from a workout at the gym.

I swallow a nervous lump. "Hi," I say. Memories of our heated encounter last night flood into my mind as I look over the contours of his biceps that highlight his lean muscular build, and my skin starts to feel warm.

He hikes a thumb over his shoulder. "Just caught your brother."

I exhale a shaky laugh. "Yeah, Mom wouldn't let up on him dropping off some supplies to me. You know how it goes."

Dane leans a palm on the door frame. "Maybe I could assist in some way?"

"No, it's putting together centerpieces for my dad's restaurant. I couldn't bore you like that," I joke.

Dane pulls his palm away from the door frame and leans his shoulder on it while he shoves both hands in his pockets and crosses one foot in front of the other. "Well, judging by last night, I don't think you could ever bore me."

I guess I didn't expect Dane to mention last night in such a casual, nonchalant way, because as soon as his admission makes my stomach flutter, it makes my stomach turn upside down. I run a hand through my hair as I avert my gaze from his, stretching my lips into a shy smile.

"We're allowed to talk about this," Dane says.

His defensive tone activates my own defense mode, and I turn my head back to him. "Well, maybe I don't want to talk about this on my front porch where anyone can eavesdrop."

"Then where do you suggest we have this conversation? You're not exactly inviting me inside your house at the moment," Dane responds. Dane's observation makes me realize I didn't welcome him inside, almost like Dane is a stranger, and I'm treating him in a way he doesn't deserve to be treated because of my own uncertainties.

Shame rocks through me, and I know I'm going to have to face our situation head on at some point. Maybe I don't have to this second, but I know I'm running out of time. I convince myself that the least I can do is know exactly what I want to say and have answers for him when we do have this conversation.

"Dane, can we talk later?" I say just above a whisper, pleading with him with my eyes.

Dane looks at me for several seconds before nodding once. "Sure," is all he says.

He peels his shoulder off the door frame and turns around to walk down the porch steps. I stare at his back until he's out of view, and then I hear his front door close. I'm left staring out into the street, wondering if my head will be any clearer tonight than it is right now.

Unfortunately, I have a grave suspicion that it won't.

I perch my forearms on the wooden railing of the pier. "I don't know what's happening, Kyle," I whisper to myself. "But I haven't forgotten about you or the love we shared. I promise." A lone tear sneaks out, but I wipe it away as quickly as it slides down my cheek.

It's been so long since I've physically cried that I feel like I'm regressing from all the great leaps I've made this last year when I feel that stray teardrop. The harsh reality is, I can't help but feel lost in a labyrinth of emotions, struggling to find my way out and my due North.

I lick my lips as I hug my beige cardigan sweater across my body. Tears continue to build behind my eyes, and all I can do is look up to the stars. Try to find a sign that tells me what to do in this situation. My heart and brain are wrestling to have the last say, and I wonder if there will ever be a true victor of this match. The question is so simple, but the answer is so complicated.

Do I want to be with Dane?

My feelings for Dane come at a price. An expense that might be too great for me to pay back the debt, and I exhale as I lean my elbows on the wooden ledge and run my hands through my hair.

My body jerks when I feel my phone vibrate in the back pocket of my high-rise denim shorts, and when I pull it out, I notice I have a text from Kate.

> Kate: Hey, what happened last night? I meant to text you, but I got a little too drunk at Shippers and Trent had to take me home. And before you ask, no we didn't sleep together. But Trent said you and Dane left early? I wanted to make sure everything was okay.

The dreaded text.

Last night, Dane and I discussed what our little white lie would be if Trent or Kate asked why we left Shippers so early. Let alone, without a goodbye. Although we had a plan devised and I should feel prepared for this text and conversation, I don't. Instead, I stare at Kate's text in emotional disarray, and my hang-ups about Dane and I are clearer than ever.

Kate's text only reminds me of the guilt that casts a shadow over my heart that begs to shine. My heart feels like it's being held captive in my own body as it beats for Dane, and every heartbeat meant for him feels like it's being silenced a little more each time.

Until the beats for him can't be heard anymore.

Agitation claws at my soul when I think about being forced to live with a heart that beats mechanically rather than authentically. Like a machine carrying out necessary functions to keep me breathing, instead of *living*. Like the parts of my heart that beat for Dane are being dulled and pushed back on.

Finally, my thumbs type out a message to Kate.

> Me: Hey, hope you're feeling better. Everything is fine, I just wasn't feeling well so Dane took me home. Nothing to worry about. :)

I place my phone back in my pocket and prop my elbow on the railing ledge as I rest my chin in my palm. The wind laces through the loose waves of my hair as I inhale the salty air of our beach town and look and listen to the waves collide on the shoreline. Screams of excitement and laughter sound off from all angles around me, and the happiness taunts me once again.

It's so close to me, but so out of reach at the same time.

My face starts to tighten with tension, and soon enough, another lone tear glides from my eyelid and down the length of my cheek. One single tear that represents the sorrow that comes along with the weight of my world.

The weight of my past.

When do I get to walk through life without dragging the chains that have been fastened around my wrists?

I feel another vibration from the back pocket of my denim shorts, and I pull my phone out to look at Kate's response.

> Kate: Ugh, that's the worst! How are you feeling?

> Me: I'm alright now. It was just one of those random headaches that pop up out of nowhere.

I swallow as I place my phone back and rest my elbows on the ledge of the railing as I place my hands on top of my head. I'm looking at the wooden planks of the boardwalk as I submerge myself in self-condemnation. The more I lie to Kate, the worse I feel. And the worse I feel, the more I blame Dane and I for being so careless.

Because Kate is just the tip of the iceberg our ship is about to crash into, and my throat constricts as I think about my family finding out about Dane and me. The thought strangles any shred of optimism I may have possessed beforehand.

Then Kyle's blue eyes flash before me.

And I suffocate.

When I approach my house, I gasp when I see Dane sitting on the top of my porch steps, his elbows perched on his bent knees as he hangs his head down to stare at the ground.

I pause my movements momentarily and swallow a nervous lump in my throat before moving my feet toward the house again. When I'm only inches away from Dane, he doesn't bother to pick his head up to look at me, so I just break the silence.

"Hey," I say softly.

Seconds go by before he responds, and my nerves start to make my heart race with anticipation. "Where did you go?" Dane asks while still looking at the ground.

I inhale as I smooth over my fitted white short-sleeved crop top. "Out on the pier."

Still not looking up at me, Dane responds. "To go be with him?"

I furrow my brows. "I wasn't with Blake."

Finally, Dane looks up into my eyes from where he's perched on my porch steps. "I wasn't talking about Blake."

I stare at Dane in surprise. Not only am I taken aback that he's bringing up Kyle, but I'm surprised he knows exactly what's going on in my head without me having to explain it to him. Then I exhale an exhausted breath and turn my head to the side, trying to piece together my next words before looking back in Dane's direction. "You can't do this. You can't use Kyle against me."

Dane holds my gaze as he starts to slowly shake his head. Keeping his voice calm and controlled, he says, "I'm not using him against you, Ari. I just want to know that at some point, maybe I could be considered in this equation of yours."

I immediately feel offended that Dane is throwing my guilt in my face. "Well, maybe I should remind you that I'm not the only one who should feel guilty," I counter.

I seem to have struck a nerve when Dane looks away from me, then sighs as he hangs his head back down to stare at the ground. A few moments of silence linger between us before Dane starts to speak up. "I never said I didn't feel guilty," Dane confesses.

Just above a whisper, I ask, "So what's the difference?"

When Dane looks back up at me, he stares straight into my eyes. "My guilt isn't strong enough to keep me away from you."

I swallow thickly as I digest Dane's words, and just as my heart hums at his admission, it becomes torched with feelings of bitterness because he's not making this easy for me. I turn to the side as I run both hands through my hair and let out an exhausted sigh. "God, can't you understand that there are other factors to consider here? This isn't exactly easy for me."

Dane's up on his feet when I hear him speak only inches behind me, making me turn around to face him. "I understand there are other factors here. I understand that very well. But the problem is, you're not considering the one goddamn person that matters here."

"Which is who? You?" I retort.

Dane shakes his head. "No." I just stare up at him waiting for him to explain further. "You."

I exhale a breath as I stare into Dane's bold hazel eyes, not expecting him to respond the way he did. Unable to look at him anymore, I shy my eyes away by averting my gaze to the ground, and Dane takes a few steps toward me to close the distance. I hear Dane inhale before speaking just above a whisper. "When I was with you last night, everything made perfect sense at that moment in time. I didn't care about anything else but being with you. Tell me I wasn't the only one who felt that."

I feel tears threaten to leave my eyes, and my breathing becomes more ragged as I find it harder to defend my original case. I keep my gaze downward as I shake my head and play with my hands as they're interlocked with one another. I'm mentally pleading with him to not make this more serious than it has to be. Before speaking with him, I could have chalked up last night to sexual frustration and fulfilling each other's needs, but the more he expresses his feelings, the more mine rise to the surface. It dawns on me that within the last twenty-four hours, I've been trying to suppress what I'm truly feeling, because as he speaks the words he is now, it's like he's describing how I feel about him. And we're so eerily in sync with one another it chills me to my core.

"I'm not listening to this," I say as I storm off toward my porch steps. But my effort is short-lived when I feel Dane's hand on my upper arm, forcing me to face him.

"No, Ari. You're not getting off easy this time," Dane demands.

I throw my hands up in anger, forcing him to release my arm. "You can't just leave this alone, can you?"

"Yeah, I bet you would love that." I narrow my eyes at him, but Dane continues on his tangent. "Then your precious feelings wouldn't feel threatened, right?"

I let out a tiny sigh before Dane wipes a palm down his mouth as he looks off to the side, seemingly deep in thought. Then he rests both hands on his hips, still looking away from me as he says, "You know what I was thinking about today?"

I stay silent until he decides to answer his own question. "I thought about how I made you feel last night." A surge of heat rushes over my body as memories of last night flash through my mind. "It made me feel on top of the world that I could make you feel so good. After everything you've been through." Dane pauses for several seconds and then looks back to me. "But as soon as I felt that satisfaction, I felt defeated."

I inhale as I witness Dane's vulnerability. He's taking down his walls in front of me and unveiling his insecurities. "Why?" I breathe out, unable to hide my curiosity any longer.

His eyes hold mine as he swallows a nervous lump in his throat and gives the last answer I ever expected from him. "Because I know what I'm competing with," he says. "And sometimes I think that a passionate encounter like last night is all I'll ever be able to give you."

As soon as the words leave Dane's mouth, my heart breaks. Not only do I hear the pain in his voice, but I can see the hurt in the depths of his hazel eyes. I want so badly to tell Dane how incredible he makes me feel, and how alive I felt under his touch. Not just because he physically made me feel good, but it's like he put air back into my lungs last night and broke the ice that contained all my frozen emotions. Yes, Kyle was the best I've ever had, but being with Dane last night was so undeniably *different*. It felt ravenous, erratic, and *powerful*. Dane's untamed, aggressive nature contrasts so much from Kyle's gentleness, that it wouldn't ever feel like a competition between the two of them. The passion I felt with Dane is like nothing I've ever felt, and all I know is that I didn't just *want* him last night.

I needed him.

And as much as I may want to deny it, I think I still do.

As Dane confesses his rawest emotions to me, I realize that last night wasn't just pivotal for me, but for him as well, and I can no longer use Dane's sexual past as a crutch. Before, I could always fall back on the notion that Dane just wanted me sexually, and he couldn't ever give me anything more than great sex. But now? Now he's taken that crutch away, and without it, I know it's only a matter of time before I fall into him.

Literally and figuratively.

But as much as I want to pour my heart and soul out to him, my conscience is restraining me from taking the leap. "You're different," I whisper. It's the only thing I can muster up the courage to admit without sacrificing my morals.

"But do you want me? Do you want me like I want you?"

My mouth parts slightly at Dane's bold question. "It's not a simple answer."

"It's a yes or no question. If the answer is no, then I can walk away knowing there's someone out there better suited for you than me. But if the answer is yes…" Dane trails off. "If the answer is yes, then I think we have a right to be a little selfish here."

"You make it sound like we're owed this. We don't have a right," I say.

Dane turns to the side and runs his hands frustratingly through his hair. Once he lets out a sigh, he turns back to face me. "I guess that's my answer then."

I furrow my brows. "I didn't give you an answer."

Dane nods in defeat. "Yes, you did."

Anger simmers as my defensive walls shoot up into action. "Then why make this harder? Go!"

Dane's jaw clenches as he watches me start to unravel, but I keep going anyway. At this point, I understand I have nothing left to lose, and thinking about losing Dane stirs chaos within me. I ball my palms into fists, and hit Dane once in his chest, barely knocking his large figure off balance. "Just leave," I say through gritted teeth, and I look up at him as I continue on by throwing my arms aimlessly in the air. "I can handle it, alright? My past has been keeping me from any kind of happiness the last year, I think I can take one more let down. So go!"

Tears start to pool in my eyes, and my breathing becomes erratic as the rage inside me continues to build. I clench my fists and hit into Dane's chest again. "Dammit, just leave!" As soon as I get the words out, Dane grabs a hold of my fists. I try to yank them out of his grip, but he's too strong. I'm being held in place and feel myself become transparent right in front of Dane's eyes. I know I'm wearing every emotion I have on my face, and if I thought Dane was vulnerable before with his words, I'm putting him to shame right now. The tears start to fall down my cheeks of their own free will, and my chest heaves up and down from my outburst. Dane's palms release my wrists and quickly cup my face so he can wipe away my tears with his thumbs, and I lay my palms flat against his chest.

Dane places our foreheads together as he wipes the last bit of moisture under my eyes. "Stop. I won't let you shed tears over me," Dane whispers.

I curl my fingers into Dane's shirt like he's my lifeline, and the one who can make all my hurt go away. The image of Dane walking away from me strikes a dagger through my heart. Thinking about not having Dane's arms wrapped around me, and having to lock away last night as a distant memory is unbearable. There's so much more to explore with Dane, and I'd be living a shallow life if I didn't let myself experience everything I could with him.

I feel Dane press his forehead into mine as he whispers, "You can push me and tell me to leave you as many times as you want, but it's the last thing I'm going to do. You understand?"

Unable to restrain myself any longer, I nod my head and place my hand at the side of his face, pulling him in for a bruising kiss. Our moans stifle as our lips mold together, and we make out in front of my porch steps under the moonlit sky, not caring about anything else but each other's embrace.

This was the beginning of a new chapter, and even though I wasn't sure how it was going to end, I was willing to go all in for a chance at happiness.

Maybe it was selfish.

Maybe it was reckless.

But it was *freeing*.

CHAPTER
Thirty

DANE

Thursday, July 28, 2022

Aria and I agreed to go out to dinner Thursday night. I sift my fingers around my hair to make sure it's styled just enough on top, and I'm wearing a black three-quarter sleeve Henley and tan pants. I'm also sporting just enough scruff on my face, so I don't think she'll have any complaints.

When I'm ready to go, I leave my house to go to Aria's and knock on her door. I wait a few seconds before Aria opens the door, and my god does she look *beautiful*. She's wearing her long hair down in soft curls, a red spaghetti strap floral fit and flare dress, and black wedge sandals.

"Hey, I'm just about ready," she says as she walks back into her house. "I just have to put my earrings and lip gloss on." I walk in as Aria stands in front of the foyer wall mirror to put on her earrings and lip gloss. "Can I get you something to drink?" she offers.

My hands are in my pockets as I pace the small foyer, trying to relieve some of my nerves. "I'm good, thanks."

"Well that works out." Aria turns to me with a smile. "I only asked because I was trying not to seem like a horrible hostess."

I smile back at how adorable she is and walk over to her as she grabs her clutch off the foyer table. "Such a gentleman," she says as she takes my extended hand.

When we get to her door, I turn so she can exit the door first. "Something like that."

When we are both off the porch steps, I wrap my arms around her from behind as I put my face in the crook of her neck. She giggles and squirms a little, but I place my mouth to her ear and take on a serious tone. "You look beautiful," I whisper.

She stops walking and looks back at me from over her shoulder, and I think she's surprised at my serious tone in the midst of all the joking. "Thank you," she says as she swallows a lump in her throat. Eventually Aria turns her head forward, and I walk in front of her to open the passenger door of my Mustang.

Aria smiles as she gets in my car, and I walk around to my side to hop in the driver's seat. Luckily Russo's is not as crowded as it would be on a Friday or weekend, so outside seating is very much open. When we are seated at a table right next to the railing of the terrace, we have an open view of the water.

"If I knew you were going to pull out all the stops tonight, I would've asked you to have the Backstreet Boys sing live here," she jokes as she takes her seat, and places her cloth napkin in her lap.

"Yeah, totally. I hear they're what, sixty now?" I say.

She drops her jaw a little. "No. Kevin is fifty."

I roll my eyes with a smile. "I was *way* off there."

Aria shakes her head with a smile as she takes a sip of water, then looks through the menu, and I choose to do the same. "Burrata and tomato is a must, so that's happening," Ari says.

"I won't argue with that," I respond before the waiter comes over to take our drink order. Aria and I order a bottle of Cabernet to split, and a minute later our first glasses of wine are being poured for us.

"Cheers," Aria says as she holds her glass up. I clink my glass with hers and we both take a sip. "So what's your move?" Aria asks. I furrow my brows to indicate I have no idea what she's referring to. "I've always wondered what Dane Hudson's move was to pick up a girl," she confesses as she takes another sip of her wine. "So what's your move?"

"Ah," I say with a tight smile. I run a hand through my hair before responding. "Honestly, it varies from time to time, and it depends on the situation."

She's resting her chin on her palm. "Uh-huh…"

Getting the hint that she wants me to pick a specific situation, I sigh and continue on. "Let's say I see a girl at Shippers, and she doesn't have a drink in her hand, I'd probably say something like, 'Can I buy you a drink?'"

Aria rolls her eyes. "Ugh, you're no fun."

I chuckle. "What? I don't have *moves*, I just go with the flow," I say while making a swimming motion with my hand.

The waiter comes back to take our dinner orders, and we both take another sip of our wine as Aria narrows her eyes at me like she's looking intently.

I narrow my eyes back at her. "Uh oh, you have that look in your eyes."

"I was just wondering if you truly never felt a connection with any of the women you've brought home. I guess I can't fathom the idea, having been in a long-term relationship," she says.

I take a sip of my wine while keeping my eyes on her, and when I swallow, I decide to respond. "I have."

"Who?" Aria's eyes widen.

"I'm looking at her," I say.

Aria just stares back at me as her cheeks flush, and she stretches a nervous smile before looking off at the water over the terrace.

I place my forearms on the table as I interlock my hands. "Hey, I'd like to take you somewhere after this, if that's okay?" I say.

Aria turns her head to face me, and at first, she looks questioningly at me like she thinks I'm up to no good. "Sure," she says with a hesitant smile.

She's intrigued.

Our appetizer comes and then our entrees, and the conversation over dinner is light as always. We skip out on dessert, and once I pay the bill, we walk back to my car so I can take Aria where I've been dying to take her all night.

As we sit in the car, Aria is the first to speak. "My mom and dad know where you live if you are planning on disposing of my remains tonight. Just saying."

I chuckle while keeping my eyes on the road. "Man, I shouldn't have taken you to dinner then. So many witnesses know I was with you tonight." Aria giggles back, and we fall silent near the end of the drive as Aria looks intently out the window trying to figure out where we are going.

When I pull up to the Bloom Rose Garden entrance, the gazebo is lit up with white lights since it's dark out now, and there are only a few other cars here.

Perfect.

ARIA

The Bloom Rose Garden is located off the beaten path, almost like a hidden gem. When we pull up, there are only a few cars besides Dane's in sight, and I slowly get out of the car to take in the sight in front of me. The rose garden is about one green acre of land, and in the center is a lit, wooden gazebo covered in ivy. Surrounding the gazebo are six arched pathways. From an aerial view, it's as if the gazebo is the sun, and the pathways are the rays.

My lips turn up in the corner as I look back at Dane, who's walking up to me with two hands in his pockets. "How did you find this place?" I ask.

"It's amazing the things you find out when you talk to people. Or use Google," Dane says with a smirk.

I just stare up at him with a smile, in awe that Dane went out of his way to bring me to this beautiful place. Especially since I know the reason he did. Dane never fails to listen to everything I tell him and never ceases to surprise me. He's opened up a whole new world for me in just one month, and it's a month I know I'll be forever grateful for. After several moments, I turn my head to look back at the garden, and I feel Dane take my hand in his.

"Let's go," he says as he guides me through the entrance.

As we walk closer to the gazebo at the center of the garden, I look around at all the arched pathways, the colors of the roses jumping out against the stark nighttime sky. I exhale a breath as I admire the scenery all around me, my feet following Dane on their own accord. Each pathway represents a different color rose; red, pink, orange, yellow, white, green.

While walking up the red rose pathway, I stretch my arm out to touch a couple roses, needing to feel the beauty between my fingers. Once we make it to the middle of the garden, I step up into the gazebo after Dane, and walk around taking a look at all the arched pathways of color from the central point. Dane leans a shoulder against a wooden post of the gazebo as he crosses one foot in front of the other, looking like he's about to stand back and watch from afar.

"This is wonderful," I say as I continue to look out around the acre of land. I walk up to the wooden railing on the opposite side of the gazebo from where Dane is standing and stare out into the garden for a few silent moments.

"What are you thinking about?" I hear Dane ask from behind me.

I don't turn around to face him but answer his question anyway. "Did you know there is a specific meaning for each color?"

"No, I didn't know that."

I swallow as I continue to stare into the distance. "Yeah."

I hear Dane's footsteps tread closer to me, and when he reaches me, he cages me in from behind by placing his palms on the railing on either side of my hips.

Before he can say anything, I point to the red rose pathway and say, "Love and admiration." Then I point to the pink rose pathway to the right as I say, "Gratitude and appreciation."

"Fascination," I continue on when I point to the orange rose pathway to the left of the red rose pathway. "Friendship," I say as I point to the yellow rose pathway that's to the left of the orange rose pathway. "Innocence," I say as I point to the white rose pathway that's to the right of the pink one. Both of us are silent for a few moments before I turn around to face Dane. "Not the most interesting information, I know," I joke.

"I'm still listening," Dane reassures me as he looks into my eyes.

His sincere tone makes my heart beat faster, and knowing Dane is fully present in this moment with me makes my feelings for him that much more profound.

"I know you are," I whisper, reassuring him that I appreciate his attentiveness.

Dane's lips stretch into a smile as he grabs my hand and wraps his other arm around the small of my back. I place my free hand on top of his shoulder and throw my head back in soft laughter when I realize he's slowly moving us into a small circle. "Dane, we don't have music," I say.

Dane's eyes scan my face curiously. "Since when do you, the dancing queen of Crestside, need music to dance?"

I look around at a few other couples walking around the garden. "Since we easily could be the center of attention."

My head is still turned when I feel Dane's lips hover over my ear. "We own the night," he whispers. When he pulls his head back, I turn mine so I can look up into his striking green eyes. His smile has faded slightly, and he evokes a more serious emotion than before.

I inhale as I tip my lip up at the corner and release my hand from his. I wrap both my hands around his neck as he rests both palms around my waist, fully embracing this silent dance with him, and we start swaying in sync. "Just tonight?" I ask as I peer up at him.

Dane swallows thickly as he considers my question and what I'm actually asking.

Is our time together limited?

"In a perfect world, no," Dane says.

"And this isn't a perfect world," I add.

Dane averts his eyes downward as he shakes his head. "No, it isn't." I eye Dane curiously as we continue to dance in a slow circle, waiting for him to continue on. Waiting for him to give me hope.

Hope for us.

Eyes still cast downward, Dane says, "But we can chase happiness." Then he picks his head up to lock his gaze on mine. "We can chase the light."

"The roses," I say.

Dane's lips tip up into a small smile as he says, "So I've been told."

I hold Dane's eyes for several moments, speechless at this grand gesture he's made tonight. For me. If I was any bit unsure how Dane felt about us, there's no shred of uncertainty that plagues my mind now.

I lean forward to rest my cheek on Dane's shoulder, and I keep my eyes open as they trail a view of the rose garden with each step of our small dance. I'm so grateful for this chance we're being granted, not worrying about the repercussions, or how wrong or careless this may be. We're submitting to the wonder of this moment, and consuming every drop of it until the glass we're drinking from must be taken away from our lips. We're doing what we feel in our hearts, and the beauty of that outweighs all the beauty there is in the rose garden itself. I feel my arms press more firmly around Dane's, and I feel his palms sink into my lower back just the same. Like we're physically clinging onto this dance. A dance we fear is eventually going to end too soon.

I'm actually coming around to the idea that there is no song we're moving our bodies to, because we get to determine when this particular tune ends. And I'm definitely okay with having that control.

My skin starts to form goosebumps from the featherlight touch of his soft lips on my shoulder, and the way he rubs the small of my back with his thumb. I finally let my eyes close as I rest my head against Dane's shoulder, and my heart feels put back together again. I don't hear the box of rattling pieces anymore, but instead, the first beats of a new heart.

"Rebirth," I whisper.

I feel Dane pick up his head, causing me to do the same. "What?"

I gesture with my chin, tilting it upward toward the green rose pathway in the garden.

"The green rose. It means rebirth. New beginnings."

Dane looks over his shoulder to find the green rose pathway outside the gazebo, and when he turns back around, his eyes scan back and forth between my own. I can visibly see his mind retreating to a memory and piecing something together. Something he didn't understand at first, but he certainly does now. "That's why you commented on my eyes," Dane states.

"What?"

"Fourth of July," Dane starts. "You stopped and stared into my eyes. You were enamored to realize my eyes were green, and I had no clue why."

I lick my lips as I listen to Dane reminisce. Even though I don't remember what he's talking about, it feels like my own memory too because it's something we shared together. And as I stare into his eyes now, I see the color I've grown to adore so much over the past year.

Hope.

Green is the color of hope.

And it's been in front of me all along.

He's been in front of me all along.

Dane's eyes focus on my face for a few quiet moments before he speaks again. "You know the song 'The Lady in Red'?"

I eye Dane with a deadpan expression. "I'm an old soul when it comes to music. Of course I do."

Dane chuckles. "Okay, silly question."

After our chuckles die down, I look at Dane questioningly because I know there had to be a specific reason he brought that up. "Why are you asking?"

"It's the song that's been playing in my mind this entire dance."

I smirk as I respond. "That makes sense. I am wearing a red dress."

"That you are," Dane says as he trails his eyes down my body and up to my eyes again. Then he shakes his head. "But that's not the reason I was thinking of it."

"No?"

"No," Dane responds as he brings a hand up, and grazes his knuckles across my cheek as his thumb touches my bottom lip. "No matter what happens between us, I'm never going to forget the way you look tonight."

I let out the tiniest breath as his words touch my soul. He's not referring to my physical appearance. He's referring to this night together, and these memories we're creating. If only we had a time capsule to bury this moment and revisit it when times get rough for us. But I don't even think there's a need. Because the meaning of this night is strong enough to lay in our hearts forever, and I don't think it can ever be chipped away.

My eyes drop to Dane's lips, and I pull his head forward so that our lips connect in a slow, deep kiss. No amount of words will ever sum up what I'm feeling, and so my actions take the driver's seat. When I feel our lips caress each other's, and I feel Dane hug me closer to him, I feel the invisible shackles around my wrists unlock.

Maybe they're not completely off my wrists just yet, but tonight brought me hope.

Hope that I'll escape my dark room.

CHAPTER
Thirty-One

DANE

Aria and I are holding each other's hands as we walk up my porch steps, and when I open the front door, I allow her to go in first before I follow suit. Aria steps into the foyer and I close the door behind me. We both just stare at each other across the way, silently telling each other we're more than ready to take this next step, but we're also very nervous. Aria stands there so purely stunning as her wide eyes and pouty lips are begging me to make love to her, and *god do I want to.*

But something plagues my mind.

I know Aria isn't a virgin, but she hasn't had sex in over a year, and the last person she had sex with was the man she was going to marry. Am I going to measure up? I suddenly feel an immense amount of weight and pressure on my shoulders, and it unsettles me.

I guess I'm too deep in thought right now because Aria's voice cuts into the silence. "Dane, we don't have to do this if you don't want to…" Aria trails off as she plays with her hands anxiously.

Just hearing her voice and looking back at her makes my head screw on straight again, and she's the only encouragement I need. I peel myself off the front door and slowly walk toward her. I cup the side of her face with my hand, and she places her hand on top of it as she leans in to trail light kisses on my palm as she looks up to me.

My god.

I lean to trail kisses down her neck and onto her shoulder as I let my free hand slide her dress strap down. I take my hand away from her lips to slide the other strap down her shoulder, then I cup both sides of her face in my hands as I lean down to kiss her awaiting mouth. She opens her mouth instantly to invite my tongue in, and as our tongues dance, I feel her weight shift from one foot to the other. When Aria removes her wedge sandals from her feet, I reach behind her to find the zipper of her dress to slowly drag it down.

I swipe my hands over her dress straps and down her arms so that the dress slides off her, and Aria picks up her legs to step out of her dress that's pooled at her ankles. She's left in a strapless black lace bra and panties, and my dick stirs at the sight of her. Aria bites her lip when she reaches for the hem of my shirt and drags it up over my head as I lift my arms to help her. Once my shirt is on the floor, I hoist her up from behind her thighs, and Aria wraps her arms and legs around me so I can walk us upstairs to my bedroom.

When we reach my bedroom, I lay her gently on my bed, and I'm standing at the foot of the bed as our eyes are locked on each other. Aria lays with her feet flat on the comforter and knees bent. Normally, I would venture into some dirty talk right away, but I can't do that with Aria right now, so I try to think of a cleaner avenue that still drives the point home. As I start to unbuckle my belt, I notice Aria's breathing starts to pick up.

"How do you want me to take you?" I ask.

"On top of me," she whispers. I can't peel my eyes away from her body, with her perky breasts spilling out of the top of her bra, and her flat, toned stomach rising and falling with every nervous breath she takes. She's a fucking goddess in front of me, and as much as I want to ravage every inch of her body and *own* her, I know I have to take this slow and make this perfect for her.

I can't mess this up.

I can't.

Then my own breathing starts to meet her pace as our eyes lock, and I slide my pants down my legs to step out of them. When I'm left in my black boxer briefs, I climb onto the bed to settle between Aria's legs.

ARIA

My breathing is coming out erratically as Dane climbs onto the bed to settle between my legs. He's on his knees when he grabs both my thighs and drags me down to him. I gasp at the way he effortlessly and dominantly shifts me, and it makes me so incredibly turned on and nervous all at the same time. Dane lifts one of my bent knees and trails light kisses from my knee up the inside of my thigh. The contrast of the feel of his scruff against my soft skin sends my mind into a delicious spiral, and I start to tremble as he nears the apex of my thigh. But Dane pauses just before and hooks his fingers in the waistband of my panties to gradually drag them down my legs, his fingertips leaving goosebumps with each brush across my skin. I bite my lip as I move my legs to help him get my panties off, and once they're on the floor, he bends to start trailing light kisses up over my stomach, between my breasts, and up my neck.

I grab the back of his neck to bring him in for a searing kiss, and I eagerly open my mouth for Dane to massage my tongue with his own. Dane removes his lips from mine, kissing down my chin and neck until he gets to the top of my breast. He pulls down a bra cup to expose one breast and sucks my nipple into his mouth.

I gasp in response when Dane starts to swirl his tongue around the taut bud, then gently bites down on it. "Mmm," I moan, my head leaning further back into the mattress.

I feel Dane smile in victory against my breast, and then he slowly moves his lips downward over my stomach until he's hovering over my sex. Without hesitation, Dane picks up one of my thighs to drape it over his shoulder, and once I feel his tongue touch my entrance, I cry out.

He drags his tongue upward to swirl around my clit and then sucks on it slowly. I arch my back as his warm, wet tongue works my bundle of nerves, and with one thigh still draped over his shoulder, he lays his palm flat against my other thigh to spread me out more to him.

My hand goes into his hair so my fingers can thread through it as he continues eating me out, and Dane instinctively reaches for my hand to gently interlock our fingers together. Even though his mouth and tongue are touching the most private part of me, holding his hand in this moment seems like the most intimate gesture of all. It's like we're saying we're in this together, feeling the exact same emotions at the same exact time, but no words have to be spoken between us.

With each suck on my clit, my breathing becomes more inconsistent, and I squeeze his hand as my legs start to feel a little wobbly. "Dane, I need you," I breathe out.

Dane moves his lips to the inside of my thigh that's curled over his shoulder and starts to place kisses there. I can feel my juices on his lips being smeared against my skin, and it's so erotic to feel how much he pleasured me in just seconds. Dane gets up from the bed to go to his nightstand to pull a condom out and then comes back to the foot of the bed. As Dane pulls down his boxer briefs, I sit up to remove my strapless bra. We're admiring each other as we each remove our last bit of clothing, knowing we're about to give ourselves completely to the other, and my stomach knots into excitement just thinking about it.

Once he removes his underwear and I remove my bra, we stare at each other for several seconds in awe. Dane's broad shoulders, and tan, chiseled chest fuel the ache between my legs even more, and when my eyes dip to his delicious "V," I can't help but swallow the nervous lump that forms in my throat. Dane is well endowed and thick. It's been over a year since I've had sex, and I feel like I'm a virgin again as I stare at his size.

Dane notices my fear, so he climbs on the bed with one knee and reaches to cup the back of my neck, planting kisses down my throat to one of my breasts. He latches his hot mouth onto my hard nipple again and starts sucking, then flicks his tongue back and forth over it. I'm so incredibly aroused that I surrender to his touch, and I'm no longer focused on Dane's size, but concentrated on how much more I want him to do to me.

What I need him to do to me.

Dane trails kisses back up the side of my neck, and when he reaches underneath my chin he whispers, "Lay down for me."

I lay flat on my back with my knees bent, and Dane is on his knees in between my legs as he rolls the condom onto his length. I hold my breath for a moment as I watch him, knowing I'm at his full mercy and he's about to be inside me, filling me in a way I so desperately need.

It's such a rush.

Dane palms the backside of my knee to lift my foot off the bed, opening me wider for him. His other hand grips his cock to slide it over my entrance in an "up and down" motion, and the sensation of his cock gliding easily across my wet folds makes my head whirl. I gasp as he repeats the movement again, and flickers of heat go off throughout my entire body.

I ache for more of him.

As much as he'll give me.

And however much I can take.

I feel Dane position himself at my entrance, and we both stare at each other as he slowly slides inside me. Both our mouths slightly part as we look into each other's eyes, silently communicating how perfect it feels to be connected in the most intimate way we can be.

Like we've been waiting to do this.

Like we were meant to do this.

His thickness battles my tight threshold, and I have to bite my bottom lip to brace myself. I slightly wince from the initial pain as I continue to look up at him, and once he is mostly inside me, he kisses up the inside of my thigh he's holding up. After a few moments, Dane closes the little space between us and thrusts forward, and he immediately drops his forehead on my thigh. "*Fuck*," he gasps.

He remains still for several seconds, allowing me to adjust to his size, and himself to get used to the new feeling. I can feel Dane's breath tickle my thigh as his cock tauntingly expands me in a way that makes my body quiver with need. When he teasingly pulls his cock out and gently thrusts back inside, I let out a strained moan as I toss the back of my head against the soft surface beneath me. I can only arch my back to take in more of him, praying he'll put me out of my misery and take me harsher.

Another moan slips free from my throat, and I can hear the slightest groan escape his own lips. "You want more?" Dane's husky voice echoes from above me as he continues his tantalizing, rhythmic pumps.

"Mmph," I whimper, unable to form comprehensive words.

Dane brushes the pad of his thumb over my clit as he buries himself to the hilt, and my eyes flutter in delirium. "Yeah, I know this little pussy likes that," he whispers.

I contract around Dane's cock as my reserve cracks at the thrill of his change in demeanor, and an inferno ignites wildly under my skin. Blazing hot and out of control. "Please," I whisper as I place my fingertips over his thumb to try to get him to apply more pressure.

Before I know it, Dane palms the back of my thigh that he's been holding up to push it forward so I'm spread wider for him, and he leans over me with one forearm against the mattress. He thrusts deeper, keeping his pace intentionally steady, and I wrap my hands around the back of his neck to look directly up at him.

My breath comes out in shallow pants as I feel every single inch of him fill me up, deliciously stretching me with every deep pump. I bring his forehead to mine and look between our bodies as his abs flex with every upward thrust inside me, and I can feel myself get more wet at the sight of him pleasuring me. I take a hand away from behind his neck and place it on his stomach, feeling the contours of his abdomen melt against my skin, and then I snake my palm around his backside to cup his firm ass cheek.

"You like watching my cock give you what your pussy needs?" he whispers.

I slightly pick my head up against his forehead, and nod shyly.

Dane cups the side of my face with his free hand and brings his lips to mine in a molten kiss, our tongues immediately seeking the other. When he breaks our kiss, he takes his palm off my thigh to settle it between us. I remain spread out for him as I start to feel two fingers circle my clit while he pumps into me with deeper, more purposeful strokes. My body is fully exposed to Dane as he's able to fill me up completely with each thrust of his cock and work my clit. The simultaneous satisfaction Dane's giving me is making me see stars, and he's making sure I'm feeling the utmost amount of pleasure from the way he's positioned me and himself. It's like he knows exactly what my body needs, better than I do, and that thought alone is enough to make me come undone.

"Oh, god," I moan. Dane starts to hurry his thrusts as he continues to stroke my sensitive nub in an even momentum, and I start to feel a gradual pressure rise in my lower belly.

Dane grazes the tip of his nose playfully against mine. "You gonna come all over my cock for me?" Dane breathes against my lips.

"Yes," I pant. My thighs start to tighten and shake as the force builds more and more, and I know any second, he's going to be my undoing.

Dane nods his head against mine with a slight smirk. "Good girl. Just like that," he rasps in encouragement.

I'm incapable of molding a verbal response, my eyelids becoming heavy as I pant in sync with his pumps inside me and assault on my clit.

"Aria, look at me," Dane whispers. "Let me have you. All of you."

I'm finding it hard to keep my eyes open because I'm so high on rapture, but I give into his demands. Whatever he says, I'm fully submitting to. With a few more thrusts and circles around my clit, I finally explode around him as I lock my gaze on those gorgeous green hues.

I gasp as I look at him through hooded eyes, but the sensations coursing through me are so all-consuming that I finally give in and lean my head back to relish in the ecstasy. I tighten around his cock as my orgasm shatters through me, and I arch my back off the mattress, feeling every vibration of my climax as I drift off into another world.

"Fuck yes, give it to me," Dane groans. He slows his thrusts inside of me, my body spasming as the ripple effects of my orgasm send shockwaves throughout my body. Dane places his forehead to mine. "God, you're so fucking beautiful," he pants as he languidly continues to pump inside me. I rake my fingers through Dane's hair as our breaths desperately tangle together, and once I completely come down from my high, Dane starts to chase his own release. He starts picking up speed again, and it's not long until he releases himself inside me.

"*Fuck. Holy shit,*" Dane rasps as he slightly drops his head to the side. My hands lay tenderly on Dane's damp back as his body involuntarily jerks from the effects of his orgasm, feeling every jolt of pleasure I've inflicted upon him.

It's breathtaking.

I think I find his orgasm just as addicting as he found mine.

We both stay where we are as we catch our breaths, our ragged breathing filling the silence of the room for the next minute. When Dane picks his head up to look at me, we stare at each other with lazy smiles, exhausted from our lovemaking. Dane gently pulls himself out of me, and I whimper from the loss of the feeling. After discarding the condom, he turns around to lay on his side, and pulls my back against his chest as he pulls the sheets and blankets up over us. He's spooning me and kissing my shoulder from behind as I just lay my head down in complete satisfaction. Dane reaches around my neck to cup the side of my face so I can look up at him, and we just stare at each other for a few seconds. It looks like Dane wants to say something, but if he does, he holds it back. Instead, Dane grazes his nose on mine before going in for a long, tender kiss, and then we cuddle to drift off into satiated slumber.

CHAPTER
Thirty-Two

DANE

Friday, July 29, 2022

After we throw on some clothes and brush our teeth, Aria sits in my living room while I'm in the kitchen preparing coffee. Once I pour coffee grinds and water in, I place the cap back over the machine and press the start button. As the coffee starts to brew, I turn around and rest my palms behind me on the edge of the kitchen counter with my sweatpant joggers hanging low around my waist. As I look down my half naked form, I'm met with images of Aria and I in bed together last night, and my heart warms.

Last night felt *different*.

Aria wasn't just some girl I took home to have mind-blowing sex with. When it comes to her, the amazing sex is just a bonus for me. Like she's the missing puzzle piece. Like she's the answer to an unknown prayer I made a long time ago. A smirk sneaks up on me as I think about how gorgeous she looked in my arms, and how the only thing I want to do is just be in her company.

Every day.

Every hour.

Her and me.

I decide to leave the coffee brewing by itself and make my way to where Aria is. When I reach the entrance of the living room, I stop when I notice Aria standing and looking out the window behind the sectional. Her shoulder is leaned on the window frame, and her head is tilted as she looks out the window with a blank stare. She's not frowning, but she's not smiling either. I slightly furrow my brows as I watch her for several more moments, trying to make sense of her body language and figure out what's going on in her mind.

A few thoughts run through my mind, thoughts I want to voice out loud, but I chase them out as quickly as they come. Instead, I quietly turn around and head back to the kitchen to grab two coffee mugs out of the cabinet, and place them on the counter. I brace my palms on the edge of the counter as I look out the window over the kitchen sink, still immersed in my own head. I guess my greatest fear right now is Aria regretting last night, and I can't even begin to fathom how much that would absolutely destroy me.

"Hey."

I turn around to see Aria at the kitchen entryway in just my brewery t-shirt that hangs low enough to cover her ass, but high enough to show off her toned legs. Her hair is tousled to one side, and she's staring at me with a slight smirk that makes my heart flutter repeatedly.

Her effortless beauty never ceases to take my breath away.

I walk toward her and stand in front of the kitchen island, resting my palms on the counter behind me. I lean back and tilt my chin up at her as I say, "That's a good look for you."

Aria playfully raises her brows as she walks toward me. "Good enough that I can keep it?"

I squint my eyes as I tilt my head. "I didn't say that," I say teasingly.

Aria chuckles as she comes up to me and wraps her hands around the back of my neck.

I bite my lip as I lift the hem of her (my) shirt up with one hand to reveal her panties, and I knead her ass cheek in one of my palms. Aria bites her lip as she slides her palms from the back of my neck, down my pectoral muscles, and over the rippled contours of my abdomen.

"You know you can have whatever you want of mine, right?" I say.

Aria tilts her chin up so that her lips graze mine. "I think I want something of yours right now," she coos, gently biting my bottom lip as she finishes her sentence.

As much as Aria's turning me on, I feel *unsure*. I start to wonder if Aria felt the same way I did last night. If last night meant everything to her as it did to me. But what if she's just craving sex because she hasn't been intimate in so long? What if it was Kyle she was thinking about when I saw her by the window just now? Was he really the first person she thought of the morning after our first night together?

Before getting in my mind too much again, I decide to channel my thoughts into my next actions. The reality is, I can't resist Aria who's standing in my embrace half naked, but there is still a feral urge building inside me that needs to get answers to all the questions I have. It's like an itch I have to scratch even though I know when I itch it, it's only going to make the scab worse.

I have to know I'm good enough.

I have to know I stand a chance.

I have to know I can live up to what she once had.

"You gonna tell me what you were thinking about by the window?" I ask.

Aria bites her bottom lip, and I can't tell if it's her nervousness or horniness making her do it, but something snaps within me when she doesn't respond right away. I may as well use my strengths to my advantage to make me the focal point of her thoughts, because if she's not going to think about me of her own will, I'm going to make sure I'm the only one on her mind right now.

I take both my hands to bunch up the hem of the t-shirt she's wearing, and lightly trace my fingertips back and forth along the waistline of her panties. "If you don't want to talk, maybe you should just tell me what you want," I taunt.

"You," she whispers as her fingers curl into my chest.

I slowly bend down and hoist her up from behind her thighs. Aria gasps as she wraps her hands around my neck, and I turn to sit her on the edge of the kitchen island counter.

I peel her hands from around my neck and bring them around my waist. When I cup one side of her face, I bring her lips to me for a deep and sensual kiss. Aria moans against my lips as our tongues seek each other, and then I hook both my hands into either side of her panties.

I break our kiss as I start to slide her panties down her legs. "Take your shirt off," I rasp.

Aria's hands go to the hem of her shirt to lift it over her head, exposing her full, ample breasts, and I toss her panties on the floor right after she completely discards her shirt. My cock stiffens painfully against my boxer briefs at the sight of Aria completely naked on top of my island counter, and the last thing I want to be is a gentleman right now.

I take Aria's chin between my thumb and forefinger, bringing her in for a few light kisses, and then I pull back just enough to graze my nose against hers. "Spread these legs for me," I whisper.

Aria exhales a breath against my lips, and I can tell by her timid movements she wasn't expecting my dirty talk, but she's turned on, nonetheless. Aria leans back on her palms and timidly slides her knees further apart, not fully committing to what I just requested. I tighten my jaw as I hold her gaze and palm the backs of her knees up to plant her feet flat on the edge of the counter, and Aria's eyes widen in apprehension as I spread her out. I rest my hands at her knees to spread them open for me, and without any warning, I lower myself to one knee, and just feast on her.

"Oh, god!" Aria cries out as she throws her head back.

I attack her clit, wanting to bring her to an orgasm quickly, so I can bring her to another one when I'm inside her after. I suck deeply, making sure to alternate my suction with flicking her sweet nub back and forth with my tongue.

I feel Aria arch her back as she whimpers, and I drag my tongue down to her entrance, thrusting in and out a few times, before gliding my tongue back up to assault her clit. I'm pulling moan after moan from her, and every pleasured sound drives me fucking wild.

Aria runs both hands through my hair to get my attention. "Dane, stop. I'm gon-"

Immediately, I rip her hands off my head and Aria submits to the pleasure as she leans back again on her palms. I know she wants me inside her, but I want to make her come more than once and in more than one way. My need to claim her body in any way I can is blurring everything else around me.

I feel Aria's legs start to shake under my hands, and I know she's about to shatter all over my tongue. I increase the suction on her clit and give it a few quick lashes with my tongue until she gifts my starving mouth what it wants.

"Oh, god! Yes! Yes!" Aria cries out as her body trembles over and over again, absorbing every jolt of pleasure. When her body goes limp, I tilt my head so I can look up at her from the side and start to slowly lick her clit again. My hands are still keeping Aria's knees spread, and Aria's body jolts at the hypersensitivity of the feel of my tongue.

I smirk deviously as I move my lips to kiss the inside of her thigh and drag her feet off the edge of the counter so her legs can dangle. When I stand up, I gently push on Aria's chest so she's lying with her back against the granite, then hook her right leg over my shoulder. I tug the waistband of my sweatpants and boxer briefs down my thighs, then guide the tip of my dick to her slick entrance.

"Do you think we need something?" I ask, but my question is teasing as I slowly trail the bare head of my cock up and down her entrance.

Aria swallows thickly before shaking her head. "I want to feel you," she whispers.

I hold her gaze as I rest the tip of my cock inside her, then hook my forearm under her left leg. I bite my bottom lip as I slap the side of her upper thigh, then knead the skin there in my large palm.

"You want a gentleman, Aria?" I ask tauntingly. "Or should I show you just how much this pussy was made for me?"

"Show me," she breathes.

I set my jaw and in one swift movement, I thrust into her all the way. Aria cries out, and then my cock is pumping into her hot and fast. "Play with that clit, let's go," I rasp.

Aria doesn't hesitate to reach two fingers down and circle them around her clit. "Oh, god," Aria whimpers as she succumbs to me, tilting her head back and arching her back off the counter.

It's such a blatant contrast from how we made love last night.

Carnal.

But there's still such beauty in the way we need each other because it's *us*.

Two people who were living in dimness, but together, our lights shine brighter.

"Come on, you can take it. Show me you can handle it," I breathe.

Aria looks back at me through hooded eyes and parted lips as I feel her continue to play with herself, her fingertips brushing my cock every now and then in frantic motions. Shallow breaths escape her plump lips as I thrust into her, and I never let up on my movements.

Needing to know we're one and the same.

Needing to know we belong together.

Needing to know she's *mine*.

Aria gasps as she lazily rests her hand at the top of her head and continues to rub herself. My thrusts are fervent and deep, and after a few more pumps into her, I feel Aria's velvety walls clamp down on me, and her lower abdomen start to convulse. Aria throws her head back as she cries out, arching her back off the counter. She's shaking uncontrollably underneath my palms at her legs as her orgasm erupts through her, and her tremors set my heart on fire.

As Aria gradually comes down from her high, I let her leg down from my shoulder, and lean over her to take her lips in mine, and Aria instantly grabs the sides of my face to return my kiss hungrily. "I can't get enough of you," Aria whispers against my lips.

"Good. Because I'm nowhere near done with you," I whisper.

I snake my free arm around Aria to sit her up again at the edge of the counter, and I pump my cock inside of her to chase my own release. Aria pulls my lips for a molten kiss, refueling the pace of my thrusts into her, and it's only a few moments until I come unraveled too.

"*God, yes,*" I breathe out against her lips. I feel my body stiffen and jerk against her as I spill myself inside her. Aria's lips gently place a kiss to my forehead as I writhe under her touch, and I return her tender gesture by placing my hand over one of her wrists, letting her know I'm *in* this moment with her.

Once I'm fully spent, her hands are still wrapped around my neck as I slowly ease myself out of her, and my fingertips lightly trace a line from her wrist to her elbow, feeling goosebumps forming on her skin from the contact.

After several moments, Aria's voice breaks through the silence. "The Ferris wheel."

"What?" I ask as I look down at her.

Aria inhales and explains herself. "I'm not going to lie to you. I had a lot on my mind this morning."

I pause as I register the crushing weight of her words that feel like they're flattening my heart. She's admitting what I hoped wasn't true when I saw her look out my living room window, and I try my best to suppress the rising frustration building up within me. I think Aria senses the tension in my body, and so she brings one hand from the back of my neck to cup the side of my face, and the other to lightly brush a few slick strands of hair off my forehead.

"But I thought about that night on the Ferris wheel. When you held my hand and made me feel safe with you, even though I was a ball of nerves that night," Aria whispers. I swallow a lump in my throat as I hold Aria's gaze and wait for her to continue. "That's exactly how you made me feel last night. Safe and protected. And when you held my hand last night during such an intimate moment between us, I thought about how we held hands that night on the ride. It was the start of *everything*." The walls around my heart start to recede downward. "Maybe our story was written in darkness, but it's being told through rays of light. No matter how complicated things are, those rays of light are the scenes of our story that won't ever leave my heart."

I swallow as I look at Aria in awe, struck speechless. When I hold her brown eyes, I see streaks of hope, adoration, and desire. The feelings I have for Aria are reflected in her own eyes, and it's like our souls are sewing together to become one. Whatever tiny reservations I had before are erased with Aria's words, and unable to resist any longer, I cup the side of her cheek to sear my lips to hers.

Damn, what a morning this was.

Later that night, Kate and Trent are meeting Aria and I for drinks at Shippers. Aria and I already discussed that we need to be conscious of what we say and how we say it so there are no suspicious flags raised. We know that eventually we will have to start telling people, but we aren't quite ready to do that just yet.

"So can we all keep the claws away tonight?" Trent jokes before taking a sip of his beer at the table we're all sitting at. Aria and I are sitting across from Kate and Trent, and we're making an effort to keep our distance in our chairs, so we don't inadvertently touch each other in an affectionate way.

"Sounds great," Aria says as she throws a thumbs up and takes a sip of her drink.

Kate shrugs as she directs her gaze at me. "I will if Dane apologizes for being a complete asshole last week."

I slightly roll my eyes. "Kate, I'm sorry for being an asshole. Are we done with that now?"

Kate throws me a face.

Aria shakes her head as she cuts in. "Okay, let's just change the subject."

Kate jumps in. "Great! Ari, I see two *hot* guys at the bar that we ought to be mingling with right now." Kate points in the direction she wants Aria to look.

Aria's smile drops as she looks over to where Kate is pointing and starts to scrunch her face. "I don't know, I'm not really in the mood to pick up a guy tonight."

Kate's eyebrows furrow. "Were you not looking at the guys I was looking at?"

Aria shrugs nonchalantly. "I was, I just don't feel like talking with random guys right now."

I'm inwardly smiling in victory as I put the rim of my beer glass up to my lips. "Kate, if you're so interested, why don't you just go talk to them? We'll provide you with all the moral support from a distance."

Kate narrows her eyes at me. "Because it's more fun when I'm hitting on guys with Ari."

Trent chimes in now. "I gotta say, Kate does have a point. It's nice to have the wingman or wingwoman around."

"Oh, god," I say.

"Speaking of hot people, Shippers is looking filled with some options tonight," Trent says as he nods over to a group of women at another table and takes a sip of his beer.

I take a sip of my beer to hold off on responding because I have to think of a way to answer Trent without acting weird about it. I decide to just go with short and sweet as I shrug one shoulder. "Nothing I haven't seen before," I say.

Kate finishes her drink off, then stands up from her chair. "Okay, well, I'm going to hit on some hot guys at the bar while all of you continue to talk in circles."

Aria lets out a small laugh as she rests her chin in her hand over the table. "Well, now I have some great entertainment for the night."

I smile, and then Trent is the next to speak. "So you two left Kate and I high and dry last weekend."

Trent's voice is weaved with a hint of accusation, and it catches me off guard. I peek over at Aria, and she's just staring at Trent at a loss for words. I think she's taken aback that he's even mentioning anything, and so am I to be honest. Between our heated argument and the rising tension last week, I guess Aria and I were sloppier than we even considered. But maybe I'm overanalyzing this. Maybe Trent's just being a concerned friend right now.

The last thing I want is more weight to be placed on Aria's shoulders, so I decide to respond for both of us. "Yeah, Ari wasn't feeling well, so I drove her home, and Ari already explained this to Kate."

Trent takes a sip of his beer before continuing. "Well it would have been nice if you two said something beforehand."

"Okay, I should have said something. Is that all?" I say.

"I don't know. You tell me," Trent says.

My wise-ass self kicks into high gear as I let out a chuckle and run a hand through my hair. "If you have a question, Trent, maybe you should just ask it."

"Or maybe you guys can start telling me what's really going on," Trent says before looking over at Aria. "Ari, would you like to jump in at some point?"

I immediately take the burden off her. "Hey, you don't need to get snippy with her. You're annoyed with me right now, so have it out with me."

Trent lets out a frustrated sigh as he looks off to the side, then looks between Ari and me. "So my gut feeling is right."

I lick my lips as I look downward for a second, and I'm about to say something when Kate comes back over to our table with the two guys from the bar.

"Hey, guys! Charlie and Luke, this is Aria, the girl I was just telling you about. Isn't she gorgeous?" Kate says with a smile and wink.

It's evident in Aria's face she's going through the same emotional whiplash I am, but still throws a reluctant smile their way. I feel my blood start to simmer knowing Kate is trying to hook Aria up with a guy right in front of my face, but there isn't a single, damn thing I can do about it. My hands are tied behind my back, and I know I have to keep my cool before this night turns into utter chaos.

"I'm sorry, I'm just going to go to the bathroom for a quick second," Aria says as she gets up from her chair and beelines it to the back of Shippers.

I'm left sitting in my chair with my elbow on the table and two fingers on my forehead, trying to find the right way out of this situation. Kate points to each of us as she introduces our names to Charlie and Luke. "This is Trent and Dane." Trent says hello and I just throw a tight-lipped smile because I don't feel a need to say hello. They're lucky they're even getting an acknowledgement from me.

Too frustrated with the given circumstances, I get up so I can go to the bathroom area and check on Aria, but Trent stands up at the same time and pulls me aside. "Look, man, I don't know how to feel about this yet, but this can get real messy for you and Aria. I mean, do you honestly know what you're getting yourself into?"

I swallow a nervous lump before responding. "Not really, but I guess I'll find out," I admit, and then I walk away to go find Aria.

Just as I'm walking in the bathroom hallway, Aria is exiting the women's bathroom. We lock eyes, and then I walk up to her to grab her hand to lead her outside. We walk through the crowd of people at the entrance of Shippers, making our way to the side of the building, and Aria's hands are over her face as she sighs. "We shouldn't have come here."

I'm leaning one shoulder on the side of the building as one leg is crossed in front of the other, and I'm facing her as I talk. "Ari, what does it matter if it was now or a month from now?"

"This guilt is exhausting me," she breathes.

"I know," I whisper, but then I shake my head as I sigh and look up toward the nighttime stars. "I've been so wrapped up in us I didn't even think about how our quick exit the other night may have raised a red flag."

Aria leans further back into the brick wall as she crosses her arms over her chest. "Me either. It was stupid," she whispers.

"Good to know where you stand," I remark sarcastically.

Aria turns her head back to me as she narrows her eyes. "Don't do this. Don't twist my words to feed your insecurities."

"Well, give me a choice then. Your emotions are like a ping-pong ball, it's a little hard to keep up," I retort.

Aria exhales as she puts her fingers on her forehead and looks downward. "Dane, you know what I meant when I said it was stupid."

I place a palm flat against the brick wall as I stand up straighter. "It was stupid. But that stupid decision led me to one of the best nights of my entire life."

Aria picks her head up to look at me, and when her eyes lock on mine, I can see her doubt lifting. "I feel the same way," she whispers.

I see her eyes glisten, like tears are begging to leave them, and I walk over to pull her in for a hug. I cross my arms around her shoulders as I kiss the top of her head, and she slides her palms up my back to accept my embrace. The scent of her strawberry shampoo overwhelms my senses, and I feel at peace having her in my arms. I can feel the tension slowly leave our bodies as we hold each other, and it's such a tragedy we haven't been doing this our whole lives. Being with Aria is so natural, and it's the sum of everything. It's like all the roads of my life have led me to this destination, and every bump and dip in them was worth it.

After getting ourselves together, we make our way back into Shippers to catch up with Kate and Trent at our table. Charlie and Luke have now occupied seats at our table as well, so Luke is next to Kate across from us, and Charlie is sitting right next to Aria on our side of the table.

Great.

"So, Aria, Charlie was just telling me he's a teacher too," Kate says with suggestive eyes.

Aria looks at Charlie as she takes her seat. "Where do you teach?"

I take a sip of my beer before I say something really inappropriate, and just let her converse. I know Aria doesn't have a mean bone in her body, and she's just going through the motions of being a civil acquaintance.

"Tannerville School District. I teach Social Studies. You?" Charlie replies.

Aria points to him quickly. "Oh, I have a college friend who works there. Gina Reyes?"

"Yes! She teaches Math. I'm assuming you're a math person too?" Charlie says with a smile.

My god, gag me.

I continue to take generous sips of my beer in hopes we can get the hell out of here soon, because my patience is wearing thin as every tortuous minute passes.

"Guilty," Aria admits with a friendly smile.

"So Kate tells me you guys like to take it to the dance floor from time to time. I could show you a good time on the dance floor later if you'd like. I've got some moves of my own," Charlie says as he throws Aria a playful smile.

Okay, we're done here.

"Hey, Charlie?" I ask.

He looks over at me. "Yeah?"

"We both know you couldn't show her a good time if you tried, so please stop talking," I say and then take a sip of my beer.

Kate shouts. "Dane!"

"You know what, we appreciate meeting you guys, but it's time for you both to go," Trent says as he gets up from the table. After a few exchanged puzzled looks between everyone at the table, Charlie and Luke understand they've overstayed their welcome, and leave the table with their drinks.

Kate's jaw is clenched tight as she points to me. "You're going to tell me why you have such a huge stick up your ass lately, Dane!"

"Dane and I have been seeing each other," Aria cuts in.

An umbrella of silence instantly encases the four of us, and all of our eyes go directly to Aria. Every single noise in the dive bar drowns out, and every single movement in our line of vision is blurred. Aria's playing nervously with her hands as her eyes are averted from all of our gazes, and none of us utter a single word or move an inch.

Finally, Aria takes a nervous gulp before looking at Kate and Trent. "We've been *with* each other. No one else knows."

Kate's jaw drops while Trent just sits there and takes it all in. I shift so my elbows are on the table and my hands are interlocked in front of my lips as I stare blankly in front of me.

"Ari, how could you?" Kate whispers.

I instantly cut my eyes to Kate, jaw tense. "That's not fair, Kate."

Kate lets out a fake chuckle. "Fair? How could you talk about what's fair? Kyle was your best friend!" Kate stands up. "This is why you two left early last week, isn't it?"

Trent wraps his hand around Kate's wrist. "Calm down."

"No," Kate says as she yanks her wrist out of Trent's grasp, and looks between Kate and me. "So the both of you have just been sneaking behind everyone's backs, fucking each other with no regard for anything else?"

I hold Kate's eyes. "That's not how this is."

Kate narrows her eyes in disdain. "I'm so disgusted with you two. I can't even look at either of you right now." Kate storms off, and we're left in dreadful silence once again.

Aria has one hand over her face, and she looks like she's trying to hold back tears as she closes her eyes tightly. My eyes are trained on Kate's now empty chair, refusing to make eye contact with Trent, and I just lazily brush my thumbs against my bottom lip as I attempt to organize what the hell just happened.

"She'll come around," Trent says, and then pauses before speaking in a low voice. "But you have to understand, this is a big pill for people to swallow. You two need to start talking about what you want out of this, before both of you get really hurt."

I inhale a deep breath and hang my head with my hands on top of it as I exhale.

"I think it's best if we call it a night," I say, and then lift my head back up to Trent. Trent responds by giving me an understanding nod, and then we all head out of the bar.

CHAPTER
Thirty-Three

DANE

Once Aria and I are on the road in my Mustang, she's the first to speak. "This is how it's going to be with everyone, isn't it?" she says.

I have one hand on the wheel as my opposite elbow is propped on the windowsill and my fingers are on my lips in contemplation. "You don't know that, Ari." I say the words, but I'm not sure if I fully believe them.

"It's not fair," she continues in a whisper.

I'm at a loss for words because I don't have any words to provide her solace right now. In an attempt to console her, I grab Aria's hand across the center console and interlock our fingers together. "Maybe we should take a break from all this tonight. I'll understand," I say as I keep my eyes on the road.

Aria rests her elbow on the door of the car as she rests her palm on her head. "No. I'm tired of listening to my head." I glance over at Aria, surprised yet so elated by her response. She peeks over to me and says, "I don't want to go home."

I tip my lips up in the corner and turn my head to put my eyes back on the road. "Feel like seeing some stars again?"

When I peek a glance over at Aria, I see her mouth stretch into a genuine smile as she says, "Sure."

She knows exactly where I'm taking her.

As my tires roll over the gravel of Crestside Landing, I take a quick look around to see that no one else is here. When I park and turn off the engine, Aria opens her door to get out of the car, and I follow suit after I pop the trunk open. I go straight to the back of my car to retrieve a blanket and bring it over to the hood of the car.

"What's that?" Aria asks.

"Ari, I know you teach math and can forget other pieces of knowledge, but this would be a blanket."

She rolls her eyes as she smirks at me. "I meant to ask if you've been keeping that specifically for a night like tonight."

I shrug as I start to unfold the red flannel blanket and lay it out flat on top of the hood of my car. "I hoped for it."

Aria smiles as she pulls the side of the blanket that's spread out toward her and helps stretch it across the hood. "No other women better have been wrapped in this blanket."

I look her in the eyes and gesture an "X" across my chest with my finger. "Cross my heart."

Aria smiles back as she walks around the hood to meet me where I'm standing and wraps her hands behind my neck. I bend my head down to kiss her, but as soon as our lips meet, I grab the backs of her thighs and sit her on the top of the blanket on the hood of my car.

Aria bites her lip as she scoots herself back until she's sitting up against the windshield, and I hop up to sit beside her. I bend one knee and rest my elbow on it while my other bent leg is tucked sideways underneath.

"Why did you tell the truth?" I ask as I turn my head to look up at Aria, who's sitting straighter than I am.

Aria inhales as she looks out at the water in front of us, and she slowly shakes her head as she prepares her words carefully. "As fearful as I was of Trent and Kate finding out, I was so angry." My brows furrow slightly as I look at her. "It made me so angry to realize I'd never be able to fully enjoy my happiness because of other people's opinions." Aria shrugs. "I guess I just wanted to take some control back."

"How do you feel now?" I ask.

Aria stays quiet for a few seconds before responding. "Like a weight has been lifted. But-"

"There's still more to go." I finish her sentence for her.

"Yeah," she whispers.

I turn my head as I wipe a palm down my mouth, trying to think of how to proceed with this conversation. I can read the subtext she's giving me, and I almost wish I wasn't that intuitive with her. It seems like the more I can read her mind, the less I want to know. On the other hand, maybe now is the time to confront my fears head on. Maybe if I get her to open up to me, I can feel more comfortable with the complexity of our situation, and it'll make us that much stronger.

Or maybe it won't, and maybe it'll make me feel even less secure than I already do.

But here goes nothing.

"Sometimes I look at you, and I can't tell what you're thinking. It's the worst unknown," I ask as I stare out in front of me.

Aria looks between us and places her hand on my thigh. When she gets up on her knees, I shift so Aria can straddle my hips, and I tentatively grab her hips as she rests her palms on my shoulders. Aria leans her forehead against mine as she whispers, "Let me help ease your mind."

I forget what I even wanted to talk about when Aria suggestively grinds against the growing erection underneath my jeans as she undoes the buttons of my button down. When she reaches the button at my hem, her elegant hands slide under the collar to drag the shirt off my broad shoulders and rest it on my biceps. Aria bites her bottom lip as she visually drinks my chest and stomach in, and my heart rate picks up as blood rushes to my groin.

When I feel her soft palms press against my bare chest, I breathe against her lips. "Ari, wait."

Aria furrows her brows as she peels her forehead from mine. "What's wrong?"

I swallow thickly. "Can we just talk for a minute?"

Aria slides her palms down my upper body. "I think we've done enough talking for tonight," she whispers.

I lick my lips as Aria's touch becomes harder to ignore, but I try to stay focused. "We haven't," I rasp. Aria looks down and reaches for the belt buckle of my jeans, and I immediately grab Aria's wrists to halt her movements. "I'm talking to you," I say with more assertion.

When Aria looks up at me, her eyes are laced with a blend of sadness and lust. "I need you," she whispers.

"You need my body," I challenge.

Aria bites her lip nervously as she looks off to the side. "For so long, I've felt like I've been suffocating. Like I've been chained down in an emotional prison. And after everything that happened tonight, I feel like my shackles have been wound tighter." Aria turns her head back to look at me. "When I'm with you, I feel *free*."

I guess my grip on her wrist loosens because Aria slides her palms up over my stomach and chest until they land on my pectoral muscles. Then Aria looks up at me as her fingertips trace the flames and ashes tattooed on my right pec. "When I'm with you, I feel like I can rise from my own ashes. Like I can be a Phoenix," she whispers as her eyes darken with a mission.

My emotional reserve breaks as she clings to me for salvation.

I grab the side of Aria's face and pull her lips to mine in a bruising kiss, my tongue darting into her mouth to lap the words she just uttered to me.

Words that give me new meaning in this life.

Purpose.

My fingers coil tightly in her hair at the back of her head, and I yank her hair just enough to expose the length of her neck. I'm kissing and softly biting a trail down her tender skin, grazing over the sensitive flesh with my teeth, making her gasp at the sensation. "Take off your underwear," I rasp against her neck.

My hand drops from her face as Aria raises her hips off me so she can slide her panties down to her knees. I use both hands to release my belt strap from the buckle and start to unzip my jeans as she frees each leg from her underwear. I slide my jeans and boxer briefs just low enough to release my aching cock, and Aria resumes her straddling position over me.

I keep one hand at the base of my dick as she bunches her floral mini skirt up, and when I guide myself to her slick entrance, Aria wastes no time easing down my cock in one swift movement.

"*Fuck,*" I hiss as I drop my forehead against her chest.

Aria's hands wrap around my neck, and she starts to slowly rock her hips in a back-and-forth motion. I curl my fingers into the v-neckline of her black crop tank top and pull the fabric down to expose her breast to suck her nipple into my mouth.

"Mmm, yes," Aria moans as she continues to work her hips over me in a steady rhythm.

But her moan doesn't make me feel satisfied.

It makes me resentful.

Bitter.

As much as I want to physically please her, and as much as she's plea-suring me, I become more aware that she's using me for a release. I want Aria to confront what exactly this is between us and stop hiding behind her sexual appetite. I want to crack the stone wall she's built around her heart and start removing each dense stone one by one.

Until her heart is bared to me.

I cover her breast back up and dig my fingers into her hips as I look up at her. "If you want to get off, you better ride my dick like it's the last thing you're gonna do," I rasp.

Aria bites her lip as she tightens her fingers in my hair and continues rocking her hips back and forth over my dick in a gradual motion. She takes one hand from the back of my neck and places it on her clit to start rubbing herself to ecstasy.

I grab her wrist and place her hand at her side. "No."

"Dane," Aria whimpers.

Still holding her hand at her side, I cup the side of her face to bring our foreheads together. "You wanted my cock so bad, let's see how well you can use it," I whisper against her lips.

Aria holds my eyes as she releases her wrist from my grasp and leans back to place both her palms behind her on the top of my thighs to balance herself. She slightly arches her back at a better angle and starts moving her hips in an upward scooping motion.

Fuck me.

I place my palms on the tops of her thighs, kneading the skin there to control my urge to lay her down on the hood of my car, and fuck her until she's screaming my name over and over. I take one hand to bunch up her skirt so I can watch her encompass me in her warmth, and I have to bite my own lip when I see her bare pussy leave a shiny, glistening trail along my cock.

Then I feel Aria's hand hover against the back of mine at her skirt. "Dane, please. I need to feel you," Aria whispers.

I grip her hips to bring her forward, halting her movements, and Aria gasps as she steadies her palms on my shoulders. "By the looks of it, you're feeling me nice and deep, so what else do you need?"

"I want it to feel like every time you've been inside of me," she breathes desperately.

"How did it feel?" I ask as I look up into her eyes.

Aria closes her eyes and gently nudges her forehead with mine. "Like you were making love to me," she whispers.

Her words revive me.

I feel my boiling anger lower to a simmer as we hold each other's gaze. I needed this validation more than I needed air, and it feels like my strength has been renewed inside of me. Even if it's temporary, I know for certain that at this moment, I'm the only person she wants.

I'm the only one she *needs*.

I slide my palms from her hips to her ass cheeks under her skirt and start to gently push her back and forth over me. Aria gasps as her forehead rests against mine, and I feel her fingers tighten in my hair at the back of my head. I tilt my head up to meet her lips, and Aria greedily takes my invitation as our mouths mold together, breaths mingling in between kisses as our pleasure climbs higher and higher.

I move my hands back up to Aria's hips, grasping her firmly and rocking her at a faster pace on top of me. I'm moving her feverishly, needing to make her come, and chasing my own climax at the same time. Following my lead, Aria starts working her hips hurriedly, and it's like we're racing against time.

Even though we aren't saying it, we both know our time together is fragile and our circumstances are far from perfect. There are so many unknowns to tackle when we come out of this trance we're in, but we're seizing the moment. We know what we feel in our hearts, and if we get to express our feelings for a single moment as beautiful as this one, that could be enough for us.

Because our story isn't being written on crisp, white paper.

No.

Our story is written on crumpled pieces of paper with stains.

Our story was tainted before it was written.

Our bodies move frantically, and our lips hover against one another in desperate pants, trying to fill oxygen into each other's lungs with each thrilling connection of our bodies. Our movements are a mixture of *need* and *hope*. Need to let go of everything that holds us back and hope that we can come out of this alive. We're trying to take back the pen and re-write this ending. It's like we're the characters who have to endure the journey and fate that's already been planned for us. Because sadly enough, we aren't the authors of this story.

Our story was written for us.

"Come for me. I need to see you come," I breathe against her lips as my palms snake around to her ass, massaging her soft skin as I rock her to ecstasy.

"Come with me," she says breathlessly.

I peel my forehead from Aria's just enough to look up into her eyes, and time freezes. I see Aria's beautiful brown eyes staring back into mine as her dark, loose waves cascade over one shoulder, exposing her long, elegant neck on the other side. Above her, I see the indigo, starlit sky, like a halo around her form.

I take one of her hands from the back of my neck and place it over my heart, resting my own on top of hers. Then I cup the side of her face with my other hand, surrendering complete control to her. Aria pants against my lips as she moves her hips on her own accord, and I nod my head in encouragement as I breathe against her lips. "That's it, take what you want from me. Ride my cock like you own every fucking inch of it."

"Dane," Aria pants. I feel Aria's legs start to quiver around me, and her whole body tightens with her pending orgasm, and I know she's going to crumble any second.

I press my palm into her hand at my heart. "Tell me I stand a chance," I rasp.

Aria nods her head as her shallow breaths knot with my own. "Yes," she chants as her hips move faster, and I pull her forehead to mine as a slow rising pressure starts to brew within me.

"Break us, Aria. Break us so we can assemble the pieces right this time," I whisper. I feel her hand snake from around the back of my neck to cup the side of my face, and her gentle touch unravels the both of us as she tightens around me, and I pour myself into her.

All of me.

She has a hold of my heart, and it's like I'm giving it to her in this single, precious moment. We're looking into each other's eyes as our bodies jerk in-step with one another. Like two bodies molding into one, feeling every crevice of the same exact feeling, at the same precise second.

It's complete and utter oblivion.

We're making love to each other.

As Aria and I control our breathing, I pull her face down to catch her lips on mine. Our tongues dance around each other, and we're saying everything that isn't being said with our lips and tongues. It almost feels like we'll never be close enough to each other, no matter how much our lips are closely pressed together. We're each other's lifeline now, and there is no other way to survive in this world without the other.

It's us against the world.

CHAPTER
Thirty-Four

ARIA

Saturday, July 30, 2022

The next morning, Dane and I go for a jog along the boardwalk. Something unspoken passed between us last night, and our eyes said a million words to each other in those sacred, blissful moments. But no words were actually spoken.

Does Dane love me?

If he did, wouldn't he have said it?

For me, I'm hesitant to take that next step and officially say or acknowledge that I love somebody. It's one thing to have sex after Kyle, but loving someone after Kyle?

Do I love Dane?

"Hey, I gotta say, you've become a much better sport about running," Dane pants out.

"Practice makes perfect, right?" I pant out in response.

We jog the last quarter mile, and then we stop to catch our breath. I'm bent over with my hands on my knees, while Dane hangs over the wooden railing of the boardwalk, looking out at the beach.

I adjust my black spandex shorts and stand upright so I can place my hands on my hips. "You think you can carry me back?" I ask.

Dane turns around. "Oh, yes, after a two-mile run I always look forward to carrying one-hundred-twenty pound people on my back."

I shrug. "Don't knock it 'til you try it. It could be a blast, you never know."

Dane walks toward me. "I think someone just wants me to get handsy," he says as he scoops me up like a groom would carry his bride, and he starts to playfully nip at my shoulders.

"Okay, okay! Never mind!" I say through a fit of giggles.

Dane smiles as he lets me down, and when I finally get my bearings on steady feet, we walk alongside one another to make it back to our houses.

"So when is your dad's restaurant officially opening?" Dane asks.

"Two weeks from tomorrow, actually. Isn't that crazy?" I respond.

"Damn, I feel like you just told me the news yesterday," Dane says.

I look up at him. "Well, you obviously need to come for the opening. My family wouldn't want to miss you there."

Dane swallows a nervous lump in his throat like I just said something wrong. And then I realize he's probably thinking how much my family would dislike him after they find out about us. "When are you planning on telling them?" Dane asks.

I answer truthfully. "To be honest, I don't know."

Dane continues to look forward but doesn't say anything, and as the silence between us commences, the tension thickens. I place my hand on Dane's arm and stop him so we can actually face each other and have a real conversation. "This isn't easy for me, Dane. Telling Kate and Trent wasn't a walk in the park, imagine how my family is going to react." I start to shake my head before elaborating further. "But this has *nothing* to do with you, or my feelings for you."

"I'd just like to know that it's somewhere on your radar, Aria."

I narrow my eyes at him. "I never said it wasn't on my radar, I just don't know when I'm going to tell them."

"Maybe you don't want to tell them because then it becomes more real," Dane says, and then he shrugs. "I don't know."

"How could you think that?" I ask.

Dane inhales as he holds my eyes, seemingly considering the fact that he's overreacting. But as I stare back at him, I start to wonder if he's over-reacting or if he's reading me correctly. As much as I hate to admit it, I'm not so sure Dane's completely off-base here, and maybe on some subconscious level, I don't want to shed light on our newfound relationship. Maybe I want to continue to live out this fantasy in our own little bubble for a few more days or weeks without judgment.

"You're right. I'm sorry." Dane's voice flings me out of my head, and he grabs my arm to bring me in for a hug.

Wednesday, August 3, 2022

I'm sitting on my porch reading a book with a glass of wine. My legs are curled at my side on the wooden bench as I absorb the words off each page, and it's calming to have some down time. As Dane and I progress in our feelings, it's almost like I can feel a slow-moving vortex in the pit of my stomach that threatens to pick up speed and cause mass destruction. Like a tornado of unsettled emotions brewing turmoil within me, but the gusts of wind aren't violent just yet.

They're whirling and waiting.

My relationship with Dane has developed exponentially. Accelerating gradually at first, and then faster as time goes on. But the more time passes, the more our sanity starts to chip away, and it seems like the rate of our relationship is too rapid for us to get a proper footing.

Sometimes silence is the loudest sound of all in the smallest instances, and it seems to be a common theme between the two of us lately. Unfortunately, silence isn't a blessing in this situation, but rather a curse, and the absence of sound equates to the absence of a resolution.

How does this end for the both of us?

I hear my phone vibrate against the seat of the bench next to me, and I turn to flip it upward to see the screen with a new text message.

Mom: Start freeing up your weeks, because we have a lot to get done at the restaurant! Your father needs all the help he can get. :)

Me: Already planned on it. Let me know when to come down, and I'm there. :)

I place my phone face down on the seat of the bench again and go to take a sip of my wine, but just as I do, I see Kate's Toyota Corolla pull up to the curb of my house. I squint my eyes as I drag the rim of my wine glass away from my lips and set it down on the floor of my porch. I close my book and place it next to me, then stand up to iron out my high-rise jeans and tucked in slub white tee as I swallow a nervous lump. Once Kate gets out of her car, she closes the door to look at me over the roof and stretches a tight-lipped smile over her lips. Naturally my lips stretch just like hers, mimicking the hopeful, yet unsure expression on her face.

"Can I come up?" Kate finally asks.

"Of course," I say.

Kate holds the strap of her crossbody at her shoulder as she walks around the hood of her car in her black polka dot long sleeve dress with black heels. I eye her with trepidation as she walks up the pathway to my porch, not really sure what she's about to say.

Is she going to lash out at me again?

Is she going to ask questions?

Is she going to forgive me?

When Kate reaches the top of my porch, she leans her shoulder on one of the posts, and I anxiously shove my hands in the back pockets of my jeans as I wait for her to say something.

"I'm on lunch now," she says.

"Oh," I say as I nod my head. "How's work been today?"

Kate shrugs as she says, "Laid back. We finished our end of the month closing tasks last week, so this week is sure to be a breeze."

"That's something to look forward to at least," I say with a shaky smile.

Kate swallows thickly as she nods in agreement, and her eyes just lock on mine for a few quiet moments, and I inhale as I feel her mind retreating back to that night at Shippers. "I couldn't stop thinking about you," Kate says.

"Hopefully not because you hate me," I respond honestly.

Kate starts to shake her head. "I could never hate you, Ari."

I stretch a small smile as I look downward and play with my hands in front of my stomach. "That makes me really happy to hear," I say, and then I lift my head up to look at Kate. "I needed to hear that. I've missed you a lot."

"I've missed you too." Kate stares at me for a few seconds, and then she sighs a long breath as she looks off to the side. "Ari, I know I said some really awful things last week. I guess I just felt betrayed. I don't know..." she trails off.

"I know, Kate," I say as I sigh and look off to the side with her. "This whole thing with Dane has been crazy, and I'm still trying to wrap my brain around it. But the only explanation I have is that it just *happened*. I know that's not going to be enough for anyone, but it's the truth. I swear."

When I finish my explanation, I turn my head to look at her, and then Kate's eyes meet mine. "You guys have spent almost every moment together this summer. I guess it was only natural," Kate offers.

I softly gasp in disbelief. "It seems like a lifetime ago. Everything happened so fast," I admit.

"I guess I was just thinking about it from Kyle's side of it," Kate adds, and when she mentions his name, the shadow over my heart darkens.

It takes me a moment to collect my thoughts, and I have to look away from her for several seconds. "I think about him every day. It's not like I've forgotten him," I say and then I turn to face her. "All I know is that *right now*, I want to spend time with Dane. I know it's wrong, and he's the last person I should ever want to be with, but I can't help my feelings. I can't just turn them off, as much as I wish there was some magical switch."

"Do you love him?" Kate asks.

I don't answer right away, but I'm not entirely sure why. Her question throws me off, and I don't know if it's because I didn't expect the actual question, or because I'm fearful of my answer.

"I think I could love him. If I let myself," I say.

"What's stopping you?" Kate asks.

I avert my eyes downward as I answer. "It seems like betrayal is a common feeling these days. I feel like I would be betraying Kyle or my heart in some way."

271

"But if it wasn't for Kyle?"

"Yes," I answer as I look up to Kate, and she looks surprised by my quick response. "But my life isn't black and white."

"Have you and Dane talked about your feelings?" Kate asks.

I shake my head. "Not really. I think we're both avoiding that elephant in the room."

"Ari, you have to try. Otherwise, this will be an even bigger mess than it already is."

"I know. I'm just not ready."

Kate holds my gaze for a few seconds before speaking. "Ari, I'm really sorry. For everything," she whispers.

"I'm sorry too," I whisper as I step forward and bring Kate in for a hug.

I don't really know what I'm apologizing for.

My relationship with Dane? Is that what I'm apologizing for?

If that's the case, it's not a great feeling.

DANE

I tell Aria I got caught up at work tonight when she invites me over for dinner. The truth is, I'm not caught up at work. I leave the office at five o'clock on the dot, hop in my Mustang, and drive to a place I've been avoiding ever since I started feeling something for Aria.

St. Mary's Cemetery.

Once I find Kyle's location, I park my car at the curb, and sit down on the grass in front of his gravestone, elbows resting on bent knees.

"Oh, man." I sigh as I hang my head downward. "I was looking out for her, Kyle. Making sure she was okay when she moved back here. Making sure she had a friend she could rely on."

I swallow thickly before continuing. "And somewhere along the way, I started to see her the way you always saw her. Beautiful, smart, funny, witty, goofy, and just a light to be around. Who wouldn't fall for her?"

I run my hands through my hair trying to collect my thoughts. "I know my words seem insignificant at this point, and I know if I sit here and say I still care for you and think about you, it doesn't seem believable."

I feel tears starting to well up behind my eyes and I sniffle before con- tinuing. "But it's true. I miss you. I miss the life we once had together. You, Aria, me, Trent, and Kate." A single tear streams down my face as I try to think of my next words. "Things were so much easier, and things made so much sense back then. I'm not even sure Aria and I make sense right now."

I pause before continuing. "Because I know she still loves you. I can feel it." Another tear streams down my cheek. "And why wouldn't she? There's never going to be anyone like you. You were one of a kind, and I was fortunate enough to be your best friend in our lifetime together. A lifetime cut too short."

I inhale before I exhale my next words. "I'm sorry if I've failed you as a friend."

I run my hands down my face, pulling myself together, and I just sit and think. Think about how so much has changed, and how things are so complicated now. Then I lie back on the grass and look up at the clear blue sky as I keep Kyle company for the rest of the evening.

CHAPTER
Thirty-Five

ARIA

Thursday, August 4, 2022

The next night, Dane and I decide to watch the sunset as we take a walk along the beach. I have my hair slicked back with a white floral print headband to match my white tank top that's tucked into my high-rise denim shorts.

Dane grabs my hand and brings it up to his lips, and when I turn to look at him, he just smiles and puts our hands down so our fingers are woven between us as we walk.

"Surprised you aren't begging us to go to Disco Doughnuts right now," Dane teases.

"That's tempting," I laugh out. "But I think I have everything I want, right here."

Dane bends down to nudge my forehead with a smile for a brief moment, and I swear I can feel my heart sprout wings as it flutters uncontrollably. I'm grinning wide when Dane stands up straighter and we resume walking alongside one another. "But, that's not to say I won't bother you ever in the future," I joke.

He chuckles as he looks ahead. "I expected that."

I smile as I look out in front of me, and then lick my lips before starting the conversation back up. "Kate came to visit me."

I see Dane turn his head to look at me in my line of vision. "What happened?" he asks.

I'm still looking ahead as I speak. "She wanted to apologize. Although I don't really know if there's anything she should have to apologize for."

I notice Dane turns his head to face forward again, and we continue to walk through our stewing thoughts until he finally voices his. "Do you think we have something to apologize for?"

"Do you?" I ask as I look over at him, and the way the evening sunrays illuminate the gorgeous contours of his face makes me crave his rationale that much more.

I want to be convinced this is okay.

I want to be convinced that we deserve this.

Dane licks his lips and slightly narrows his eyes as he ponders his response. "An apology implies that you regret something." Then he turns his head to look at me. "I could never regret you. I could never regret *this*."

I exhale the faintest breath as I stop walking and stand in front of him to place my free palm on his chest. Dane places a hand over mine as our other hands are still interlocked between us, and I just stare into Dane's olive-green crewneck t-shirt. "How do you know the right thing to say every single time?" I whisper.

"Because I'm giving my heart a chance to win," Dane says.

I swallow thickly as I look up at him. "Against?" I ask softly.

"My guilt." I'm rendered speechless, and just hold Dane's green hues against my brown ones. "I carry the same burden as you, Ari. But maybe if we carry it together, the weight will be less painful."

I inhale as I look down and flip my palm upward against his chest so our fingers can tenderly play together. "Maybe we need to start living for small moments instead of the big ones."

"What do you mean?" Dane asks above me.

Keeping my eyes trained on our fingers, I elaborate. "Maybe we need to stop focusing on what's going to happen tonight, tomorrow, or the next day. Maybe we need to just enjoy being in the present." Then I look up at Dane. "Maybe then we can accumulate enough happiness to win against the storm."

"I'm liking this moment," Dane whispers.

My lips tip up at the corner as I whisper back. "Me too."

Dane bends to press his forehead against mine, and both our eyes close as we let the ocean breeze shield us from the chaos that lurks in the background. "Can you promise me something?" Dane asks.

"Anything," I say.

"If you ever feel like I'm not making you the happiest you could possibly be, I never want you to feel trapped."

I shake my head against his forehead. "I'd never feel trapped with you. It's the exact opposite," I breathe.

Dane lets go of both my hands and cups the sides of my face to bring me in for a passionate kiss, letting our lips tenderly complete the conversation. I melt into his touch as my feelings liquify from their previous ice-bound state, and my palms press into his firm chest as I curl my fingers into the fabric of his shirt. When our lips pull away, Dane's the first to speak. "Don't stop fighting," he says.

I tilt my head to look up at Dane as I snake a palm up to cup the side of his face. "You give me all the armor I need," I say before placing a single, light kiss to his lips. I graze the tip of my nose against his, allowing us both to sink into the moment for a few more needed seconds, and he returns my gesture with just as much care. Then I peel myself off of him and start to walk backwards with a playful, devious smirk.

Dane eyes me curiously. "What are you doing?"

"Come and find out," I tease as I turn around and walk to the shoreline where the waves meet the sand. My bare feet press into the mushy sand, coarse and wet, and the tip of the waves crash against my ankles before receding back. Then I purse my lips as I spin on my heels to face Dane, who's standing in the same spot with his hands shoved in his pockets.

He shakes his head with a smirk. "No."

I gesture a "come here" motion with my finger, and when Dane doesn't bite, I decide to egg him on a little more. I drop my hand to my side and sigh. "Not for nothing, Dane, but you're kind of being a vagina."

Dane laughs. "Are you seriously calling me a pussy right now?"

I scrunch my face. "You can't use that word outside of the bedroom."

Dane walks a few steps toward me to close the distance. "Is this some sort of unspoken rule of yours?"

I nod my head confidently. "Yes, it is. It's not allowed."

Dane chuckles as he just peers down at me. "You do know you were the one that just called me out?"

I hold my hands out to drive my point home. "But I used a less vulgar term. Read the room." Dane's lips curl up in the corner as he holds my eyes, but at the same time, he shuffles on his feet to remove his sneakers and socks. I look down in question, and then back up to Dane. "I thought you only took your sneakers and socks off when you were getting in the water?"

Dane smiles knowingly as he half-turns to chuck his sneakers and socks farther up the sand, so they don't get wet, and I gasp when he turns around and hoists me up by the back of my thighs. My arms snake around his neck while my legs wrap around his khaki shorts, and I bite my bottom lip as I look down at his bright green eyes.

Eyes that give me all the hope I'm ever going to need.

"Maybe I spoke too soon," I tease with a smirk.

"I can agree with that," Dane says.

"Maybe you should shut me up then," I challenge as my palms snake from around his neck to the sides of his face. As if my words reel his lips to mine on a fishing line, Dane's chin tilts up to catch my lips in a sultry kiss. We're further into the water since our weight has shifted, and the waves are knocking us back and forth as we make out. Unexpectedly, a big wave comes. Dane is unable to keep himself upright from the power of the crash, and we yell at the same time as the wave takes us with it.

"Shit!" Dane yells.

"Ahhh!" I laugh out.

We topple over in the water, the current taking us deeper and submerging us in the salty water. When we both come up for air, we're laughing hysterically, and immediately start swimming closer to the shore. Dane extends his hand out to me in the water, and I take it gratefully as we make our way out of the waves and onto the dry sand. We're completely soaked from head to toe, Dane's t-shirt sticking to his rippled six-pack, and his shorts molding to his thick, muscular thighs.

God, *he's so undeniably sexy.*

"Mmm, I could get used to that look on you," I say as I run my hands through my wet hair and devour Dane with my eyes.

"Hey, Miss!"

A voice calls out from behind me.

When I turn around, there is a guy about my age walking up to me with my white floral print headband in his hand, but it's not the hair accessory that keeps my attention.

It's his face.

He has dirty blonde hair and blue eyes that feel like they're staring into my soul.

He reminds me so much of him.

Kyle.

I just stand there and don't say anything as I scan over his facial features, trying to decipher if this person is Kyle reincarnated. I know that's not possible, but my mind starts to believe that maybe this is Kyle sending me a message.

"Miss?"

I shake my head slightly to thwart my thoughts. "Oh, thank you," I say breathlessly as I take the headband from him.

The guy throws me a smile. "No problem. Have a good day," he says as he waves and walks away.

My eyes follow this man's retreating form, and I'm cemented to where I'm standing as I feel the re-tightening of my invisible shackles. My emotions will always be in a constant tug-o-war battle, no matter how many steps forward I take with Dane, and I'm not sure how much longer I'll be able to fight.

Don't stop fighting.

Can I truly keep the promise I just made to Dane?

I feel an arm come around my shoulders. "Hey, you alright?"

I look up at Dane. "Yeah," I say as I nod reluctantly. "Let's go home."

If Dane recognizes my emotions, he chooses not to say anything, and we just wrap our arms around each other to walk back home.

CHAPTER
Thirty-Six

ARIA

Friday, August 5, 2022

I'm finishing putting the breaded chicken cutlets and asparagus in the oven when I hear a knock on my front door. I open the door and am greeted with Dane, his hair slightly messy on top, and he's donning a little scruff on his face.

"Impeccable timing you have, I just put dinner in the oven," I say as I wrap my hands around Dane's neck and bring him in for a kiss.

"Mmm, to think this isn't my dinner is disappointing," Dane says as he nips my shoulder playfully.

I giggle as I wrestle out of his grasp and am now walking in front of him to the kitchen. I hand Dane the glass of Cabernet I poured for him, and I clink his glass with mine before we each take a sip.

"How was work?" I ask as I place my wine on the counter and start washing the mixing bowls and colander in the sink. "Pretty slow today. I've finished a couple big projects yesterday, so it was nice to have a break," Dane answers as he takes a seat at the eat-in kitchen table.

"Lucky you, I had such a stressful day," I say with an exaggerated sigh. Dane plays along. "Oh, yeah?"

"Yeah, you know, reading my book outside on the porch for a couple hours, then coming in here to make a sandwich for lunch, then having to prepare dinner. It was really overbearing," I say with a smirk. I stop the water once I finish cleaning the colander and wipe my hands with the dish towel.

"Well, maybe I need to help you relax then. From all this unbearable stress," Dane says as he walks up behind me and places his hands on my hips, resting them on my high-rise denim shorts.

I lay my head to the side to give him access to my neck, and Dane takes the invitation to trail featherlight kisses down my neck. "Mmm, you keep doing that and we won't be eating dinner soon," I moan.

I'm making a joke and expect him to make a playful remark back, but he doesn't speak. Instead, he continues to place kisses on my neck as his hands come up under my crop top to grab my breasts over my bra. He purposefully grazes his thumbs over my hard nipples, and I bite my lip as I tilt my head back into him, appreciating the pleasure he's giving me. Then his lips graze my ear as he speaks in a husky voice. "You still thinking about dinner?"

I reach behind me to grab the back of his neck, and I shake my head in response.

Dane smiles devilishly against my ear. "No?" he asks as he removes his hands from under my shirt and starts to slowly undo the top button on my short sleeve crop top. "What are you thinking about?" he whispers in my ear.

"You," I breathe out as I close my eyes, and then Dane unfastens the second button on my crop top. His movements are tantalizingly slow, and at this point he knows he's torturing me. Dane grabs the side of my face and kisses my lips from over my shoulder, deep and wet as our tongues instinctively seek each other's.

When Dane pulls away from my lips, his hands go to undo the third button on my shirt. "Let's take this to the bedroom," Dane whispers.

I freeze at Dane's request, and the blood in my veins runs cold. I can physically feel all the pleasure from the last-minute drain from my body, and I'm positive Dane is witnessing it slip from my face as silence consumes the air around us. I haven't slept with anyone in our old bed, and I don't think I ever truly thought about it until this moment when Dane suggests we make love in my bedroom.

Like clockwork, guilt grabs hold of my heart and squeezes the life out of it.

I feel short of breath.

Dizzy.

My lack of words seem to be enough of a reaction as realization dawns on Dane's face. He swallows a nervous gulp as he peels himself away from me, and I turn my head to stare out the window above the sink as I place two palms flat on the countertop in front of me. Dane's now turned away from me so his back is leaning against the kitchen counter beside me.

"I'm sorry," I whisper.

I can see in my peripherals that Dane's gaze is averted downward, and his stance is rigid as tension radiates from his body. "It's Kyle you're think-ing about, isn't it?" he asks.

I lick my lips, keeping my eyes trained out the window as my emotions create a building pressure behind my eyes. "What does it matter? If I say yes, you'll be pissed. If I say no, you'll think I'm lying. I don't win with this question."

I see Dane turn his head to me in my side view. "Can you ju-"

"Yes." I don't let him finish his question. I know this truth is going to hurt Dane, but I can't lie to him. I close my eyes, trying to compile my thoughts carefully. "But it's not what you think."

He lets out a small laugh like he doesn't believe what I'm saying. "No? Could've fooled me."

I throw my hands up and step away from the counter, the pressure of my emotions too great to keep pent up inside me anymore. "What do you want, Dane?!" I yell. "Just tell me what you want me to do!"

Dane shakes his head as he stands up from the counter. "Don't do that. Don't make it like I'm being completely unreasonable."

I sigh as I run both my hands through my hair and turn to walk around my kitchen. "I guess it's me who's being completely unreasonable then, huh?"

"I never said that," Dane says harshly.

I stop and face him as I drop my hands from my head. "You didn't have to!"

"Well excuse me for wanting to make love to you without you thinking of someone else. I guess it's just the price I have to pay after vying for the one woman who's off limits to me," Dane snaps back. Toxicity poisons the space between us as Dane's hostility fuels my own rage.

"You know what, you're right," I say as I walk the few steps toward Dane, and as soon as I'm right in front of him, I start to bunch the hem of Dane's shirt up. "I should just give you what you want."

Dane places his hands on my wrists to pause my movements. "Stop," he says, but his demand only powers my anger more as I drop my eyes downward to move my hands to his belt buckle and unloop the leather strap. "Knock it off, Ari."

I can hear Dane's clenched jaw as he speaks, but it doesn't faze me, and when I start to unbutton his jeans, Dane's hands take my wrists in a firm hold as I jerk forward. "I said cut it out," he gruffs.

I push my forearms outward to release my wrists from his grip, and then I start to undo the rest of the buttons on my crop top that Dane didn't get to earlier. When I shrug the sleeves off, my shirt falls to the kitchen floor, and I'm left standing in front of Dane in my red lace bra and high-rise denim shorts. I swallow my nerves down as I take a step forward and place my small palms on his chest, grazing one up to cup the side of his face.

"Take me to bed," I whisper as I peer up at him. Dane inhales a shaky breath as he places his palm over my hand at his chest, and I can tell he's contemplating taking my invitation. "It's what you want, isn't it? To know you've won?" I breathe out.

I gasp in surprise when Dane scoops me up from behind my thighs, and I wrap my legs and arms around him, not thinking my little charade would put us in this predicament. Dane starts to move us out of the kitchen, and with each step he takes, my heart skips with distress. I close my eyes as I lean my forehead against his, uncertain if I'm going to be able to take this next step.

I barely sift through my thoughts when I feel Dane lower me on to something soft as he stays hovering above me. My eyes remain shut because I'm sure I'm going to throw up once I see my bedroom walls encasing us. But when I start to sink into the cushioned surface I'm lying on, I realize we're not on my bed.

We're on my living room couch.

When I open my eyes, Dane's green hues stare back at me, and the only emotion I see weaved within them is *understanding*.

He's not bitter.

He's not resentful.

And he's most certainly not angry with me.

The panic inside of me loosens its grip on my heart, and I'm able to breathe more steadily as Dane brushes a few hair strands away from my eye with the pads of his fingers. Then Dane cups the side of my face, and his thumb strokes my cheek in a back-and-forth motion as he says, "I only win if I have your heart. But I'd never *take* your heart. I want you to choose to give it to me."

My eyes glisten as I take in his beauty.

Not the beauty of his looks.

The beauty of his heart.

This man. This beautiful man, who knows me so intricately well, satisfies my body and soul in every single way that's humanly possible. He knows just what I'm thinking and what I need at every moment. Whether we're being intimate, having a conversation, or whether we're having an argument. Sometimes it's scary just how well he knows me, and maybe that's because he's the last person I ever expected to understand me as wholly as he does. And with that, he's absolutely taken my breath away.

I think a part of me has hoped that my attraction to Dane was purely physical and was just a side effect of our passionate lovemaking. But when I look into his eyes now, my body isn't the only part of me coming to life.

I feel my heart beat differently.

It beats like a crescendo, and the louder my heart beats, the more positive I am of what I'm feeling. Being in Dane's arms now feels so undoubtedly right, and I almost forget what we were arguing about because all I know is this is where I want to be.

I feel my body start to light up, and an all-consuming need starts to take over. It's carnal, but it's necessary. Neither of us are saying the words we truly want to say, but I know there's a way we can *feel* everything we want to say to each other. It's our way of giving in, but not kicking the chair out from under us. It's our way of coping with the unfortunate circumstances we've been placed in and taking control back.

It may be toxic, and it may be poor judgment, but it's all we have for now.

And anything I can get from him, I'll greedily take.

"Take me," I whisper as I grab the hem of his shirt and lift it over his chest. Dane stands up to completely remove his shirt, and then he unbuttons and drags his jeans down his legs and off his ankles. When he comes back on the couch, I spread my legs wider for him to settle between, and a surge of heat rushes through my body as I stroke my palms over Dane's carved chest and abdomen. A pool of wetness puddles into my panties, and the ache between my legs throbs for attention. Dane unbuttons and unzips my denim shorts, and I lift my bottom off the couch cushion to help him slide my shorts and underwear down my legs.

When my clothing is finally tossed to the floor, Dane hovers over me and cups the side of my face as he caresses my cheek with his thumb. "I try to think about the moment I fell for you, Aria. I think it was when we made love for the first time. Or maybe it was when we first kissed under the stars on the hood of my car," he whispers. "But I think it was even sometime before that. When we danced together for the first time at Shipper's. When I watched you in the pouring rain on the pier. Maybe even when I held your hand on the Ferris wheel." He swallows a nervous lump in his throat, and all I can do is exhale a shaky breath. "Because falling in love with you can't be measured in a single moment. I fall every day, every hour, every minute. And although I might plunge empty-handed, it's the greatest dive I've ever taken."

His confession heals me.

It's like the last piece of my broken heart stitches back into place, and it feels like my heart is whole again.

All because of him.

When I bring a hand up to palm the side of his face, Dane molds his lips to mine, capturing them in a blinding possession that makes me see stars. We moan into each other's mouths, and I feel Dane's weight shift as he starts to push his boxer briefs over his erection. My hands immediately go between us to help him out, our hands a hurried mess, not seeming to get his underwear off him quick enough. Once they're completely removed, Dane guides his cock to my entrance and pushes through my velvety walls, thrillingly stretching me.

Our lips never disconnect as his hand goes to my hip while one palm is still at the side of my face, and he starts pumping into me deep and fast. Both my hands are cupping the sides of his face now as I whimper against his lips, savoring every second of pleasure he's gifting me. With every thrust, he's hitting my clit at just the right angle, and the simultaneous sensation sends my mind spinning.

I pull my lips back from his, desperate to feel his love and ownership over my heart. "Give me more. I need more of you," I whisper against his lips.

Without hesitation, Dane slips himself out of me and flips me over so I'm on my stomach. I gasp when he raises my hips up off the couch, and I brace myself against the couch cushion by laying my palms flat against the plush surface. Dane bends one leg on the couch, so his knee is resting on the cushion, while his other leg stands straight with his foot planted on the floor.

I cry out when Dane thrusts his cock through my slick folds, and my fingers curl into the soft fabric beneath me. He slowly glides himself out to his tip, and plunges his full length back into me, only to repeat this over and over as I gasp with each aggressive pump he drives forward. Every hard and intentional thrust causes me to yelp in a blended squeal of pain and rapture, and the stars I was seeing before have turned into a spiral galaxy, and I'm lifted to another universe only he has the power to bring me to.

Dane's fingers dig into my hips, surely leaving bruises in their wake tomorrow, and he continues to ruthlessly fuck me as he savagely tries to own my body. But I don't even think it's a matter of him attempting anymore. Because he owns every crevice of my body, including the very muscular organ that thunders beneath my chest right now, palpitating in anticipation for him to eventually destroy me.

Break me.

Break the stone wall I've built around my mind, body, and soul.

I need him to take the sledgehammer and crumble it to pieces to re-mold me. Shape me into the person I was meant to become if I wasn't meant to live the life I had before.

I need him to give me *life*.

I need him to give me a new purpose.

I feel Dane's slick chest hover over my back as his hot, minty breath tickles the shell of my ear, and I cry out when he rails into me again. "Is this the 'more' you wanted?" he rasps. "Me railing out this sweet fucking pussy like it's the only salvation I'm ever gonna need?"

"Y-yes," I gasp, my voice hoarse and winded. A thick fog takes over my brain, and the only part of me that can effectively respond is my body. The demand of my body is too fierce to ignore, and I've never wanted to tip over the edge into euphoric bliss as much as I do right now. The knotted ribbon in my lower belly starts to unravel, and when it completely unwinds, I know it's going to shatter me.

Just like I need him too.

Just like I once told him to.

I gasp when Dane wraps one arm around my stomach, and he pulls me up so that my back plasters to his steel chest. I wrap one arm around his neck as he starts to thrust hard and fast into me. I turn my head to the side so our eyes can lock together, and with my free hand, I grab his palm from my hip and place it over one of my breasts, kneading the top of Dane's hand to encourage him to squeeze me there.

"I can always give you more," he breathes against my lips, his affectionate words a stark contrast with his harsh thrusts into me. "Anything in this life, I'll fucking give to you," he rasps.

As our breaths mingle together, Dane brings his hand down from my breast to place two fingers on my clit, and the tight knot in my stomach is starting to uncoil at a quicker speed now.

"You've ruined every single part of me, Aria," Dane whispers, and I look into his eyes as my fingers wrap firmly in the dark locks behind his head. My toes are sliding off the cliff now, and I'm just waiting for the rest of my feet to follow suit before I take the leap.

"Let me feel you fall with me," Dane whispers.

My fingers clutch Dane's hair, and my orgasm crashes through me like a tsunami, erupting from my lower belly and knocking over my chest, just as he spills his hot seed inside me. We cry out, my hand tightening in Dane's hair as his palm presses against my midsection. My body spasms of its own accord, each jolt breaking a piece of my old self off.

When the ripples of our highs start flattening, it's like Dane and I are standing on crumbled pieces of my old soul. It wasn't just Dane's sexual expertise that brought me to an earth-shattering orgasm, it was his *words*.

He's the light that's outlined the doorframe of my dark room, waiting to open the door when I was ready to accept the light. Accept color into my world again. And as treacherous and agonizing as my journey has been, he resurrects *hope* inside me. Hope that I can heal from the venom that I've ingested from my past.

"*God, yes,*" he grunts into the crook of my neck, digging his fingers into my hips as his body jerks a few final times from the shockwaves of his climax. I place my palm over the top of one of his hands at my hip, and I place a light kiss on his temple, tasting salt from the droplets of sweat that bead his skin there.

Dane picks his head up and cups the side of my face to bring my lips to his. Our lips are sleek with beads of moisture from our exerted energy, but I don't care. I need his lips now more than ever as I dip my tongue into his mouth for him to stroke it with his own. When we break away from each other, Dane playfully nudges the tip of my nose affectionately as he carefully slips out of me, and I whimper at the emptiness I suddenly feel.

I wince as I register the soreness Dane left behind on me, but grin just as quickly when he embraces me from behind and lays us on our side on my couch. Dane spoons me as he grabs the throw blanket off the back of the couch, and drapes it over both of us. I snuggle my backside into Dane, and I feel a featherlight kiss touch my bare shoulder.

I turn my body around enough to look Dane in the eyes, and notice a sleek tendril of hair sticking to his forehead, evidence of our intense love making just minutes earlier. I gently palm the side of his face when I say, "I'm going to tell my family tomorrow."

Dane starts to shake his head as he says, "I didn't say what I said earlier to push yo-"

"I know," I interrupt. "I want to tell them." I'm stroking his cheek with my thumb as I stare into his eyes that promise redemption. "I'm *alive* when I'm with you, Dane," I confess, my feelings sliding off the tip of my tongue with ease now. Dane grabs my hand at his face, kissing the inside of my palm, and the corner of my lips tip up before I continue on. "You've restored my faith in everything I lost. Happiness and the will to live on. You've brought me hope in despair and protected me from hurting any more than I already have. There's no denying the fire that burns within me burns for you, and I don't want to run from the storm anymore. I'm ready to take shelter with you."

Dane closes his eyes and inhales sharply as he nudges my forehead with his, kindly pushing against it. "*This* feels so right to me. How could this ever be wrong?" he whispers.

I close my eyes as I'm swallowed in the same thoughts as him, willing myself not to retreat two steps after taking one huge leap forward. "This world isn't perfect, remember?" I whisper back.

"It feels perfect right now," he whispers.

I let a small smile creep on my lips. "Yeah. It does," I breathe out.

We're glued in each other's arms, forehead to forehead, for the next few moments when time stands still. The blanket that covers us is like our security from the outside world. We're confronting our emotions and tackling them head on, but how will my family react when I tell them? Can they accept this? If they can't accept it, can they still support me? If they can't support me, can they still respect our relationship? Or will there always be a crow perched outside the window, looming over Dane and me?

As I'm about to drown deeper into my thoughts, I feel Dane peel his forehead from mine, causing my eyes to open. "What if they can't accept this?" he asks.

Like two bodies connected to the same soul, it's clear he was thinking the same thoughts I was, and as much as the question unsettles me, it reassures me. Reassures me that Dane and I are in this together, and there's a possible winning chance for us.

"I've been through worse, right?" I say, but there is a hint of uncertainty in my voice that reveals itself a little too much. Yes, I have been through much worse than what we're discussing, but I'm not so sure if I can be with Dane if my family can't welcome him with open arms.

How would that be fair to either of us?

It wouldn't.

Dane's knuckles graze my cheek. "It doesn't lessen the importance of needing your family in your life," he says.

My eyes swell with emotion, glossing over as Dane's response helps me keep one foot forward on this journey. This amazing and incredible human being before me understands my heart without me having to utter a single letter to him.

"I love you," I whisper.

The words leave my mouth so fluidly it's not lost on me how effortless it is to tell him, and I can see and hear the slightest breath escape through Dane's lips.

"I love you too," he whispers. Then he pulls my face to his, and our lips connect like we're trapping our admission between us, hiding it from anything or anyone that dares to snatch it.

He tastes like a sanctuary, and I take refuge.

CHAPTER
Thirty-Seven

DANE

Saturday, August 6, 2022

I have one foot propped up on my coffee table as I lean back into the couch with my head turned up toward the ceiling. Aria is on her way to her dad's restaurant to help finalize some preparations for the grand opening in two weeks and made it clear last night and earlier today that she was going to tell her family about us. As much as her leap forward pleases me, fear churns in the pit of my stomach.

When Aria first suggested this last night, I wasn't expecting to feel as unsure as I did in that moment, and as I still do now. For a while, I thought this step would be the answer to a huge hurdle Aria and I have been trying to successfully jump over. But there's an ominous question that lingers in the background of this picture.

Could I be so selfish to continue to love Aria if her family doesn't accept this?

A sour taste seeps into the inside of my cheeks as I realize what possible repercussions lie ahead today. Specifically, in an hour or two.

I swallow the nauseous feeling in my mouth down, trying physically to suppress reality and the weight I'm carrying on my shoulders. Last night felt like only the beginning for us.

Don't we deserve just a little more time?

Even if our story wasn't meant to be permanent, I know it wasn't meant to be this abrupt. Like our story is slipping between my fingers as soon as our hands wrapped securely around it. Because once Aria takes this next step, there's a great chance it's a step backwards for the both of us, and we'll have to start from square one. That is if Aria even decides she wants to refight all of the battles that have led us to this point.

I exhale an exhausted breath as I run both my hands through my hair, and mutter to myself. "*Fuck.*"

Before I can change my mind, I throw on a black pullover hoodie and khaki shorts with white sneakers. Then I find myself heading out the door to greet my Mustang, and I'm driving over to Aria's dad's restaurant.

"Ari!" I yell as I get out of my car and jog toward her in the parking lot.

Aria turns around with two boxes in her arms and furrows her brows when she realizes I'm the one approaching her. "Wha-" Aria starts.

"Let me," I breathe as I take both boxes from her and set them on the ground. Then I inhale as I take a quick glance around me, making sure the coast is clear. I'm not sure where her family is yet, but I *really* don't need them sneaking up on us unexpectedly. Once I realize we're free of possible bystanders, I cup the sides of Aria's face as I shake my head. "Don't tell them today," I say.

Aria draws her brows together. "Why? What's going on?"

I blow out a small breath before looking into the depths of her light brown hues, needing her to understand what I'm saying without me having to speak it. "I just…I need more time with you," I say.

Aria pulls away slightly and shakes her head in my palms. "They don't have to understand. It's you and me. That's all that matters."

I lick my lips, knowing that deep down, Aria doesn't mean what she's saying. Deep in my heart, I know her family's opinion will matter, and in order for her to be absolutely happy in our relationship, she needs their support. And the painful truth is, if she can't be happy in our relationship, I am of no purpose to her. If I can't make her smile and laugh and live, I refuse to be the reason she lives a shallow life. Aria doesn't just deserve the world, she deserves the whole goddamn universe. And even though I won't let go of her hand without a bloody fight, I'm not ready for our worlds to crash and burn just yet.

Not now.

Not today.

Not when we just said "I love you" to each other less than twenty-four hours ago.

Instead of agreeing with her, I just reiterate what I said earlier, driving my point harder. "Can we just have *today* at least? That's all I'm asking."

Aria swallows thickly as she reads my pleading eyes. "Okay," she whispers, and then slides her hands under my arms and up my back to embrace me in a hug. I sink into her by resting my lips on the top of her head, and close my eyes to take her in. Inhaling her scent and letting it float through my veins so that my blood can be marked by her.

So that she can consume me when she's not around.

Because if my days are counted with Aria against my own will, at least I could make the most of every single second with her.

"We probably should head in before someone sees," Aria whispers.

It takes a few seconds until I reluctantly open my eyes, and as we pull away from one another, I grab the two boxes from the ground so we can make our way toward the restaurant. When we head through the front entrance, Helen and Ronnie are taking supplies out of boxes, and setting them on the bar and tables around them. When I set the boxes I'm carrying on the floor, Helen is the first one to see us, and she walks up to me to give me a big hug.

"Dane! Thanks so much for coming," she says.

"It's no trouble at all," I say as I hug her back, and then Ronnie comes up to bring me in for a handshake-hug.

"Dad's not here?" Aria asks.

"He's at the bank finalizing the payment plan on the loan for the restaurant," Helen responds.

"So what can I do?" I ask.

Helen is the first to speak. "If you don't mind, we have boxes of glassware to stock behind the bar. The boxes are out on the terrace because I thought they were the string lights for the pergola."

I smile at her explanation before walking to the back of the restaurant to grab the appropriate boxes to bring back inside. When I set the boxes down on the bar and start opening one, I'm looking over every couple minutes to watch what Aria's doing. She's taking out lantern centerpieces, making sure each works properly after being lugged around in a cramped box, and Aria's apparently interested in what I'm doing because I catch her glancing over at me from time to time. When we lock eyes, we just smirk before going back to focusing on what we're supposed to be doing.

"I just finished taking inventory of the silverware, let me give you a hand," Ronnie says as he approaches me behind the bar, and he doesn't waste any time before he starts taking glasses out of the boxes and stocking them onto the shelves. "So what's new?" Ronnie asks.

"Not much. How about you? How's Cheryl?" I respond.

"Can't complain. We started renovating our bathroom last week, so that's about as exciting as it has been this summer," Ronnie says.

I chuckle. "Hey, at least you're prioritizing the house. Can't say that about many people."

Ronnie just laughs, and then stands up as he takes the boxes we've emptied with him. "Are the rest of the boxes still on the terrace?"

I furrow my brows. "I only saw these two there."

Ronnie looks confused, then walks to the back to check the patio. When he comes back inside, he directs his statement at Aria and Helen. "We're missing a few boxes of glassware."

Aria and her mom look up from their tasks, and then Helen's eyes flash. "Oh, no! I must have left them at the house. I have to go back and get them."

"Don't be silly, you can get them later in the week," Ronnie reassures.

Helen sighs as she runs a hand through her hair. "I can't believe I did that."

Aria chimes in. "Mom, it's drinking glasses that can be stocked in two minutes. I think we can manage to fit that in the schedule some time within the next two weeks." Then Aria looks and points over at Ronnie and me at the bar. "I don't see them drained from a brutal job of stocking glasses," she jokes.

Aria has a curl to her lips as she looks back at her mom, and Helen gives Aria a deadpan stare. "You always like to poke fun, don't you?"

"Alright we know you aren't letting this go, so what can Dane and I do to help so that you're less stressed?" Ronnie asks.

Helen points to the sliding back doors as she looks at Ronnie and I. "Lights. Pergola."

We playfully salute her as we make our way to the outside deck, and I hear Aria suggest taking out the linens to set up the tables inside.

When I start unloading one of the boxes on an outside table, Ronnie comes beside me to help unravel the light string. "Didn't have anything better to do today, huh?" Ronnie jokes.

"I wouldn't exactly consider this cruel labor. I'm honestly happy to help," I say as I focus on the task at hand. "Gotta say, the interior designer who was hired knows what they're doing. This place looks phenomenal."

Ronnie turns to climb up one of the step stools he set up by the pergola. "Yeah, my dad did effective research on that part," Ronnie replies as he scopes out the layout of the hooks under the pergola.

I walk behind him with a string of lights in my hand. "Are we taking opposite sides?"

"Yeah, that's probably best. I'll take this first beam."

"Sounds good," I say as I lift my step stool to the other end of the pergola. Once I climb up, I busy myself with linking the string of the lights in the mounted hooks, and the only sound that fills the patio is the shuffling of our wires, tapping of the Edison bulbs against the wood, and the sliding of the step stools across the wooden planks of the deck.

But with each passing second, the silence mocks me. Ridiculing me for not taking advantage of this opportunity to be the bigger man and do the right thing by Aria and Aria's family.

"How's she been?" Ronnie's voice interrupts the silence, slicing through it like a chainsaw.

I inhale and swallow as his words taunt me. "She's good," I breathe out, and I slightly shrug as my voice softens to a lower decibel. "At least I think so. "

Ronnie pauses his movements for a second and looks across to me, our step stools facing each other from opposite ends of the pergola. "Sorry, I feel like I'm always asking. I just worry about her."

My jaw tightens with tension, and my tongue feels a little too big for my mouth right now. Like my throat is clogged, and I can't find the right words to choose to escape my lips. So I cower and look upward to resume hooking the string lights in place. "Hey, I understand. She's your sister."

In my tunnel of vision, I notice Ronnie is also resuming hanging the string lights on his side. "I'm really glad she's had you to be there for her. She looks almost as happy as she used to be."

My hands slow their movements above me when I hear Ronnie's voice, and my heart plummets into the pit of my stomach. Like the cushion it's been resting on has been tossed aside, and my heart no longer has the necessary support to reside comfortably.

I decided that if mine and Aria's relationship couldn't be accepted, it would be selfish of me to keep her to myself in spite of that. But it turns out *this* is selfish. Omitting information and keeping truths from Aria's family. Ronnie trusted me enough to come to me and ask me to look after Aria, and all I have to show for it are lies upon more lies. Here he is constantly thanking me for befriending Aria, and supporting her in her time of need, when he has no clue I've stepped over a forbidden line with her.

That same line that's a line of betrayal with him.

And let's not forget that one word.

Almost.

The insides of my cheeks salivate with a sourness again. As much as Ronnie's appreciation towards me makes my stomach crunch uncomfortably, there was no way I could miss the way he said Aria looks *almost* as happy as she used to be. Maybe I'm overanalyzing this because the stakes have been raised, but it doesn't make Ronnie's observation cut my heart any shallower. The cut is deep, and the knife twists in the wound, lowering the high I've been on all the way down to rock bottom. I'm brought back down to a reality I should've considered more carefully before driving down this compelling road.

A reality where I can't win against *him*.

My lungs were filled with new oxygen earlier, determined to squeeze more time in with Aria if things didn't go our way today. But now my lungs deflate until all the air of my determination leaves me. Because if my love can't bring her as much happiness as someone else's love once gave her, what good am I to her?

I inhale, trying to regain concentration on the physical task at hand. "You know, I wasn't actually planning on coming here today to help out."

"I don't blame you. There're definitely better things to do on a Saturday in the summer," Ronnie jokes.

"Maybe that's true," I chuckle as I finish hanging the last of the lights on my end. "I actually came because of Aria."

Ronnie finishes hanging his lights at the same time and starts stepping down his stool. "Dane, I know I asked you to look out for her, but I didn't mean you had to pick up the slack around here," Ronnie says apologetically as he walks back over to the table where the boxes are.

Once I climb down my step stool, my heart starts beating a little faster, and I tread cautiously up to Ronnie. "When I said I wasn't planning on coming, what I really meant was that Aria didn't want me here today."

Ronnie turns to look at me as he narrows his eyes. "What? That doesn't sound like Aria."

I swallow a lump in my throat as I make sure to look eye-level at Ronnie. "It would if you knew the truth about Aria and I." I inhale as my jaw remains tight with nerves. "I owe you that much."

Just as Ronnie looks my face over trying to crack the mysterious code in front of him, we hear the sliding door to the terrace open, and Aria's faint voice interrupts. "Hey."

Ronnie and I both turn to look over at Aria, and our secret is written all over her face as she looks between us with trepidation. My eyes apologize to her, and I think I take her in for a second too long as I sense Ronnie looking back and forth from me to Aria. I swallow hard as I turn my head to look back at Ronnie, but as soon as I do, I feel his solid fist connect with the left side of my jaw.

"Ronnie!" Aria shouts.

I brace myself with both my palms on a table as I try to alleviate the sting of Ronnie's punch by moving my jaw around a little. If this is what it will take for things to be right between Ari and I, so be it.

I start to feel a tinge of metal in my mouth when Aria comes between us and pushes Ronnie. "This is my choice too goddammit!"

"Your choice?! Ari, you can't possibly think this relationship is going somewhere. He preyed on you in your most vulnerable state!"

"It wasn't like that," I cut in with a hard tone, keeping my head trained downward.

Aria is standing in front of Ronnie, and he's pointing over her at me. "You shut the fuck up, Dane!" I respect him enough to peel myself off the table and look at him. "I don't think you have any right to talk right now," he seethes out.

Aria is the next to scream, as she flails her arms in Ronnie's face. "What're you going to do, Ronnie?! Beat the shit out of Dane because we care for each other?! That's bullshit!"

"Come on, Ari! He's not in this for any reason other than to get his dick wet! That's who he is!" Ronnie screams.

I see red.

I duck and rush into Ronnie to hug him by the waist, and I take him down to the floor. I get one good punch in, but then he's able to flip us over, connecting another punch to my face.

"Stop it! Stop it!" Aria screams as Ronnie gets up.

"You think Ari will ever feel for you the way she did for Kyle? You're a fucking fool," Ronnie pants out.

I sit up with my elbows propped on bent knees, swallowing down the metal taste in my mouth, as if I'm swallowing the harshness of Ronnie's words. The pain in my jaw pales in comparison to the pain I feel at hearing the truth. A truth I've been trying to deny for as long as I can but am being forced to confront head-on now.

As I eventually lift myself off the ground, Helen shouts angrily. "That's enough! I won't have this shit in your father's restaurant!"

Ronnie points to me. "I asked you for a favor. To look out for my sister, and you took that as an opportunity to take advantage of her. You're dead to me." With that, Ronnie storms off and out of the restaurant, leaving me,

Ari, and Helen on the terrace. Aria's palm is over her mouth, and her eyes flash with shock and sadness at the wreckage that just occurred.

"Dane, I think it's best you leave," Helen says.

I blow out a breath as I run my hands through my hair, and then nod before walking off and to the parking lot.

ARIA

"What is this?" my mom asks.

I turn to look her in the face as tears stream down my cheeks. Now that the shock of the situation has subsided, my bottled emotions are slipping free. "I know this seems wrong. I know it doesn't make sense. But all I can tell you is that I need him, Mom. I *need* him."

"Ari," my mom treads.

I throw my hands in the air in defeat, my voice strained with frustration. "What?! What are you going to tell me?!" I feel my face heat with rising anger, ready to burst out of me and strangle this life of mine. But I feel weak and powerless against it, and my fight can only take me so far, so I blow out a small breath as I run my hands through my hair and look at the ground. "We became really close over the summer, and things just started to develop from there," I breathe out. When I keep my eyes laser focused on a wood plank below me, my mom's silence is so loud it booms in my ear, and when I can't bear the noise anymore, I look up with a snarky expression. "I guess you think I'm some inconsiderate slut, right?"

My mom's face scrunches. "I never said that, Aria, don't you dare put words in my mouth."

"But it's what you're thinking isn't it? It's what everyone thinks or is going to think," I affirm.

My mom sighs exhaustingly. "Well, I'm sorry for being a little taken aback. This isn't exactly a normal situation."

I huff a mocking laugh out as I shake my head and look off to the side with my hands on my hips. "Because my life has been so normal up until this point. My life's been *absolutely wonderful*," I say with blatant bitterness that I can taste at the tip of my tongue.

"No, life hasn't been great to you, Aria. I kno-"

I whip my head around, flailing my arms in the air again. "No, you don't know! Nobody *knows* the pain and misery I've endured this past year! So how is it fair that you all get to judge who I choose to love and be happy with?!"

My mom's brows draw in as she takes in my hurt and confession at the same time, studying me for a few moments before speaking. "You're in love with him?"

My jaw clenches just enough to show my offense. "Oh, I guess you thought with Dane's background we couldn't love each other? That he could never love me back?"

My mom's brows furrow tighter, and this time she's in defense mode. "I never said that, Aria! But I'd be lying if I said I wasn't a little skeptical. You haven't seen Dane in practically a year, and you've fallen in love in such a short amount of time? Not to mention the circumstances don't make it easy for you or Dane. I worry about you getting hurt."

I look up to the sky as my palms rest on my lower back, inhaling a controlled breath to restrain myself from lashing out again. "I'm not a child. I can make my own decisions." Then I tilt my head forward to look back at my mom. "And if Dane and I can't make this work, that's for us to figure out," I breathe out, my voice hoarse.

"You're right, but something like this doesn't just fit into place. Ronnie's not looking through the same lens as you two," my mom reminds me.

"I think you seem to forget that Dane was the one who owned up to the truth just now, yet he still got a punch to the face. Go figure," I retort.

My mom points aimlessly in the direction of where Ronnie and Dane were going at it minutes earlier. "I'm not agreeing with how Ronnie handled that, Aria! But Dane had opportunities before this to speak up when Ronnie was asking about you. Your brother feels fooled."

"I'm not sticking around for this," I say as I walk quickly past my mom.

"Aria!" I hear my mom call behind me.

I whip my body around once I reach the sliding doors of the terrace. "If you're so worried about Ronnie's feelings, chase after him. Clearly you don't give a crap about mine."

"That's not wh-" my mom responds, but I'm inside the restaurant and storming out the front doors before I can listen to another word.

When I reach the parking lot, I find Dane leaning his back against his car door with his hands in his pockets and head hanging downward. I pull him in for a hug when I reach him, and when his arms wrap around my shoulders, his warm touch alleviates the irritation that's crawling under my skin.

"I'm so sorry," I whisper.

Dane kisses the top of my head as he tightens his grip on me. "It's okay," he breathes against my hair, and then he rests his chin on the top of my head. "Believe it or not, I can take a punch," he says lightly.

I pull away just so I can look up at him, and he wipes my tear streaks with his thumbs as I reach up to gently graze his cut lip. "I feel so terrible," I breathe.

Dane swallows hard as he holds my eyes, and there's regret and hesitation emitting from them. His warm embrace cools, and I can practically feel a chill run through me as the temperature lowers between us. "Ari, I don't want to be the one who makes your life more complicated," Dane says, his voice just above a whisper.

I slowly bring my hand down from his face as I cut a hard stare at him. "You won't."

Dane sighs as he looks downward, and then he looks back up at me. The cool temperature drops a little more, descending with every look he gives and every sentence he speaks. "I'm adding more stress. More pain. I can't keep doing this to you," he continues.

"They can get over this. It'll be fine," I grit out.

"It's not just about your family. Even though I can't bear to keep you to myself, knowing you're at odds with them." The cold temperature turns to freezing, and the blood in my veins solidifies to ice. "Maybe I can't accept the idea that our love can't be like it was for you and Kyle. A love that was pure, with no questions asked."

I shake my head as tears painfully sting my eyes, and I push on Dane's chest with two angry fists. "No. Our love can be that way."

Dane curls his hands around my fists and holds them closer to his chest. "But it shouldn't be like this," he whispers.

As tender as his touch is, it feels brutal.

I bang my fists into Dane's chest again. "Like what, Dane?!"

Dane matches my tone. "Like we're never going to escape the past! There are moments when I look at you and see a glimpse of hesitation or guilt." His grip tightens over my fists when he continues on. "I don't want your love for me to come at that expense," he admits and then places one hand over my heart. "There's always going to be a part of your heart that still beats for him. I'm never going to have your whole heart."

I shake my head as I scrunch my face, tears flowing from my eyes as the frozen streams in my veins shatter to pieces, leaving my heart abandoned of a life source.

"Can you honestly tell me you're all in with no reservations?" Dane whispers.

"Dane, don't do this, please," I breathe out.

"Hey," he whispers as he starts to swipe my wet cheeks with his thumbs, but he barely gets to complete his mission when I aggressively swat his hands away and pull back.

"No! You don't get to do this to me! You don't get to coddle me while you break my heart!" Dane just stares back at me as he swallows a nervous lump, and I just continue on. "You're faulting me for my past, but the reality is this isn't my fault!" I wipe my own tears from my cheeks with my fingers, and then cut him a firm stare as my jaw becomes rigid. "The truth is, you don't truly love me. Because if you did, you would accept my past and the flaws that come with it."

Dane takes a step to try and pull me to him, but I reject him instantly.

"No!" I scream as I push him off me. "I'll make this easy for you. We're done."

With that, I turn and walk to my car, and with every step I walk away from Dane, a piece of my soul breaks off, cracking under my foot.

CHAPTER
Thirty-Eight

DANE

"Here, man, I think you could use this," Trent says as he hands me a beer and ice pack on the porch of his apartment. After everything that happened outside Aria's dad's restaurant, I couldn't bear to be home tonight. I needed to just get away from it all. Luckily, when I called Trent, he offered me his couch for the night.

"Thanks," I say as I take a sip of beer and place an ice pack to my jaw. I wince at the applied pressure but know it's necessary.

Trent takes a sip of his beer as he takes the seat next to me. "So does Ronnie look as good as you do?"

"Not quite," I say honestly as I stare out at the courtyard of Trent's apartment complex, reliving everything that happened only a couple hours ago.

"So what're you going to do? What're you and Ari going to do?" Trent asks.

I put my beer down on the table in front of me and lean my forehead on my hand as I continue to ice the side of my face. "I really don't know," I answer, and then I let out a breath. "The thing is, I want her love the way she gave her love to Kyle. You know?"

Trent is silent for a few moments, and then he leans his elbows on his knees as he turns his head to me. "You may be asking for too much, Dane. And I know that sucks to hear, but you need to be willing to accept that."

"I know," I breathe out as I lean back in my chair with a huff. "But I don't know if I can accept it. That's the problem."

"He's always going to be part of her. This is on you now. You have to decide how much being with her is worth to you," Trent says.

I chuck my ice pack at the porch railing in front of me. "Goddammit!" I yell as I stand up and run my hands through my hair. "How the fuck did this happen to me?" I turn to face Trent. "I fell for the one girl I can't have. How's that for fucking irony?" I ask as I let out a frustrated chuckle.

"You *can* be with her," Trent responds.

I look away from him and sigh as I put my hands on my hips. "Not the way I want her."

Trent gets up from his chair and starts lecturing as he spreads his arms out. "Dane, what did you expect?" he says. "Did you have blinders on this whole time up until now?"

I'm still looking away from him as I shake my head in disbelief. "Nothing mattered to me other than just being with her," I whisper. "Or maybe I was just fooling myself, I don't know. I don't fucking know."

Trent comes up to me and pats the side of my arm. "You need to talk to her, Dane."

I shake my head. "Not now. She couldn't even bear to be next to me when I was trying to tell her how I feel."

"Eventually, you need to," Trent says.

I look up at Trent and throw him a tight-lipped smile. "Yeah. Eventually," I say.

As I lay on Trent's couch later that night, I think about what Trent said.

How much is being with Aria worth to me?

Can I accept her not being able to give me all of her?

Can I accept her love knowing it has reservations?

Right now, I honestly don't know the answers to these questions, and I'm starting to wonder if I'll ever find them.

After leaving Trent's house in the morning, I decide to go to the gym to kickbox. I'm ready to take my anger out on something and luckily, I keep a bag of gym clothes in my car. Once I change into my navy tank top and black gym shorts, I throw on boxing gloves and go straight to the freestanding punching bag. Every punch and kick I connect to this bag is powered by my internal suffering.

I think about how unfair it is for Aria and me to be denied a great relationship because of circumstances.

Whack.

I think about how Ronnie accused me of only being with Aria for sex.

Whack.

I think about all of Aria's tears and sadness caused by this situation.

Whack.

I think about how I have no control over the fact that she can never love me without doubt, guilt, or hesitation.

Whack.

I think about how for the first time in my life I've fallen madly in love, but I've fallen in love with the wrong girl.

Whack.

Sweat trickles down my face as I keep beating the shit out of this punching bag. I'm starting to grunt out my breaths so I can channel as much aggression as I can into this fucking bag.

I hate this bag.

This bag represents my life right now. My life that's been flipped upside down and pulled down into emotional hell. This bag represents all the reasons why I've avoided loving anyone.

When I decide to chill out, I turn away with my hands over my head.

Inhale, exhale.

Inhale, exhale.

Inhale, exhale.

When some of my rage leaves my body, there is one question that remains.

How does this end for us?

In order for me to answer that question, I need a sign.

I just haven't been given one yet.

As I turn on my block and pull up to the front of my townhouse, my stomach drops at the sight of Aria reading on her porch. I wasn't expecting her to be outside because I wasn't expecting to have to face her so soon. Or maybe because I just don't want to face her.

But as soon as I see her, memories of our summer together come back to me, and I just take her beauty in. Her long dark hair softly blows in the light breeze, as she's wearing a light pink tank top tucked into high-rise denim shorts around her petite figure. She's curled her legs beside her on the bench so she's comfortable reading, and she hasn't picked her head up yet to notice I'm home. Or maybe she just doesn't care enough to.

That's an excruciating thought.

I swallow a nervous lump as I open my car door to get out, but my eyes are on her the whole time. It's at this point Aria acknowledges me, and she just stares back at me for a couple seconds. Before I even have a chance to say anything or walk to her, she closes her book and gets up from the bench to go into her house. The front door shuts behind her, and I'm left just staring at the empty bench she was sitting on two seconds ago.

I stand at my car door as my heart falls to the floor, breaking to bits, and the hurt I feel is immense. Not hurt because she's ignoring me but hurt because I know I've caused her so much pain in such little time. Then I start to think about the things she said to me out in the parking lot, and I think of how I never got a chance to respond to her.

No matter how much she may hate me right now, I have to let her know something.

I close my car door to start walking up to her front porch, and once I reach her door, I knock.

I'm waiting twenty seconds before knocking again, and another twenty seconds pass by.

"Ari, please open the door," I say loud enough that I know she can hear me.

Nothing.

I knock and speak again. "Ari, please."

Nothing.

I'm bracing my palms on either side of the door frame as I lean forward to say what I need to say, and I speak loud enough so she can hear. "You were wrong yesterday."

I pause, waiting for her to hopefully open the door or talk through the door. Even if it was just to tell me to go away, at least she would be talking to me.

When I realize neither of those things are going to happen, I continue on. "I do love you," I say. "I love you with every ounce of my being. Nothing will ever change that."

I purse my lips, waiting to see if by some slight chance she will open the door.

But when I accept that my waiting is futile, I eventually nod my head in defeat before peeling my hands off the door frame to walk back home.

CHAPTER
Thirty-Nine

ARIA

"I love you with every ounce of my being. Nothing will ever change that."

I'm sitting on the floor against the foyer wall as I hear Dane speak through my door. Tears slide out of my eyes, and I just let them fall as I listen to his voice, letting the droplets coat my skin in inevitable misery. I'm hurt, angry, skeptical, embarrassed, and I refuse to face Dane right now. It's agonizing knowing that even though we care so much for each other, circumstances are keeping us apart.

My family.

Dane's insecurities.

My past.

That's the common denominator of it all.

Isn't it incredible how one event can change the entire course of your life indefinitely? How one event can destroy your original destiny and affect your future destinies in its wake?

My past is my prison, and it's given me a life sentence.

As I sit on my floor after Dane leaves my porch, I wonder if I'll ever find the key to unlock me from the chains of my past.

A couple days after the porch fiasco, I go on a jog with Kate on the boardwalk. We jog for two miles before stopping to catch our breath as we're bent over with our palms on our knees.

"Ugh, remind me never to agree to work out with you," she grunts out.

"Lucky for me, I have so much on my mind I wasn't even thinking about the physical pain," I pant.

"Have you spoken to him?" Kate asks as she stands upright and stretches her quad.

I stand up with my hands on my hips and shake my head in response.

"Has he tried talking with you?" Kate asks.

I shrug. "Not really. I mean if you count talking through my door as trying."

Kate switches to stretching her other quad. "Huh?"

I sigh before answering. "I was on the porch reading and he pulled up in his car. We saw each other, but I sought refuge in my house and completely ignored him."

Kate lets her leg down and stares at me for a couple seconds before speaking. "I'm sorry, Ari."

I shrug as I start walking, and Kate follows suit. "I've been through heartbreak before. I'm kind of immune to it at this point."

Kate places a hand on my arm and stops me. "Ari, you can't just chalk this up to being destined for heartbreak. If you really love Dane, you need to fight to be with him then."

I pause before responding. "He can't handle the fact that I've loved someone so strongly before him," I say, and then throw my hands up as I continue to walk. "Why is this only falling on me? He has to work for this too."

Kate looks forward as she speaks. "I agree that Dane does need to get out of his head," Kate says, and then she turns to me as she's walking. "But can't you understand where he's coming from a little?"

I purse my lips as I hang my head down. "That's the problem. We're at a stalemate." I turn to look at Kate as I continue. "I can't change my past. My past is with me forever."

"But you can change the future. You control that."

I stare at Kate for a solid moment, then face forward as I walk. We walk in silence for the next few minutes as I take in what Kate just said to me.

Does that kind of power live in me? Despite all the odds against me?

Maybe my past is tied to me, but it doesn't have to define me.

I start to think of how sweet it would be to seek revenge on my misfortunes. How good it would feel to be able to take my life back.

To take my destiny back.

Later that night, I'm cooking dinner as I'm pan-frying cubed chicken breast and sweet peppers in teriyaki sauce. I was happy to see that Dane's car was gone because I still can't bring myself to speak with him.

Not yet.

Not until I know what I should say or do.

As I'm tossing the chicken and peppers in the wok with a spatula, I hear a knock on my door, and my heart instantly falls into the pit of my stomach thinking it's Dane.

I slowly turn and tiptoe out of my kitchen to peek through the beveled glass of my front door, and if I thought I was nervous for Dane to be behind my front door, I'm even more anxious when I see who's actually there.

Ronnie.

I swallow a nervous lump and turn the handle of my front door as I greet him with a blank expression. Everything that happened at Dad's restaurant comes flashing through my mind, and I can't help but feel infuriated as I look at him. *Anger* because he's the catalyst for Dane and I being in the situation we're in right now.

"Can we talk?" Ronnie says.

I narrow my eyes at him. "I don't really have much to say to you if I'm being honest."

"Well I do. Can I please come in?" Ronnie says as he motions his hand forward.

I sigh as I open the door, welcoming him into my home. I shut the door with a little extra force than needed, and then walk past him to resume my cooking in the kitchen. Ronnie follows me and leans his back on the kitchen island, but I keep my back to him as I stir my dinner in the wok.

"Ari, I know I didn't handle things the way I should have."

I let out a sarcastic laugh but keep cooking my dinner. "Understatement of the century."

There's a pause before I hear him speak from behind me again. "Do you love him?"

"What would it matter? He's only with me for sex, right?" I respond.

"I honestly don't know what his intentions are," Ronnie says. I keep stirring my dinner, ignoring my brother, but he continues on anyway. "But if you love him, you need to make sure his intentions are right. If he wants to be with you long term. If he wants a future with you."

I slam my spatula in the wok as I turn around and glare at Ronnie. "Well, it's no longer a concern. Thanks to you and your brotherly protection, Dane and I had a fight after you left Dad's restaurant. We're not speaking right now. I ended things." I throw him a thumbs up. "So great job, big bro, I really appreciate it."

Ronnie looks away from my face as he purses his lips, but he has no right to feel sympathy now, so I shake my head as I speak again. "I'm not interested in an apology from you if that's what you came here for. Your damage is done."

Ronnie turns his head to look at me. "Ari, you have to see this from my side o-"

Oh, no.

He doesn't get to play victim.

I throw my hands up in the air. "Your side?! It's always about everyone else's side! Everyone else's but my own!" Tears start to well up in the back of my eyes as I lose the controlled grip on my emotions. "No one gives a shit that I finally learned to love again. No one gives a shit that someone loves me the way that I love them. No one gives a shit that I was *happy* again." I set my tears free. "He made me *happy*. He made me feel *passion*. *Love*. But no one cares! All everyone cares about is that he's the *wrong* person!" I put my head in my hands and sigh, and after a few seconds, I pick my head back up and speak in a calmer tone. "But the truth is, he was the *right* person," I breathe out as my body wracks with sobs.

Ronnie's hand grabs my arm, and on instinct, I clutch onto the sleeves of his t-shirt like an SOS as he lets me sink into his embrace.

CHAPTER
Forty

DANE

Sunday, August 14, 2022

It's now Sunday, and I am meeting my mom for a coffee date. Aria and I still have not spoken since a week ago, and I've been spending later days at work and more nights at Trent's to avoid being in Aria's presence. Not because I don't want to see her, but because I can't witness her ignore me or reject my attempts to speak with her.

It's too much to handle.

I leave the house to pick up my mom, and we drive to Roasters Cafe. Once we order our drinks, we take a seat at a small table by the window, and my elbows are leaning on the table as I take a sip of my cold brew when my mom is the first to speak.

"Thanks for taking me on a coffee date. It's not often I get to see my son on Sundays. It's nice," my mom says with a smile.

"I'm always happy to take you out," I say, and then I lean back in my chair while holding my drink on the table. "But you're right, I don't see you as much as I should on the weekend. Maybe we should make this a monthly thing."

She dismisses my comment by waving her hand. "Oh stop, you're young. You don't need me to crash the party on weekends."

I take a sip of my drink and then respond. "My life isn't too much of a party right now, so you wouldn't be crashing much," I admit as I look out the window to avoid her inevitable questions.

My mom furrows her brows. "Dane?"

I shrug. "I just bit off more than I could chew with Aria."

"What are you talking about?" my mom asks.

I lean my elbows back on the table as I sigh. "I caught feelings for her."

My mom's eyes light up. "See, I knew when I saw your smile that day, there was something about this girl that was giving you that special feeling."

I hold out a hand to my mom before she gets ahead of herself. "Things didn't work out."

"Why not?"

I purse my lips as I shake my head, trying to think of a way to explain everything that's been going on in a "Cliffs Notes" version. "I let my head win out. I can't help but think of all the craziness us being together has created. Her family is upset, Aria's upset because they're upset…" I trail off.

My mom nods sympathetically and places her hand over mine. "You have to understand their reactions."

I take another sip of my cold brew and lean back in my chair as I run my fingers through my hair. "I do. I definitely do," I say as I exhale a long breath and stare out the window again.

"Do you still want to be with her?" my mom asks as she tilts her head like she's trying to read my mind. I swallow as I stare out the window, and I don't respond right away because I still don't know the answer.

It takes a few moments to collect my thoughts, but then I start speaking. "I can't be with her the way I want to be with her." I turn to face my mom. "She'll never love me the way she did Kyle, and I can't spend our whole relationship comparing our love to what they once shared."

My mom nods as if she understands what I'm trying to say, and I shrug before taking another sip of my drink. "I'm sorry, Dane. I know how much you must've cared for her for you to confide in me."

I place a hand over my mom's in an appreciative gesture. "I know you are. Thanks." I sigh as I change the subject. "So enough with my sob story, what's going on with you? How's the new puppy?"

"Oh, my god, this pug is the most rambunctious thing in the world. Cute, but spiteful," she says.

I chuckle. "Oh, yeah? How does a small runt like that cause so much chaos?"

She waves her arms with a laugh. "I have no idea. Chris and I came home from dinner to find that Pepper had ripped up his wee wee pads to shreds in his cage."

"This is why you must properly train the dog," I say with raised eyebrows.

My mom rolls her eyes. "We're trying, okay?"

I just smile. "So how's Chris? If he's not making you happy, I'll have to kick his ass."

"As a matter of fact, I've never been happier in my life," she says with a big smile and takes a sip of her latte.

I return her big smile. "That's great, Mom. I'm really happy for you."

She nods her head. "It's definitely been a long time coming, but it was worth the wait. We're actually planning to go to Las Vegas in September."

"Yeah? Well if that's the case, I'm crashing the trip," I joke.

"Oh, no. I don't want to be babysitting you after clubbing all night, and then having to take care of you while you're throwing up in the bathroom," she says as she shakes her head.

I furrow my brows when I respond. "Clubbing? Throwing up? I'm not twenty-two anymore, Mom."

She shrugs. "Whatever. The point is this trip is for Chris and me only."

I hold my hands up. "Okay, I can take a hint."

"Glad we have an understanding," she says with a smile.

There are more small laughs here and there, and when we finish our drinks, we head on out. As we drive back to my mom's house in my Mustang, our drive is a little quiet for the first few minutes until my mom speaks. She's looking out the passenger window as she says, "If you keep comparing your love, you'll never have your own beginning."

I turn to my mom for a second to see if she's talking to me or herself, but she's staring out the window and I have no idea what she's referring to. "What?" I ask.

My eyes are back on the road as she turns to face me now. "If you keep comparing the love you and Aria have to what she once shared with Kyle, then you two will never have your own beginning." Again, I look at her for a second, then turn my eyes back to the road. I narrow my eyes slightly as I comprehend what she just said to me, and when I don't respond right away, she continues. "He'll always be with her, Dane. That part of her won't go away." Then she turns to look out her passenger window. "You can't rewrite her story, but you can give her a new story. A new beginning."

My eyes are looking at the road, but I'm not seeing what's physically in front of me. Memories of our time together in the rose garden shine in my mind. Aria explaining the meanings of the different colored roses, Aria sharing the quote her therapist read to her, Aria expressing her mission to find the beauty in this world, and then I think about the last time we were together intimately.

This whole time, I thought the only way our love could survive was if Aria felt the same way about me as she did for Kyle. I wanted us to have that same kind of love because I knew how strong and powerful that love was between them.

But the reality is, that's not what she wants.

She wants a second chance at love itself. She wants a different story. She wants *a new beginning*. And if I could give her a new beginning, then I wouldn't have to worry about her love being as strong as it was with someone else. Because if I am able to give her a rebirth in this life, her love would come on a clean slate.

It would be a different love story.

It would be *our* love story.

When I pull up to my mom's house, I turn to my mom and pull her in for a tight hug. "I really appreciate you being there for me."

We hold each other for a few seconds longer than usual, and then my mom pulls away and touches the side of my face. "Everything is going to work out the way it's supposed to. I promise." I throw her a small smile, and once I make sure my mom is back in her house, I stare out at the road before me.

Life has a funny way of throwing you signs. I was looking for answers this last week, and I was looking for answers to questions I didn't necessarily know to ask.

But I know that this was my sign.

This was my answer.

Aria is my answer.

As much as I want to run to Aria and tell her everything I've now learned, I know there is something that has to be taken care of first.

When I come to that conclusion, I start my car and drive to my next destination.

As I pull up in Ronnie's driveway, my stomach twists into a tight knot. I'm not exactly sure what I want to say to him, but all I know is this is what I need to do before anything can progress with Aria. If Aria and I are going to be together, I need to make sure her family understands the weight of our relationship.

I need their acceptance.

I still have two hands on my steering wheel as I hang my head down and blow out a breath. After a few moments, I manage the courage to open my door and step out, and with each step toward Ronnie's front porch, anxiety simmers within me. I don't know how he'll react, what he'll say, or what he'll do. For all I know, Ronnie can throw ten more punches at me, but it doesn't matter.

I've said it before, and I'll say it again.

I'll take every punch and kick from him if it means Aria and I can be together.

That much I am sure of.

I inhale a deep breath as I ring the doorbell and I wait a few moments until the door opens.

It's Cheryl.

I hesitate for a moment trying to collect my thoughts. "Hi, Cheryl, is Ronnie home?"

Just as I ask for Ronnie, he comes walking in the foyer behind Cheryl, and we lock eyes.

"I got this," Ronnie says to Cheryl.

Cheryl gives Ronnie a tight-lipped smile, then turns back to me. "Nice to see you, Dane," Cheryl says with a smile as she walks away to let us be.

I lift my chin to her. "You as well." When it's just me and Ronnie left in the doorway, I rub my neck nervously. "I'm not expecting to come inside or anything, I just wanted to talk if that's okay."

"Sure," Ronnie says as he steps out on his front porch, closing the door behind him.

I throw my hand out. "Look, I know what you think of me. That this was some sexual conquest, and I took advantage of your sister. If I had a sister, I probably would've reacted the same way."

Ronnie shoves his hands in his jeans pockets as he stares at me intently, waiting for me to continue explaining myself.

I sigh as I look off to the side. "When you gave me the responsibility to look after Ari, I wasn't too thrilled. I was nervous and felt like it was too big a burden for me to bear." I chuckle as I say, "I actually dreaded it to be quite honest." Then I turn my head back to face him. "But I'm truly grateful you gave me that responsibility, because it brought me to her. Your sister is the most beautiful person I've ever known. She's kind, funny, smart, easy-going, witty, I mean the list goes on. She's as beautiful on the inside as she is on the outside." I let out a breath as I drop my head for a moment, then I look back up at Ronnie. "I'm in love with Aria. I love her with everything that I am, and I want to be with her. But I can't be with her knowing I'm causing her world to be flipped upside down. I can't be with her knowing her family won't be supportive. Because if you guys aren't supporting her, she's not happy, and if she's not happy, there's no way I can be happy. I don't want Aria selfishly. I want her to be with me knowing she has her family behind her."

Ronnie just stares at me for a few moments, digesting everything I just said. "What if my family or I can't support this? What then?"

I swallow a nervous gulp as I look off to the side, and take time to let that notion sink in. I feel my heart rip open, but I turn to him to respond anyway. "Then I would live an unfulfilled life. Because I'd be living without her."

Ronnie inhales a deep breath as he places his hands on his hips. "I went to visit Aria the other day. She wasn't in the best of shape. In fact, she cried in my arms."

I look away from Ronnie as I purse my lips, trying to control my emotions. "I tried talking with her, but she won't talk to me," I whisper.

"Well maybe you should try again," Ronnie says.

I turn my head to him and furrow my brows slightly. He doesn't answer my silent question, but he continues on. "That's my advice to you." Then Ronnie turns to open his front door and before he walks in his house, he turns to me and says, "She needs you just as much as you need her. I can learn to accept that."

He throws me a small smile, and I sigh out a small smile of my own, knowing that he's telling me he's giving us his blessing. We give each other an understanding nod, and then Ronnie is back in his house.

CHAPTER
Forty-One

ARIA

It's Sunday night, and I'm pulling up to the front of my townhouse after having dinner with Kate. I'm getting out of my car when I notice Dane on his front porch. He's in a navy crewneck and gray joggers, sleeping on the bench of his porch, and a wave of rage flows through me. I haven't heard from him in a week, and now he's trying to grovel at my feet?

No thanks.

I spitefully slam my car door loud enough to wake him from his beauty rest, and he picks his head up trying to assess where he is. It only takes him a moment to get his mental bearings and realize that I'm outside, but I start to walk up the pathway to my front porch.

"Hey! Ari, stop," Dane calls out as he jogs over to me.

I continue to walk forward. "Dane, just leave me alone."

"I just want to talk to you," Dane says.

I turn around and let out a chuckle. "Oh, yeah? Where the hell have you been this past week?"

He narrows his eyes at me. "Last time I checked, I tried talking to you, but you completely shut me out."

I sigh as I run a hand through my hair. "It's late, Dane, what do you want?"

He seems surprised by my dismissive tone. "Okay, well can we talk inside? Please?"

"No. I'm tired and I have a bunch of stuff to do this week for my father's restaurant opening. So if you don't mind, just say what you have to say."

He shakes his head and gives me questioning eyes. "Why are you being so cold?"

I glare at him with a hard stare. "Me cold? You break my heart because of your own insecurities, and I'm the cold one?"

"Okay, I get it!" Dane sighs as he places his hands on his hips. "I never wanted to hurt yo-"

"I can't listen to this." I let out an exhausted sigh as I turn around to head up the steps of my porch.

"Dammit, maybe you should!" I immediately turn around from the top step of my porch to look down at Dane on the bottom one. "I want to be with you, Ari."

"Only until the next time you have a meltdown, right?" I let out a frustrated sigh. "I'm never going to be free," I say as tears well up behind my eyes. "I've been thinking a lot over this past week. Yes, I've had my reservations about us because my past is a part of me. I can't change that. But it's not who I *am*. *This* version of me fell in love with you, and this version of me doesn't have loyalty to the past, it has loyalty to the future." I shake my head as I look away from Dane, trying to stop my tears from coming out. "But I can only be so strong, and my strength has been chipping away with every hurdle we've had to jump." I pause to look back at Dane. "Maybe our challenges are just a sign that we aren't meant to be. We should have known that from the beginning."

Dane sighs as he runs both hands over his face, and then walks up the porch steps so he is eye level with me. I start to turn away to go inside my house, but he gently grabs my wrist. "I see you, Ari. I saw it that night when you were looking up at the stars on your porch. I saw it that evening on the pier when you embraced the rain. And I saw it that night in the rose garden. I know you want something more out of life than what you've been given. You think if you just give up now, you won't have to be disappointed anymore." Dane shakes his head at me. "But that's not what you want." He pauses before continuing. "You want the roses." I lick my lips as my tears threaten to leave my eyes, and I have to tighten my face to make sure my emotions don't shed in front of Dane. "And no matter how many thorns are between us, I know I'd prick myself a thousand times just to get to you. I wonder all the time if you feel the same way." Dane hangs his head down and licks his lips to gather his next words together, and when he looks back up at me, he looks into my eyes as he says, "That's been the question that's been plaguing my mind this whole time, and why I've second guessed so much of what's happened between us."

I just stand staring at him, trying my best to analyze what Dane's saying in real time. Is it possible for us to survive all we've been through, and come out of this journey happy and more in love than ever?

Then I start to think of Dane's analogy.

Does every thorn that pricks you actually draw blood? If I chose to walk through the thorns to meet Dane on the other side, could I come out unscathed? If not, how many scars am I willing to wear for him?

When Dane realizes I'm not going to respond, he drops his head down and nods in acceptance. "Alright," he whispers, and then he turns around and walks back to his house.

Once Dane is out of view, I stand frozen on my porch, the only movement being the current of my tears flowing down my cheeks.

CHAPTER
Forty-Two

ARIA

Saturday, August 20, 2022

The ivy-covered roof of the gazebo stares down at me as I lay in the middle of the rose garden. I think about how one moment, one single moment, can change everything. It changes how we feel, how we live, and the direction of our journey.

Some people are lucky enough to experience a moment that brings greater meaning to their life. A moment that brings joy, hope, and purpose. But what about those of us who aren't so lucky? Those of us who experience a devastating moment that shatters our entire world. A moment that wreaks havoc on all of our hopes and dreams that once were.

It's like that single moment morphs into invisible shackles around your wrists and you're chained to the corner of a dark room. The door closes, and as your eyes adjust to the dimly lit space, you see the key to your shackles on the other side. It's like that scrappy piece of metal represents the wonderful moments that were once in your reach.

At first, your instinct is to tug at the restraints with every ounce of strength you possess, even though you know your efforts are pointless. And as time goes on, you start to tire physically, and eventually your mental exhaustion catches up. At some point, you're not tugging frantically at the restraints, but you're embracing them. Accepting them as your fate and wardrobe accessory for life. Finally, you lay limp on the floor with your cheek flat against the cold concrete, and you stare at the door to the room. As time starts to slow down, you're willing someone to walk through that door and pick up the key to release you. But when minutes turn to hours, and hours turn to days, despair starts to consume you and you forget what it ever felt like to live unchained.

These are the ripple effects of just one moment.

One moment that's caged me for so long, it feels surreal to be lying flat on this wooden bench, surrounded by endless beauty. I can see hints of the starlit sky above, and I feel my lips tip up ever so slightly at the corners. I inhale as I turn to look toward the green rose pathway, keeping my eyes trained on the bold, green petals. Flashes of scenes from the past couple months shine in my mind. Moments I thought I could never experience again.

And then I think of *him*.

I think of how his arms were wrapped around me as we danced under this very gazebo that night, savoring every second together. The images are so vivid, like the memories have been inked into my veins and forever etched into my soul. It was the first time we listened to our hearts instead of the sand pouring in our hourglass. Some would say you can't hear the sand anyway, but when you're on borrowed time, it's the loudest sound of all. And if I had to relive that night again, I would make the same decision every single time.

Because that night, the door to my dark room finally opened.

He represents my liberation.

My salvation.

My key to freedom.

I exhale a breath as I turn my head away from the green rose pathway and look back up to the roof of the gazebo. I think about how Dane and I went from a sweet and tender moment in my living room, to arguing on my front porch about the future of us. I haven't spoken to Dane since the night on the porch, and it's because I've been consciously avoiding him. Yes, there are a few times when I'll peek out the window to see if I catch him walking to his car or walking the pathway up to his house.

Sometimes I see him.

Sometimes I don't.

The times I don't, I'm let down. Because the truth is, I miss him.

I miss *us*.

When I take a step back and think about our journey together over this past summer, it's overwhelming. After Kyle, I never expected to feel something so profound again, let alone love.

Love.

The heart is truly an incredible phenomenon. When we experience tragedy, our heart breaks into thousands, maybe millions of pieces. And we start to wonder if we'll ever find the glue to put the scraps back together again. But even if we do find the glue, is our heart ever truly the same? If we try to rebuild something, can it ever be as good as the original?

Over the last year, the fragments of my heart have been slowly stitched back together. Being with Dane was like the final needle and thread I needed to make my heart whole again. But although my heart was put back together, I was still living life for my stitches and scars. I held back, I hesitated, and I was unsure.

I could never give Dane one hundred percent of me because I was still living as if my heart was broken. I could still feel every inch of thread that was sewn into my jagged organ. But there was one thing I failed to realize throughout all of it. Even if the scars don't completely fade, they're never as ugly or profound as they once were, and our bodies are still able to function after.

Can the heart do the same?

Does it have the ability to love immensely again after heartbreak?

Some scars have completely faded from my heart over the last year, but Kyle's death and memory are marks that will stain my heart forever.

Then I start to think about what Dane said to me. He said that a part of my heart will always beat for Kyle. And he's right in a way. Dane can never have my whole heart because a part of it will always lay in memory of Kyle.

But does that part still beat for Kyle?

I'm not so sure.

I'm not so sure my heart works the way it used to. That's the thing about stitches and scars. They enable you to still function, but the function might not be the same. Maybe my heart doesn't function like it used to. Instead, my heart has been renewed and remolded, and the beats of my heart are different now. Yes, there are scars, but I can't let those scars hold me back. They're just physical evidence of what I've been through, and I know my heart still has so much left to give and take.

Scars can't stop that.

CHAPTER
Forty-Three

ARIA

Sunday, August 21, 2022

It's the night of my dad's restaurant opening, and I'm putting on an emerald-colored maxi dress with a deep V-neckline, mid-thigh split, and tie-back detail. The spaghetti straps have ruffles on them to add a little flattery to the dress, and I slip on nude strappy heels to complete the outfit. I run my fingers through my long hair to soften out the curls I just made in my hair before putting on eyeshadow and mascara in my mirror. Once I finish my makeup and give my reflection one last look, I grab my gold clutch off my dresser and make my way downstairs. I peek out one of the windows in my living room to make sure I am in the clear from running into Dane, and once I verify I'm good to go, I hop into my car and head to my father's restaurant.

As I walk up the wooden ramp, there is a huge balloon arch surrounding the front doors, staggered with blue, white and gold colors. When I walk through the doors, I find my parents, Ronnie, and Cheryl standing off to the right side where there is a table of champagne glasses, and guests scattered about *everywhere*.

It's amazing.

"Hey," I say with a large smile.

My mom is the first to turn around and hug me. "Look at you, you look beautiful."

I shrug with a smirk. "I try."

I throw my dad a big smile as he's dressed in a navy tailored suit. "But not as good as you!" I exclaim as I bring my dad in for a bear hug. "I'm so proud of you, Dad. Everything looks perfect."

He hugs me tighter. "Thank you, Ari." When he pulls away, he jokes. "Let's just hope everyone thinks the same. As long as they are fed and there is an open bar, I think we'll be in good shape."

I smile and reassure him as I say, "It's going to be great. I have no doubts."

My mom grabs my father's arm. "Jared, we should probably go make our rounds so we can keep our head above water."

When my parents walk away, I'm left to stand with Ronnie and his wife, and I automatically smile and hug Cheryl.

"How are you, love?" Cheryl says as she returns my embrace.

"Good. How about you?" I say as I pull away.

"Not much to complain about," Cheryl replies.

I'm suddenly very aware that Ronnie is standing with us, and I realize I haven't said hi to him. I decide to swallow my pride and throw him a smile, because after all, this night is not about me.

"That's good to hear," I finally say as I look back at Cheryl.

Cheryl turns to Ronnie. "Do you want something from the bar? I'm going to get myself water."

"No, I'll get a drink later. But you go," Ronnie replies as he gestures to the bar.

Once Cheryl walks away, I'm the first to speak as I grab a champagne glass off the table. "We can put our differences aside tonight. Tonight is about Dad."

He throws me a small smile and looks over at our parents mingling with guests. "He's like a kid in a candy shop, look at him."

I smile as I watch Dad mingle and laugh with guests, and he does look genuinely happy. "Yeah, he does."

I'm still looking at my parents when Ronnie's voice cuts in. "I really am sorry, Ari."

I take a sip of my champagne and look back at him with a shrug. "Like I said, it doesn't matter anymore."

Ronnie shoves his hands in his pockets. "Well, it matters to me. I can't have my sister despise me the rest of her life."

I look down into my glass. "I don't despise you. I'm just hurt, I guess."

"I was really convinced that Dane had ill intentions," Ronnie continues.

I'm still looking down at my glass as I slowly nod with a smart remark. "I think everyone knows that. You made it very clear."

"Well, my opinion changed when he came to visit me last Sunday," Ronnie says.

I pick my head up and furrow my brows, waiting for him to explain. Ronnie rubs the back of his neck, trying to find the right words to say. "He came to the house and sort of poured his heart out."

I start to feel my face tighten with emotion, tears threatening to leave my eyes, but I refuse to allow it. Instead, I look away from Ronnie and just take another sip of my drink to compose myself.

"For what it's worth, he's head over heels in love with you, just like you are with him," Ronnie says as he walks up to me, but I'm still facing away from him when he places a hand on my arm. "And no one should stand in the way of that. Not even me."

When Ronnie voices his last words, he walks off to meet Cheryl at the bar, and I just stare mindlessly at the back wall of the restaurant as my lips morph into a frown. Guests are probably wondering what the hell a psychopath is doing at Jared Tate's grand opening, and before I bring down everyone's mood with my melodramatic life, I down the rest of my champagne in one gulp.

Then I hear a clinging sound.

I turn and see my dad holding a microphone in the back right corner of the restaurant where the guitarist is set up to play music.

"Good evening, everyone. First, I'd like to thank you all, from the very bottom of my heart, for coming tonight. When you become a chef, the big dream is to own a restaurant one day. Tonight, I'm living out my dream. But my dream couldn't have been possible without the ever-loving support of my family. My beautiful wife, Helen, my overbearing but loveable son, Ronnie, and my gorgeous daughter, Aria." There are small chuckles from his description of Ronnie, which is an accurate description, nonetheless. "We've worked tirelessly this past year to open a restaurant to the public that wouldn't just offer delicious cuisine, but great ambience as well. I truly hope we can make the town of Crestside proud. It's my honor to officially invite you to the grand opening of Bistro Eighty-Six."

I'm smiling wide as guests applaud my dad, and all my turbulent emotions are shoveled to the side for now. My dad places the microphone on the stand, and the guitarist announces that the buffet is now open, and people start to make a line to get their food. I walk right over to my dad and congratulate him, and Ronnie and Cheryl do the same.

After we all get our food and sit at the head table as a family, we all dig in, and I'm sitting next to my mom when she starts the conversation. "Getting ready to go back to school?"

"Ugh, don't remind me," I say before taking a bite of the skirt steak I have on my fork.

Ronnie narrows his eyes. "You literally get two months off."

I swallow my steak and narrow my eyes back at him. "Well if it was so easy and everyone wanted two months off, everyone would be a teacher, wouldn't they?"

Cheryl chimes in as she points to me with shrimp scampi on her fork. "That's right!"

I give Ronnie a victorious expression that someone agrees with me.

My mom then diverts her attention to Ronnie. "How are the renovations at the house coming along?"

He takes a sip of his beer then responds. "Our contractor just needs to refinish the tub in the bathroom and put the countertops in. Another week to go, maximum."

My mom's eyes light up. "That's great. And maybe there will be a baby in the refinished tub soon?"

Cheryl and Ronnie look at each other with smiles, and then my mom and I look at each other with furrowed brows. When we look back at Ronnie and Cheryl again, I'm the first to speak. "You're pregnant?!"

Cheryl nods her head eagerly.

"Oh, my god!" my mom yells as she gets up to hug the both of them, and I follow suit.

We find out Cheryl is six weeks along, and I give Cheryl a big hug before I turn to Ronnie. We look at each other with tight-lipped smiles before putting our arms around each other, and he pulls me in for the biggest bear hug.

"I'm so happy for you," I say as the side of my face rests on his shoulder.

"I want you to be happy too," he says.

I nod with a smile as I pull away. "I will be. A lot of great things in my future between Dad's restaurant and having a niece or nephew."

Ronnie smiles, and we pull completely away so that the four of us can converse back at the table. An hour passes at the table as we talk about the baby room, baby names, gender reveals, and baby showers. We have some really great laughs, and I step outside of myself for a quick second to look in on this scene.

Two weeks ago, our world was chaotic.

Now, our world seems settled.

Maybe everything can be okay in the end if Dane and I decide to be together.

Ronnie and Cheryl head out right after dessert, and I am left at the table with my mom. My elbow is on the table as I prop my chin in my hand, and I look around at all the people immersed in conversations and laughter as I listen to the instrumental versions of classic songs played by the hired guitarist.

My mom's voice cuts into my thoughts from my side. "What are you thinking about?"

I swallow a nervous gulp as I decide what I should say. Should I make something up, or go with the truth? "Him," I respond as I look straight ahead.

My mom pauses before speaking. "Who?"

I furrow my brows at my mom's question as I keep looking forward. She knows who I'm talking about, so why is she acting like she doesn't? Why does she need clarification?

And then it dawns on me.

For the first time since I've been with Dane, my mind didn't wander to think about Kyle or what emotional repercussions there are. Instead, my mind was thinking of Dane.

Just Dane.

"He came to visit your father earlier. Even dressed up for the occasion," my mom says with a smile.

I turn to look at my mom. "Dane was here?"

My mom nods her head. "Yes. He wanted to congratulate your father."

I let out the faintest exhale as I hold my mom's eyes, touched by this new information. It was a small gesture from Dane, but the meaning of it is grand. The parts of my heart that beat for Dane beat more prominently now, fighting against being suppressed by my past.

"You'll figure it out," my mom says as she rubs my back, and then she excuses herself to take more pictures with my dad on the terrace.

I prop my chin back in my hand and look around again. I look at the entrance door, telling myself I'm just looking here because it's in view, but I know the truth. I'm wishing that any minute I'm going to see Dane walk through that door. But the seconds turn into minutes, and with each passing minute, the only person who I want to walk in, never comes.

The guitarist is starting the introduction to a song, and when I listen intently for the first few seconds, I realize it's the acoustic version of Journey's "Don't Stop Believin'." Memories slide into my mind like a montage. Dane and I holding hands on the Ferris wheel, him coming over to my house for dinner and being his obnoxious self, our first workout together on the boardwalk, our stroll out on the pier at sunset, Fourth of July, our night at Duke's, Dane teaching me salsa at Shippers, our passionate arguments outside our homes, the angst between us until we submitted to our feelings in his hallway, our dance under the rose garden, the first night we made love, then our lovemaking every time after.

Each moment with Dane was physically different, but what I felt in my heart was a common denominator.

Happiness.

Love.

Freedom.

A single tear slides down my cheek as the montage of the most wonderful summer continues to scroll on repeat through my mind. I wipe the tear and force myself to stay strong for the remaining hour of the opening. Eventually, my mom comes back to the table, and we fall back into easy conversation as the guest count dies down.

Once my parents and I are the only ones left, we're standing in the middle of the restaurant. "It was a successful evening, Dad. I've never been prouder of you," I say as I hug my father.

"None of this would be possible without you, your mom, and your brother," my dad says before giving me a kiss on my cheek.

"I'm going to start taking down the decorations inside. Then I'll work my way outside," my mom interrupts.

I place my hand on my mom's upper arm. "No, Mom, I got it."

"Thanks, that's a huge help. Otherwise, your father and I might never leave here," my mom says as she walks to the bar area to start taking down the balloons and banners we have.

When I walk out onto the patio of my dad's restaurant, the evening sky is illuminated with yellows and oranges as the sun is about to set. It's not too hot on this August night as the wind tickles my skin, and whispers through my hair. Then I walk up to the wooden railing and rest my forearms on the ledge to close my eyes, smiling at the feel of the wind on my face and the evening glow illuminating it.

Never stop fighting.

I remember Dane's words to me when we were walking along the beach. I've fought a continuous uphill battle this past year, never really knowing when or where the end of the battle is. But maybe there is no end, and life is meant to be fought for. If life was just a single, paved pathway to easily walk through, how can we cherish or value the good that comes our way?

It's the battles we endure that make the victory that much sweeter, and it's the battle wounds that show how much the victory means to us. They show what we're willing to give up, and how far we'll go to reach the top of the hill.

Are Dane and I meant to be fought for?

We weren't brought together through easy circumstances, but we were certainly brought together by our hearts and what we feel for each other inside.

If we aren't living for our hearts, then what are we even living for?

Aren't our hearts worth being fought for?

When the canvas for a love story has blemishes before it's even painted, it's not so simple to cover up.

That's how it's felt for Dane and me. We felt defeated from the beginning because of the flawed canvas that was given to us. But maybe that just means more technique has to be used to make sure the imperfections don't take away from the incredible artwork. Instead of seeing how we could work harder to fade the blemishes into the background, Dane and I saw them as the focal point of our painting. I've never taken up painting as a hobby or cared for it that much, but I'm suddenly wishing a paintbrush was the only thing in my hand right now.

I push off the railing to walk to the post in the corner to start undoing the string of the "Grand Opening" banner, and then I move to the tables to collect the centerpieces to bring them inside to place back in boxes.

It's dark out once the chaos of cleaning up dies down, and I give my parents one last hug before making my way to the parking lot to get in my car. As my heels hit the pavement, I register the pain from being in them for so long, so without a care in the world, I stop in the middle of the parking lot and bend to unbuckle my heels. I flick them off in one swift movement and pick the shoes up in one hand as I hold my clutch in the other.

"Note to self: always bring a change of shoes," I mutter to myself as I make my way to my car door. Exhausted from the shoegate extravaganza in the parking lot, I toss my clutch and shoes on the passenger seat before hopping in my car and driving off barefoot.

I know, I'm a mess.

At least it's not a far drive, and it's only about ten minutes until I'm pulling my car up to the curb in front of my house. I feel a slight frown form on my face as I see Dane's usual parking spot empty.

He's not home.

Disappointment settles over me.

At least when I was at my dad's grand opening, I thought I may have a conversation to look forward to afterwards, but that doesn't seem to be the case. I inhale sharply and let out a large exhale as I hook my heel straps around my fingers and grab my clutch in one hand. I open the car door to step outside and decide to let a little of my frustration out on my car door when I slam it shut.

Yeah, I'm definitely going straight for a glass of wine tonight.

As I'm walking up the pathway to my porch, I bend my head to take the barrette out of my hair with my free hand and shake my fingers through the soft waves. When I pick my head back up just as I reach the bottom step to my porch, I immediately halt in my tracks as my breath catches in my throat.

My eyes are greeted with a single, fully bloomed green rose tied to the column post of the stair railing. I drop my heels and clutch to the ground as the beauty of the rose pulls me into a trance. I slowly take a step forward and extend a hand out to brush a green petal with my fingertip, and tears sting my eyes as soon as I make the contact.

I feel like I'm touching *him* instead of this flower, and like a moth drawn to a flame, I raise my fingers to my parted lips and close my eyes. I'm instantly brought back to that night where Dane and I danced silently under the gazebo of the Bloom Rose Garden. Every detail is vibrant and vivid behind my eyes. I can smell the roses, I can see all the bright colors, I can feel Dane's touch, I can taste his kiss, and I can hear our conversation replaying in my mind.

There was so much beauty in that one moment.

So many roses to be grateful for.

Suddenly, I hear a faint sound coming from the right of me.

It's a song.

I furrow my brows slightly as I start to recognize its melody, and my heart starts to beat a mile a minute as I listen to the instrumental introduction of "The Lady in Red". And I know without a shadow of a doubt that when I turn around, I'm going to see the one person I've been praying to see all night.

He never forgot that night.

Just like he said he wouldn't.

I exhale as I open my eyes, and when I turn around, my soul sings.

Dane's leaning one shoulder on the column post of his porch steps, with one leg crossed in front of the other. He holds my eyes as he turns his lips up in the corner, and he's never looked more handsome. I didn't think that was even possible until this very moment as he's wearing a tucked in white button down with the sleeves rolled up and the top two buttons undone. He's paired his dress shirt with khaki pants that hug his long, thick legs just right, and his hair is styled on top more than it usually is.

When Dane starts to walk toward me, he says, "You know, I never knew how rare green roses were."

I let out a breathy laugh, and nothing can prevent the smile that spreads across my face. Dane stops when he's only inches away from me and reaches around me to untie the rose from the column. "It took me five different visits to florists before I found what I was looking for." When he successfully removes the rose, his eyes meet mine as he shrugs slightly. "I thought it was worth mentioning. And also the fact that I parked my Mustang the next block over."

I narrow my eyes slightly, as if to ask him why on earth he would do that.

He smirks as he says, "If you thought I was home, there was a small chance you could knock on my door. I wasn't taking any chances ruining such a grand gesture. I don't exactly do this often."

I let out a laugh as a tear slides down my cheek, and Dane hands me the rose. As soon as I take the rose in my hand, Dane wipes my stray tear away with his thumb as he continues on. "Aria, I've been really stupid." He shakes his head at me. "Too stupid to see everything that was right in front of me all along. I thought our love needed to equal what you once shared with Kyle. I thought that our love had to be the same or else we wouldn't stand a chance." Dane averts his gaze downward. "I've been so focused on comparing and measuring our love that I failed to give our love a chance to grow." Then his eyes meet mine again. "And I overlooked the most important detail of all."

"What's that?" I say.

"That we're meant to write our own story." He looks down and touches the rose as he places his forehead against mine. "I'm your new beginning. I can set you free," he whispers, and I close my eyes. "That's what I should have said to you all along." Dane pulls back just enough to bring his free hand to cup the side of my face, and he starts wiping away at my tears with his thumb again.

"You once told me that you'll never have my entire heart because a part of it will always beat for him," I say. "The part of my heart that belongs to Kyle is a treasured memory, and yes it belongs to him," I admit before shaking my head. "But it doesn't beat for him. The parts of my heart that beat? They beat for you."

Dane's lips purse into a grateful smile as his nostrils flare from built up emotion, and he bends down to kiss me. I instinctively wrap my arms around his neck, green rose still in hand, as we get lost in each other's kiss.

A kiss that's deep, passionate, and free of all reservations.

I can hear the clanking of my shackles as they drop to the concrete floor of my dark room, and the light shining through the door frame comes into focus as I take confident steps toward it.

I open it to walk on the other side.

This is the start of something new.

This is my rebirth.

Isn't it amazing how powerful a single moment can be? A single moment can change our story in the blink of an eye and rewrite it without receiving our permission. That's the harsh truth about life. Things come and go, events happen, and life goes on. Life doesn't wait for a perfect moment to insert tragedy and pain. Life doesn't wait for us to be ready for the hardships it's going to throw at us. The expectation is for us to just accept our fate and try to make it through our days as best as possible.

But life isn't about *getting by* or *making it through*.

It's about *living*.

See, I used to think life itself held all the power. It was so natural for me to surrender to the darkness because what was happening was so blatantly out of my control.

But when we accept this fate, what's left to live for?

Some might say nothing.

Some might say *everything*.

Our power lies in the fight we're willing to give. Life may deal us some really shitty hands and throw a few punches, but no one ever said we had to stand defenseless on the other side. Even if we can't avoid the first few jabs, we can avoid the ones that come later on because we're more prepared.

Life may control the layout of events in our story, but it can't control *how* we write the story. We have the power to succumb to the tragic nature of it, or we have the power to fight back and uncover a new theme.

Knowing what I know now, the answer to Dane's question rings clearer than ever. Given all the thorns between us, would I prick myself a thousand times just to get to him?

No.

I'd prick myself a thousand times, and then some.

THE END

ABOUT THE AUTHOR

Writing is a hobby of mine. I started writing this precious book at the beginning of the summer of 2022, and completed it at the end of the Fall. Because of reasons I cannot disclose, I wish to keep my identity secure. At least for now.

I started this journey of becoming a new romance author as a way to escape from reality and indulge in stories I truly believe in. Yes, stories! Since Hunt for the Roses, I have written two more romance novels that will be launched in the near future, and am excited for all my stories to be set free from my mind and fly into yours. I only write what I believe in, and these characters that speak to me, I keep very close to my heart.

So I'll end with this…

When I finished writing this book, I said, "If just twenty people I don't know read my book and fall in love with it, I know I've done what I set out to do."

Anything else, is just a bonus.

xo Drea Scott

Printed in Great Britain
by Amazon

26644471R00198